THE SECOND AWAKENING BOOK ONE

# DEAD WRONG

ALEXANDER C. EBERHART

# DEAD WRONG
## The Second Awakening Book One

www.alexanderceberhart.com

Copyright © 2025 Alexander C. Eberhart

All rights reserved. No part of this publication may be reproduced, stored in a retrieval system, or transmitted, in any form or by any means (electronic, mechanical, photocopying, recording, or otherwise), without the prior written permission of the publisher.

This book is a work of fiction and does not represent any individual living or dead. Names, characters, places, and incidents either are products of the author's imagination or are used fictitiously.

Cover and Interior Design by We Got You Covered Book Design
www.wegotyoucoveredbookdesign.com

FOR THOSE WHO KNOW THAT LOVE
TRANSCENDS ALL THINGS, EVEN DEATH.

# GLOSSARY

**Magi:** a person granted with the ability to use magic. Gifted with longer-than-mortal life spans, Magi are born of four different bloodlines, the Adored, the Unseen, the Hallowed, and the Reviled. Each bloodline has innate talents unique to them, though a large proportion of the Magi lack magical aptitude beyond the most basic of spells.

**Mortal:** a person not gifted with the ability to use magic. Mortals still make up a majority of the workforce in the Magi society, so some Magi see them as lesser-than.

**Adored:** the wealthiest and most politically powerful of the Magi bloodlines. The Adoreds' innate talents allow them to impose their will upon others, but only the most powerful families are able to wield it with much success.

**Unseen:** the servant class of the Magi. Unseen's animalistic appearances have been a stigma for generations amongst the Magi. These animalistic traits are displayed in a variety of forms, but most often in the presence of animal features such as tails, fangs, claws, wings, scales, etc. All Unseen are traditionally male-presenting, and are capable of reproducing with another male Unseen. The Unseen's innate ability allows them to wrap themselves in magic to become invisible, as well as grants them traits of their animal-like personas, such as enhanced speed and strength.

**Hallowed:** the religious class of the Magi. Hallowed worship the Source of all magic and govern the Church of the Source. These devout believers' innate abilities allow them to use their magic to cure disease and heal wounds.

**Reviled:** the exiled branch of the Church of the Source, Reviled are thought to be extinct in the modern Magi world. These powerful practitioners possessed rituals that could bring the dead back to life, conjure spirits of the deceased, and even project their own souls from their bodies. Driven from the Church of the Source during a schism, the Reviled are pariahs of the Magi community.

**The Source:** Believed to be the source of all magic by the Hallowed, the Source is the recipient of the Church's worship, and serves as their deity.

**The Awakening:** the inciting event that originally granted magic to the mortals many centuries ago. A popular belief among the modern-day Magi is that a second Awakening is coming.

**Glamour:** A low-level illusory application of magic that most Magi can use.

**Veil:** High-level illusory magic that can disguise a person's appearance, voice, and tactile sensations. Only Reviled Magi are able to utilize these skills.

**Distortion:** a being of myth in the Magi society. A horrible creature, twisted by magic into shapes unrecognizable.

# ONE
## DEAD TO THE WORLD

A warmth like I'd never felt before. A weighted blanket layered over my skin like swaddling. Or perhaps a cocoon of sorts, preparing me for a metamorphosis, an evolution to strip away all of my flaws, transitioning me into a flawless nubile state.

Yes. That was it. I would be made anew.

How long had I been here, wrapped in this comforting warmth? A day? A week? An eternity? All of them seemed likely answers in the crushing darkness.

There was no viable way for me to gauge the passing of time, as even my lungs had fallen still in this state. My heart rested motionless in the cavity of my chest—which most would find alarming—but the weight bearing down on me smothered any anxieties before they could seize my mind.

A voice, tenor and familiar in its cadence, buzzed around my ear. The words didn't land cleanly but muddled themselves into nonsensical mutterings that grated against my nerves. Irritation bloomed in my tranquil mind, ripples distorting a still pond.

Who would disturb such blissful peace with their aimless ramblings?

Yet, the intruder's voice continued, even after I had exhausted all efforts to ignore it. The volume only increased until it was no longer a bothersome insect flitting about my ear but a thunderous rumbling that rattled my bones.

I would never know solace again while this damnable noise droned on.

Something had to be done.

Pulling against the weight of my limbs, I struggled to free myself from the invisible cocoon, but my restraints kept me immobilized, locked in place under a warmth that now grew stifling. Another rumbling wave of noise jolted me, and my lungs inflated to the point of pain. Breathing through the smothering blanket was nearly impossible, yet I gasped and wheezed, forcing air through the tight mesh that covered my lips.

This wasn't right. I wasn't supposed to feel pain. Pain was something that I'd left behind in this new form of mine. Did it finally catch up to me here, pursuing me into the darkness like a wild beast stalking its prey?

A pressure against my chest drew my attention next, increasing till my ribs groaned, threatening to crack. That damnable voice sounded in my ears once more, closer than ever. Words slowly began to seep through like drips of honey.

"—until it stops… even if we do… Lenny won't be found… going till we get somewhere…."

Recognition flared in my mind, igniting dormant connections like lightning hitting brush. I knew that voice. I was certain of it. A character from a life before the cocoon. From before I was nothing but darkness and absence. Another wave of searing strength and my limbs moved, muscles coiling against the restraints until they cried out.

"Coming to… doesn't react well… for most it's jarring…."

The incessant voice was driving me mad! My fingers curled at my side, nails digging into the meat of my palms. My lungs inflated once more, pushing out the heavy darkness that filled my chest. Just as I tried to locate my tongue to voice my distaste for this agony, a burst of color exploded into my vision. Clouds of shapeless purples and greens swirled over me, replacing the colorless void. My muscles tensed again, an oppressive pattering rhythm battering my ears.

What was that infernal pulsing?

It took an endless collection of time to realize it was my heartbeat hammering away.

How bizarre it felt in place of the stillness.

"Breathe," the tenor voice commanded, hot breath nipping at my ear. "Breathe, Tobias. You're almost through it."

Another gasp ripped through me as my body contorted, a fiery heat rushing through my veins. I'd never known such pain. It was as if every cell in my body was being ripped apart, only to be hastily stitched together again with jagged needles. The dancing colors slowly faded from my vision, replaced by a dull red glow that flared with each beat of my aching heart.

A sudden lurch in my stomach forced my body into motion, rolling onto my side as stinging bile choked me, and I wretched.

Strong hands gripped my shoulders, holding me in place as I heaved a second time. An acrid bitterness coated my tongue as I negotiated another agonizing breath.

"Is it always this messy?"

A second intruder to my peace. The higher pitch wasn't familiar to me like the tenor was.

"Yes," rumbled the lower voice. "My magic is starting to take hold. It shouldn't be much longer now."

"What a relief. He's getting shit all over my rug—"

Fresh pain radiated through me in a wave, swallowing the voice in a dull, rushing sound. Pins and needles stabbed at my dormant limbs, the once pleasant numbness replaced with static discomfort as my heart continued to hammer, pumping white-hot agony throughout my body.

A low, guttural moan welled in my chest, escaping through clenched teeth.

"Tobias," the familiar voice rang in my ears. "Stay with me."

Tobias. The name lingered, bringing with it a sense of revelation. I was Tobias before the smothering darkness took me. A life that I couldn't recall through the crushing darkness. But if that's who I was before, would the same still be true after I woke?

A sputter in my newly beating heart and the light behind my eyelids dimmed. The tension in my aching limbs released, pain withdrawing slowly as a pleasant numbness took hold.

That was better. I wanted to sink back into the comforting darkness, away from that persistent voice and its tortuous tone.

"Tobias? Tobias, can you hear me?"

The voice was getting farther away. Or perhaps I was. Either way, I was relieved at the slowing of the alien beating in my chest. I much preferred the stillness. The quiet. The comfort of weighted shadow as it began to settle over me once again, squeezing the air from my lungs.

"What's happening?"

The other voice was distant, too. A tweeting songbird, miles away.

It wouldn't be long. Sweet oblivion would soon take hold. I just had to make it through a few more moments of misery.

"—allowed to die, you son-of-a-bitch."

A pressure on my chest, but it wasn't as sharp as before. The numbness was close to completing its task. Soon, all that would be left was blissful nothingness.

"—working. Step back. I said step back!"

White-hot light filled my senses, sending shockwaves of pain through my body as every muscle contracted. My eyes sprang open, blinding brightness searing them. The smell of ozone filled my nostrils as the convulsion ceased, my heavy limbs falling still as the horrid beating of my heart assaulted my ears, louder than ever.

"Oh good, his eyes are open." The staccato of heels clacking against smooth flooring assaulted my ears, then it spoke again, "I was starting to doubt you, handsome. Glad to see you're not all talk."

Blurred shadows moved against the background of searing light. Over the constant thumping of my own anatomy, other noises began to bombard me from all directions. The hum of electrical lights overhead, the rush of air from vents, the drumming of footsteps against wooden floorboards. They all felt like spikes jabbing into my skull.

"Can you hear me?"

The familiar voice wasn't as sharp on my senses. It didn't assault me like the clacking noise coming from the opposite direction. My head lulled to the side, moving slowly to catch a glimpse of whomever was speaking. But my eyes hadn't adjusted to the light, and all I could make out was the vague outline of a broad face.

"Blink twice for yes, once for no. Can you hear me?"

I blinked once, then again.

"Good," the tenor cajoled. "Focus on the sound of my voice. I need you to take a deep breath for me."

I inhaled, lungs expanding to the point of bursting.

"Great, he's breathing," the unpleasantly sharp voice stated. "Can you speed this up, please? We're losing precious time."

"No," the tenor answered flatly.

I exhaled, the edges of my vision sharpening. Sunlight streaked in from windows opposite me, casting a large pool of gold light across the dark wooden floors. Exposed beams of wood ran along the ceiling overhead, and standing on the edge of an ornate rug, leaning against the arm of a plush-looking leather sofa, a woman with honeyed curls down to her shoulders watched me, her arms neatly folded over her navel.

"I don't have to remind you what's at stake here, Bastien," said the woman, her full lips drawn into a pout.

My freshly beating heart skipped at the mention of the name, then—

It burst through my mind like a dam rupturing, memories rushing in to fill the void left behind by the expansive darkness, too quick to make sense of: *A bristly blanket atop a hill of crimson flowers bobbing in a gentle breeze. A moonlit stroll along a river of starlight. Soft fingertips pressed into the most sensitive parts of melanated flesh—*

"Look at me."

Warm hands cupped my face, steering me till I found a pair of golden eyes. I knew those eyes.

*Bastien.*

The name rippled through me, driving heat through my aching limbs.

"Keep breathing."

I tried to form words, but my mouth was so dry, and my tongue buffeted against my teeth like sandpaper. I managed to coax a string of broken noises, but none of them hardly resembled words. I reached for Bastien, pushing through the agony of my screaming muscles, longing for the warmth of his honeyed skin—but another flood of memories halted me in place: *Bastien, standing in the doorway, jacket tossed over his shoulder as he turned away, delivering words that bit into my skin like shards of glass. Tears, hot and plentiful, streaming down my face as I watched Bastien walk away from me, taking with him all but the hollowed-out shell that remained. Emptiness. Then nothing at all.*

I was wrong. This Bastien was not mine, after all. At least, not anymore. If only I could remember why.

"Keep breathing," Bastien repeated, hands drifting from my face to my chest. His fingers sunk into the skin, leaving trails of burning heat. "He'll need a few more minutes before we can move him, Lorelei. But he should be ready soon."

The woman huffed, her heels scraping against the floor as she straightened. "Fine. I've got some calls to make anyway. Get him out front as soon as you can. We're burning daylight."

Her clattering steps faded as she exited. Bastien let out a sigh, his chest deflating and shoulders sinking inward like a sagging foundation. He looked exhausted; the usually smooth angles of his face pulled taut with a frown, and deep bruise-like patches bloomed under his eyes. His fingers moved along my chest once again, and I struggled to lift my head enough to catch the motion of his hands. Bastien moved slowly, deliberately, peeling away layers of a thin linen that covered every bit of my body that I could see. As he pulled a long strip away, I noticed the faint green aura coming from his hands.

Was that magic? It couldn't be. Bastien was a mortal—

"I know you have a lot of questions." Bastien's voice was low, and he looked away when he spoke, like he was afraid someone was watching him. "But I cannot answer them. Not yet. For now, know this: We're searching for your sister. She's not been seen since the day of your death."

My death? What was he on about? I wasn't dead….

Flashes of memory churned in my mind like roiling waves, but much like water, they slipped through my grasp. Grunts dug their way up my parched throat, formless words tumbling over my lips but finding no purchase. I needed him to explain. Explain what happened to me. Hell, explain just *who* I was. The turbulent nature of my mind shielded the knowledge from me. But I couldn't manage any of those requests, aside from gibberish noises. So, instead, I was forced to watch the man remove strips of translucent material from my body.

"That woman—Lorelei—was hired by your mother to find your sister," Bastien continued, still not meeting my gaze. "The Madame will not rest until Lenny is found."

Lenny. Another name that summoned a fountain of memories. My head ached as the torrent of scenes broke free from the roiling sea of confusion, drowning me in melancholia so heavy I wasn't sure I'd be able to escape. My life sliced into bite-sized pieces that ricocheted through my consciousness, exploding like fireworks at each collision: *Lenny—Lynette—my sister, my twin, her face round with a youthful glow, staring at me across a table stacked high with scrolls of parchment. She mouthed words I couldn't recall, her brilliant emerald eyes shining with dew. Then we were dancing, her hair down and the curve of her body fuller than before, her face obscured by a mask embellished with glittering sapphires in every shade of the rainbow. We glided along a polished marble floor, captivating all who would dare to steal a glance at the Greene twins. The ballroom shifted then, leaving us alone in an empty sitting room, watching the dwindling flames of a fire. I held her pale hand in mine as she wept, the source of sorrow lost among the endless waves that battered my mind.*

"Lenny…."

Her name was fire in my throat, but I spoke it anyway.

Bastien paused, his dark eyes finding mine at last. "Are you with me now, Tobias?"

I managed a nod. But the light around him was dimming, the edges of my vision darkening until Bastien's face was a halo against the encroaching shadows. Bastien leaned in closer, bringing with him a familiar scent of spice.

"Good. We've got work to do." He looked back over his shoulder before his eyes returned to me. "And once Lenny is safe, I'm putting you right back in the ground where they found you."

# TWO
## DEAD AHEAD

"Another cup?"

Bastien held up the half-empty coffee pot from across the kitchen, giving it a gentle shake. Sunlight streamed through the open, floor-to-ceiling windows, washing the cherrywood floors in patches of sepia and honey. The heat of summer had finally loosened its grip on the city, and the first cool breezes of autumn drifted in, caressing my exposed skin. Gooseflesh rose across my arms, so I pulled the sleeves of my robe down further.

"That's okay, love. If I have any more, I'm afraid I'll burst through my skin. And while it would be incredibly entertaining, Mother would not see the humor in my ruining her soiree."

Bastien filled a mug for himself, returning the pot to the burner before sauntering back to where I waited in the breakfast nook. My spare silk robe hung from his body like a sheet of moonlight, concealing far too much of his warm umber skin. The urge to peel it off of him left me leering. I would do it slowly. Deliberately. I would feast on all the delicious places hidden underneath the fabric.

He planted a kiss on my forehead, dulling the ravenous thoughts left unchecked, then returned to his seat across the table, his hands cupped around the steaming mug. My mind must have been singularly focused because all I could imagine were those hands wrapped around other things. But the morning was already wearing thin, and I could not afford to be late.

# THE SECOND AWAKENING

*Not when it came to Mother.*

"Are you still hungry?" Bastien eyed me from over the rim of his cup, his deep golden eyes bright with amusement. He was always looking at me this way. Like he was in on a joke that I didn't understand. Not cruel—never cruel—just amused.

"Hmm?" I looked down at the half-eaten breakfast on my plate.

Bastien's grin was tantamount to an act of seduction. "You were staring at me like you wanted to gobble me up. Should I make you another egg?"

"Really?" I mused, trying to play coy even though my voice spiked an octave. I cleared my throat, then continued, "That can't be true. I would never be so lewd at the breakfast table. I adhere to a strict moral code, you know."

"Mhm." Bastien cocked an eyebrow, which sent a biting heat prickling across the nape of my neck. Suddenly, the cool breeze didn't feel quite as refreshing. "And where was this moral code when it came to last night's activities?"

"Completely absent," I admitted, the rush of blood to my face far more successful in rousing me than the coffee had been. "But I don't remember hearing any complaints."

"There was no chance to complain. You kept my mouth so busy."

My face was no longer the destination of the blood pumping frantically through my veins. Bastien sipped his coffee, a smug smile curling his lips around the rim of the mug. He was especially wicked in the mornings, and it seemed today was no exception. Not that I minded, of course.

I shook the heated thoughts from my head, a shiver creeping down my spine from another burst of cool air washing over my flushed face. With a simple wave of my hand and a shower of golden sparks, the windows flew shut.

Bastien flinched, his mug tipping forward, but he managed to catch it before it toppled over.

Damn my distracted impulsiveness. I knew better than to use magic—even simple magic—so flippantly around Bastien. It was so second nature to me I hardly had a moment to reconsider. Magic was as much a part of me as using my hands or feet. But for Bastien, who had grown up outside of the Magi City, in a town of mortals, being so close to magic was an adjustment.

"Forgive me," I offered, giving a weak smile. "I'm trying to be better about that."

Bastien waved off my apology. "It's fine. I promise. Maybe I shouldn't have poured myself a second cup. I'm already jumpy enough as it is."

There was something else underneath his words. A shadow that settled across his features and obscured the brightness I had grown so accustomed to. It spurred a twinge in my chest to see his luminescence dim.

"Are you sure I couldn't convince you to tag along today? The look on Mother's face alone would be well worth any recourse. And selfishly, I so desperately wish to show you off. Parade you around all those dreadfully boring princelings who flock to me."

"I have a shift," Bastien replied, fidgeting in his chair. "And we've talked about this. I don't think it would be a good idea."

"But why? I've already told her about us—not that she didn't already know. What's the worst the old hag could do?"

I knew all too well there was a lot that Mother could and probably would do to me if I showed up to her event with a mortal in tow. I could just imagine the gasps. The clutching of pearls. The sordid whispers.

It would be glorious. If only for a moment.

"I don't belong in that world," Bastien said, cutting through my mask of sarcasm. "And I have no interest in getting involved with your family politics. I won't be reduced to some headline in the gossip column for a bunch of Magi socialites to gawk over just so you can piss off your mother."

I flinched at the force behind his words.

"That was never my intention," I said slowly. "And I apologize if I made it seem so. Your comfort is far more important to me than any of those assholes that Mother spends her time wining and dining. Why should they deserve a chance to feast their eyes on such beauty?"

Bastien's lips curled into a slight smile. Flattery was a weakness that I knew how to leverage.

"But just to be clear, if I keep showing up unaccompanied, Mother is going to make me dance with all of those awful Adored bachelors in some poor attempt at marrying me off." I covered my face with my hands, slyly peeking through my fingers. "Are you okay with that?"

His smile blossomed into a mischievous grin. "Maybe I will attend, then. If only to watch you longingly from across the room. You never want to dance with me."

"Not true!" I argued. "I distinctly recall there being dancing last night."

"Writhing in ecstasy and dancing are not the same thing."

"Writhing in ecstasy?" I repeated with a laugh. "My, someone thinks highly of themselves."

Bastien shrugged, clearly holding back his own laughter. "I merely speak the truth."

"There should be a consensus from all parties before such claims can be corroborated."

"Have you forgotten so quickly, Tobias?" Bastien asked, setting down his mug and rising from his seat. "It sounds like someone could use a refresher."

I glanced up at the clock just as Bastien swept me up into his arms, hoisting me over his shoulder.

"Fine, fine, but we better make it quick!"

"Stop touching that."

Bastien steered my curious hand away from the sparkling green gem embedded in my chest. The facets pulsed with acidic green energy in time with my heartbeat, and even though the edges sunk into my flesh, there was no pain at my poking.

Maybe it was the effects of death lingering in my veins. The numbness had only just left the tips of my fingers a few moments prior.

"Could you at least find me a shirt to cover up with?" I asked, still fixated on the pulsing protrusion. "I'm going to stare at the damn thing all day if I don't get it out of my sight."

"Patience," Bastien retorted, his voice lacking any of the familiar honey I had once been accustomed to. Bastien firmly gripped my arm, tracing prodding fingers down to my wrist and then back again. Once he was satisfied, he jotted a note in a leatherbound journal lying on the table next to me.

"And?" I watched him now as he stared down at his notes, his taut jaw revealing more than words ever could. He was upset. Whatever strange magic he'd used to bring me back to life must have had a hitch. Some unforeseen side effect. That certainly would explain the chaotic condition I found my faculties in. And perhaps the insatiable itch coming from the soles of my feet.

"The Viridian gem is taking hold," Bastien said finally, snapping the book shut and stuffing it into the chest pocket of his button-down. "It will keep your body moving, keep magic pumping through your veins. But it won't help far beyond that. Your magic had already seeped from your body by the time I was called, so this—" he tapped the gem embedded in my chest, "is filled with a portion of my magic. It's not a lot—I don't have much to begin with—but it'll keep you going until we find Lynette."

"My magic is gone?"

I reached into that space in my chest—the hollow where my magic usually thrummed, filling my veins with vigor—but found a cavernous emptiness. Well, maybe not entirely empty. It took a moment, but I was finally able to detect the abnormal magic Bastien had given me. I reached out for it instinctually. It was like a familiar song, played in a foreign key, recognizable but eerily wrong. Sorrow, muddled with a wave of panic, swelled in my gut. My fingers wrapped around Bastien's forearm, anchoring me to him.

"Please," I pleaded, my voice splintering. "I can't—I don't understand what's happening. How did I die?"

"Allow me," another voice interjected, the clacking of heels returning as the woman with yellow-blond curls glided into view. She was a few inches shorter than me, which meant that next to Bastien she almost appeared as a child. Her piercing blue eyes looked me up and down, and I silently cursed Bastien for leaving me so exposed, especially under her chilly stare. "Your sister is missing, Mister Greene." The woman's voice was matter-of-fact as if she were discussing sales data and not vanishing loved ones. "She was last seen leaving the residence of the VanDoughtens after her Ascension ceremony three nights ago. You were reported to be with her at that time. The day after, your body was discovered in an unmarked grave outside on the outskirts of Adoracia Cemetery in the upper Magi City. The Council of Magi has launched an official investigation into the whereabouts of Lynette

Greene. However, the Madame has retained me to locate her daughter as soon as possible and by any means necessary."

The Council of Magi. I at least had enough faculties to remember the collection of high-powered Magi who acted as the governing body of Magi society. My mother, Adoranda Greene, had been a part of the Council for decades. Depending on who you asked, she would be considered its defacto leader.

It was odd that I could recall the intricacies of Magi politics, yet anything leading up to my supposed death was scrambled to near oblivion in my mind. If these two were to be believed, and I'd been dead for the last three days, then the strangeness was only beginning.

"Well, that's right shit," I concluded, scratching my stubbly chin and longing for a shave. "I would have at least expected them to provide a headstone for me."

The corner of Bastien's mouth twitched. It didn't go unnoticed. In fact, I reveled in the realization I could still draw out that reaction. I'd take any small victories I could.

"I'm looking for Lynette," the blond woman continued, stepping between me and Bastien. "And we're hoping you can help us in locating her."

"How exactly would I do that?" I asked, failing to understand the woman's logic.

"All I need is the truth," she replied, her stern voice commanding my attention. "What were the two of you doing the night of her disappearance? Why were you at the VanDoughtens?"

Her words gnawed at the soft tissue of my brain like vermin, radiating a nauseating pain down my spine. "Look, I haven't the foggiest idea what you're talking about."

"His memory has been affected," Bastien interjected, placing a hand on the woman's shoulder and steering her out of the way. "Hopefully, it's only temporary, but I told you this could happen with a revivification this late. I can't guarantee it will come back at all."

I let out a shuddered sigh. The news was less than comforting. Then again,

Bastien had already promised to put me back into the ground once Lynette was found, so maybe I wouldn't have long to lament over the missing pieces of my life.

I was already dead. And what's worse, I couldn't even mourn the life I'd lived before. Not when the details of it lay shattered in a heap.

The woman muttered something I couldn't catch, shaking her head hard enough to send her curls bouncing. "Fine," she spoke up, turning to Bastien. "Then let's focus on what we can get out of him. It's better than nothing. Can you see—"

"Don't speak about me like I'm not in the room," I snapped, pushing myself up into a seated position. Immediate regret sunk in as I swayed, the room spinning around me.

Bastien was at my side before I could topple, steadying me with warm hands. "Easy," he coaxed, the edge dissolving from his voice. "You can't rush yourself."

The woman stomped her foot with a huff. "You can, actually. And you should. The longer this situation drags on the less of a chance we have of finding Lynette alive. You do want your sister to be alive, don't you?"

"Would you care to fill me in here?" I addressed the woman, bracing both hands on the edge of the desk to hold myself upright. "Preferably starting with who the bloody hell you are? You said that the Council had launched an investigation, so why would my mother go out of her way to hire you when there are teams of Magi trained to track targets down?"

The blond woman's eyes narrowed. Her lips pursed as if she found the question so far beneath her it didn't even deign a response.

"Some details might help speed up the recovery of his memories," Bastien said, digging through his duffle bag on the floor and retrieving a small blanket. He wrapped it gingerly across my shoulders and I quickly pulled it tight around my exposed flesh.

The familiar scent of pine and musk filled my nose, and for a moment, I was transported miles away to a room far cozier than my current surroundings—*A crackling fire roared opposite a plush, velvet sofa. Wine glasses sat on the low table, half empty. Legs wrapped around my torso, painted by firelight in coppery hues—*

Heat built at the nape of my neck, spilling over to trickle down my back. I pulled the blanket tighter, letting the corners of the fabric bundle across my lap.

Why would these memories be the first to return to me? Surely, my addled mind needed to check its priorities.

The woman huffed once more, folding her slight arms across the buttons of her striped vest. "Fine. In the interest of saving time, my name is Lorelei Orion. I was retained by Madame Greene to locate her daughter in a discreet fashion. As I'm sure you are aware, Lynette was to officially assume the role of Head Councilwoman of the Magi Council yesterday. Because of her absence, the position now sits vacant, leaving other houses chomping at the bit to fill the vacuum of power. They will hold a special election if Lynette is not located in time, so you can imagine that Madame Greene has stressed the importance of locating her as quickly as possible. Which is why she came to me."

Odd that she would go behind the Council's backs. Perhaps Mother suspected treachery from the other Council members. If they could stall the search for Lynette long enough, they could replace her with another candidate. Mother must have suspected a coup d'état in the works.

"Orion," I repeated, scouring the fragments of my mind for any recognition of the name. "That doesn't sound like an Adored surname. Are you one of the Hallowed?"

"Mortal, actually," Lorelei answered.

Laughter bubbled up and out of my mouth before I could process it. A mortal? There was no way Mother would have anything to do with a mortal in any capacity—even this. She'd rather die than rely on someone of mortal blood. Then again, perhaps that's why she insisted on discretion, if only to save herself from the embarrassment. Wouldn't want it to get out that she had to rely on a mortal.

"I'm the best at what I do, Mister Greene," Lorelei continued as if privy to the unvoiced comments bouncing around my head. "Of that, I can assure you. And I charge a small fortune, which the Madame respects." Her attention shifted to Bastien then, "Is he ready to move? Time is not on our side."

"Almost," Bastien replied, rummaging around his bag once more. "He just needs to get dressed."

Lorelei nodded, pulling a device from her pocket and flipping it open—a communication device popular amongst the mortals, I recalled—she pressed it to her ear, rattling off a greeting in a language I didn't understand. The staccato of her steps faded down the hall, leaving the two of us in silence.

I was still reeling that Mother would involve a mortal in family affairs, even if the mortal was as supposedly impressive as this Lorelei woman proclaimed. It showed a desperation that I had thought beneath her. Was she starting to show a glimmer of humanity in her advanced years?

The idea fled from my mind with a shake of my head. There was no love left for the woman. Even from my jumbled stasis of that, I was sure. Any affection was extracted from me long ago by her own hand. If I'd been brought back for any other reason besides helping Lynette, I would have told Bastien to put my back in the ground right then and there.

But I supposed that would happen sooner or later, so all that was left for me to do was help my sister. She was the innocent one in all this.

My thoughts and gaze returned to Bastien as he gathered the stripped bandages into a pile on the desk. A new ache flared in my chest—a squeezing sensation that stole the breath from my lungs. Whatever happened between the two of us, I couldn't recall, but that fact did little to quell the urge to reach out and touch him.

I needed to know why he was here. Why *he* was the one who brought me back. There must be others out in the world who could have performed the task. Why did it have to be my Ex?

"How did you get wrapped up in all this?" I asked him as he worked.

Bastien didn't answer as he removed to final bandages from my legs, adding them to the growing pile. The line of his mouth with tight, as if he were holding himself back.

"Bastien?"

He retrieved a pair of jeans and a wrinkled T-shirt from his bag, setting them on the desk beside me. "Get dressed," he said, still avoiding eye contact with me.

I moved, no longer able to resist the urge, catching him at the wrist. "Please, Bastien. You must help me out here. I'm just trying to make sense of—" I motioned back and forth between us, "*this*."

"I'm sorry," Bastien replied, his voice a whisper. His eyes—warm pools of amber—flitted down to his knuckles as his grip tightened on the handle of the bag.

Pain. I was sure that's what I saw in his expression. But was I the cause? What had I done to warrant such a response?

Releasing my hold, I grabbed the T-shirt and pulled it swiftly over my head. My stiff muscles ached with each movement, and I had to stifle a groan.

"Could you at least tell me what's wrong with my brain?" I asked, unfolding the jeans. "My memories… they keep coming in waves. It's impossible to keep them straight."

Bastien turned his back to me as I finished dressing. "That's a bit less complicated. It's one of Death's Touches. My grandmother called them that, at least. Side effects that manifest in the resurrected in an endless number of ways. Memory loss is supposed to be the most common."

"Lucky me," I mumbled, fastening the button of the too-loose jeans. They hung from my hips like a curtain. "I don't get to remember who murdered me."

Bastien glanced over his shoulder, a flicker of softness peeking through before his guarded expression returned. "We should get going."

"Did I know about you?"

My tongue formed the question before my mind could catch up. Bastien's warm eyes found me again, spurring me on. "I can piece together that we're not—that things ended between us. But did I know you're a Reviled?"

Reviled. Even speaking the word made the hair on the back of my neck prickle. The banished Magi who could manipulate life and were supposed to be extinct. And Bastien was one of them. How had I not seen it? Was I really so blind?

"I never told you," he answered, tone flat. He reached down, grabbing the bag from the floor and slinging it over his shoulder. Then he was beside me, wrapping a strong arm around my waist and hauling me to my feet. I stumbled, my legs numb through the first few steps. Bastien held fast, supporting my weight with ease. There was a part of me—someplace deep down—that relished in that moment, Bastien's warmth pressed to my side. But it didn't last, and as soon as I was able to stand on my own, Bastien removed himself.

By the time we'd made it to the door leading out into a marble-floored hall, the pins-and-needles sensation in my feet had abated almost entirely.

"What is this place?" I asked, glancing down the long corridor. The floor was polished to perfection, reflecting the intricate, prismatic design of the ceiling panels above us. The effect was dizzying, and I had to shut my eyes for a moment to keep from swaying.

"This is Lorelei's home," answered Bastien, hovering a few steps behind me as if he were waiting for me to fall out. "The Orion Manor. She wanted to make sure no one would interrupt the revivification, so she insisted that I come here."

"Manor, huh?" I echoed, following the path forward and trying to keep my eyes level to the ground. "What kind of a mortal is she?"

Bastien shook his head, slowly rounding the corner behind me. I pushed myself to keep pace, my lethargic limbs cooperating more with each step. The hallway opened up around us, the ceiling vaulting as we approached the landing of a dramatic, curved staircase leading down to an opulent foyer. A crystal chandelier hung overhead, refracting beams that streamed through half a dozen skylights, casting pools of rainbow light across nearly every surface.

It was like stepping into a kaleidoscope.

The beauty rivaled any Adored chateau—at least the ones I could recall—and I struggled to believe a mortal family was capable of such wealth.

"And you're sure she's mortal?" I questioned, unable to tear my gaze away from the articulate carvings on the pillars of alabaster that rose to support the vaulted roof. Scaled beasts twisted along the surface, frozen in pale beauty as they coiled toward the sky.

# THE SECOND AWAKENING

"Does it matter?" Bastien asked, already halfway down the marble stairs.

The question caught me off guard. Did it matter? I wasn't even sure what compelled me to ask it in the first place. It was maddening, not being able to understand my own inclinations. Where did this contempt for mortals come from?

My legs quaked under me as I clung to the railing, beginning my descent. Bastien didn't rush me, waiting patiently at the foot of the stairs, watching me with a steeled expression. Fiery needles stabbed into my calves with each impact, a sheen of cold sweat building along my forehead by the time I'd landed on the fifth step. I clenched my teeth to stifle the noises rising from the back of my throat, but it did little to dampen the sound.

"How's the pain?" Bastien asked the slightest trace of warmth buried in his deep voice. At least, that's what I hoped it was.

I cleared my throat. "What pain? I'm fine and dandy."

"You're whimpering."

"Am not."

"I think I remember what your whimpering sounds like."

My foot slipped on the smooth tile, forcing me to clutch the railing with all my might to stay upright. "Stop distracting me!"

Bastien sighed, dropping his duffle on the polished floor and retracing his steps up to meet me. "You're a stubborn asshole, even in your second life. Here."

He offered a hand out to me, and I reached for it without a second thought. It's like my body didn't care for the forgotten details of our breakup. It longed to touch Bastien, no matter the reason.

Bastien's warm hand enveloped mine, and for a moment, I thought he was going to brace me again like he'd done before, but then he swooped down, pressing his strong frame into my thighs as he heaved me over his shoulder as if I were a sack of flour.

"Put me down!" I protested, my head dangling inches from the small of Bastien's back. I lacked the strength to be anything but a ragdoll in the man's clutches.

Bastien ignored my request, refusing to even offer a reply as he carried me down the rest of the stairs with little effort.

"How wonderful," Lorelei's voice echoed as we crested the foot of the staircase. "Here I was thinking you were only good for revivification, Bastien. Maybe I'll put those muscles to good use as well."

"My services were laid out clearly in the contract you signed," Bastien retorted. "Tobias is my only concern for the duration of his second life. You can hire a lackey if you want something heavy carried around."

My heart fluttered involuntarily. I was Bastien's *only* concern. Why did that make me so… happy?

"What a shame." Lorelei's voice was closer to us now, and I strained my neck at a painful angle to catch a glimpse of her as she circled Bastien. "I'm so curious as to why you showed up at my doorstep in the first place. You know who I'm working for. And I was under the impression that Reviled, like yourself, are considered a pariah to other Magi. What happens if you get caught, handsome?"

"Money is money. And any other reasons are my own," grumbled Bastien. "None of which are relevant to you or your work."

"Are you sure about that?" Lorelei pressed, her eyes gleaming with amusement. "Because I've got a few theories of my own as to why you're here."

"Keep them to yourself. I'm not interested."

"Can you please put me down?" I interrupted, taking advantage of the lull in their sniping. "All the blood is rushing to my head."

Bastien's hold tightened, tipping me forward to allow me to slide off his shoulder. Lorelei's eyes found me, icy blue judgment sizing me up. It was the first time we'd met eye-to-eye. A shiver shot down my spine as she sniffed.

"The car is out front," she said plainly while Bastien retrieved his discarded bag. "We need to get a move on."

"Where exactly are we going?" I asked, already missing Bastien's presence beside me.

Lorelei turned her back, making for the grandiose wooden door at the entrance.

"Wonderful. Good talk."

# THREE
## DEAD AIR

"*One hour to midnight!*"

Cheers rang out through the claustrophobic hole-in-the-wall bar as the countdown clock hanging over the dance floor chimed the first of eleven ear-splitting gongs. Decorations made from flashy holographic plastic adorned nearly every nook and cranny, streaming down into the flushed faces of intoxicated patrons, who swatted them away with grins of stupefied bliss. Bodies packed the space, sweaty and pressed together like rats swarming over a piece of rancid meat.

The was no elegance here. No refinement to show the value of one's status, only bedlam surrounding me from all sides. I should have expected this when my "date" for the evening suggested we come to this hovel on the Mortal Row, but it had been so long since I'd set foot outside of Magi society I'd forgotten how those without magic behaved. This bar was absolutely barbarous, and I could only hope that I wouldn't have to stay a moment longer than necessary.

"Are you certain you don't want to join me, Tobias?"

I wiped the expression of disgust from my face, swiveling on my barstool to face the reason for my presence in this hellscape. The young man's brow glistened with perspiration, the strange silver conical hat jutting out from atop his sandy blonde locks pointed directly at me like a unicorn's horn. He hopped up onto the stool next to me—which I'd been holding vacant during his absence through a blend of surly stares and a touch of magic—and lifted his empty glass to catch the bartender's attention.

"I'm perfectly content watching you perspire from a distance," I replied, reaching out and taking him by the shoulder to steer his attention. "Edward, wouldn't it be better if we went someplace a little quieter so we could talk?"

Edward's well-sculpted brows drew together. "And miss the fun? Absolutely not! We've only got an hour left before the New Year! After midnight, the party really gets roaring."

I had to exercise a great deal of restraint not to strangle him in the middle of the crowded bar. Mother had told me that the Rothwind sire would be a vain little twerp, but my briefing was nowhere near as detailed as it needed to be. How was I supposed to convince this nitwit that his family needed to align itself with Mother's latest campaign if he wouldn't sit still for five blasted seconds?

An itch twinged in the palm of my hand as if to answer the question. The truth was I knew exactly how to bend this waif of a boy to my will. I could mold his very thoughts like wet clay coaxed between my fingers and sculpt them into any shape I desired. Even now, I could feel the pitiful defenses surrounding Edward's subconscious. It would be almost nothing to crush them.

But that would mean I'd have to forfeit my bet. And I would be damned before conceding to Lynette, even if it meant spending all night in this mortal bar.

I just needed to pour on the charm.

My hand slid down from Edward's thin shoulder to his elbow, gripping it gently. I pulled him close enough to whisper in his ear, "Are you sure, Edward? I've been waiting such a long time for the two of us to share some quality time together."

I poured as much honey into my words as they would carry, setting the bait to draw in my prey. Now, I'd have to just sit back and wait for him to take it.

Edward looked over at me, the stupid grin fading from his lips. "What about the party?"

"Damn the party," I said, trying to keep the playfulness of my tone from spilling over to frustration. "Let the mortals celebrate another cycle around the sun. We have more important things to discuss."

Edward shrugged my hand off, grabbing the drink the bartender placed in front of him and taking a gulp.

*Well, shit. That wasn't the reaction I had hoped for.*

"I'm kidding," I added quickly, doing my best to salvage the mess before it completely imploded. "Of course we can stay for the silly little countdown. Where do I get one of those gauche hats?"

Edward looked at me then, a glimmer of sadness in his eyes. Or was it... pity? I bristled at the idea. Where the hell did this boy get off, looking at me like that?

"You don't get it, do you?"

"Get what?" I seethed, frustration reaching a boiling point.

"Why I want to be here. Why it thrills me to be caught up in the excitement. To be at the center of so many emotions that you can feel them electrifying the air around you. You can feel it, Tobias, can't you?"

Would he ever shut up? The air in the bar felt no different than any other place packed to the gills with mortals—tinged with desperation and misery. Nothing I would want to expose myself to longer than necessary.

"It's too bad," Edward concluded, then downed the rest of his drink as he slid off the barstool. He leaned in close enough that I could smell the alcohol on his breath. "You're so damn pretty, Tobias. It's a shame you can't see past your own misery."

Edward turned to walk away, but I caught him by the elbow before he could slink out of reach.

"You stupid little shit," I muttered just between the two of us. With a deep breath, I reached for the magic brimming under my skin, projecting it outward and over the blond. Edward's magical defenses—the pitifully thin layer of magic that he wrapped himself with—crumpled under the swift assault, and his body went rigid. "Looks like I just lost a bet."

Edward's features twisted in confusion for a moment before the shroud of my magic fully engulfed him, his expression then dissolving into blank compliance.

I leaned forward, speaking directly into the man's ear. "Tomorrow morning, you are going to convince Madame Rothwind to abandon her plans to extend protections to the Unseen. If she does not agree, then you are to use any force necessary to persuade her. Is that understood?"

Edward started back, unblinking.

"Yes."

"There's a good boy. Now, take off that ridiculous hat and go home."

As I withdrew my shroud of magic, Edward's trembling hand removed the cardboard hat, setting it on the bar. Without another word, he turned from me, weaving his way through the crowded dance floor toward the exit. I lost sight of him from there, but my work was already complete.

I waved to the closest bartender, motioning to close out my tab, but they were too absorbed in a conversation to notice me. By the time I was able to finally able to flag someone down, the barstool to my left had been filled.

"Where are you off to, Tobi?"

I didn't have to look to know who had taken Edward's place. She must have been close by, counting on me to break tonight.

I let out a heavy sigh. "I really did put in the effort, Lenny. You have to give me some credit."

Lynette propped an elbow on the bar, resting her chin on it. Her emerald eyes shined with an amusement that only came from teasing her brother. "Do I now? I'm fairly certain I still won our little wager, no matter how you want to frame it. So, pay up, little brother."

As much as I didn't want to admit my defeat, I knew she had me dead to rights. Reaching inside the pocket of my jacket, I retrieved the golden foil-wrapped rectangle and placed it on the bar in front of Lynette.

"To the victor goes the spoils."

She swiped up her prize, hastily unwrapping the top half with a giddiness that I would never understand. The sweet smell of chocolate wafted into the air, mulling with the stinging stench of spilled alcohol. Lynette snapped off a square of the chocolate, raising it to her mouth and taking a long, exaggerated inhale before biting it. A soft groan rumbled through her chest.

"It tastes so much better when suffused with the joys of winning."

"You're disgusting," I snickered, pulling at the lapels of my jacket to straighten them. "Where is your decorum?"

"Back at the consulate with Mother, where it belongs. Where's your date?"

"You've already won, Lenny. No need to gloat."

She leaned in closer, her teeth stained with chocolate and her breath sweet.

"Unfortunately, you've yet to learn your lesson, so I'm allowed to gloat as long as I wish."

I exhaled, rubbing at my temples. "Our schooling ended ages ago. Why must you torture me with these asinine lessons of yours?"

Lynette didn't answer right away, taking her time to watch me with eyes that mirrored my own. Although we weren't identical, Lynette and I shared more features than not. The same warm, coppery curls, though hers draped down to her shoulders while mine were cut short. The same alabaster complexion, complete with a smattering of freckles that burst to life with only the slightest coaxing of the sun. The same arched brows, constantly reaching for the sky as if they were always slightly amused—though that often couldn't be further from the truth.

"Did Mother tell you to wear that?" she asked, decidedly ignoring my question.

I looked down at the sapphire-colored double-breasted vest, working my fingers under the edge and giving it a gentle tug to make sure it wasn't riding up. "She might have suggested it. Why do you ask?"

Her hand moved, subtle enough that most wouldn't notice, but I clearly clocked the golden shimmer of magic ripple along her skin as the buttons burst from my vest, scattering across the floor and disappearing into the crowd. The ignorant bar patrons didn't notice the magical maneuver as someone across the room erupted in a rallying cry, a gaggle of beverages being raised above heads in response.

"Was that absolutely necessary?" I asked, running fingers down my tie to ensure it wasn't also a casualty of my sister's impish game. "Those buttons are sterling silver."

Lynette snorted a laugh. "And? Since when do you care?"

"Since Mother put me on an allowance," I snapped, causing Lynette to recoil. "Not all of us have the privilege of being a Successor. I still have to prove my worth to stay in Mother's good graces."

Lynette groaned, reaching across the bar to nab a glass and a clear bottle of spirits. The bartender closest to her doesn't bat an eyelash, too absorbed in conversation with a brunette clad in leather to notice. She poured herself a shot, slurping it down before saying, "Trust me, you have the better deal."

"Right," I scoffed. She couldn't be serious. "Yes, flirting and fucking my way through Adored nobility at the behest of our mother is far better than wielding *immeasurable power."* I tipped forward, sliding off the stool and once again trying to get the attention of the bartender. I weighed the pros and cons of leaving with my tab unpaid. It may be worth it to rid myself of this place that much sooner.

"You're wrong," Lynette said, pouring another round and sliding it over to me. "We're both whoring ourselves out. But at least your whoring can be a little fun. Edward wasn't the worst person to look at."

"He's an idiot," I corrected her, taking the offered drink and downing it in one go. The alcohol burned the back of my throat—a byproduct of cheap liquor—and I coughed before adding, "The biggest idiot of his family, which is really saying something."

Finally, one of the bartenders caught my eye, and I motioned in the air to pantomime signing the check. The bartender gave me a brisk nod before disappearing around the corner. Maybe this one would actually come back.

Lynette raised her glass to me in a toast.

"To the fucked-up things we do for family."

She knocked back her drink, reaching for the bottle again.

"You're in a cheery mood," I said, grabbing the little black book offered by the bartender. They didn't even blink an eye at Lynette pouring her own drinks. I stuffed a fistful of bills into the book, snapping it shut with a finality that I hoped Lynette would pick up on. I wasn't in the mood to tolerate any more of her teasing. I needed to get home and scrub the squalor of this bar from my skin. "I'll leave to your bottle, then."

I turned to leave, but she snagged me by the sleeve. "Wait, don't go."

Pulling myself from her clutches, I knocked shoulders with the person beside me, but they didn't seem to care or even notice, for that matter. These mortals were all so oblivious, so wrapped up in their impotent little lives. They clung to whatever absurdity would secure them the smallest fraction of contentment. Which, at this point, meant wearing those ridiculous cardboard hats and blowing on noisemakers that caterwauled like dying animals.

"I need a bath," I told my sister. "Before the stench of this place seeps into my pores. It reeks of piss and sadness."

Lynette's lip curled with a sneer. "Gods, when did you become such a stuck-up *prick?"*

Her words bit into my skin like thorns, sticking and digging their way inside. How could she sit there, casting judgment on me when I was only doing what Mother required of me? I was the same as her, albeit without a lot of the pomp and circumstance of a position of power. She was the Successor, after all. Being stuck up came with the territory.

"That's smart, coming from the Successor of the Greene family name. In just a few years, you'll be the one stepping on people's throats and pimping me out for your own agenda. So why don't you come down from your high horse already and admit that you're no better than I am?"

Lynette held my gaze even as she poured herself another drink, stoicism in motion. But then, she softened, her emerald eyes growing round and the lines of her face smoothing with an exhale.

"I've missed you," she said, soft enough that I almost missed it amongst the noise of the bar. She abandoned the glass on the counter, stepping forward and wrapping her arms around my waist. Lynette buried her face into my chest, her mouth moving to form words that I couldn't possibly hear above the din.

Any flames of frustration contained within me sputtered out, smothered by the rare sincerity of my sister's gesture. I sighed, resting my hands on the small of her back.

"I'm sorry," I apologized, my chin settling on the crown of her head as she clung to me. "It's been a long night, and I'm not myself."

Releasing her hold on me, Lynette wiped at her face, turning her back to me while she cleared her throat. "I haven't felt like myself in a long time." Her hand lingered on the edge of her glass. "Too much time with Mother, I think. Her poison is slow, but it's powerful."

"Afraid you'll turn into her?" I asked in a teasing tone. But when Lynette turned back to me, I knew that I'd struck a nerve. "Sorry again. You're nothing like her, Lenny. And you never will be. That much evil stuffed into a pair of sensible pumps is a once-in-a-millennia event."

She cracked a smile. "Thank you, Tobi. I needed to hear that tonight."

There was more behind her words. Something that she kept for herself. Years ago, back when our lives were simpler, she would never have withheld something from me. But those days were a thing of the past. And, although I was itching to slake my curiosity, I knew that it would be better for both of us if I dropped the topic.

"It's been good seeing you," Lynette said, raising her glass to me. "Enjoy your bath."

And even though I'd been waiting to make my escape since the moment I set foot in this mortal bar, I found myself saying, "Ugh, fine. You've got me until midnight." I snatched the drink from her hand, downing the pungent liquid with a gulp. "Let's go dance those troubles away."

Lynette brightened, the creases at the corners of her eyes smoothing as she took my hand, pulling me toward the dance floor and the flashing lights. And there, spinning on that sweat-stained floor, my sister cackling with glee as pockets of colored light washed over us, I found myself happier than I'd been in a very long time.

I'd never experienced such pain.

The dull ache sunk deeper into my muscles with every step, each movement. A cold sweat slicked my forehead, even as I reclined on the posh leather bench of the town car Lorelei had summoned to take us to the destination I wasn't allowed to know. The car had been spelled to drive itself, which only added to my suspicions of this so-called mortal. Spelled vehicles did not come cheap and required regular magical maintenance to keep them from driving you off a cliff. She'd have to have connections in the Magi community to even procure one to begin with.

We rolled over a bump in the road, and another wave of nauseating pain washed through my system. It was enough that I had to concentrate on stifling the groans that built in my throat.

It was only pain, I reminded myself. Temporary. All I needed to do was focus on something else. Distractions would prove themselves my savior.

But looking out onto the passing streets only intensified the nausea, so instead, I allowed my gaze to drift over to Bastien. He was facing the tinted window, gazing through at the banal scenery, which streaked by in a blur of greys that refracted across the shine of his dark eyes. The line of his jaw was taut as if he were clenching his teeth. Flashes of memories surfaced in my mind, cycling through like a carousel, all blurred faces, figures, and places in constant motion. With a bit of effort, I was able to sift through for signs of Bastien. I had seen him from so many different angles, it turned out. Watched him from across the room and from beneath his strong frame. From a balcony high above as he traversed the busy sidewalks below and through the window of a car as he drove away.

There was something different about the way he looked now. Something alien in the movement of his body. I couldn't place a finger on the exact anomaly. Perhaps I had just grown unaccustomed to the melancholy that seemed to cling to Bastien.

Where had it come from?

The car bounced again, and a hiss escaped through my teeth.

Bastien's trance broke, his attention quickly drawn to me as he unleashed the full intensity of his stare. "Are you okay?"

"Not quite sure how to answer that," I said, the pain forcing a bluntness I typically strayed from. Exhaling through my teeth, the throbbing pain dulled slightly. "Am I going to feel like this the entirety of my second life?"

Bastien chewed on his response for a moment, then reached out to me.

"Give me your hand."

"That's quite all right," I said quickly, folding my arms across my chest. "I'm not a child. You can just answer my question."

Bastien didn't lower his offering, staring me down with fingers outstretched. I would be lying if I told myself that I didn't want to take it. To feel Bastien's skin against my own, even in this small way. A shock of electricity ran along my spine as I imagined those fingers wrapped around mine.

But I was certain things would never be what they once were. It wouldn't mean anything to Bastien. I'm not even sure what it would have meant to me at that point. What I wouldn't have given to recall the details of the schism between us. Maybe then, my body would calm down around Bastien. But what if I'd never stopped having feelings for him? Bastien could have been the one to call things off. Abandoning me, just like all the others that came before, like all the so-called friends who didn't seem to care that I was in a grave.

None of them came for me. Only him.

A new heat flashed under my cheeks, radiating down into my chest. Anger, red-hot and building like a wildfire now, raging through my system.

Why was I allowed to die? I was Magi, for gods' sake. Not only that, I was the son of the most powerful Adored in existence today. Even the most inept of healers should have been able to bring me back from the brink of death. It was so rare for one of our kind to die from anything other than old age. So, why was I left for dead?

Something wasn't adding up.

I swatted away Bastien's hand, causing him to recoil, the line of his jaw going taut once more.

"I was only trying to help."

A cruel laugh bubbled up over my lips. "I'm certain you were."

My mind—more organized than it had been since the moment I awakened on that frigid desk—raced, grasping any scrap of information I could about the time leading up to my death. It wasn't that I couldn't remember what happened. It was more that all of my memories were jumbled together. Like a box containing every bit of my life had been dumped out, piled high enough that all I could do was sort through them one by one and give my best guess at the chronology.

"You're flushed."

Bastien's stupid, smooth voice disrupted my concentration.

"I'm fine," I assured him, sliding as close to the door as was physically possible. I rested a cheek on the cool window. Water droplets clung to the exterior, the fine mist that had been falling from the ominous grey sky conjoining across the smooth surface until it formed bulbous spheres large enough to streak across the window. I could only hope the fragments of my life would behave the same. Once enough of them emulsify, they would streak through my consciousness, catching the rest and pooling together. Then maybe I'd be able to find some answers before Bastien put me back in the ground.

*The ground.*

A flash of recognition ensnared my mind, followed by blinding pain splitting my skull in half. I doubled over, sucking in air through my teeth—

*I was falling forward, head over heels, tumbling onto a mound of soft earth, twisted and dazed. I struggled to find purchase on the loamy ground beneath, but couldn't seem to orient myself, couldn't figure out which way was up as more earth rained down from above. My body was on fire, my limbs twisted in unnatural angles as I tried to claw my way out, but darkness soon overwhelmed me, choking my senses as dirt filled my mouth, my eyes, my lungs. I thrashed in the pitch black, fighting to keep myself above the churning earth, but all too soon, I was pinned, blinded and sputtering under the crushing weight.*

*Then everything was quiet.*

*I was alone in the ground.*

*Surely, someone was coming to save me. They would be here soon, yes?*

*Gods, someone save me!*

"Tobias."

My eyes fluttered open, the details of the town car coming back into focus as I fought the urge to wretch. I could still feel the dirt in my throat, the grit of it between my teeth.

Bastien uttered a string of words that buzzed in my ears, pressing his palm firmly against my chest. Soothing heat radiated from the gem embedded in my skin, pulsing through my limbs and calming the agonizing ache.

"Your body can't take this much stress," Bastien said, his hand lingering on me even after the waves of heat had ceased. "Tell me what's happening. Let me help you."

"I remembered," I choked out the words, hands still clawing at my throat. "The way I died."

Bastien's hand retracted slowly. I turned to him, suddenly seeking the weight of his stare. But he was looking down at his hands, his expression stoic. "I'm sorry," he said quietly, tracing the lines of his palm with his index finger. "I know it must be painful."

"It's horrible," I corrected him. "Who did this to me, Bastien? Does anyone even care that I went into the ground? Did my mother even shed a tear for me? Or is everyone too caught up worrying about who will step in if she can't name a new Successor?"

The questions spilled from me one after the other, a dam of frustration bursting. My mind was only getting sharper by the second, and I couldn't halt the anger that built along with the clarity. I had been wronged. Murdered. Discarded. And the only ones who seemed to give a damn were the ones who could profit off my death.

What was worse, in the back of my mind, I couldn't escape the feeling that maybe the murder was deserved. That I must have done something truly awful. But it was impossible to know until my mind was whole again.

The partition between the back and front rows of the town car lowered, revealing Lorelei's expressionless face. "We're here," she announced in a bored tone, seemingly oblivious to the tension in the air of the backseat.

I tried the handle of the door, desperate for fresh air, but it didn't budge. I looked back to find Lorelei giving me a pitying smile. "It's probably a good time to mention that if you try and make a run for it, Mr. Tall, Dark, and Handsome here can make that gem in your chest go supernova and blow you straight back to Hell. So, do behave yourself while we're in public, yes?"

I ground my teeth, glowering between my two captors. "So be it. Just get me out of this fucking car."

"My, my," Lorelei tutted, wagging a finger at me. "That language is so unbecoming of someone from your upbringing."

My stomach twisted, bile rising in my throat.

"You wouldn't believe how wrong you are."

# FOUR
## A DEAD END

*T*he crowded coffee shop bustled with life, even in the dying light of the late afternoon. I checked the time on my watch before scanning the rows of tables and cushy chairs in search of today's assignment. Mother had briefed me on the topics of discussion I was to bring up during my "date" with the son of an influential Adored matriarch, but already, I could feel the tedium sinking in as I stood in line to order. Another afternoon of vapid conversation and subtle influence as I charmed the pants off an insipid socialite.

These days, I felt more escort than envoy.

But such was my lot. It was how I could prove myself useful to Mother and stay in her good graces. And the job wasn't without its perks. Being in the favor of the figurehead of the Magi Council opened endless doors for me, even if I did still have to wait in line for coffee.

"Next, please."

The person standing ahead moved, making room for me to approach the wooden counter. A woman with pale pink hair and an impressively detailed sleeve of tattoos nodded at me. "What can we get started for you?"

"Double espresso over ice," I ordered, eyeing the mouthwatering pastries in the bakery case before deciding better. It would be too difficult to steer the conversation in the necessary direction if I had a mouthful of scone crumbs. Even though they looked incredibly tasty....

I handed the woman a bill, waved away the offer for change, and slid down the counter to the waiting area, maneuvering carefully around the other patrons queued for their caffeinated concoctions.

"Here you go, Larry."

A deep-timbered voice drew my attention as the barista handed a short, round man his order over the counter.

"Thanks, Bastien," the portly man replied, grabbing the mug and carefully turning on his heel to retreat to a small table in the corner covered in newspapers.

The barista—Bastien, as confirmed by the name stitched on the front of his apron—returned to the polished chrome espresso machine, humming under his breath as he pulled the next shot of rich, dark liquid. His arms were the first thing that held my attention. The sleeves of his white shirt were rolled past the elbow to reveal sinewy flesh, just a few shades lighter than the rich coffee he masterfully poured from a small glass. The next was his hair, rows of tight, dark locks stylishly swept to the side. They bobbed with each confident movement the man took, every step a gracefully choreographed loop of motion.

I forced myself to look away as the barista handed out the next beverage, if only because I was concerned he'd catch my lingering gaze. But as soon as the patron stepped away with their order, my eyes were drawn right back to him.

He smiled as he worked, humming an aimless tune. I couldn't quite catch the melody in its entirety from where I stood, but what I picked up made the corners of my mouth twitch upward.

"Double espresso," Bastien announced, scanning the line of customers before his sights narrowed in on me. "Here you go, friend."

I stepped forward, an irregular heat building behind my cheeks. Without a word, I swiped the glass from the counter, reeling to move as quickly as I could away from the barista and into the café.

What in blazes was that? Perhaps I was coming down with something? I would seek out a healer as soon as my duty pertaining to this "date" was finished.

"Tobias!"

A lean, brunette-haired figure waved at me from across the room. My target had been spotted at last. Now, all that remained was the manipulation. It was a simple enough job, really. If my words and looks weren't enough to sway the man, I could always rely on magic to get my point across. But that required a certain risk on my end, as other Adored matriarchs could possibly detect my influence on their sons, so it was best to keep it in reserve as a last resort.

I pushed the barista from my mind and set my focus on the target.

"Corinth, I do hope I didn't keep you waiting long." I maneuvered around the table, pulling out the chair opposite the brunette. His smooth features masked his true age—just a year younger than myself—and he wore a loose poet's shirt with golden string lacing the top that displayed the supple flesh beneath.

He was easy prey that was for certain.

"Not at all," Corinth replied, flashing a bright smile. "I was so glad to hear from you. It feels like I've been twisting your arm for ages to get some one-on-one time. Your mother must keep you quite busy."

"I'm lucky to be so useful," I replied, settling into my seat. From this angle, I could still see the handsome barista each time he served a beverage over the counter. "But today isn't about business," I continued, leaning over the table to take Corinth's delicate hand in mine. "I'd like to keep to the topics of pleasure if that's alright with you?"

Corinth's cheeks flushed as he nodded, bouncing curls momentarily obscuring his sapphire-like eyes. He was cute. I would award him that. If it weren't for my duty, I could see myself wooing this man for entirely different motives. Unfortunately, that fact did little to alleviate me from my responsibility to Mother. This man held something that she needed, and my orders were to take it.

But that didn't mean it had to be entirely unpleasant.

"Has anyone ever told you that your eyes favor the depths of Lake Veranova?"

Corinth's lashes fluttered as he batted those crystalline eyes at me, then shook his head. "I can't say they have. I've never been to Veranova if you can believe it. Mother always wants to vacation in the mountains, so I usually end up bundled in three layers of coats, pretending I like to ski."

I let out a light chuckle, stroking the back of Corinth's hand with my thumb. "The mountains are beautiful too, of course. Think of it: a cozy cabin with a warm fire, wine flowing as easy as conversation, and we'd spend the evening *curled up—"*

"Here we go, sir." A glass pot of coffee landed on the table, severing my hold on Corinth's hand. I looked up, flustered, to find Bastien standing at the edge of the table, a warm smile spreading his full lips. He pulled out a small hourglass from the pocket of his apron, flipping it over so the red sand began to trickle down. "Your aero press. Once the timer runs out, press down on the plunger, and you'll be ready to enjoy."

Corinth nodded at the barista. "Thank you. Could I bother you for some cream and sugar?" His gaze fell back to me, and he added, "I like things on the sweeter side."

"No bother at all," Bastien replied, turning to direct his smile at me. "I'll be back in just a moment."

"Sorry about that," Corinth apologized sheepishly, his fingers wrapping around the empty mug in front of him as he watched the sand fall through the hourglass. "What were you saying?"

"It doesn't matter," I replied, brushing off the interruption. I leaned closer once more, lowering my voice. "Why don't you tell me more about these ski trips?"

Corinth launched into an incredibly unamusing recollection of his family's latest trip to the Crested Mountains, and I did my best to appear interested in the details of places I'd never been to and people I'd never met. By the time Bastien returned with a small pitcher of cream and a ramekin of sugar, I was almost relieved to see him if only to take a breather from the mundanity of Corinth's ramblings.

"I think you're ready," said Bastien after setting down the accompaniments. He pressed the stopper down on the small pot, and a stream of rich-smelling coffee poured into the bottom reservoir. "If you'll allow me." He motioned to the empty mug, and Corinth nodded enthusiastically.

Bastien deftly poured from the pot, filling the mug but still leaving enough room at the top for Corinth's additions. As he returned the vessel to the center of the table, he eyed my untouched beverage.

"Was the espresso not to your liking?"

"What?" I looked down at the glass in front of me, a bead of condensation rolling down the side and pooling on the surface of the wooden table. "Oh, I'm sure it's fine."

# THE SECOND AWAKENING

Bastien didn't move, still eyeing me expectantly. Corinth watched me as well, a curious expressing twisting his smooth features.

I was beginning to feel like an oddity to be gawked at, so I grabbed the glass, raising it to my lips, and drew a long swig. The bright, floral flavor of the espresso danced along my tongue, bold at first but dissolving into the subtle sweetness of chocolate.

Bastien's smile grew wider, obviously satisfied with my reaction to his work. Maybe it was just the way the light hit them, but I could have sworn I could see something glimmering in behind those honeyed eyes as the man looked at me.

"Do let me know if I can assist you further," said the barista, pulling his attention back to Corinth. With that, he departed, leaving me floundering as an electric trill shot down my spine.

"They're so friendly here," said Corinth, stirring a heaping spoonful of sugar into his cup. "I'll definitely be back."

I watched as Bastien returned behind the counter, his golden eyes finding me once more from across the café.

"Yes, I imagine I will, too."

The car door opened from the exterior, blinding sunlight pouring into the cab as Bastien reached in and offered me his hand. I ignored the offer, gripping the doorframe to steady myself as I climbed into the warmth of the afternoon. The air was still humid from the earlier rain, but a break in the clouds overhead was enough to douse the area in glowing light.

When I was alive—the first time—I never gave much thought to my affection for sunlight. How it wrapped around me in a warm embrace but never felt smothering. How it danced along the ends of my curls, transfiguring them into flames that fell into my eyes. The gentle way it coaxed open a budding flower in the gardens around the chateau or guided twisting vines as they stretched for the heavens. It was a constant companion to all who thrived in the light.

Now, I only wondered how long I'd have to enjoy it before I returned to the dark.

"Do you remember this place, Tobias?"

Lorelei watched me, her thin brows raised with a sort of bored curiosity. In the sunlight, her hair was golden thread, weaved into spiraling coils.

Pulling myself away from my re-acquaintance with the sun, I looked up at the iron gate across the sidewalk, wrapped in strangling ivy. Beyond the gates, rows of rosebushes bloomed in a cacophony of colors, the grounds sloping upward until they reached a beautiful structure of grey stone in the distance. A soft wind drifted over the wall, bringing with it a sweet, floral aroma that lifted memories to the surface of my mind, like buoys bobbing over waves.

"The Floating Gardens," I answered, my voice almost swallowed by the breeze.

"That's right," Lorelei confirmed with a nod. "This is one of the last places your sister was seen before her disappearance. My reports say that the two of you left together. Now, I need you to walk me through what happened that night."

I concentrated on the flashes of memory that came with the next breeze, but they were too sporadic to try and form a timeline—*Lenny and I stood on a balcony, our mother beside us as she addressed the gathered crowd below. The next, I leaned against a bar, my glass filled with a swirling green concoction as I chatted with the handsome bartender. He gave me a wink, and I gave him a tip. Next, I was running my hands along the soft petals of red roses as I moved through the garden. In the golden light of dusk, the bushes came to life around me, rising into the air as their translucent roots dislodged themselves from the soft earth, drifting upward until a thin rope attached to their base pulled taut, keeping them from drifting too far. Then, there was a man before me with salt and pepper hair and a tie of glittering gold. He spoke of deals made behind closed doors, and his breath reeked of onions. Then, another face, another conversation of broken details, none of which seemed important. And more faces, each washed of detail until they were reduced to a parade of mannequins draped in finery, circling me in a carousel of silk and satin.*

A steadying hand on the small of my back rocketed me back to the present moment. I shied away from Bastien's touch, ignoring the traces of heat that it left on my skin. "It's too jumbled," I said through an exhale, my breathing shaky. "I can recall bits and pieces, but it'll take me forever to sort it into anything coherent."

"We don't have the luxury of forever," Lorelei said, pulling the small notebook from her vest pocket and flipping it open. "Every moment, Lynette's fate grows grimmer. So, might I suggest you find a way to speed things along?"

"Are you not some grandiose detective?" I queried, a heated frustration rising in my gut. "My mother wouldn't waste her time with someone who was inept. Surely, you've already parsed out the details of what happened that night. What do you need me for?"

Lorelei's notebook snapped shut as she leveled a glare at me. "I have testimonies, yes. I know where the two of you went after the celebration. I know the food that was prepared. I know the family history of the woman who served Lynette dinner—they've got a nice farm not too far from here. What I lack, Mr. Greene, is *context*. Those invisible threads that tie everything together. I need to know what Lynette was feeling leading up to the event. If she mentioned being worried about anything in particular, or if anyone from outside her usual cohorts was hanging around. Those are the details I'm interested in, so stop wasting my time and start talking."

"Don't push too hard," Bastien interrupted, which did little to elevate my mood. "His mental state is still fragile. You don't want him to fracture."

"What in blazes does that mean?" I questioned, temper flaring. I was growing weary of the barrage of ominous afflictions I had acquired during my short second life. I'd been ill fewer times than I could count on one hand, yet now I was moments from falling apart at every turn.

Bastien sighed, thick fingers rubbing the slope of his brow. "It's a complication from Death's Touch. If you place too much stress on your psyche, it can fracture. You'll end up losing yourself permanently."

"Losing myself?" I repeated, a chill running up my spine. "What, like I go off my rocker?"

"Something like that," Bastien replied, averting his eyes.

"Then what do you suggest we do, corpse peddler?" Lorelei asked with a huff, the toe of her shoe tapping against the sidewalk in an impatient staccato. "This is obviously a problem rooted in your expertise."

"We can walk him through the space," Bastien replied, moving toward the iron gates and pushing on them. They groaned in protest but swung open. "We'll give his memories the opportunity to resurface naturally. It's the best chance we have to avoid lasting damage."

"Why bother?"

The question leaped from my mouth before I could stop it. The others turned to look at me, Lorelei grinning and Bastien looking like he was going to be sick. Overhead, the sun was obscured once more behind a wall of grey clouds, matching the shift in my mood.

"Why are you so hellbent on keeping me intact?" I continued, stretching out the collar of my shirt to poke at the sparkling gem protruding from my sternum. "I'm dead, Bast. What does it matter if I end up broken in the end? It won't change anything."

"See?" Lorelei positioned herself beside me, placing a dainty hand on my shoulder. "He's willing to do whatever it takes. It is his sister we're trying to find, after all."

Bastien glowered, the darkness of his expression accentuating the growl in his voice. "You don't know what you're saying."

"Of course I don't!" I shouted, arms flailing with frustration. "I'm only the one who was murdered, then dragged out of my cozy little grave and tossed into a clusterfuck of butchered memories and mind-numbing pain. So, you'll have to excuse me if I've become a little disillusioned with this shitty second life. You can't blame me for being interested in speeding up our hellish little field trip so I can get back to my dirt nap."

Bastien blinked, the lines of his face smoothing. Lorelei grinned like a madwoman at my side, white teeth against crimson lips as if she'd been waiting for me to hit my breaking point.

"He's willing to take the risk," she said, pushing past the two of us and stepping through the open gate. "So, let's get on with it, shall we?"

"Slow," Bastien warned me as I trudged through, following Lorelei into the gardens.

The sun peeked through the clouds above, beams of golden light streaming down over the expanse of greenery. We were on the far side of the garden, the large building crafted from grey stone resting atop a verdant hill overlooking this place of beauty. Rows and rows of vibrant flora lined diverging paths of swirling design, intended to keep one wandering for hours. Another breeze kicked up, and I was wrapped in the honey-sweet aroma of roses.

It was peaceful here in the waning sunlight. The soft sounds of the branches swaying in the wind, the chittering of tiny animals that dashed under bush and trees, the thousands of blooms, each facing the bashful sun, the entity that brought them life.

I couldn't help but feel the same way. Except, it wasn't the sun's warm rays that brought me back. No, it was the handsome man standing six feet away, watching my movements like a hawk. I was fully aware of it, the distance between us. Almost as if there was an invisible cord tethering me to Bastien. And perhaps there was. I knew little about the ways of the Reviled's magic. Did it make sense that I would feel drawn to the man whose magic brought me back to the world of the living? Whose magic quite literally ran through my veins?

It made all the sense in the world to me at the moment.

"Anything?" Lorelei stood under the shade of a fir tree, arms crossed and looking at me expectantly. The chill from her icy blue eyes set the hair on the back of my neck standing. She could freeze a sweltering afternoon with that stare.

"Not yet," I replied, pausing as my eye was drawn to a particularly beautiful rose—a deep and sultry orange. A bumblebee hovered over the open bud, its body covered in yellow specs of pollen. I watched, transfixed, as it disappeared, only for a moment, into the petals, then resurfaced, perching atop the edge of the flower. It watched me, too, with large bulbous eyes staring up at me like it knew I didn't belong there.

Then again, perhaps that was a bit much to infer from an insect.

With a gentle buzz, the bee took flight, circling me lazily before changing trajectory upward and becoming a streak across the sky. As I watched it go, a sudden chill settled around me. The bee illuminated, bursting to life as a pinprick of light across the now-darkened sky. The sun had fallen impossibly fast, and the garden had come to life around me with lamps of swirling green fire suspended over the paved walkways. The bee flashed again, and I realized that it wasn't a bee at all but a glowing firefly dancing on the gentle night breeze. There were more of them now, fluttering between the rows of flora and shedding their candescence across the ground below, each a burning star against the backdrop of deep purples and blues.

The fireflies weren't the only thing to move amongst the darkness. Figures draped in clothing made from shadows stalked around me, drifting on soundless steps as they went, seemingly undisturbed by my presence.

"What's going on here?" I asked, turning to where I expected to see Bastien, only the sidewalk was empty. Lorelei had vanished, too, which did little to quell the panic rising in my chest.

"Hello? Can anyone hear me?"

The shadows paid me no mind, continuing on their way without hesitation. One drew near, but when I reached for it, whispers brushed against my mind, soft as a caress but unintelligible.

I spun in place, grasping for anything recognizable. If I could get back to the gate, perhaps I could find the others. But dusk had robbed me of my bearings, and even though I was certain I was heading in the correct direction, it didn't take me long to become lost among the winding paths.

My thoughts raced. Had my mind fractured, like Bastien warned? Had I been sent into the shadows of madness?

Panic swelled in my gut.

"Come along, Tobi! Mother is going to mount my head if I keep her waiting any longer."

The words shredded through the shadows around me, coming from another figure that moved in the distance. Where all of the others had been ghostly apparitions, this one was an ethereal being haloed in golden light.

As she approached, she smiled at me, hesitating long enough for recognition to kick in.

"Lenny?" I choked on her name.

She snatched my hand, dragging me alongside her. Her lavender dress billowed out from her waist—an antiquated silhouette popular amongst the Adored—with layers of ruffled fabric lending her the illusion of a physical presence far larger than reality.

As she pulled, I felt my body snap into place—as if something or *someone* were controlling it—and I followed her lead, clutching her arm.

"Let her squawk." My lips moved along to the words. "Her days of tyranny are nearly over. What can she do now?"

Lynette weaved us through the faceless crowds, squaring us on the path up to the looming stone building at the top of the hill. The windows glowed with an inviting, soft amber light. "Just because she's giving up her title doesn't mean she can't still make our lives a living hell, Tobi."

My lips moved again, my voice sounding like it was coming from somewhere behind me in a fashion most disorienting. "And how would that be any different from the last twenty-some-odd years?"

Lynette looked back at me, her blood-red painted lips spreading wide. But something touched her eyes then. Melancholia appeared like a stranger in the dark, then slipped away as she turned from me, the mask of her smile firmly in place once more.

"It won't be that way much longer, Tobi. I promise."

Her words struck me like a sour note in a chord. What did she mean by that?

We passed others as Lynette moved us through the garden, weaving our way towards the observatory. Shadowy figures went by, illuminated briefly by the shimmering golden light that radiated from us. As the light washed over their features, they came into sharp detail, and it took me only a few moments to put things into place.

This was my memory from the night Lynette disappeared. The shadows hid the details I couldn't recall—the faces of those I didn't interact with or objects that didn't capture my attention. But the golden light brought illumination—both literal and figurative—to all of the details I *did* remember.

How clever of my fractured mind to lay things out so cinematically.

"You'll never guess who decided to show their arse at the bar earlier," my lips continued to move while my body dodged a floating silver tray of hors d'oeuvres. My hand snatched one of the puffed pastries as they went by. "And after everything I did to show them a splendid time last fall—"

A strong grip on my shoulder yanked me backward, and I was blinded by a sudden flash of light. I raised my arm to shield my eyes.

"Tobias!"

I blinked, Bastien's features seeping through the brightness that assaulted my senses. He was panting, a droplet of sweat beaded on his dusky brow. Gone were the murmuring voices of the faceless shadows, the shapeless figures, and Lynette. I was standing in the sunlit garden once more, the memory of that night fading with each second, sifting through my grasp like the details of a dream.

"What happened?" I asked, still regaining my bearings from the whiplash of the changing scenery. "How did I get back?"

"Back?" Bastien repeated, his brow furrowing. "What are you talking about?"

His grip on my arm slackened, and it was only then that I noticed that Bastien had been holding me in place. My skin ached from the touch, a dull throb.

"I was with Lynette," I explained, turning around and half-expecting her to be there, waiting for me with outstretched arms, her lavender dress glowing brilliantly in the daylight. But there was just a topiary and an empty path weaving its way towards the clubhouse.

Bastien's golden eyes were wide when I turned around.

"What do you mean you were with her?"

"Did you find him?" Lorelei poked her head over a rosebush—a feat for one as vertically challenged as she—then rounded the corner to meet them. "Oh, thank the gods."

"I saw her," I answered Bastien's question with a huff, heated frustration burning behind my eyes. "I don't know how I did it. Nothing here is making sense. One moment, I was staring at a blasted rosebush, and the next, Lynette was pulling me through a sea of faceless shadow people, chattering on like nothing has changed."

Lorelei tensed at Bastien's side. "You saw her?"

"Yes. And no. I don't think she was actually here. Or maybe *I* wasn't actually here. It was like I was—"

"Reliving a memory?"

Lorelei and I both turned to look at Bastien.

"You know what this is?" I asked, ashamed that I was still letting myself be surprised. "Let me guess, now you'll tell me it's a death thing, right? Then you'll warn me about how dangerous it is, and blah, blah, blah. Can we skip to the part where you explain whether or not this is going to help us find Lynette?"

The edges of Bastien's mouth twitched as he held back a smirk. "I actually have no idea if it's dangerous, but I do know there's a name for it."

My eyes rolled back in annoyance. "Is it ominous?"

Bastien's teeth sunk into his lower lip—another sign he was holding back laughter.

"Call it whatever you want," Lorelei interrupted, "does this mean you can recall what happened that night? Can you go through the details?"

"They're fuzzy," I said, shaking my head. "I didn't get that far before I was pulled out."

"You were about to walk head-first into a topiary," Bastien defended himself. "Was I supposed to let you impale yourself on a sword made out of boxwood?" He motioned to the sculpted knight figure behind me, its weapon drawn and pointed down at chest level.

Lorelei exhaled, a deflated sound like an exasperated mother whose children had worn her down to the last nerve. "With every wasted moment, the odds of us finding Lynette dwindle."

"I don't need reminding," I sniped, rubbing an irritating pain from my temple.

Lorelei stepped in front of me, planting herself before unleashing a baleful stare. "Obviously, you do. Now stop gawking at me like a petulant child and get on with it. This may be the last chance for you to do something good with what's left of your life. I'd hate to see you squander it."

Bastien winced, but Lorelei's words didn't strike me anywhere deep enough to cause lasting damage. I didn't need reminding of my inadequacies. Mother seemed to take enough enjoyment from doing that herself when I was alive.

Instead of rising to her goading, I turned to Bastien and asked, "You know something about this magic, yes?"

Bastien nodded slowly.

"Can I take the two of you with me? Into the memory, I mean. I have enough going on trying to piece together the details as I go. Like I'm trying to cross a bridge while building it. It would be helpful to have others there to help keep things straight."

"It's theoretically possible," Bastien said, folding his arms. "But I can only guess it would take a significant amount of magic to hold together—"

"Save the warnings," I interrupted, holding a hand up. "Just tell me how to do it."

"There's no telling how much of a strain it'll place on you," Bastien answered, his voice tight. "I could only put a finite amount of magic into that gem. Should it run out completely, you'll start to die again."

How fitting that my existence in this world would be tied so directly to the magic I held. After all, it was my family's magic that made my life what it was. Without it, I was nothing. A husk of the person I was before the grave. But I would use every bit of what I held to save Lynette if that's what it took.

Even through the jumbled chaos of my mind, I knew the sentiment was true. And someplace deep down inside me knew that if my life must be forfeited for hers to continue, it was still an exchange of astronomical disparity.

Lynette had always been more important.

"Let's give it a go," I said, a certain boldness flooding my veins as I looked to Bastien. "What should I do?"

"Extend your aura to Lorelei and myself," Bastien said, stepping closer. "Then, we just have to make you sink again and hope for the best."

"Sink?" I repeated, raising a brow at him.

"I told you there was a name for it."

"Well, forgive me for thinking it would be a cooler name."

"I'm not in charge of naming magical phenomena, Tobias."

I sucked in a breath as a heat flared in my chest. I wasn't sure if it was only because I'd reached for the magic in my veins or if Bastien's banter was stirring something deeper. I pushed those thoughts away, focusing on the task at hand. It was odd, flexing the intangible muscles of my power for the first time since my resurrection. Normally, my aura was wrapped around me at all times, a blanket of power to keep me shrouded from prying scryers and fending off the magical influence of others. It was the first application of magic I'd learned from Mother—a way to protect myself and the secrets that she used me to collect.

Now, as I dug into the pitiful reserve of magic seated in my chest, what once felt like liquid lead wrapped around my body was a fragile sheet of lace. What's more, I could feel that invisible thread connecting me to Bastien twinge, as if someone had reached out and plucked it.

Sweat beaded on my brow as I finished weaving the aura around me, my breaths coming in rasps from the effort. If Mother saw me now, she'd have more than a few choice words to share.

"Take your time," Bastien said, reaching out to steady me.

I shrugged off his touch. "I'm fine. Ready to project."

Bastien nodded, looking over to Lorelei, who was once again tapping her shoe against the sidewalk.

"Any day now."

If this idiotic idea didn't kill me, I was going to rip those shoes from her feet myself.

Pulling at the edges of the shroud I'd managed to conjure, I pushed the boundaries of the magic outward, focusing it first over Bastien. The air between us shimmered like a heat wave as it made contact. The warmth of Bastien's skin was a calming presence as my aura settled over him.

The taste of honeysuckle danced along my tongue—a familiar sensation, I realized.

"Good job, you're nearly there."

Bastien's voice caused a shiver to shoot down my spine. The connection between us thrummed with another intangible pulse.

I wanted to linger in the moment, with Bastien's warmth washing over me in waves. It was the gentlest sunlight, his presence. Not harsh like summer noon, instead the first caress of springtime coaxing open the buds of roses and lilies alike.

But I knew that Bastien's sunlight no longer shone for me. I couldn't even be certain it ever truly did, if I was being honest with myself. Would Bastien have kept his true self hidden if I had been a better lover? A better person? I understood the need to hide the fact he was a Reviled to others in the Magi community, but had we not shared our deepest secrets with one another, wrapped in silken sheets?

I couldn't be sure. Not now, at least. And the thought that itched its way through my conscious was this—would things be any different if I weren't already dead?

"Okay, now Lorelei."

She bristled at Bastien's instructions, taking a step back from me.

"Are we sure this is the only way? I'm not too keen on the idea of—"

"We could always leave you behind," Bastien interrupted, raising an eyebrow. "I understand if you're scared."

Lorelei leveled a cold stare at him, her lips pursed. "Just do it."

Pushing the boundary once more, I willed the shroud of my aura over her. The woman recoiled at first contact as the magic brushed against her consciousness, but then she lowered her guard long enough for it to envelop her.

Lavender filled my nostrils, followed by an acrid smoke on my tongue. I had to force myself not to gag.

I'd experienced hundreds of auras in my first life, but hers was the most repulsive by far.

"I'm ready," I told Bastien, swallowing back the bile that rose in my throat. "Now, how do I 'sink' or whatever it was?"

"We need to identify the trigger from the first incident," Bastien said, moving till he was all I could see.

"It wasn't anything special," I admitted, thinking back. "I was just looking at the roses."

"But it was a place you'd been before," Bastien confirmed. "That's what drew you down. Try looking around again. Let your mind wander till you've found something to latch on to."

I did as I was asked, though not without a touch of skepticism. I allowed my mind to drift as I turned in place, taking in my surroundings. We were standing in the center of the gardens now, flanked by hedge walls on either side of the path. Topiaries broke the sidewalk at regular intervals, each meticulously shaped into unique characters or objects of striking detail. A green knight stood closest, its helmet and armor seamlessly sculpted from twisting branches and verdant leaves. Further down the path, a dragon rose up above the scenery, wings of scarlet leaves stretched toward the sky and a maw of sharp, thorny teeth.

"Nothing feels familiar," I confessed after a moment.

"Then we'll keep moving," Bastien replied, staying close by. Even though he wasn't touching me, through the aura wrapped around us, I was under the near-constant barrage of sensations radiating off of him—pulsing their way down the thread.

The sweet smell of coffee. The dulcet tones of wind chimes. The calming comfort of a blanket warmed by the fireside.

Shaking off the fuzziness, I started down the sidewalk in the direction of the looming building, feeling more like a disgruntled tour guide with every step as Bastien and Lorelei fell in line behind me.

Even though I was supposed to be letting my mind wander over the landscape, I couldn't help but be drawn back to Bastien, a moth to the flame of his magnetism. Did he notice the way my eyes kept drifting over him? He paused by another topiary—a full-figured woman holding a tipped urn that spilled clean water into the pond at her feet—and my gaze lingered on the way the light seemed to bend around the contours of Bastien's body. Like even the sunlight wanted to embrace him.

I halted my steps, squinting to make sure I wasn't hallucinating. The light really *was* bending around Bastien. Darkening above, the sun's light was extinguished, and torches illuminated the pathway once again with flickering green light as we sunk into the folds of my memory.

Lorelei hastened to my side, her heels now muted against the pavement. "Is this it?"

I nodded as Bastien joined us, and a faceless shadow emerged in my periphery. Before I could speak, my body went rigid, limbs seizing, then propelling me forward on the path. The others hurried after me, keeping stride with the forced pace. One of the faceless shadows—this one in a billowing dress—materialized in front of me, my hand raising to meet theirs.

Layers of black smoke peeled away from the figure, revealing Lynette's pale face.

Lorelei and Bastien sucked in a synched breath.

"There you are," murmured Lorelei, closing the gap between us as if she feared Lynette would slip away again.

"So, you're coming tonight, right?" Lynette asked, dragging me along behind her as she weaved around more faceless figures. "To Amelia's."

A groan built in my throat. "Why does that dullard always get to play hostess? She's so plain it hurts. A rice cake has more personality."

"Because she is a dear friend," Lynette reminded me, a twinge of attitude creeping into her voice. "And I do think that you'd find tonight's activities *very* entertaining."

I felt my posture straighten as I placed a hand over my chest in a dramatic flair. "A thousand apologies, but I'm afraid I must decline. I'm dreadfully busy tonight, so you'll have to enjoy the blandness of Amelia's all by your lonesome."

Lynette snorted a laugh. "You're an awful liar, Tobias."

Lorelei made a choking sound to my right.

"At least when you're lying to me," Lynette continued. "You should know that by now."

And maybe I did know it once, this connection between Lynette and I that made it impossible to hide the truth from one another. Why was it then, looking back at this memory, that I ignored the shadow of something darker behind my sister's smile?

What was she hiding?

"Fine, but if she brings out those hideous dolls of hers, I will gnaw off my own arm if it means escape."

"Who is she talking about?" Lorelei asked, her voice echoing over Lynette's chatter as she continued to pull me toward the looming stone building.

"Amelia VanDoughten," I answered, my voice reverberating against the shadows that lurked in the periphery. A dull ache thrummed behind my eyes, but I dismissed it as merely a strain from my concentration. "She's one of Lynette's oldest friends. Another Adored nepo-socialite."

Lorelei nodded, her lips pursing into a straight line as she scribbled a note, muttering to herself. It sounded like she was shoring up the timeline. So far, she didn't seem surprised by anything discussed between me and Lynette. Maybe she was better informed than I had first thought.

We reached the bottom of a long stone staircase leading up to the pavilion attached to the stone building that overlooked the gardens. Lynette hesitated at the bottom stair, and her attention pulled to a recess tucked between the pavilion's support pillars where a tall, handsome gentleman lurked, his dark eyes trained on us.

Familiarity pawed at my mind as I watched the man, but between Lorelei's muttering and the throbbing ache in my head, it was hard to focus long enough to figure out why. The angles of the man's face and his stern posture stuck out like the details of a long-forgotten dream. His hair—the color of crimson autumn leaves streaked with strands of white sunlight—was pulled back tight from his face, his thin frame lending itself to a life lived in libraries and his complexion to hours spent indoors. He was dressed in finery like the rest of the guests, a tunic of pale blue complete with a golden half-cape draped across one shoulder and down the small of his back. But it was his eyes that held my attention, two dark orbs that drank up the light around them, drawing you in like the hypnotic stare of a viper.

"Is he here for you?" my memory asked Lynette, nodding my head toward the voyeur. "I have to say that I approve, but I don't think there's enough time for the two of you to get very far if that should be your intention—"

Lynette's snorted laugh cuts me off, her eyes drifting over to the stranger. "He's not my preferred flavor, dear brother. But I'm afraid he *is* here for me. If you'll excuse me for just a tick, I'll be right behind you."

"Are you certain?" I asked, not yet relinquishing the grip on my sister. "How do we know he doesn't have nefarious intentions?"

Lynette grinned up at me, gently pulling her hand away. "I'll be fine, Tobi. Wait for me at the landing above. I promise it won't be long."

I wanted to stop her. To pull her away from whatever shadowy game began on this night, but I was powerless as the Tobias of the past let her go, ignorant to the dangers that lurked in the near future. The memory turned from her to continue climbing the stairs, taking me along with him.

"Who is she speaking to?" Lorelei's voice bounced off the smooth stairs, piercing and too loud. The stabbing pain behind my eyes intensified.

"I don't remember," I replied as the three of us crested the top of the staircase. There were more faceless figures here on the balcony, but they didn't approach the group, keeping a polite distance. "I know him, but I can't put a finger on it."

"He's part of the Hallowed," Bastien interjected, suddenly standing very close to me.

"How do you know that?" I asked, willing the memory of my body to move further from Bastien.

Bastien pointed at the collar of his shirt. "The pin on his lapel. It was the crest of the Cardinal, Saint Sancha. Didn't you see it?"

"I guess not. But what are the Hallowed doing here?" I asked, curiosity spinning. It wasn't commonplace for the upper echelon of the holy church to be seen fraternizing with those outside of their congregates. Plus, this wasn't just some party they were crashing. Every Adored family in the Magi City was in attendance to witness Lynette's ceremony, so it wasn't like Mother to have been lax in restricting the guest list.

"There are only two Hallowed on the guest list," Lorelei said, flipping through her tiny notebook. "Including the Cardinal herself."

"The Cardinal was here?" Bastien questioned, brow furrowed. "That can't be a coincidence. Do you think she's involved somehow?"

"I can't rule anything out," Lorelei muttered, marking something down with her golden pen. "Our mysterious friend's name is Cirian. He's—"

"The Cardinal's acolyte," I finished for her, the name triggering a flood of memories alongside my throbbing headache. That's why he looked familiar. I'd first met Cirian nearly two decades ago when we were mere boys.

Lorelei nodded, continuing, "If rumors are to be believed, he will soon inherit the Cardinal's position. They say he was chosen by the Source itself."

"How convenient," Bastien scoffed, folding his arms across his chest. "To be chosen by something no one can see or hear. Makes it kind of difficult to disprove, doesn't it?"

"What would he want with Lynette?" I asked, trying to piece together the scraps of knowledge about the Hallowed fluttering around my head. It was like trying to wrangle a bird with my bare hands.

"He's one heir apparent speaking with another. Maybe he's simply assuring that alliances carry over to the next generation?" Lorelei tapped the end of her pen against her chin, seemingly not convinced of her own theory.

"Here she comes," Bastien interrupted, motioning towards the stairs.

Lynette crested the landing, the lavender fabric of her dress settling around her as she spotted me. She was smiling once she rejoined me, the tips of her cheeks slightly ruddy, though it could have just been a trick of the light.

"Did you miss me, dear brother?"

"Like one misses their own excrement after the flush, dear sister."

Her smile widened, crinkles surrounding her emerald eyes. "If only Mother were here to witness your quick wit. You know how she *adores* your low-brow touches of humor."

"The night is still young, Lenny. I'm sure I'll find ample opportunities to offend Mother dearest."

Lynette took my hand once more, seemingly no longer in a rush to reach her destination, as she meandered us across the balcony at a lackadaisical pace. Maybe she wanted to savor these last few moments of normalcy between us, or perhaps she knew even then that there was something sinister lurking in the shadows ahead.

"Speaking of ways to torment Mother, it's a shame that your mortal boy toy isn't around any longer to—"

Her words were drowned out by an intense pressure building bearing down on my skull. The scene flickered around me, sounds muffled and distorted as the shadowy figures who danced around us slowed to a stop. I glanced over to Bastien, only to find the space he and Lorelei had been occupying empty. It was just me and Lynette now, the shadows at the periphery of my vision pulsing was the only movement in sight.

"What's happening?" I asked Lynette, my own voice swallowed up by the encroaching darkness. It smothered my words like I was trying to speak underwater.

Lynette turned to me then, her eyes wide. The lavender dress shredded from her body, the encroaching shadows wrapping around her pale form. She opened her mouth to speak, but a wave of noise filled my ears, blotting out all other sounds.

"Lenny?"

The shadows crept closer, but I surged forward, grasping at Lynette's hand. It was ice-cold in my grip.

A heaviness seized my limbs, and my knees nearly gave in as the ground swayed under my feet. The pressure in my head spiked again, my vision blurring.

Her lips were moving, more soundless words, her eyes pleading as she clung to me.

"I can't… I can't hear you."

The shadows were nearly on top of us now, swallowing my lower half in a chilling embrace. I held onto Lynette as best I could, but with a final tug from the dark, she was ripped from my grasp, and I tumbled backward into endless shadow.

# FIVE
## DEAD WEIGHT

"Again, Tobias. With feeling."

Mother's voice was calm, but the contempt radiating off her was like a miasma, thickening the air inside her office till it was suffocating. Rows of heavy books lined the walls, and the portrait of mother hanging behind her desk stared down at me with the same look of disappointment.

I did as she instructed me, pressing out the aura of my magic until it butted against the presence beside me—a boy with wide, violet eyes and fuzzy lupine ears that rose from the crown of his head. The boy bristled at the contact, his tail of purple fur puffing up to twice its normal size and his lips trembling as he stared back at me.

Taking a short breath, I gave the order, the heat from my magic spiking.

"Kneel."

A burning sensation ignited in my throat as power suffused the word. The boy didn't move in response. He merely watched me, his dark, orb-like eyes reflecting my own tortured expression.

I had failed. Again.

Mother clicked her tongue. "No, no, no. This will not do, Tobias. Again."

"Could I have a moment to—"

A sharp sting bloomed across the back of my legs, and I swallowed the words. Mother flicked the end of a thin whip back into her hand with a smooth flourish, her expression frigid.

"Again."

I blinked away the building tears, taking a deep breath as I expanded my aura once more, wrapping around the other boy. His eyes—lavender at the edges—stared back, not in defiance but... disappointment?

He didn't seem that much older than me. Even with his pointed, furry ears and the claws protruding from the ends of his fingers, our similarities far outweighed the differences.

Except, of course, he was an Unseen. Part of the lower class of Magi. And I was an Adored. It was all the difference that mattered to most.

Especially Mother.

"Kneel." My voice cracked around the word as another surge of heat filled my throat, but the Unseen didn't budge, his sad eyes trained on me.

Mother's hand gripped my shoulder, her long nails biting into my skin even through my shirt. "You are not trying hard enough, Tobias."

I didn't argue. I knew better than to talk back to Mother. People had disappeared for far less around the chateau.

She bent at the waist, leveling her cold gaze with mine. "You know why this is important, yes?" The stench of her perfume was cloying, her face close enough that I could feel the heat of her breath.

"Yes," I whispered, wishing I could look away.

"Our family has a duty," Mother continued. "And even though you are a male, that doesn't excuse you from that duty, do you understand?"

I nodded.

"That's a good boy. Now, show me your strength."

My hands clenched into fists at my side. The aura of my magic expanded from me, wrapping around the Unseen boy tight enough that his posture straightened. This was my chance—to show Mother that I belonged to this family. That I could be useful, even though I was only a male.

All I had to do was focus.

"Kneel."

The heat in my throat smoldered like coal, and the Unseen's knee buckled for a split second, but then it straightened again, the boy's eyes squinting to a glare.

"Enough, Tobias," Mother sighed, releasing her grip on me.

"Please, Mother," I pleaded, acrid tears stinging my eyes. "I can do this. Give me one more chance."

"Enough."

She crossed behind her desk, settling into the plush leather chair before resting her elbows on the edge of the polished wood. When she turned her gaze back to me, it took everything I could not to shy away. "Perhaps the fault lies with me, Tobias. I expected too much. You may share my blood, but you only inherited a fraction of my power. Your unfortunate disposition has made you a liability, and I'm beginning to fear there's no place for your weakness here."

Fear swelled in my gut. No place for me here? What did that mean?

"I can do better."

"No, child, I don't think you can. And that's what troubles me. Your sister can bend a dozen soldiers to her will, and yet you struggle with even the basest of creatures." She motioned at the Unseen boy, causing him to flinch.

Mother continued unbothered, "How can you expect to garner the respect of our community if you lack the resolve to demand it from them? I can assure you, child, they will not give it willingly. You must take it from them."

I didn't have an answer.

"A reminder, then. This is what true power looks like, Tobias. Observe." Mother's gaze shifted to the Unseen. "Step forward."

No magic was necessary for the boy to do as he was instructed, his steps silent as he approached the desk.

"Kneel."

A wave of pure heat washed over me as the Unseen dropped to their knees in a fraction of a second, a grimace washing away his stoic expression.

If Mother felt any strain from the terrifying display of magical strength, she didn't show it. The lines of her face were smooth, the smallest hint of a curl at the corners of her mouth. It was the closest Mother had to a smile most days.

"You may leave us," she said, motioning a dismissal to the Unseen boy. With a brisk nod, his body shimmered, the faint halo of light obscuring his features. Then he vanished completely. Mother didn't move from her seat, but her gaze drifted over to me, and I couldn't help but cower under the weight of it. She reached into a drawer of her desk, pulling out a long wooden pipe, which she ignited with a wave of her hand. After taking a long drag, she exhaled a cloud of purple smoke that smelled of lilac and maple. "Weakness is not a flaw easily overcome, Tobias. It takes dedication. Sacrifices. An unwavering spirit. If you truly wish to take your place in this family and sit at your sister's side, you must prove that you deserve to be there!" She took another long inhale, the smoke billowing from her wide nostrils. "Now, tell me. Do you believe you possess the resolve?"

My knees quaked. Even at ten years of age, I knew that I didn't. I wasn't special, like Lenny. Like Mother. I was just a boy. What could I possibly do?

"Y-Yes, Mother."

Rising from her seat, she moved around the desk to tower over me. "You are so fortunate, child, to have a mother who loves you enough to speak the truth to you. There are those in our community who believe that males are to be coddled, nothing more. But I know the value of being underestimated—" She hooked a sharp nail under my chin, pulling it upward to meet her fiery gaze. "A tool with a subtle edge can carve deeper than anyone expects. Hone your edge, child, and you will earn the privilege of being at my side as I lead our people into a new chapter of prosperity."

The power of her words smothered me, squeezing the air from my lungs as I nodded in agreement. I had been training my entire life to please my mother. To make myself useful to the Greene family.

"I'll make you proud, Mother."

She offered me a rare smile. It was not something of warmth nor affection but more of a tight-lipped grin, pulling at the edges of her taut face. But I lapped it up, nonetheless.

"Yes, child. You will."

A knock on the door spared me from my mother's attention long enough that I was able to suck in a breath.

"Enter."

The heavy oak doors swung open, an older Unseen holding it ajar as a woman glided gracefully into the study. She wore robes of pale blue that shimmered at the edges, embroidered with threads of gold. The clothing billowed out from the woman's full frame, giving her an air of importance before she even opened her mouth to speak. Her dark skin contrasted the pale fabric that framed her face, the rest of her head wrapped in a tight-fitting habit.

The Unseen cleared his throat, announcing, "Her Eminence, Saint Sancha, Cardinal of the Hallowed Church."

Mother moved from my side to greet the Cardinal, dipping into a low, seasoned curtsy. "Apologies, Your Eminence. My afternoon has run off, and I find myself behind the clock." She motioned for me to join her, and I quickly did so, bowing as I'd rehearsed a thousand times before. "This is my son, Tobias."

"Source's blessing be upon you, child," the Cardinal responded, her voice a deep contralto. Her dark eyes watched me with an amusement I didn't understand. "You have grown in the Source's favor since last we met."

"Thank you, Your Eminence."

"Tobias was just leaving," Mother continued, ushering me toward the door.

The Cardinal nodded as I passed her, then addressed me. "Tobias, my new acolyte is waiting in the foyer, and I worry about the trouble he'll find if left alone for too long. Perhaps you would be kind enough to show him around the chateau? Even the grand cathedrals of the Cradle pale in comparison to the Greene estate."

I looked to Mother, and she gave me the slightest of nods.

"It would be an honor," I replied, bowing once more before leaving the study. The Unseen attendant closed the door behind me, slipping back into an invisible state.

Glancing around the foyer, I spotted a boy standing at the base of the grand staircase, staring up at a marble statue of my great-grandmother. He was dressed in the same pale blue as the Cardinal, a tunic and billowy pants that pooled at his feet. Unlike the Cardinal, his skin was fair, and his hair was crimson with streaks of white blond. He didn't look much older than myself, which meant he had also not yet come of age.

I took a steadying breath before approaching, muting my anxieties as Mother had taught me to do.

A first impression was the first opportunity to gain the upper hand.

"Do you find the statue to your liking?"

The boy turned to face me, his eyes wide but a look of amusement twisting his features. "Quite," he replied. "There are few in our cathedral that could rival its beauty."

"I'm glad it brings you joy," I said, giving a small bow. "That is my great-grandmother, Adoracious Greene. She built this place."

The boy bowed his head in return. "I'm Cirian," he introduced himself, then leaned closer, lowering his voice, "Tell me, Tobias. Do you know the reason for the Cardinal's meeting today?"

"No," I admitted. "But it's not really my place to know such things."

Cirian nodded, folding his arms across his chest with a frown. "Aren't you curious?"

"Why should I be?"

"Because knowledge is the most important currency."

I raised an eyebrow. "I'm not sure I follow."

With a sigh, Cirian deflated. "You're hopeless."

Heat built behind my cheeks. Mother's disapproval was one thing, but I would not suffer the sting of this louse's rejection. I needed to move quickly.

"The Cardinal asked me to show you around the chateau," I said, pushing down the squirming sensation in my gut. "We could start out in the gardens where—"

"No, thank you," Cirian scoffed, his eyes rolling. "I am not interested in the unholy opulence of your family, Tobias Greene." His gaze moved from me, focusing on something across the foyer. "Nor the slaves you keep in your halls."

"What is that supposed to mean?" I questioned, irritation modulating the practiced volume of my voice.

Who did this Cirian think he was?

"It means fuck off, pretty boy," Cirian muttered, his gaze drifting back up to the statue.

There was an undercurrent of darkness in his expression now, I realized. And a radiating contempt that clouded my mind till I turned on my heel and stalked away from the strange boy.

"—warned you this could happen! We're lucky he's still breathing!"

Bastien's voice was the first thing to break through my consciousness, his words ringing in my ear, vibrating with anger.

"Yeah, yeah, cut the phony self-righteousness and tell me if his brain is officially pulverized or if we can wring any more info out of it."

Lorelei was just as charming as always. Good to know that I couldn't escape these two, even in death. Or whatever happened to me.

"Could you keep it down, please? You're ruining my nap."

Bastien let out a deflated sigh, and Lorelei sucked her teeth.

"Tobias?" his voice was closer now. "Can you hear me?"

"I can hear both of you just fine now please shut up."

A dull, droning noise under the conversation and an occasional jolt told me we were back in the town car. I cracked an eye open to catch a very concerned Bastien looking down at me.

For someone who claimed to be excited to put my back in my grave, he sure did seem worried. It twisted his brow and carved lines across his beautiful face. I had to actively stop myself from reaching out to smooth the lines with my fingers.

"Look, we didn't completely melt his brain. Maybe he can finish walking us through the night?" Lorelei craned her neck to peek through the divider between the front and back of the town car. Her eyes lacked any of the concern that filled Bastien's.

"What happened to me?" I asked, attempting to sit up. The world lurched under me, my head spinning, so I quickly abandoned the idea and fell back onto the cushioned bench.

"You fractured." Bastien's hands worked the buttons of my shirt, unfastening the top half and peeling back the fabric to uncover the gem embedded in my chest. He held his palm over it, eyes closed as he muttered a string of words that buzzed in my ears like a swarm of insects. A painful, searing heat forced the air from my lungs with a gasp as the gem glowed white-hot. Bastien frowned. "The strain from your magic use caused the gem to crack," he explained, pointing to the edge of the gem where a fissure ran along the facet.

"So, is that it? Am I going to die again?" I asked, my voice unusually calm for someone asking about their life ending.

I guess the second time around, anything would feel old hat.

"It's not a structural fracture, thankfully," Bastien replied, pulling his hands away and taking that insufferable heat with him. "And a trace of my magic managed to stay contained. So, no. You're not going to die. Not yet, at least."

I was relieved at the news. Or maybe relieved wasn't the right word. There was more time now. Time to figure out who killed me and what happened to Lenny. I needed to know that she was okay. I didn't think I could give up my second life before I was certain she was safe.

"What did Lynette say to you?" Lorelei asked, seemingly unconcerned with the state of my well-being. "The two of you were talking just before the shadows ejected us."

Lynette's soundless words replayed in my mind. Her frightened expression was burned in the back of my eyelids when I closed them.

"I don't know. I couldn't hear her. She did mention you, though." I looked up at Bastien, his brow furrowing as I locked eyes with him. "She said it was too bad that we'd broken things off. It sounded like… it was a recent incident."

Something flickered behind Bastien's eyes, but he quickly reined in his reaction, expression wiped clean.

"Was it?" I pressed him, desperate for the answers I'd been trying to parse out. "Recent, I mean?"

"Yes," Bastien replied, his voice even.

"What else did she say?" Lorelei interrupted.

"Nothing." I watched as Bastien's shoulders relaxed a fraction. "There was a lot happening all at once, so it was hard to focus."

Bastien averted his eyes from me, staring out the window with his jaw clenched. I knew that reaction. It felt familiar. What was he hiding?

"How long has it been, Bastien? I haven't been able to sift through that part of my memories yet."

"A little while," Bastien replied, still not looking at me.

He didn't elaborate further or offer any details.

"We're not here for you two the drudge up a lover's quarrel," said Lorelei, turning around to face forward once again. "We'll be arriving at the Cradle shortly, and Bastien needs to prepare."

"The Cradle?" I echoed. Even with my memories in shambles, I could recall the seat of power for the Church of the Source. "Why on earth are we going there?"

"Because that's where Cirian is," answered Lorelei, flipping through her notebook. "And at this point, he's the best lead I have."

"But they'll never let me set foot on their holy ground," I argued. "Or Bastien, for that matter. The Hallowed won't tolerate a Reviled in their midst or his reanimated ex."

"We're aware," Bastien replied, rolling up his sleeves past the elbow. "That's why I have to build a Veil around the two of us before we enter."

I stared after him in disbelief. Bastien was powerful enough to create a Veil for both of us at the same time? The magic required to obscure someone's identity was no small sum. The Adored aren't even able to perform such illusory magics, and the most powerful of the Hallowed struggled to uphold a convincing glamour longer than a few minutes. Just how powerful was Bastien's magic? And how did he keep it concealed from me the entire time we were together?

"You're staring," said Bastien, folding his hands together in the shape of a seal. The air around us began to prickle with the electric sensation of magic.

"I am." I didn't shy away when he glanced over at me.

"Why?"

"Because I'm trying to understand how I didn't see your magic before. There must have been so many signs I missed. Or maybe I wanted to overlook them. Either way, I'm sorry."

Bastien shifted his hands, forming another seal as motes of light burst into existence, hovering over my body like fireflies. "I've concealed my magic my entire life, Tobias. A Reviled like me can't just flaunt their power. We have to be cautious. We have to be certain of who we can trust."

"Which means you didn't trust me."

It wasn't a condemnation but more of an acceptance on my part. Whatever happened between me and Bastien, I was almost certain it was my fault.

Had I been unfaithful? Did my work for Mother interfere with the relationship? Was there something more insidious lurking beneath the pile of jumbled memories rolling around in my head? It was maddening, going through the endless what-ifs and scenarios. I needed Bastien to fill in the gaps for me.

But what did it matter? I was dead. Or at least, I would be dead again soon. There was no use in spending what little time I had sifting through the shambles of a life already passed. I should focus on the task at hand—finding Lynette.

Bastien and I were over. I needed to accept that.

"For what it's worth," muttered Bastien, his voice low. "I would have told you about me. Eventually. But it seems like fate had other plans for us."

A flare of heat swelled in my chest under the sparkling gem.

Bastien continued his work, stitching together the Veil through a series of seals. By the time the car came to a stop, sweat beaded on his forehead. His hands, which had been twisted into unnatural angles during the spell weaving, relaxed, and he let out a deep sigh. The air around us shimmered for a moment longer, then stilled, and Bastien's visage blurred at the edges, morphing his appearance into one of a man that I didn't recognize. Deep wrinkles set into his usually smooth face, his eyes lightening to a pale blue, and a scraggly grey beard protruded down from his chin.

"How do I look?" he asked, voice unrecognizable. He dabbed the sweat from his brow with a handkerchief from his pocket.

"Like a history tutor Lynette and I used to torture as children."

Bastien's new face grinned, more creases spreading across the weathered skin. "Just wait until you see what I've cooked up for you."

With a bit of effort, I finally managed to sit upright, straining to catch a glimpse of myself in the rearview mirror. My skin was still pale, but the smooth complexion of my face was now riddled with pockmarks. The bend of my nose was crooked, and my hair hung into my eyes in greasy brown clumps.

I was someone else entirely. Running a finger over the bumpy flesh of my cheek, I marveled at the sensation. It felt real.

Lorelei eyed the two of us from the front seat. "Good work, Bastien. Once again, proving yourself to be even more useful than I imagined."

"I live to serve," said the disguised Bastien in a dry, mocking tone.

"What exactly is the plan here?" I asked, avoiding my reflection in the tinted windows. "Are we just going to waltz in and demand to speak with the Cardinal's acolyte?"

"Yes, actually." Lorelei flipped down the visor overhead using the small mirror to apply a fresh coat of blood-red lipstick. "I'm officially acting on behalf of Adoranda Greene, so there's little they'll do to stop me. All I have to do is drop your mother's name, and they'll bend over backward to make way."

The logic was actually fairly sound. Mother's name carried significant weight. It was a power that I frequently flaunted during my first life.

"You two stick close to me," Lorelei continued, snapping the lipstick closed before opening the door and climbing out of the car. Her head appeared again through the opening to bark, "Get a move on!"

Bastien and I put our new forms in motion, clamoring out of the back seat and onto the sidewalk in front of the intimidating building. The Cradle Cathedral rose high above us. Dark stone spires jutted up into the sky, windows crafted from stunning stained glass adorning the front façade, and an arched entrance of grey stone that feigned humility.

Figures dressed in a familiar pale blue moved along the sidewalk, some in flowing robes while others wore more modern adaptations of vests and suit jackets emblazoned with the symbol of the Hallowed.

Lorelei was already on the move, heading up the stone steps to the main entrance of the Cradle. Bastien and I hurried after her, catching up by the time she hit the landing of the stone steps and pressed forward.

The doors swung up as we approached, beckoning us inside. As we entered,

I couldn't shake the feeling of being a fly fluttering directly into the maw of a carnivorous plant.

Once inside, a figure wrapped in draping fabric robes and sporting a mask of white porcelain addressed us, bowing as they did so.

"Good day, travelers. Have you come to commune? Our next service begins in—"

"No." Lorelei stepped forward, shaking her head hard enough to send her curls bouncing. "We're actually here to speak with the Acolyte, Cirian. Could you please direct us to him?"

The figure hesitated, their head tilting to the side. "My apologies, but Master Cirian is currently in the presence of the Source. I'm afraid he'll be unreachable for the foreseeable future. Perhaps I could summon one of the priests to come and—"

Lorelei held up her hand to silence the attendant, then reached into her jacket pocket and produced a small, round emblem that she held up to eye level. "It's in regards to the disappearance of Madame Greene's daughter."

The attendant's shoulders slumped, and they bowed again. "Of course, my apologies. If you'll please wait here for just a moment, I will contact His Grace."

I snickered quietly as the attendant scurried away. The Greene family crest had always proven a reliable tool when it came to intimidation. I always preferred flattery and infatuation, but when a hammer was the only solution, a quick glimpse of that emblem would prove more than a convincing argument to anyone aware of its significance.

"This place drains the life right out of you," Bastien muttered, pulling the edges of his coat tighter around him. He glanced up at the cavernous cathedral ceiling, his strangely-colored eyes reflecting the kaleidoscope of hues from the stained glass.

I wasn't surprised to hear him say this. To a Reviled, stepping into a Hallowed space would be like entering a lion's den.

"I enjoy its chilly severity," Lorelei replied, her lips curling into a smile. "It reminds me of home."

"That explains so much," Bastien replied, still peering up at the splendorous sight.

Another of the robed individuals strode past, their pale eyes lingering on me long enough to trigger an unease in my stomach. "I'm starting to think that this was a bad idea," I whispered, inching closer to Lorelei. "Do you know what will happen if they find out the truth about me?"

"They'll destroy you, I'd imagine," Lorelei answered plainly. "Incinerate you with holy fire, or perhaps tear you limb from limb to discourage any further resurrections. But don't worry so much. I have full confidence in your former lover's Veil. From what I can tell, it's nearly seamless."

I opened my mouth with a retort, but the attendant returned at that moment, offering us another timid bow. "His Grace is expecting you in his quarters. Please, follow me."

The three of us trailed after the robed figure, Lorelei leading the way while Bastien and I kept a comfortable distance as we moved deeper into the Cradle. From the main cathedral, we maneuvered through a series of hallways that snaked their way in a dozen directions. The flat, grey stone walls blended in with the floor, leaving little to differentiate one path from another, yet the figure continued forward with an even, confident stride.

The longer we traveled, the more I couldn't help but think that we were descending into the belly of the beast. Just as my anxieties reached their apex, we stopped in front of a simple wooden door, the swirling symbol of the Hallowed carved into the center of it.

Stepping aside, the attendant bowed once more, gesturing for us to enter. Lorelei moved first, wrapping a delicate hand around the knob and opening the door with a twist. Bastien gave me an encouraging nod before following her inside. I crossed to join them but stopped just shy of the door as the figure's head snapped up, their pale eyes locked on me through the porcelain mask. A shiver shot down my spine as I hastened through to the other room, the heavy wooden door closing behind me with a resounding *thud*.

Releasing a deep exhale, I took in my new surroundings.

The acolyte quarters were sparse in their furnishings, certainly nowhere near as elaborate or ornate as Mother's office back at Chateau Greene. A plain wooden desk devoid of clutter or technology. A simple highbacked chair, upholstered in a blue-grey. Rudimentary lamps mounted to the walls at regular intervals shed a pleasant, warm light. A shelf of tomes, each swollen to bursting with Hallowed knowledge hidden behind simplistic covers.

It was all so obscenely plain. Unsurprising for a Hallowed, I figured. Always ready to play the humble martyr.

"Well, where is he?" Bastien asked, standing behind one of the two modest seats opposite the desk.

"How the hell should I know?" Lorelei snapped, huffing a breath before lowering herself into the other chair. She pulled out her device, her lips curling into a sneer. "No connection. They must have powerful wards in place."

"The disciple outside was staring daggers at me," I said finally, running a hand through my alien, stringy hair. "Do you think they recognized me or something?"

"Your own mother wouldn't recognize you right now," Lorelei replied, tapping her foot against the stone floor. "Well, maybe *your* mother could, but you know what I mean. Bastien's Veil is strong."

"Was that another compliment?" Bastien asked, raising a wild eyebrow.

Her face twisted in disgust. "Don't sound so surprised. I dish out compliments all the time."

"You mean out loud?" I added, mirroring Bastien's bewilderment. "That's not exactly been my experience."

Lorelei's eyes narrowed on me. "Don't presume for a moment that you know a single iota about me, Tobias Greene. If I've not complimented you, it is simply because you have yet to do anything worthy of commending. You should take it upon yourself to do better. Then again, knowing your reputation, maybe you're already doing your best."

Anger flashed in my gut as I stepped forward. "I just hope that we find Lynette soon because, at this point, I'm yearning for my grave—"

The door opened behind me, and I swallowed down the rest of my tirade as a man sauntered in. Heat rose in my cheeks, spurred by the display of flesh. The man was every bit as handsome as he had been in the vision from my past, with crimson hair streaked with white pulled back from his face, though several strands had escaped from their bindings and fell to frame his angular face. He was bare from the waist up, the alabaster color of his skin disrupted by a pattern of brown freckles that trailed up along his chest and bloomed across both shoulders, which glistened with a sheen of sweat. His stature was lean, with wiry muscles pulled tight across his lithe frame, his movements equal parts grace and confidence.

"Apologies," said the man, crossing quickly to the door in the corner of the space and pulling it open. "I did not intend to keep you waiting." He removed a tunic of billowy fabric from the closet, pulling it on and fastening it at the waist. "The Source had already taken hold of me when Augustus informed me of your arrival. Once that happens, I'm afraid there's no stopping my communing until the Source has spoken its piece to me."

"It's no trouble, Your Grace," Lorelei spoke, any annoyance in her expression having evaporated. She smiled politely, crossing her ankles. Her posture was immaculately rigid, like a carved statue. "I appreciate you agreeing to see us on such short notice."

Cirian turned to face us, shutting the closet behind him and taking his place at the desk. "The Council has been friends of the Church for centuries. I am honored to welcome you into the Cradle of the Source." His dark eyes moved from Lorelei to Bastien, then finally landed on me. His stare carried a weight to it. A sort of pressure that butted against me and squeezed a bit of air from my lungs. "Who do I have the pleasure of addressing this fine afternoon?"

"My name is Lorelei Orion. These men are my associates. I am acting as a personal attaché to Madame Greene of the Adored. I have been tasked with the location and retrieval of her daughter, the presumed successor to Madame Greene's position on the council. I'm sure you've heard of her recent disappearance."

"Indeed, I have," Cirian replied, a certain amusement lilting his voice. "It is a tragedy to lose such a bright light in this dark world. May the Source be with her."

"I was hoping you could answer a few questions for me pertaining to the conversation the two of you had at her inauguration ceremony."

Cirian's expression darkened, the air in the room taking on a weight that settled against my skin. "I would hope, Ms. Orion, that you are not under the assumption that the Church had anything to do with the young Ms. Greene's disappearance?"

Lorelei didn't falter, her gaze remaining trained on the man. "I haven't ruled out the possibility. However, your cooperation today would go far in proving the church's innocence, should you provide the information I'm seeking."

Tension swelled between the two of them, tangible as a sheet of fabric wrapped around me. A playful smile danced across Cirian's face. "Ask away, Ms. Orion. You'll find no ill intent here."

I couldn't help but be drawn back to the first time Cirian and I were introduced all those years ago and the pure vitriol I felt radiate from the boy when he spoke of my family. If those sentiments remained, I could only assume that he would have a plethora of his own reasons to be pleased about Lynette's disappearance.

"What did the two of you discuss the evening of her ceremony, when you pulled her away from her brother's company?"

Cirian's eyes moved to me as he answered. "I was merely congratulating her on behalf of my master, the Cardinal, and assuring her that the Church of the Source would observe all previous agreements with Madame Greene."

Lorelei's pen scratched along the page of her notebook, filling the silence.

"You discussed nothing else?" she pressed, leaning forward in her chair.

"Not that I can recall," Cirian replied, his attention shifting back to Lorelei. "Perhaps you should confirm these details with her brother? He was standing close by and should be able to corroborate."

A shiver crept up my spine at his words.

"Unfortunately, Tobias Greene has been reported deceased," Lorelei said, her tone even. "So, you understand the urgency by which we're working to locate Lynette."

Cirian didn't betray an ounce of surprise from the statement. Instead, his eyes trailed between myself and Bastien. "Would you permit me a question of my own, Ms. Orion?"

"Just a moment, Your Grace. Now, when you say that you can't recall, does it mean that you know for a fact that the conversation between the two of you didn't stray to the topic of the Unseen Rebellion?"

Cirian blinked—perhaps for the first time since he entered the room—his lips pulling into a tight smile. "Once again, we discussed only her appointing, official council business, and nothing beyond."

"And you'd be willing to swear by that statement?" Lorelei pressed, leaning over her notebook with a grin that bordered on threatening.

Cirian leveled his gaze at her, a twinge of icy coldness seeping into his answer. "With certainty."

Another shiver shot through me, the air around Cirian crackling with the oppressive force of his magic. It rippled around the Veil Bastien had spun over the two of us, and I could feel Bastien's posture tense with concentration as he held the edges of the glamour together, keeping them from fraying under the magical pressure.

Cirian's power was not something to take lightly, though Lorelei seemed entirely unbothered.

"One last question from me, Your Grace," Lorelei continued, oblivious to the invisible struggle taking place behind her. "When you spoke with Lynette, did you happen to confide in her the whereabouts of Rudderkin?"

Another flash of recognition moved across Cirian's features like lightning streaking from behind clouds. "I do hope you understand the weight of such accusations, Ms. Orion. Even for someone in the position you find yourself. To insinuate the Church would have anything to do with the Unseen Rebellion is the ultimate blas—"

"Not the Church," interrupted Lorelei, rising to her feet. "Just to be clear, I'm not accusing the Church of the Hallowed for any part of this. Just you. There are certain rumors circling around your icy halls that suggest your loyalties may lie outside of the Church. As I see it, I'm merely giving you the opportunity to defend your good name."

Cirian smiled coldly at her, a mask of pleasant indifference in place once more. "Rumors can hardly be trusted, even within these hallowed halls, Ms. Orion. Indeed, a woman of your stature would do well to remember that. But if it is my word you're searching for, then by all means, take it. I am no traitor to the Church, nor do I conspire with the likes of Rudderkin and his pack of mongrels. To suggest such is to besmirch the holy name of the Source itself, and I will not tolerate such blasphemies within the Cradle."

The room crackled once more with energy, pressing against my skin like a swarm of angry insects. Lorelei didn't falter, her stony gaze trained on Cirian. "So, you deny the claims?"

"Deny doesn't seem appropriate to the egregious nature of the accusation," Cirian scoffed. "I rebuke it in the name of the Source. My loyalties are, as they have ever been, aligned with the Church."

The pressure in the room shifted, causing my ears to pop.

"Then there is nothing left for us to discuss," Lorelei concluded, her notebook closing with a *snap*. She moved from between the chairs, motioning for us to follow as she made for the door. She stopped short, turning to face Cirian again. "Good day, Your Grace."

With a wave of Cirian's hand, the door slammed shut in Bastien's face. He reeled back, turning to face Cirian.

"You'll indulge me with an inquiry of my own," he said, moving slowly from behind the desk. Bastien stepped in front of Lorelei, but she quickly out-maneuvered him, seeming to relish in the opportunity to stand toe-to-toe with the taller man. "Tell me," Cirian continued, "what exactly is Madame Greene playing at, allowing a Reviled and his unholy creation to defile this holy ground?"

A snap of his fingers, and I gasped as the Veil was ripped from my body. Bastien—his true form returned—shot me a worried glance before stepping in front of me, taking a defensive stance. I stared down at his arms and the spiraling black markings that wove their way from his wrist upwards till they disappeared under his sleeves.

Where did those come from?

"Ah, isn't that better?" Cirian cooed, the edges of his lips curling into a wicked smile. "I do so appreciate when a Veil is torn and we can stop all this foolish galivanting." His dark eyes found me, and the angle of his smile tweaked into a snarl. "The Madame's corruption knows no limits. She sacrifices her own children like lambs on the altar of the false god."

"What's that supposed to mean?" I stepped forward, but Bastien was quicker, moving in front of me and blocking the path.

"Stand down," Bastien warned the other man, the palm of his hand pulsing with an eerie green energy.

"And if I refuse?" Cirian questioned, voice pitched high with amusement. "It's only by my grace that you still draw breath. The teachings would have me snuff the light from your eyes here and now, Necromancer."

"You could try," Bastien retorted.

"Enough." Lorelei moved between the men. "You're not going to hurt us, Your Grace. We both know you don't have it in you. And if I were you, I would keep this little conversation of ours between the soon-to-be-three of us. If it makes you feel any better, as soon as we locate Lynette, Bastien here will be sinking the lesser of the Greene twins back into his early grave."

I huffed a breath. That was uncalled for.

Cirian's glibness faded as he straightened, arms lowering to his sides. "You're nothing like they said you'd be, Truthsayer. Adoranda must love having you under her thumb."

Bastien stiffened in front of me as Lorelei moved like a bolt, her fist gripping the fabric of Cirian's tunic and dragging him down to her level. "I'm under no one's thumb," she seethed, her careful composure evaporating into a fiery rage. "You'll do well to remember that."

Cirian's smile spread across his lips once more as he freed himself from her grip. "Oh, what wicked games we play. One with sword, the other with clay."

Lorelei turned to me and Bastien, her steely resolve settled back in. Without a word, she pulled open the door, disappearing through it. Bastien gave me a withered look before following, and under the lingering stare of Cirian, I did the same.

# SIX
## LEFT FOR DEAD

"Does this conversation bore you, Tobias?"

I blinked away the daydream of open fields of wild honeysuckle, flinching from the intensity of Mother's icy gaze. The others gathered around the meeting table watched me as well, a blend of resentment and pity, to which I'd long grown immune, tainting their expressions.

I bowed my head quickly, offering an apology of forced sincerity. "Not at all, Mother. Please accept my apologies."

Mother squared her shoulders, expanding herself to fill every bit of the high-backed chair she occupied. "Then I will repeat myself now that I've captured your attention. Was your rendezvous with Corinth Creeley a success?"

My mind drifted back to the brunette man, images of his ivory skin drenched in sweat and twisted between silken fabric as he moaned my name.

I cleared my throat. "Yes, he was quite receptive to the ideas you suggested, Mother."

To her left, Lynette snickered. "I'm sure he was very receptive."

Murmuring rippled along the table, but I didn't pay it any heed. My years of service on Mother's behalf had inoculated me to the judgment of others.

"I'm pleased to hear it," Mother continued, ignoring Lynette's jeering. "The Creeleys are the last to hold out on my initiative to quash the Unseen Rebellion once and for all. As soon as Madame Creeley caves, we must move swiftly—"

"Apologies, Mother," Lynette interrupted, the lurid chatter evaporating. Shocked stares followed from around the table. "But perhaps we could reopen the discussion of parlaying with the Rebellion leaders for a ceasefire? I've been reviewing the documentation from Rudderkin's latest demands, and I can't say they're unwarranted."

An oppressive silence settled over the room as if no one dared to breathe while they awaited Mother's response. When she did not speak, Lynette continued, "The Unseen are merely seeking fair compensation for their dedicated service to the other Magi, and I believe that negotiation may be the best chance we have at avoiding unnecessary bloodshed on both sides—"

"Enough."

Crushing weight squeezed the air from my lungs, the pressure of Mother's magic pressing into my body like a wave of sand, trapping my limbs in place. From the wide-eyed fear displayed on the other faces at the table, I could only assume that Mother's power was equally distributed across the room. A man at the end of the table clawed at his throat, a garbled, wet gasp escaping his lips.

My eyes panned to Lynette, who merely sat still in her seat, fixated on Mother. Was she under the same assault?

"You may be my successor," said Mother in a controlled tone, addressing her daughter. "But my word is still final. This rebellion will meet its end in the manner that all rebellions should. With blood and ash."

The slightest lip tremble was the only crack in Lynette's stone expression.

"As you wish, Mother."

A collective sigh filled the room as the oppressive force lifted, allowing me control of my body once more. The man at the end of the table coughed violently, and Mother tugged casually at the lapels of her blazer.

"Renata," she addressed the dark-skinned woman to my left. "Your forces must be ready at any moment to mobilize. Has Broussard been able to identify the location of Rudderkin yet?"

"Not yet, Your Grace," the woman replied. "But I am confident in his abilities. The strike force will be ready when the time comes. You have my word."

"It would seem as though your word is the only thing you can offer me at the moment," Mother said through a sigh. "I only hope that you've placed your faith in the right man, Renata. I would not have so willingly left my fate in the hands of another. Especially one so weak as a man."

Renata stiffened in her seat.

"Wise words as always, Your Grace. I thank you for them."

Just then, Mother's eyes fluttered closed, a slight twitch under her eye telling me that a message was being delivered to her directly through magical means. When she opened them a moment later, they shimmered with a mirthful glee.

"Madame Creeley has requested an audience with me," she said, rising from her seat. She addressed the table, towering over us all. "The time has almost arrived, my friends. A new era of peace. May it be the foundation on which you continue to build our legacy, my daughter."

The rest of the table, minus Lynette, stood to join in Mother's triumph. I watched my sister, her gaze distant as she stared down at her hands, lips spread into a taut grimace.

Mother's departure was like a vacuum, sucking all the air out of the room in her absence. The others quickly dispersed, each of Mother's peons hurrying off to finalize preparations for her newest act of ambition. Lynette lingered in her seat, her eyes still fixed downward.

She was a thousand miles away. I couldn't blame her. But I also couldn't deny the frustration building in my gut.

"You knew that she would never change her mind, Lenny. Why even bother?" My sister looked up, the familiar mask of bravado vacant from her face for the first time in years. She looked…scared. As if she were staring down her worst nightmares brought to life. In many ways, I suppose she was. No matter how powerful Lynette was, I knew her heart. She had always abhorred violence, while Mother wielded it like an extension of herself.

"I can't be a part of this, Tobi. I can't let this be my legacy."

I sank back into my chair, letting out a sigh. "I hate to break it to you, but it already is. For both of us. This is just the latest chapter in the fucked-up history of our family."

Lynette leveled a blistering glare at me. "How can you be so blasé? Can't you see what's going on here? This is exactly how the Reviled Exodus began. Mother won't be satisfied until the Adored are the only Magi left with power. Until she *is the only one."*

"The Reviled were menaces to society," I argued. "Everyone knows that. They were trying to upset the natural order between life and death. They forced the Council's hand."

Lynette bit back a scathing laugh. "Is that what she told you? My gods, Tobi. You're denser than stone sometimes."

"Well, excuse me for not being as learned as you, oh great Successor. I'm fortunate the little bit of magic I have is useful to Mother, or else she would have gotten rid of me ages ago."

"I'm just as powerless against her as you are, Tobi. You saw it—hell, everyone saw it today. I can't stand up to her. She's too strong."

The idea of standing up to Mother was pointless. Here, within the walls of our house, she ruled with absolute power. Lynette was a fool to think otherwise.

"Would you?" I asked, lowering my voice because I never knew who could be listening around the Chateau. "If you had the power to defy her, would you even do it? It's not just Mother that you'd have to convince, Lenny. The rest of the Council would still have to change their minds as well."

Lynette doesn't answer.

"Exactly. So, forget about it, Lenny. Play it safe until you're the one holding all the power. Then you can do whatever you want. Just like she does."

Lynette shook her head, a sad smile curling the edges of her mouth. "I know. That's what I'm afraid of."

"You're a fucking Truthsayer?"

Bastien waited till we were safely back in the car before the accusations started flying. I was honestly shocked we made it out of the Cradle in one piece without Bastien's Veil to conceal us. Cirian must have decided that we weren't worth the fuss after all.

Gods, he was such an arsehole.

"Does it matter?" Lorelei replied, closing her eyes and jamming a finger into her temple.

"Yes, it fucking matters," Bastien retorted, running a hand over the intricate tattoos that spanned up his forearms. I wanted to inspect them closer, but there were more important matters at hand. "Why didn't you tell me?"

"Wait, what's a Truthsayer?" I questioned.

"A mortal who can use small amounts of magic to detect falsehoods," Bastien replied.

A mortal using magic? That shouldn't have been possible....

"It's not something I like to broadcast," Lorelei continued. "Kind of defeats the purpose of my abilities if I go around announcing myself. And let's get one thing clear, corpse peddler. You work for me. I don't *have* to tell you anything."

"Why are you asking about Rudderkin?" I interjected, searching for answers to my own questions. "What does the Rebellion have to do with Lynette's disappearance?"

Lorelei let out a hearty laugh. "Now you have questions. Okay, Tobias. Your mother asked me to explore all avenues related to Lynette's disappearance. What, with her bleeding heart for the Unseen's plight, it only makes sense that she'd open herself up to being a target for those extremists to utilize. She'd make a great bargaining chip for negotiating with the madame."

Bastien let out a huff beside me, muttering something under his breath that I couldn't catch.

It made sense. The Unseen Rebellion could easily have been the ones who kidnapped Lynette. If that were the case, Mother would be forced to negotiate with them or risk her Successor. But if Lynette were taken by them, where did *I* factor in? Was I simply an expendable pawn standing in the way of their prize? Did I try and defend Lynette and get caught up in the crossfire? How would they even manage to capture her in the first place? Lynette was more powerful than any other Adored presently alive besides Mother. Even if they did manage to capture her, they could never hold her.

Something wasn't adding up.

I needed to recall those moments leading up to my death.

"So, what now?" Bastien questioned, his tone gruff. "You've risked exposing me to the Hallowed, and we've no more information than before."

"Not true," Lorelei argued. "My conversation with the Cardinal-to-be was incredibly illuminating, even if you couldn't see it. For instance, I know that he and Lynette discussed the location of Rudderkin, which means Lynette would have had that information beforehand. And if she had the information, why did she not share it with Madame Greene, who was waiting to give the orders to eradicate the rebellion? If we're to believe the rumors flying around Cirian, then his involvement would lead me to think that Lynette was passing along the whereabouts of Rudderkin. And, of course, if Cirian were going to help relocate Rudderkin, then he'd risk the Church being accused of siding with the Rebellion, which has a plethora of nasty implications. He must have a good reason to put so much on the line.

"Then there's Lynette. If it's true that she shared information with Cirian, that would make her guilty of high treason. Madame Greene would certainly be stuck between a rock and a hard place by having to execute her own daughter and heir to her legacy."

Bastien watched the woman, his eyes wide and mouth hanging open. I was stunned myself, though my cluttered mind made it difficult to fully digest the information being presented.

Would Lynette be that foolish? Would she have risked everything—her entire future—for a group of others? It was a dangerous game, if true. One that she knew she couldn't lose or else there would be grave consequences. There were always consequences when you defied Mother.

An idea wormed its way into my mind, causing me to shiver.

What if this was the reason I died? Had I found out about Lynette's plan and tried to stop her? Tried to convince her that she was making a mistake in throwing everything away? Would she have gone to such lengths to stay the course, even if it meant ending her own brother's life?

Bile rose in the back of my throat as my head spun.

Bastien leaned forward in his seat, bracing his elbows on his knees. "Those are some serious accusations, Orion."

"And yet, the pieces fit. You can't argue that fact." She took out her leather-bound notebook, jotting something down with a quick flourish. "Cirian all but confirmed it. Now, all that's left is locating Lynette, and my task will be complete."

The realization struck me like a lightning bolt. "You're looking for the rebellion."

Lorelei ignored my proclamation, continuing to write in her notebook.

"This was never about Lynette, was it?" I continued, stringing together the inconsistencies that stood glaring in the daylight. "Mother just wants to know where they're hiding, and she knows Lynette will be there."

"Is that true?" Bastien asked, voice tight.

"And what if it is?" Lorelei proposed. "You'll still get paid, regardless, corpse peddler. And you'll get to go back to your blissful sleep, Tobias. So, really, it's a win-win-win."

A flash of green from beside me drew my attention, but when I looked over at Bastien, he was merely checking his watch.

"What did Mother tell you to do when you find Lynette?" I asked, needing to hear it plainly.

"My job is simply to inform her when I have a visual. Once that happens, my obligations have been filled, and whatever happens next isn't my problem."

"Would she really hurt Lynette?" Bastien asked, looking over to me.

Bastien had never met Mother. Never felt the pull of a power so great it threatened to smother you at any moment. To snuff the light from your eyes, if only to watch it go. I'd felt it. I'd been a victim of the overwhelming strength of Adoranda Greene's magic. So, without hesitation, I replied, "Yes. Yes, she would."

Bastien checked his watch again.

"Well, I've just about got this wrapped up," announced Lorelei, turning around in her seat to peer back through the divider. "Tobias, I just need one more thing from you. We're headed to the gravesite that you were found in, and I'm hoping that it'll spark some more of your memory of that night. Your sister told you where she was going, of that I'm almost sure. All I need is for you to tell me what she said, and then we can get you back where you belong."

"Forget it," I said, folding my arms across my chest in a gesture of defiance. "I won't help you if it means putting Lenny in danger."

Lorelei made a pouty face, turning her attention instead to Bastien. "I guess it's time for you to earn your keep, then. Come on, corpse whisperer. Work your little magic and make the puppet do what I want."

Bastien's fist clenched at his side, and he checked his watch once more.

"Oh, I'm sorry. Am I keeping you? Do you have a date?"

I watched Bastien, too, waiting for his answer to her demand. Could he really force me to do something against my will? How strange to face the very weapon I used to wield so thoughtlessly. Perhaps it was the universe balancing the scales before my (second) final breath.

But Bastien's response never came. He merely held still, staring down at his watch, his lips moving silently as if he were counting down the seconds till—he moved in a blur of motion, sliding to close the distance between us on the bench seat and pulling one of the safety belts around him and myself. In a flash, the restraint clicked into place, and Bastien's arm wrapped around my trunk just as the impact hit.

The car spun, and Lorelei was thrown from her seat into the driver's side window, the glass splintering on contact. I clung to the bar above me as the vehicle lurched, the tires skidding across the pavement with a deafening squeal. With a second impact, the car tipped, rolling side over side and spraying the interior with shards of glass as we toppled. I shut my eyes, Bastien's grip on me slipping at some point, but the restraints held me in place well enough.

As the deafening noise subsided and the momentum of the crash halted, it took me a split second to realize I was hanging upside down as shadows moved outside the splintered windows. Pain radiated from side, and I drew a hand away from my ribs, fresh blood covering my skin in a layer of crimson. A shard of glass protruded from my side, and I tried not to shift too much. My mouth tasted of blood, and my vision blurred. Voices filtered through the ringing in my ears, shouting coming from the exterior. Bastien wasn't beside me any longer, and I frantically panned back and forth till I spotted him stirring beneath me, his body a heap of tangled limbs. Carefully, I tried to free myself from the belt holding me in place, but the release wouldn't work. I nearly yelped when a hand wrapped around my wrist.

Bastien clung to me, pulling himself upright. A long cut ran across his forehead and leaked blood down the side of his face, but his eyes were wide and alert.

"Are you okay?" I asked, breathless.

Bastien didn't answer, his free hand extending toward me as well. For the briefest moment, I thought he was going to embrace me, but then I felt the heat of his fingertips sink into the flesh of my chest. A string of words poured from his mouth as a green light filled the car.

Searing pain dulled my senses as an immense pressure squeezed my sternum. I couldn't form words through the agony, but my eyes locked with Bastien's, hoping he'd understand what I was asking. But then the pressure abated, a pleasant numbness seizing my limbs as Bastien pulled his hand away, clutching a blood-stained green gem.

"B-Bast?" I croaked as the edges of my vision darkened.

But Bastien was swallowed by the darkness, the sound of my straining heartbeat the last thing to ring in my ears before crushing silence overcame me.

# SEVEN
## DEAD TO RIGHTS

*T*he café bustled with life around me as I waited in line to place my order. Having visited the café every day for the last week, I'd grown accustomed to the traffic pattern of customers, so it was easy enough to navigate the hoard of locals clamoring for their mid-day pick-me-up. As I waited, my gaze drifted to the counter in search of the reason for my return. While others came for the lattes and scones the size of their heads, I sought out this place for a different reason.

I had not been able to get the barista out of my head since my "date" with Corinth. And now, much like the days prior, I found myself drawn back to this place, if only to lay eyes on the man once more.

The absurdity was not lost on me. I was behaving like some love-struck school whelp. And yet, there I stood. Waiting to spend a collective two minutes in the presence of this beguiling man.

"Getting the usual?" the woman behind the counter asked as I approached. I cringed at the realization I'd frequented the location enough times to be recognized, but I nodded curtly, handing over a bill for payment.

"It'll be right out," said the woman with a smile, offering me the change that I always declined before sliding it into the glass tip jar in front of the register.

I moved down the bar, still feeling self-conscious about my childish reasons for being here, but then I spotted him, and any hesitation melted away, a breath catching in my chest.

He was dressed in his usual fashion, a white button-up shirt with sleeves rolled past the elbow and a navy apron tied around his slim waist. I'd grown to appreciate the way the fabric hugged the man's form, hinting at the toned physique underneath.

I wondered what it would feel like to sink my fingertips into that waist…

"Hello again," the barista greeted me as he danced through the motions of his work. "You're becoming a regular, aren't you?"

"I suppose so," I replied, a heat building at the nape of my neck that I tried to ignore. What was it about this man that affected me this way? I couldn't figure it out.

"We don't get many Magi through here. I'm glad you enjoy my work," the barista continued, a smirk curling the edges of his full lips. "Or was there something else that keeps you coming back?"

The malignant heat spread across my face like wildfire. "The coffee," I replied, my voice wavering.

"Ah, I see." The barista nodded, sliding a mug across the counter to another patron without taking his eyes off me. "Thought so. Double espresso over ice coming right at you."

Now that I'd all but been given permission, I watched the man closely as he worked, tamping down the ground coffee and pulling the rich espresso into a glass. While he poured the velvety brown liquid over ice, swirling it gently, he looked up at me once more. "You know, I'm going to be finishing up my shift in about fifteen minutes. If you're still around, maybe I could join you for a bit?"

"Why would you do that?" I asked, instinctively suspicious of the man's intentions. What reason would this mortal have to speak with me? Was he being manipulated by another Magi to glean information about Mother?

It wouldn't be the first time I was targeted to get to her.

"I like to get to know my regulars," the barista replied, sliding the cup over to me. "Plus, I think you're cute, and you've been staring at me for the last week without asking me out, so I figured you must be shy."

Shy? I laughed at the ridiculous notion. I was the furthest thing from shy. But still, I found myself nodding at the man, my tongue unable to find the words of agreement.

The barista flashed a smile at me. "Great, I'm looking forward to it."

Retreating to the café dining room, I found a seat by the window, the reality of the interaction slowly sinking in.

Away from the barista's gaze, I could finally trust my thoughts again. What had I just agreed to? Why would I waste time sitting in some café in the middle of Mortal Row talking to one of them? Mortals and Magi lived such separate lives. What would we even talk about? It didn't make sense. None of it did. And yet, there I sat, eagerly awaiting the lapse of fifteen minutes.

It was harmless, I told myself. It's not like I would actually develop an attachment to someone—especially a mortal. Besides, my role prevented me from ever having that type of relationship. What would a lover think of me gallivanting about, seducing men to assert my family's influence over them? It was a recipe for disaster. A sure-fire failure in the making.

None of those reasons spurred me to action. I was still seated when the barista approached the table, his apron tossed casually over his shoulder. "I'm glad you're still here. May I join you?"

"If you'd like," I replied, determined to keep my cool.

"I'm Bastien," said the barista, sinking into the chair opposite me.

"Tobias."

"It's nice to officially meet you," said Bastien, his warm golden eyes alight with a sparkle that I did not find distracting in the least. "What brings you to this side of the world, Tobias?"

"My work," I replied, a calm settling over me as the conversation bloomed.

"Me too," Bastien said with a grin. "Who would have thought we had so much in common?"

I found myself laughing. And for once, it wasn't forced or a tool used to distract. It was natural. A subtle tightness in my chest eased as I took a deep, freeing breath.

I could get used to the feeling.

I fully expected the numbness to linger, so when pain returned in my chest, rousing me to consciousness, I groaned in protest.

Death couldn't keep its grip on me, it would seem.

A blanket lay over me, itchy and stifling against my clammy skin. I struggled to rid myself of it but quickly discovered that my legs were bound together at the ankle—not tight enough to cause discomfort, but enough that I couldn't maneuver my way from under the claustrophobic cloth.

"Try not to move too much, Tobi. I don't want to have to redo the bindings."

I froze, the blood in my veins turning to ice.

"Lenny?"

The space was dark, just a flicker of a lamp across from where I lay, illuminating a wall of textured fabric and a low ceiling. She moved in the shadows, lithe and silent as the grave. When the light hit her face, casting dark shapes across her features, I finally came face-to-face with my sister.

Relief poured over me like a rainstorm, soaking into my skin. I reached for her, my hands cupping her face as if I needed to touch her to prove to myself that she was real. She was here.

"You're alive," I whispered, afraid that speaking too loudly may shatter this new reality. My fingers found warm flesh as Lynette leaned into my touch. "Or we're both dead. Either way, it's good to see you."

"You had it right the first time," she said, lowering herself onto the edge of the cot, though her posture remained tensed, like she was expecting to leap away at any moment. "Are you happy to see me, Brother?"

"I'm relieved," I admitted, a tangible tightness in my chest loosening with every breath in her presence.

"Bastien is here, too," she continued. "He's over in the infirmary, causing a lot of problems while they stitch him up."

"Okay."

Lynette raised a brow at me, a curiosity behind her eyes. "Does that news not please you? What's wrong with you, little brother? Other than the obvious, of course."

I leaned back on the pillow, my head cradled in its soft down. "I don't know who I am right now, Lenny. My mind is in shambles, and I can only make sense of pieces here and there."

"Right." She nodded to herself. "Bastien mentioned there may be some lingering side effects. How much do you remember right now, exactly?"

"Not much," I answered, running a hand along the ache in my chest and stuttering when my hand passed over the vacant space where the gem had been embedded. "Everything before Bastien revived me is still hazy. I'll get glimpses, but it's hard to keep it all in order."

Another nod from my sister, and I could tell the cogs in her head were turning. She avoided looking me in the eye. "Don't fret, Tobi. I'm sure your memories will be back soon. Till then, you can enjoy the bliss of a clean slate. No one from our family has had such a privilege in a long, long time."

She smiled, but there was something else. She was holding something back from me. That much was clear. A warmth swelled in my chest at the thought of my connection with her surviving the end of my first life. She was still my sister, even if I was only a portion of her brother in return.

"What's happened, Lenny?" I asked, my voice breaking.

Exhaustion had taken its toll on my body. My muscles ached, my pulse hammered erratically, and a buzzing sensation writhed under my scalp like an infestation of insects. But I was alive. And Lenny was here, her flesh warm against mine. We'd made it, somehow.

"There's not enough time to explain," Lynette replied, pulling a golden watch from her pocket, the face opening on a hinge. "I have to run, Tobi. But I'll be back soon, I promise. Rest and recuperate, brother of mine. We will speak when I return. I want your wits as sharp as your tongue."

My pulse spiked as she slipped from the cot.

"Lenny, wait," I pleaded, but she was already across the tent, pulling a flap of fabric back before disappearing through it. I collapsed back onto the cot with a sigh, pressing the heel of my hands into the sockets of my eyes.

Lynette was alive. I had that much to celebrate. But what did it mean for me? Would Bastien now make good on his promise to return me to the grave? And what of the gem that was supposedly keeping me alive? I pawed at the spot on my chest once more, wincing at the tenderness of the flesh.

Unfastening my shirt, I observed the ring of scarred skin across my chest, the center of which was fiery red and hot to the touch. If the gem was removed then how was I still drawing breath?

More mysteries that weren't adding up to any sum of coherency.

As I lay there, stewing in my thoughts, the sounds of my surroundings seeped in through the walls of the tent.

From the direction that Lynette exited, I could make out the faint sounds of laughter. Conversations layered over one another like a symphony in rebellion, each melody playing over the other till none could be differentiated.

After a moment of effort, I detangled myself from the scratchy blanket, investigating the binding around my ankles. Rings of crackling blue light wrapped around both, fastening them together. I would be able to stand as it were, but without release from the magic that bound me, there was no way for me to make an escape.

But why was I thinking of escaping? Lynette was here. Wherever 'here' was. She was safe. And with that knowledge, I should feel at peace with my imminent return to the earth. It was the way things were meant to be.

And yet, I struggled against the thought as if it were the bindings themselves. How had I died? Was I going to be able to rest without that knowledge?

A voice drew my attention, closer to the tent than the rest of the din.

"Let me through, godsdammit!"

The flapping of fabric filled the tent again as Bastien strode through the entrance, his attention locked directly on me.

I recoiled into the padding of the cot. Bastien had come for me, which could only mean one thing—he was ready to make good on his promise. He was coming to put me back into the ground.

Instinct took over. I had to run.

Swinging my legs over the edge of the cot, I struggled to my feet, but Bastien was quick, and in two steps, he was upon me, hands firmly on my shoulders, preventing me from moving any further. He leaned down over me, and for just a moment, I feared he was going to bite me, flashing teeth like a ravenous wolf, but then Bastien's lips were on mine, the heat of them against my skin enough to cause me to shiver.

The buzzing in my head intensified as memories bubbled to the surface—

*We stood in an alleyway, the night sky above twinkling with only the brightest of stars. Bastien's hands were on my waist, fingers sinking into the supple flesh as he pulled me tighter against him, my breath coming in short bursts that steamed between us. Bastien's eyes held me in place as he drew closer, closing the almost non-existent distance between us. Thunder rumbled through my chest. The taste of coffee, bitter, then sweet against my tongue. The smell of lilacs, floral and crisp. It was everything I had been missing—this pleasure that washed over me. No strings attached. No manipulations at play. Just me and this man who ignited the smoldering heat in my chest with every flick of his tongue and every caress of his fingers—*

I shoved Bastien away with all of my strength, and he stumbled back a few steps.

"What the fuck is wrong with you?" I spat, running a hand over my mouth.

"I'm sorry," Bastien said quickly, his eyes shut as he pressed a hand to his forehead. "Gods, I shouldn't have done that. I'm so sorry. But Tobi, the last few days have been absolutely *insufferable*. Then today, being so close and not being able to touch you—it's been torturous."

"What are you talking about?" I questioned, straining further against the restraints on my legs. Was this some sort of ploy? Did Bastien intend to catch me off guard, to blindside me with this show of affection so I wouldn't put up a fight when it came to returning me to the grave? "Why would you kiss me like that? I thought… things were over between us."

Bastien's eyes opened, the edges of his mouth pulling downward. "It's complicated."

I ran a hand over the scar on my chest, the warmth steadying me. "Then I suggest you start talking. And make it quick."

"I know it must be confusing for you," said Bastien. "But I promise you, this is all a part of the plan."

My blood ran cold.

"*What* plan?"

# EIGHT
## DEAD CERTAIN

𝓑astien's hands found my waist again as he pulled me into his apartment. The door shut behind us with a thud as we wrestled back and forth for control of the kiss that pinned us together. His jacket was the first thing to go, falling to the floor by the door as he staggered back, nearly bumping into the small kitchenette set that sat a few feet into the apartment. His fingers wrapped around the scarf hanging from my neck and tugged it off, discarding it alongside my coat.

"Nice place," I muttered between breaths, and he exhaled a laugh into my mouth before diving in again.

Bastien had no trouble taking control, his strong hands on my waist, steering me further into the apartment and onto the small couch pushed up against the wall. We broke apart long enough for my back to hit the cushion, and then he crashed down on top of me, covering me up in all the delicious exuberance he could muster.

For once, I didn't mind giving up control. Surrendering to his whims as his tongue parted my lips and grazed my teeth, and his warm fingers prodded the space between the buttons of my shirt, leaving heat trails along my body.

"Is that okay?" he asked, still close enough that I could feel the heat of his words, still taste the coffee-sweet succulence of his breath.

"More than okay," I replied, unfastening the first two buttons with a single tug. That was more than enough encouragement for him to finish the job, removing my shirt a moment later and tossing it to the floor. I shuddered as his fingers grazed my bare chest, desire smoldering in my gut like the embers of a fire hungry for another round of wood.

It had been so long since I'd experienced this kind of connection with someone. Sexual activity had become rote, just another part of the role I executed for Mother. But with Bastien, everything was new again. Each caress, each swipe of his tongue electrified my senses. My head swam in an elevated stupor.

"Take off your shirt," I told him, and he grinned at my direct order, pulling his sweater over his head in obedience.

When he lay into me again, the friction of his skin against mine was a chorus of sensations, all pooling at the base of my spine. His hands explored the angles of my body, each ridge and valley a new frontier for them to discover. When he grazed my crotch, my hips bucked, grinding my cock against his touch with an urgency that surprised me.

Bastien laughed, pulling his hand away and saying, "Patience."

I pouted—I actually pouted—like a sullen child not getting their way. I don't know what came over me, but my cheeks burned with embarrassment. Bastien only grinned wider, kissing me again and trailing the inside of my thigh with his hand.

"We'll get there," he said as if comforting me. He didn't give me long to stew in my own self-consciousness as he began to press kisses down my chest and along the thin line of hair to my navel.

"Ah, oh gods," I moaned as the tips of his fingers brushed along the waist of my slacks, slipping under the fabric to skim the sensitive skin beneath. My cock strained almost painfully against my undergarments, begging for him to touch me again.

"What is it, love?" Bastien teased, flashing a wicked grin.

His head was between my legs now, fingers tangled in my waistband as he traced the lightest circles on my inner thigh with his lips. Electricity ran up my spine, jolting me as he grazed my cock again, and I couldn't help but cry out.

"Eager, aren't we?" Bastien commented with a smirk, lifting his head up from his work and resting his chin on my navel.

"Don't stop now," I whined, the haze clouding my mind building to a point of no return.

"Patience," he repeated himself, pushing on my inner thighs till my legs spread wide enough for him to sink into the space between them on the couch. He ground himself against me, and stars exploded into my vision.

It was all too much. Was he really this good, or was I just too pent up for all of this stimulation? I'd worry about it later.

"Can I taste you?" he asked me, licking his lips in a manner that unmoored me right then and there.

I nodded emphatically. He could have asked me for the moon and I would have gladly given to him.

Wresting my trousers away, I shivered once at the full exposure of my body to the cool air of his apartment, then again when his fingers wrapped around my shaft, pulling back the skin around the head of my cock as he ran his tongue around the rim. My legs quaked with pleasure.

"Delicious," he mused, grinning up at me before devouring the entire head at once. A wet heat enveloped me, and I couldn't think anymore. My hands found the back of his head, guiding him as he glided back and forth, swallowing my cock with practiced expertise. When I hit the back of his throat, he merely exhaled through his nose with a sense of accomplishment.

Gods, this man was driving me wild.

"I can't take much more," I stammered, removing my member from his mouth.

"You can finish," he coaxed me, his hand around the base of my cock, gripping it firmly. He stroked me again, and I jolted, almost climaxing on the spot. I wrapped my hands around his to keep him from moving.

"But—I can't—I haven't even seen yours—"

He leaned forward, pressing his index finger to my lips to silence me. "You can't even think straight, Tobias. Let me give you this, and then we can see about you returning the favor later, okay?"

I nodded, all at once lost for words. He asked for no pledge of reciprocation, or even promise that I would take things further with him. He only wanted to take care of me. A warmth bloomed in my chest, settling in like a cozy blanket as he lowered his mouth to my cock once more, wrapping me in ecstatic bliss.

He didn't flinch as I released inside of his mouth, his motions hardly pausing as I dug my nails into the fabric of the sofa, my toes curling and a gasp ripping through my throat.

It was everything, all at once, and I shattered under the masterful care of this beautiful man. Once my release was complete and my legs ceased their quaking, he crawled up between my thighs, hanging over me with a coy smile that kindled that heat burning in my chest.

"You're incredible, Tobias."

And when he kissed me, the taste of my own body on his tongue, I couldn't help but believe it.

"*What* plan?"

Bastien approached slowly, his hands out in front of him in the universal gesture of pacifism. "Your fracture is still affecting your memory," he said, his voice calm and reassuring. He reached for me, but I flinched away from his touch, the resurfacing memories bombarding me in a haze of heated skin. Taking a few steps back, Bastien tried again. "I'm sorry for rushing all of this on you. And for the kiss. That was selfish of me. I should have waited until all of your memories returned."

I fell back on the cot, pulling my knees into my chest and wrapping my arms around them. Fracture. Bastien mentioned it before, back in the gardens. I couldn't think of a name more justly deserving. My mind was in shambles. Bastien's kiss still lingered on my lips, trilling with electricity, as if my body craved renewed connection. Another dose of the numbing balm that Bastien had provided for me those times before. But there was more. More brokenness down to the core of what made me. So deep that it felt as if I were coming apart at the foundation.

"Can you help?" I asked, my voice swallowed by the space around us. "With my mind. Can you put it back the way it was?"

Bastien exhaled, his mouth pulling taut. "It's unlikely. If I had known about the plan beforehand, I could have told them about the dangers of waiting to bring you back. Walked them through the risks."

"Plan? Are you telling me that someone *planned* to have me killed and brought back?"

Anger flashed in my belly, igniting like wildfire. Had I once again been made a pawn in the game larger than my own understanding?

"No, of course not!" Bastien contradicted me, "Please, just hear me out. I'll tell you everything I know, but I need you to stay calm, okay? Without the Verdant gem, you won't have a lot of strength. I don't want you to waste it being stupid."

I snorted a cruel laugh. "How kind of you. Why did you take it in the first place? Back in the town car, I thought you were leaving me to die."

Bastien winced. "No, Tobias. I would never—I couldn't do that to you. No matter what happened between us. Listen, you got injured in the crash. The gem was going to siphon what little magic was left in your system to try and heal you, but it wouldn't have been enough. You would have died if I didn't take it out."

"You told me that I'd die without it," I reminded him, placing a hand over the sore spot on my chest.

"It's the truth. Without the gem, your strength will start to fail. You can probably feel it already, can't you? That lethargy is only going to get worse."

"Then give it back," I said, holding out a hand. "Don't let me die again, Bast."

His expression crumpled as he turned from me, his hand pawing at the nape of his neck. "I have to repair it, first. The crack got worse when I extracted it from you. But you're safe for the time being, Tobias. And once I'm able to rest, I'll have it fixed up. I promise you."

"If I'm so safe, then why am I bound?"

"You've fractured, Tobi. There was no telling what state you were going to wake up in. We had to make sure you weren't going to do something stupid."

"Like get myself killed?" I huffed a breath. "Yeah, I already handled that."

"You have every right to be upset," Bastien offered, turning back to me again.

"But if you're up for it, I'd like to tell you how you got here. I can't promise it'll be helpful, but it could spark some specific memories. Fill in the gaps you're looking for. I won't force it, though. If you'd rather wait, then I understand—"

"Tell me," I interrupted, a surprising desperation in my voice. "Please, help me make sense of all this, Bast. You said there was a plan—who made it?"

Bastien nodded, clearing his throat. "We'll get to that, but first there's a few things you should know. A rumored plot against Lynette started circling around the City of Magi a few weeks ago. She would be targeted on the night of her appointment once she'd officially taken your mother's mantle as Councilor. Those behind the attack would then fabricate evidence, leading the investigation toward Rudderkin as the prime suspect. The Council would have no choice but to immediately declare an all-out war against the Rebellion.

"Lenny says that she was aware of the rumors, that she was taking extra precautions that night, but that there was still work to be done. Rudderkin and the others begged her to keep hidden after the ceremony, to make herself a smaller target. Lenny told them to kindly 'fuck off' and that she had important things to take care of that night, that she couldn't let fear keep her from what needed to happen. When the two of you left the ceremony, Rudderkin had three of his best spies tailing you just to make sure she stayed safe. It must have happened so fast, though. All three of them were gone in an instant. They weren't expecting it to come from one of your own—an Adored assailant. You were the only one with her when they attacked."

An Adored? Was that who killed me? Who would risk the ire of the Greene family? Even if I was the most expendable among them. It didn't make sense.

Bastien's throat bobbed as he swallowed, his gaze falling to the floor. "I was new to the Rebellion—I guess I still am. After what happened between us… I wanted to make a difference. Call it my subtle way of coming to terms with my power, but I figured it was as good a cause as any. And I wouldn't have to deal with any of those Hallowed assholes breathing down my neck, at least. After the attack, Lynette came here. Rudderkin sent more operatives to escort her before the assassin could make another attempt on her life. She told me about what you did, Tobias. The bravery you showed when it mattered most.

"I've been around death my whole life, you know. It doesn't frighten me. But when I thought of you crossing through those doors, all by yourself, I couldn't allow it. I revealed myself to Lynette and showed her the marks that I had glamoured away, the proof of my heritage. And she—" he paused, swallowing again. "She didn't even bat an eyelash. She didn't recoil in disgust or pass any judgments. She wrapped me in an embrace and told me that it broke her heart I had to hide what I was."

My chest ached at the image. That Lynette would be the one to comfort Bastien and not me. A flare of jealousy flickered along with the hurt, but I swallowed them down.

"I offered my services. I could bring you back. If we got to your body in time, I could pull you from Death's door. She went to Rudderkin, and the two of them sent out more operatives to see what had become of your body. But it was already gone by the next morning, scooped up during the night. We kept searching, reaching out to discreet contacts to try and find you. Then, you came to us. Orion was looking for a Reviled to pay for an off-the-books resurrection with the highest discretion. I knew it was you before I even made contact. It had to be you.

"I didn't think I'd make it in time. Typically, revivifications require specific prep work. Burial rites. My Grandmother passed them all down to me. All I could think of was, what if I couldn't bring you back? And there you were. It was like you were sleeping, Tobias. Like all I had to do was reach out and give you a gentle shake. You responded right away to my magic. I created the Verdant gem and fused it to your body. It was stupid, but I thought to myself that it must be because of our history together, how I was able to call you back when you had been dead for nearly three days."

He looked up at me again, an apologetic smile bending the edges of his mouth. "And the rest was history. I planned on sneaking you away at the earliest chance, but Orion was watching us like a hawk. I'm sorry it took so long to get some help to bust us out of there."

"Why didn't you just tell me this from the beginning?" I asked, my head swimming with the onslaught of information. "We were alone at Lorelei's. You could have just told me everything."

"I didn't want to rouse suspicions before I could get you away from there," Bastien explained. "If the Adored knew that you lived, possibly with the knowledge of the assailant, your life would be at risk once again. So, I leaned into the lie. Played the part of the scorned lover, if only to keep Orion at bay. That was, of course, before I knew she was a fucking Truthsayer. Who knows what she actually believed anything I said."

It was starting to make sense. At least a little. But did that really mean that he wasn't coming to bury me again? Had it all been a ruse?

"I'm sorry, again, that it took so long to get you back here. But you're safe, Tobias." Bastien took another step closer, still cautious. "Once you've recovered from this ordeal, and I have some time to prep, I can perform the true resurrection rite, and you'll be back to your full strength."

"True resurrection?" I repeated.

He nodded in response. "Right now, you're technically revivified. That's a temporary state. With the true resurrection, you won't have to worry about fracturing any longer. It'll make you whole again."

Could it be that simple? I was still trying to wrap my mind around the deluge. More memories flashed through my mind, like bubbles rising to the surface of my consciousness, too numerous to track. They overwhelmed me, so much so that I had to sit back, resting my head against the pillow.

"You said all this was planned," I recalled, closing my eyes and letting the roiling memories sink into the background of my thoughts. "By who?"

"Lynette," Bastien answered. "She said that you saved her life that night. That you'd save us all, if we could get to you in time."

Save them all? What did she mean? I wished she was still there, if only to explain all this in a way that didn't make my head feel like it was about to collapse in on itself.

"I should let you rest," Bastien said, turning over his shoulder and moving towards the exit of the tent. "I'll come back when you're ready, and we can keep talking. I—" he stops himself, clearing his throat and finishing with,

"I'm glad you're here, Tobi. I'm glad… well, I'm just glad you're still with us."

"Wait." I tried to stand, but between the restraints and the cacophony of noise in my mind, I couldn't keep my balance. Bastien moved in a blur, catching me at the waist before I could topple over.

Heat spread across my face as I looked up at the man, the locs of his hair hanging into his ochre eyes. He helped me to my feet, making sure I was steady before releasing his hold. "What is it?"

I shook the fluttery feeling from my stomach, chiding myself for the way the heat lingered at the site of Bastien's touch.

"You're coming back, right?"

His crooked smile shone in the dark, twinkling like a star amongst the inky cosmos.

"If you wish."

# NINE
## IN A DEAD HEAT

"It can't be true."

"Of course not. Madame Greene wouldn't stand for it. Not even from her own daughter."

Rounding the corner of the hall, I spotted the two mortal staff members murmuring back and forth as they polished a set of vases. They subtly bowed their heads in my direction as I passed. The entire chateau had been abuzz all morning, whispers of some bombshell secret being passed back and forth like the exchanging of currency. I knew not who or what the target of the rumor mill was that morning, but the mention of my sister piqued my interest.

"Pardon me," I said, halting my pace and turning back to the man and woman dressed in simple emerald-shaded finery. They bowed deeper, exposing the crowns of their heads. "I've been hearing tittering conversation all morning. Would you be able to provide me with a bit of context regarding the topic?"

The woman was the first to straighten, her eyes wide. "You mean, you don't know, Your Grace?"

"Know what?" I questioned, my patience already drawing thin.

"It was all over the papers this morning. They're running a smear campaign against Lady Lynette. Saying she's a sympathizer of the Rebellion and that she's looking to bring an end to the conflict as soon she succeeds the madame."

"We know it's all balderdash, of course," the man chimed in, running fingers over the thick mustache that covered his lip. "There is no way the Lady would ever think of supporting those brutal savages."

I nodded along, my stomach tightening from the news. "Right, what nonsense. They'll print anything these days if it moves papers."

"Right you are, sir," the woman replies, giving another bow of the head. "It's a shame, really, all this violence from the minority. Most of the Unseen are very well-mannered, like the ones who work here."

The man nodded, rubbing at a stubborn bit of dirt on the vase. "They've been trained appropriately, that's for sure."

"Is there something else you need, Your Grace?" The woman looked at me once more, her brow raised.

"No, my apologies. I'm running late as it is." I flashed them a quick smile, which earned another round of bows before I continued my path down the hall.

Lynette a traitor? Surely, there must be some mistake. But why would someone be spreading these rumors? Her ascension to our mother's role won't happen for at least another two years—once Mother's two-hundredth birthday arrives. Would the other houses be vying to sow distrust this far ahead of the ceremony in an effort to steal Mother's role?

No, the idea was ridiculous. The politics of the Adored are a discipline in the art of subtle persuasion. None in their right mind would publish something lambasting Lynette like this unless….

Unless it was the undeniable truth.

Abruptly changing direction, I moved with renewed haste towards the west wing of the chateau, hoping I'd be quick enough to catch my sister.

Outside of Mother's office, I hesitated, then gave the door a gentle knock. I checked the watch in my pocket, silently counting back the minutes.

Perhaps I was too late? Mother and Lynette must have already left for their commute into the Magi City.

But then the doors swung open—the outline of an Unseen shimmering as it moved out of the way—and I stormed into the room. Lynette was sitting at the end of the long meeting table, her unbound red curls falling to obscure her face as she wrote with a feverish pace along the page of parchment.

"Hello, brother of mine," she greeted me without looking up from her work. "If you're looking for our mother, she's already retired to her quarters to make ready for our trip."

I took a steadying breath, doing my best to appear calm. "No, you're actually the one I wished to see."

She looked up at me then, brushing the curtain of hair from her face to reveal a quizzical expression. "Is something wrong, Tobi?"

I approached the table, glancing over my shoulder in the direction of the Unseen standing in the corner of the room.

"Harris?" Lynette addressed the Unseen. "Would you mind returning to my quarters and selecting a few outfits for me to choose from? Your sense of style is simply unmatched."

The Unseen materialized fully—a man with oblong ears like a hare and nostrils made of long slits. "Yes, Your Grace." He bowed, then pulled the heavy door open before exiting.

"Speak freely, Tobi."

"You are aware you're at the center of the entire estate's gossips this morning, yes?"

Lynette rolled her eyes, snorting out a laugh as she dipped the point of her pen into the inkwell beside her. "Is that what this is about? You've nothing to fear, dear brother. I'm not some rebel sent to spy on your bedding rituals if that's what you're afraid of."

"I'm serious, Lenny. Why would anyone come out against us if they weren't absolutely certain they could back up the claims? Why would they risk Mother's wrath?"

Lynette waved off the question. "Mother has already handled it. Called the editor of the Page herself and demanded they print a retraction. I can't imagine the type of dirt Mother must have on her. You could practically hear the tears running down her face as she begged for forgiveness."

"So, then, there's no truth to the claims?"

Lynette looked up at me once more, setting the pen in the holster and leaning back into the plush cushion of her chair. "And if there was?"

"Was what?" I asked.

"Truth to the claims. If theoretically speaking, someone had managed to intercept communications between me and a certain prolific member of the Unseen Rebellion, promising aid once I've stepped into Mother's role. How would that affect your view of me, Tobi?"

I swallowed the lump in my throat. "Did you do such a thing?"

Lynette laughed once more, but it never touched her eyes. "I speak merely in hyperbole. Call it a thought experiment. I'm curious what you would do if those rumors they ran in the Page turned out to be true?"

I sank into the chair nearest me, resting my elbows on the edge of the wooden table. "I would tell you that you were being an idiot."

Another laugh from Lynette, this one full and boisterous. Not the demure giggle of the girl she portrayed when Mother was nearby. "And why is that? Do you the Unseen Rebellion to be a fool's errand?"

"I think it to be suicide," I replied plainly. "For anyone involved. You know this, Lenny. Mother will not rest until the entire rebellion has been snuffed out and order restored in her eyes. She hardly tolerates the Unseen staff these days."

Lynette grinned up at me, a strange gleam in her eye. "Well, it's a damn good thing that these are nothing but unsubstantiated rumors then, isn't it?"

Her words had never wrung more false. Something stirred behind the feigned innocence she wielded in my direction.

"Be honest with me, sister. What are you plotting?"

She barked another laugh. "Plotting? You think too much of me, Tobias."

"You cannot move against Mother," I continued. "At least not while she still holds power. Wait until your succession is complete. Then, no one will be able to stand in your way. Not even her."

"But what about all the innocent people who will die in the meantime?" Lynette asked, her smile flickering like a spent candle. "What of the children who are caught up in the collateral damage of the never-ending scuffle between us and them? We're talking about thousands of lives here, Tobias. You would have me toss them to the wayside until a more opportune moment?"

"I would have you live, Lynette." My voice was quiet as it hovered over the long table. "That is all."

Lynette was silent for a moment, then reached for the pen once more, signing the bottom of the scroll before drawing a sigil in the air with the tip of her index finger. The glowing golden character burst into a shower of sparks, and a snowy white raven appeared, perched on the table in front of her. She rolled up the parchment, whispering a few words as she placed both hands on the bundle, the roll shrinking to the size of a matchbox. She fastened the scroll to the raven's leg, rising from her chair and walking it over to the gilded window. Unlatching the glass, she pushed the window open, the raven fluttering away in the blink of an eye.

"Living grows more difficult by the day, I fear, Tobi." She turns back to face me, the corners of her eyes shining with moisture. "Suffering spreads like flames amongst the chaff, and the cries of those who demand justice grow with each passing day. I can't take it much longer."

"But think clearly," I said, raising my voice. "If you want to help anyone, then shouldn't you focus on attaining the power to do so on a larger scale? Think about all of the change that can come after your ascension, Lenny. Your magic already rivals Mother's, and your heart outweighs hers tenfold."

"And she is infinitely more clever," Lynette concluded. "And dreadfully cruel. Which means I can't tarry, waiting on a peaceful transfer of power. I can't delay, Tobias. There are lives to be saved now."

"Then you must become sharper," I replied, rising from my seat. "Mother will be watching you even closer now. You can't be sloppy."

Lynette smiled then, her demeanor lightning as she reached out, drawing me into an embrace. "Your concern is duly noted, Tobi. But we're just speaking in hypotheticals, right?"

I nodded, a lump in my throat blocking the words I wanted to say.

"I wish you were coming to the city. I want to go dancing with you again before we grow too old and self-conscious for that sort of thing."

"I fear it may already be too late for me," I said with a grimace.

Lynette laughed once more, taking me by the hand and leading me out of Mother's office.

"It's never too late, Tobias."

My sleep was anything but restful.

Fragments of memories flashed through my dreams in spiraling patterns, a kaleidoscope of my life playing out in moments both mundane and poignant. But a common thread kept weaving its way through the mess, tying the pieces together like patches of a quilt—Bastien.

Those memories would linger, allowing me to hold onto them for the briefest time. Moments of kisses pressed into sensitive flesh. Evenings tangled in silken sheets. Meals shared over tables, muddled with laughter and the ache of longing that twinged each time we were forced to part.

When I woke alone in the darkness, it was these memories that planted themselves, sowing their warmth through my shivering body. The air had grown cold, and a thin layer of sweat across my forehead was the physical evidence of the fits that had raged through me during slumber.

Through the haze of recollection, I turned over on my side, expecting another body to be sharing the bed. But I found only empty space and a deafening silence. My feet were still bound at the ankle, I confirmed, pulling back the scratchy blanket and flexing my calves. The blue aura pulsed with energy, keeping my legs firmly in place.

"Hello?" I called into the darkness. "Bastien?"

The air around me swallowed the words, pressing against my ears with a weight that bordered uncomfortable. I raised a hand in front of my face, pressing fingers together to try and snap, but they made no sound.

Magic. I could smell it now, a tang in the air that itched in the back of my throat. Panic swelled in my chest as I clawed at the restraints on my ankles, blue sparks erupting at the contact as it sent an electric jolt up my arm. It was no use. The restraints held fast.

My heart hammered silently in my ears. A glimmer of silver flashed in my periphery, and I raised my hand quickly, fingers grasping the would-be assailant by the wrist and halting a blade trained on my throat. Glittering emerald eyes narrowed at me in the dark, only a stripe of ebony skin visible between the shadowy mask obscuring the assailant's face.

"Who are you?" I tried to shout, but my lips moved soundlessly, my arm shaking with the exertion of holding my swift demise at bay. My muscles ached, any strength left in them squeezed out with this final moment of self-preservation.

But then, the figure pulled back, wresting their arm from my grasp and dissolving into the shadows. I scrambled to right myself on the bed, taking a deep breath and reaching for the magic in my chest. I attempted to push my aura outward in search of the attacker but was met only with a sharp pain in my temple, blinding me with an eruption of colors. Without focus, the magic withered, withdrawing inside of me. I blinked the spots from my vision enough to catch another flash of silver as the silent blade moved again. This time, I was able to deflect it away from me, the edge catching the fabric of the pillow and ripping it open with soundless efficiency. Before I could move, another hand seized me by the throat, lifting me off the bed in a smooth motion. I gasped for air as my feet left the ground, my assailant manipulating my body with the ease of a child holding a doll. My fingers found purchase on their arm, and my nails dug into the fabric of their sleeve. The emerald eyes appeared once more, widening till they resembled orbs.

With a faint *pop*, sound returned, assaulting me in a wave.

"Tobias, is that you?"

The voice rang familiar in my head as the assailant lowered me to the ground, their grip lessening enough for me to draw a shaky breath. "Y-Yes, I am Tobias."

Pulling the mask down that covered her face, the woman exclaimed, "You're supposed to be dead!"

Familiarity sparked as I gazed down at the woman's face, a memory of her staring back at me from across the table in Mother's office rising to the surface.

"I will be soon if you don't let go, Renata," I managed, the air through my throat making a slight whistle.

Renata released her hold on me, sheathing the silver knife into the holster on her hip. "How is this possible? Madame Greene told us that you'd been killed by the Rebellion."

Before I could answer her, I was rocked off my feet by an explosion outside of the tent, the very ground beneath us rippling from the force.

"You can explain later," Renata said, drawing her dagger once more and stooping down to slice through the magical restraints on my ankles. The sound of metal striking metal rang, and Renata was suddenly very close as she spoke in a hushed whisper, "Stay close to me. Do not make a sound. The raid will be finished soon, but I need to get you to safety."

Raid? So, this was Mother's doing. She'd finally found the heart of the rebellion and was making good on her promise to eradicate them. From outside the tent, screams echoed through the night.

I wanted to argue. To tell Renata to go on and pretend she never saw me. But if the Rebellion wouldn't survive the night, that meant I wouldn't either.

Did they know Lynette was here, too? I had to get more information.

I nodded to her, shifting my weight back and forth to regain sensation in my toes. My whole body felt heavy and sluggish. I just hoped I would be able to keep up. Renata moved like a shadow ahead of me, her footsteps muted against the soft ground as she led me to the entrance of the tent. Noise washed over us again as we stepped into the cool air, the tumultuous sounds of conflict assaulting from all sides. Two bodies lay at the entrance of the tent, throats slashed open as inky blood seeped into the ground beneath. They were Unseen, I realized as I stepped over them, their glassy eyes staring up at me.

Another scream and a burst of flames erupted from the tent next to us. Renata grabbed me by the wrist, pulling me away from the structures and toward the dark trees that loomed at the edge of camp.

"This way, Your Grace," Renata encouraged me. "Your mother will be thrilled to hear of your perseverance."

Fear trickled down my spine. Was I walking toward my end no matter which way I went? If Mother had been the architect of Lynette's assassination attempt, surely she would have been informed of the cause of my death.

"Not far now," Renata muttered as we rounded the final row of tents on the outer edge of the camp. Beyond the structures, the night was nearly pitch black, the moon absent from the sky, and the stars a muted tapestry of pinpricks. "I'm going to get you to the extraction point, and from there they'll—"

# THE SECOND AWAKENING

A wet sound and Renata's grip on me slacked. She spun around to me, her eyes wide again as red blood bloomed across her chest and spilled over her lips.

"R-Run." The word gurgled from her as she slumped to the ground. A ghostly outline of a clawed hand shrank into the shadows behind, still slick with Renata's blood.

Taking a step back from where she fell, I reached once again for my aura, projecting it out in front of me in an attempt to detect those nearby, but another debilitating lance of pain skewered my head, forcing me to my knees. I exhaled a hiss as invisible claws sank into my shoulder, shredding the fabric of my shirt as they ripped into my flesh. My aura withdrew once again, but I managed to grab hold of the assailant, the claws digging deeper with a pain sharp enough to force a groan from my mouth. I swept a leg out, catching the Unseen by surprise, and the grass indented where they landed, freeing their claw from my shoulder.

Scrambling to my feet, I took off, heading for the open field between the camp and the cluster of trees. I could make it. If I just kept running, I would make it to safety—another sharp pain raked across my back as claws tore into me, and I was sent reeling forward, losing my footing in the soft earth. My ankle twisted at a strange angle, and I stumbled, rolling head over heels till I was sprawled out, looking up at the inky sky.

The tall grass around me rustled, but I couldn't see anything. Not in the darkness that seemed to seep up from the ground like a rising tide of nothingness. I braced myself, struggling to get a leg under me, but my ankle throbbed, radiating pain that I felt all the way up to my teeth. The rustling was close, a low growl permeating the air. I didn't dare try and draw out my magic again, and without it, I was defenseless.

"I'm not your enemy!" I cried into the darkness.

More rustling. I cried out as claws bit into my chest, sinking deeper and deeper till I thought they'd puncture my lungs. I thrashed futilely, unable to detach my attacker as blood, hot and wet, soaked through my front. My vision began to narrow, the sound of my heartbeat drowning out the chaotic din of the raid.

I could only hope that Bastien and Lynette made it out alive, even if I was going to perish amongst the sea of grass. Then maybe, just maybe, my brief second life wouldn't have been completely pointless.

With a flash of light, the weight of the Unseen attacker disappeared. For a moment, I thought it was Death who approached, returning for me and me alone. But the constant beating of my heart disproved that theory rather quickly. The sky above was still dim, an endless, speckled void bearing down, ready to consume me entirely.

Would Bastien find me out here, alone amongst the wildflowers? Or maybe the earth itself would swallow me up, drinking in the blood that seeped from my body and leaving the rest of my flesh for the worms.

But it wasn't Death that came for me. At least, not unless Death was a pale man with flaming red hair streaked with white.

"Still with me, Toto?"

I cringed at the nickname, a trickle of blood leaking from the side of my mouth.

"I'll take that as a yes," said Cirian, kneeling beside me. "You look like a pin cushion, and your foot is nearly backward. Just what have you been doing out here?"

More blood spilled as I attempted to curse Cirian's name.

"Ah-ah, let's not speak with our mouths full. Come now, you can't just lay here all night. Let's get you someplace safe. Adoranda will not be pleased if they find you out here."

Cirian hooked a hand under my knees, then the other under my ribcage, hoisting me into the air as if I weighed as much as a ragdoll. I groaned from the pain as gravity forced my foot to twist further, and Cirian muttered a half-hearted apology as he began to move, ushering us away from the blazing camp and sounds of Death's approach.

# TEN
## DEAD ON YOUR FEET

*I* descended the marble stairs, the early hour dragging a deafening yawn from deep in my chest that mimicked the cry of a wounded animal. I'd been summoned to Mother's office, though I was not given a reason. Surely, she wouldn't expect me to entertain some insufferable son of the Adored aristocracy at this ungodly hour. I winced as I landed on the last step, my shins still sore from a recent growth spurt.

"Your Grace," an Unseen servant greeted me at the bottom of the staircase, the outline of their body pulsing with a dim spectral energy. My tutor once spoke of the Unseen and the magic that allowed them to render themselves invisible. It was attached to their instincts, they told me. Some primal urge that magic enhanced after the Awakening blessed them. The tutor also explained that the Unseen had to spend their entire lives resisting their primal urges, or else they would be no better than beasts.

I had difficulty believing it. All of the Unseen here at the Chateau were just as proper as the rest of us.

"Good morning, Ferrin," I replied, following him over to the entrance of Mother's office. The Unseen hooked a padded hand over the doorknob, pulling it open for me.

"My child, how lovely it is to see your face before the dawn."

I stifled another yawn, bowing my head as Mother greeted me. Another woman sat across from Mother, her ostentatious blue garb spilling over the arms of the chair and pooling on the floor.

"Source's blessing on you, young one," said the Cardinal. Beside her, a boy with fiery red hair tied back from his face stared at the bookshelf behind Mother, either oblivious to or completely ignoring my presence.

I had a pretty good hunch as to which. It wasn't the first time I'd been snubbed by the acolyte, Cirian.

"Good morning, Mother," I greeted her in return, then turned to honor the Cardinal with the same half-bow. "Saint Sancha. It is an honor to welcome you to Chateau Greene." My gaze lingered on the boy with scarlet hair, waiting for him to acknowledge my existence, but he seemed entirely disinterested in pleasantries. "Was there something you wished of me, Mother?"

"Indeed, there is," Mother replied, rapping a long nail against the desk. "Young Cirian here is training under Her Eminence and has shown an impressive interest in the study of the blade. While the Cardinal and I discuss matters that would lull her acolyte to slumber, I hoped that you would take him to the gardens and have a friendly bout?"

"Really?" I questioned, unable to keep the surprise from my face. "You want me to spar with him? I would think Lynette more suited for the sport—"

"He has requested you as his bout mate," Mother answered, her voice adopting a tone that communicated her displeasure in being questioned. "Does this not please you, child?"

"Apologies, Mother. This pleases me very much." I turned my attention to the boy once again. "I would be delighted to spar with you, Cirian."

The boy rose from his seat, finally turning to face me. The years between the acolyte's visits to Chateau Greene were clearly marked in the staggering height difference between him and myself. Cirian stood a remarkable foot taller than the last time I'd spoken with him, looming under the statue of my great-grandmother.

"I look forward to meeting you on the strip," said Cirian, the hint of a smirk building beneath his usually stoic expression.

"Likewise," I replied, my drowsiness dissipating more and more by the second. "I hope to provide you with the challenge you seek."

Cirian's smile finally bled through. "I doubt it."

"Cirian," the Cardinal addressed him with a quiet timbre.

The boy nodded toward the Cardinal, wiping his expression clean. "Apologies, Your Eminence. I will try harder to curb my competitive nature."

"Do give him a good showing, young Master Greene," the Cardinal continued, turning her attention to me. "I'm afraid there are few at the Cradle who can stand against Cirian these days. Adversity inspires growth, and as my acolyte, he still has much growing to undergo."

"I'll do my best, Your Eminence."

"Yes, yes," breathed Mother, flicking her hands at the wrist. "Off with both of you, now. We are not to be disturbed until we send for you, is that understood?"

"Yes, Your Grace," Cirian said, showing Mother more respect than he did the Cardinal. In my opinion a wise decision. The Cardinal seemed much milder in temperament. He turned and strode past, not even bothering to wait for me as he headed out into the foyer.

"Good day," I addressed the adults, giving one more bow before following quickly behind Cirian. Once the heavy doors were shut behind me, I hurried to close the distance between us, falling into stride with Cirian.

"If I behaved as you did, Cirian, my mother would have cut out my tongue ages ago."

"If you behaved as I did, Toto," Cirian scoffed, "then maybe one day you'd make something of yourself instead of hiding away in this palace of pomp and circumstance."

"That's rich, coming from the Source's chosen whelp. Not all can be so blessed."

I worried for a moment that I'd overstepped the line of playful banter, but the smirk that twisted Cirian's lips put my mind at ease.

"That is true. There are few who compare to me."

"Few who think themselves so low?" I interjected, taking the lead and crossing the foyer to the large ornate doors. They swung open without a sound, and the Unseen servant guided us down the stairs and toward the garden. It was still dark, so the lamp posts guided our way, the warm firelight catching on the mist that clung to the ground.

"I haven't thanked you properly for disturbing my slumber this morning," I said as we rounded a row of hedges, entering the garden proper. A large fountain built from polished stone engraved with colorful gems sprang from the center of the garden, the sound of trickling water filling the peaceful space. "Do you prefer to be struck across the face or in the gut?"

Cirian huffed a laugh, already moving to the opposite end of the strip that had been hastily assembled beside a row of Mother's cherished rosebushes. A mask and padded vest awaited us on either end and one of the staff, an older mortal man with grey-streaked hair and jowls that hung like a hound's, stood in the center of the strip, ready to serve as the judge.

"Feel free to land a blow wherever you like, Toto. If you can, that is."

I pulled on the white vest, fastening it around my back with a quick tug and knot. "The gut it is, then. I do hope you abstained from breakfast."

Cirian pulled on his mask, flipping the faceguard up to give me a bored expression. "Well, do hurry up, man. I want to break a sweat before the sun rises."

Donning my own mask, I retrieved the fencing saber from the holster. With a flick of my wrist, I slashed the air in front of me, testing the balance, then headed to the starting place. Cirian mirrored me, lowering the mesh covering over his face as we squared off.

The grey-haired man stepped between us, holding his hand out. "The first combatant to five points will win the match. Are the combatants ready?"

"Ready," we responded in unison.

"Begin."

Cirian body was a blur of motion, the blade of his saber nearly invisible with its speed. I hardly had the opportunity to parry, and even as I swiped my weapon downward, the tip of Cirian's saber struck me in the hip, pain flaring at the impact.

"Point to Master Cirian."

"Apologies, Toto." Cirian's muffled voice sounded amused. "Are you still asleep?"

"Your company is rather dull," I replied, letting out a yawn. "I'll make more of an effort to stay awake this time."

"Ready?" the judge asked.

We took our positions once more.

"Begin."

Another flurry of motion from Cirian, but I was ready on the defensive. I stepped back on my left foot, parrying the quick thrust and directing it away. Cirian staggered a bit, his momentum diverted, and I seized my opportunity. Lunging, I drove the tip of my saber toward Cirian's chest, but the other boy was faster, knocking away my riposte with ease after regaining his footing. We squared up, the ends of our blades crossing as we tested each other's defenses. It became quickly apparent how disadvantaged I was. Cirian moved with a practiced grace that made it nearly impossible to glean his next maneuver. Not only that, but he also had the advantage of height on his side, his limbs longer than mine. But most troublesome was the ferocity of his strikes. Each parry sent a shockwave down the hilt of my saber, numbing my hands. I had to focus on not losing my grip.

It took only a few more exchanges for Cirian to overwhelm me again, knocking aside a misplaced parry to find a second touch, this time against my shoulder.

"Second point to Master Cirian," the man announced as we took a step back from one another.

"Come now, Toto. You can't seriously expect me to believe this is the best effort you can muster?"

I gritted my teeth behind the scrim of my mask. Anger flickered in my gut, and I took a deep breath, reining in the emotion before it bubbled to the surface. Mother had drilled into me from a young age the importance of controlling one's emotions. They were a vulnerability to be used against you with the greatest of ease.

We stepped back to our starting positions.

"Ready?"

Two nods.

"Begin."

Wanting to bank on the element of surprise, I lunged first, stamping my foot against the ground as I thrust my blade, aiming low on his torso. For a fraction of a second, I knew that I'd made contact, but then Cirian's body blurred, and my assault was halted by the tip of a blade pressing into my stomach.

"Point three to Master Cirian."

With a grunt of frustration, I turned from him, stalking back to the starting position once more. Heat simmered in my gut. I knew Cirian was toying with me. I shouldn't have let it bother me like this, but the more I pictured that stupid smirk under his mask, to more I wanted to abandon the blades and tackle him outright.

"What's the matter, Toto? There's no need to get upset over a little bit of sport."

"Why do you insist on calling me that?" I spat, the edge in my words evidence of my slipping control.

Cirian took his stance once more. "Does it bother you?"

"Would you care either way?"

"Ready? Begin."

Another onslaught of quick thrusts erupted from Cirian, but I was able to deflect them, only giving a few steps back as collateral. As Cirian regained his footing, having covered a long distance in his advance, I saw the opening and struck, managing to clip him on the side, the tip of my blade sinking into the fabric of Cirian's vest.

"Point to Master Greene."

Cirian flipped open the visor, a wide smile spread across his lips. "My, my, what a surprise. Have you finally decided to give winning a try?"

"Anything to wipe that smug grin from your face."

He barked a laugh, lowering the screen back into place.

"Ready? Begin."

Our sabers collided with a deafening clang! And I broke the stalemate by stepping backward, renewing my attack with a thrust that Cirian deflected with ease.

"Where did your rage go, Toto? You'll never hit me again without it."

I struck at him, and Cirian knocked it away with a disappointed huff.

"Come on! Show me more!"

I sucked in a steadying breath, willing myself to ignore his goading. Mother had been clear—true power came from giving nothing control over you. Even your own emotions. One more deep breath and I deadened the anger in my gut, smothering it like a wayward spark.

Cirian advanced on me once more, his weapon nearly invisible with speed as it clashed against my saber again and again, shockwaves of numbing pain shooting up my arm.

"Is that the best you have?" Cirian questioned, his onslaught relentless.

Gritting my teeth, my foot slid from under me, setting me off balance, and I tried to knock away another thrust, but the tip of Cirian's saber struck me in the hip. I sucked in breath as pain radiated down my leg.

"Fourth point to Master Cirian."

Cirian pulled his blade back, letting his stance fall as he pushed up the scrim. His usual cocky smile was absent this time. "Tell you what, Toto. If you can manage to win this bout, I'll tell you why I picked that darling little nickname for you."

"How kind of you," I scoffed, massaging the soon-to-be bruise on my hip.

"I'm serious," Cirian replied, taking up his position once more. "You have the ability. Don't hold back, and you'll get the reward you're seeking."

"Ready?"

Not sure if I believed him, I took my place quickly, eying Cirian.

What was his angle?

"Begin."

I stuck first, swirling my blade in a quick flourish and thrusting. Cirian deflected the attack, responding in kind, but I quickly sidestepped the attempt. Our blades met once again, exchanging glancing blows back and forth. Sweat built on my brow as the bout stretched on for longer than any previous, neither of us giving the other an opening.

"Come now, Toto," spurred Cirian, a ferocity in his tone that sunk into my skin. "You can't expect to win with timidity. Show me your mettle!"

A grunt of frustration escaped through my lips as I whipped my blade haphazardly. Cirian easily evaded the clumsy haymaker, disarming me with a blow to the back of my hand. The saber clattered to the ground as Cirian gently pressed the tip of his sword to my chest.

"The point and the bout go to Master Cirian," the grey-haired man announced in a dull tone.

Still panting from the effort of the bout, I wiped my brow after removing the mask, the sting of embarrassment lingering in my cheeks from my childish outburst. He'd defeated me in more ways than one.

*I swore he'd never do it again.*

*The red-headed boy sheathed his weapon, lifting up his visor to give me a small smile. The first streaks of daylight broke through the foliage, transfiguring the sheen of perspiration on his face to a glistening dew that twisted my insides the longer I stared. There was something almost sad in the way he looked at me, but the emotion fluttered away as he spoke.*

"Better luck next time, Toto. Want to go again?"

Cirian carried me away from the camp and into the darkness of the woods for some time, the sound of his steady breathing and my stifled grunts of pain the only noise to break up the eerie silence that surrounded us. I dared not speak till I knew it was safe to. Then again, even if we weren't fleeing for our lives, what would I say? I knew not whether the man who carried me considered me friend or foe. The last time we'd seen each other, he'd seemed hellbent on ridding the world of my existence, but there was an airiness in the way he looked now compared to then. Like a great weight had been lifted from his shoulders.

"What exactly were you doing out there, Toto?"

Cirian's deep voice rumbled against my body, sending chills across my skin like a cool breeze.

"Renata found me," I answered, taking the calculated risk of telling the truth. "The captain of Mother's militia. She was leading the assault but got sidetracked trying to get me to safety."

"And did you wish to leave?"

His tone wasn't accusatory but more so curious.

I'd have to decide which way to lean. Had Cirian been a part of the assault against the Rebellion? It seemed strange that the Church would have sent someone like him into the fray unless negotiations were in order. And I knew how Mother felt about negotiations. So, did that mean the rumors Lorelei Orion had thrown in his face were true, and he was there alongside the Rebellion? Would that be enough to change his thinking of me being brought back to life by a Reviled?

"Toto? Are you still with me?"

"No," I answered. "I wasn't trying to escape, I mean. I was waiting for someone."

"Ah, yes. Your Reviled friend."

His stoic features remained unchanged in the dim moonlight, much to my chagrin. He'd always been difficult to read, now even more so in adulthood. So, I decided to change tactics and ask some questions of my own.

"We're a long way from the Cradle. What exactly were you doing in a rebel camp, Cirian?"

"Me?" Cirian questioned, his pace slowing. "Haven't you heard the rumors? I was there to speak with Rudderkin, of course."

Relief washed over me like a wave. Maybe Cirian wasn't there to kill me after all. At least, not at this very moment.

"Didn't get a chance to make the meeting, though," he continued. The circles under his eyes were purplish and bruise-like, especially in the dim light. His skin seemed tight, pulling across the sharp angles of his face like a drum. "Your mother saw to that nicely."

"So, you're part of the Rebellion too?" I asked, wanting to be certain.

"In a sense," Cirian replied, coming to a stop. "Lynette said your mind was fractured. It's a shame, really. Just when you decided to become interesting, you flush all that away and dig yourself an early grave."

I deflated with a sigh. "Thank you for reminding me. Gods, I long for the day that I can feel like a complete person again and not this tattered mess." I winced as Cirian stepped over a log, jostling one of the deeper wounds in my shoulder.

Cirian was silent as we went, his brow furrowed.

"Have I said something?" I asked, confused.

"No one ever feels entirely whole, Tobias. You may not remember it now, but even with your memories in order, I would imagine you'd feel the same."

"Isn't that a cheery thought?" I asked, shifting in his arms once more. The throbbing in my ankle was impossible to ignore, but I did my best. "As if I don't have enough to look forward to."

"Enough with the bravery," said Cirian, walking a few paces to the base of a large oak tree and gently setting me against the trunk. Once I was out of his arms, I noticed just how much blood coated Cirian's pale clothing.

"Gods, are you alright?" I asked, leaning forward enough to earn another wince.

Cirian looked down at his tunic, his lips parting with a grin. "This is your blood, Toto. I'm afraid I escaped rather unscathed."

That certainly did explain my lightheadedness. I swayed at that moment, falling back against the abrasive bark.

"Easy," Cirian coaxed me, long fingers drifting down my leg till they brushed against my swollen ankle. "Don't worry. I'm going to make it all better, Toto."

I rolled my eyes, muttering a string of curses under my breath at this infuriating man. Cirian's hands began to glow with a pulsating aura of blue light, not unlike the color of thread woven through his tunic. A groan built in my throat as the pain in my ankle dulled, and a strange sensation crawled up my leg as tendons popped into their proper place. I felt function return to my foot in a swell of relief.

Once Cirian seemed satisfied with the work on my ankle, his hands drifted upward toward the wounds across my chest that still oozed dark blood. With the steady confidence of a battle-worn healer, Cirian tore open my shirt, letting the fabric fall in pieces to the ground and leaving my torso exposed to the cool night air. Again, Cirian's warm hands found my flesh, knitting together wounds one after the other till only the bloodstains remained.

Immobilized as I was, I watched Cirian as he worked, transfixed by the intensity of the man's focus. Cirian had always been strikingly handsome, with an arrogance that often lent itself to pulchritude. But in close proximity, under the constant attention of his umber eyes, I felt a stirring that rattled me at my core.

Maybe the blood loss had rendered me witless.

"That should hold you together," announced Cirian, wiping the bloom of sweat from his brow with a deep exhale. He stood once more, looming over me like another of the dark forest's trees.

A stiff breeze passed over us, an overwhelming shiver creeping over me as I longed for the warmth of the shirt that lay in tatters on the ground. Cirian reached up to his neck, loosening the fastenings of his tunic before removing it. He held it out to me with a smirk that bordered lewdness.

"What is that for?" I asked.

"To stop your shivering," Cirian explained, the sheen of his pale skin capturing what little light shone through the cover of tree branches. "I wouldn't want you to catch your death."

I snorted an unexpected laugh. "Was that a joke, Cirian? Here I had I thought for so many years you were incapable of humor." Taking the offered garment, I pulled it around my exposed shoulders, reveling in the residual warmth. Fresh juniper filled my nostrils, but I resisted the urge to bring the fabric closer to take in more of the heavenly scent.

"A simple oversight, I assure you," said Cirian with a chuckle. "Besides, it's covered in your blood. I think it only fair it belongs to you now." He offered me a hand, a mirthful smirk playing across his lips.

After quick contemplation, I took it, the tall man lifting me to my feet with ease. The only lingering discomfort was a strange numbness in my foot, but otherwise, I felt right as rain. Even the splitting headache that had come upon me when I tried to wield my magic had subsided.

Was it just another symptom of my fracturing?

"Are you ready to push on?"

Cirian watched me closely, his fingers still wrapped around my hand.

I nodded in response. "Where are we going, exactly?"

"A sanctuary for the time being. I'll have to make contact with Rudderkin once things have calmed down. Then we can get you back to your sister."

"And Bastien."

Cirian's hand dropped away, his demeanor cooling. "Yes, and your necromancer. Let's hope he hasn't moved onto another cold body by the time you two can reunite."

"If I didn't know any better, Cirian, I would argue you sounded like a jilted lover."

Cirian didn't respond to the accusation, instead muttering something under his breath, and a small orb of blue light burst into the space above his open palm. He held out his hand, illuminating the path forward. "Shall we?"

I let the details of his reaction sink in. Was this something more than just the normal animosity between Hallowed and Reviled?

Having no other option, I agreed, following Cirian as he led us back onto a trail. The woods surrounding us from all sides were deathly quiet, our steps swallowed by the heavy cover of leaves and hanging moss. The night's chill had even silenced the insects, so instead of dwelling on the awkward silence, I asked the question blooming in my mind.

"What is it about the Reviled that bothers you so?"

Cirian didn't look back at me, his gaze trained ahead. For a brief moment, I thought he hadn't heard my inquiry, but then he spoke, words skipping over the soft earth like stones along the surface of a pond. "If you're referring to the Church's stance, I'm afraid it's a long story. One that isn't as cut and dry as the history books make it out to be."

I hastened my steps, coming alongside Cirian, marveling at the deep shadows the orb of light cast across his face. He really was striking to look at. Like a piece of artwork, chilling at first impression but warmed the longer you stared.

"Perhaps you could explain it to me then since we've nothing naught else to discuss. Who better to help me understand than the future leader of the Hallowed himself?"

The edge of Cirian's mouth twitched, and once again, I found myself wondering if I'd pushed too far, but it wasn't long before he spoke again. "Up until a hundred and fifty years ago, the Hallowed and Reviled belonged to the same community of Magi, known as the Revered. We both worshiped the Source for its gifts and recognized our place among the Magi as spiritual leaders and healers."

"A hundred and fifty years?" I echoed. "Forgive my addled mind, but I was under the impression the schism went back centuries."

Cirian shook his head. "That is a false narrative disseminated through the Church. As is the reason for the schism. They would have you believe the Reviled to be unholy wretches without a rational thought amongst the lot. That they sought to defy the very nature of the Source and violate its most sacred beliefs, and these perversions led the late Cardinal to banish them from the cities of Magi. But that is not the truth of the matter. See, the fracturing of the Revered was not started internally, but brought about by outsiders."

"Who would wish for such a thing?"

Cirian looked at me, a quizzical expression bending his brow. "There were plenty who wished to topple the Church, I'm sure. But the prevailing theory is that these usurpers infiltrated the Revered, serving in our communities as members of the Church of the Source, spreading lies and conspiracy amongst the factions. By the time the late Cardinal realized what was happening, it was too late to stop the inevitable."

"What sort of lies?"

"The Revered were blessed as a people with many gifts by the Source. We can knit flesh as if it were fabric. Expel toxins from the body with a simple incantation. Commune directly with the Source without being driven mad. But there were those amongst us who had more powerful gifts, still. Those who could tamper with the very balance of life and death."

"The Reviled."

He nodded, attention falling back to the path ahead. "Before the schism, none of them were called as such. They bore symbols on their flesh—" he trailed a finger along his forearm from wrist to elbow— "that marked them as divine. They were the most respected members of our society at one time, some of which were Elders who had manipulated the flow of time to live nearly a millennium. Powerful projectionists who could send their souls through the ether to the afterlife and destinations beyond. And necromancers who could stay the very hand of Death."

I shivered once more, pulling the garment around my shoulders closer, though it had nothing to do with the night's chill. No wonder Bastien had gone to such lengths to hide the swirling markings on his arms. They would have given him away at a glance.

"The other Revered became jealous of those with more power than themselves. And with the outsider's influence, the fires of their animosity were flamed to the point of revolt. They crusaded against the families now labeled as Reviled, claiming them heretics amongst believers." Cirian paused for a moment, his pensive expression deepening. "The others were quick to believe such lies, if only because they saw it as an excuse to act on their basest of desires. The Reviled were rounded up and expelled from the Magi cities. Those who refused to flee were made examples of. The history books neglect to cover those torturous executions, but the Church still holds records. I've seen them with my own eyes. You can imagine the difficulty of executing someone who has sway over Death. The results were nearly always… gruesome."

My stomach lurched, and I exhaled a shaky breath. Had Bastien's family met the same gruesome end? Was he descended from one of these Elders?

"After that, they disappeared, most going into hiding out in mortal societies. Now, here we are, a hundred and fifty years later, and the animosity towards the Reviled has only increased. Parents scare their little ones with stories of necromancers who dance with the dead, and any remaining Reviled dare not show their face, lest a mob show up at their doorstep demanding blood. It's…archaic."

"Then why allow it to continue?" I asked, nearly tripping over a tangle of roots as I struggled to match Cirian's long strides. "Why not ask the Cardinal to intervene and set things right?"

Cirian glanced over his shoulder, a flicker of amusement in his eyes. "You think it so simple to shift the minds of thousands? Ah, but I suppose for an Adored, it would be. You can merely bend others to your will. The rest of us have to rely on subtler tactics to get what we want, Tobias."

I bristled at the use of my actual name. It sounded strange on Cirian's tongue. "And what is that you want, exactly?"

He halted, his shoulders slacking as he rested a hand against the trunk of a gnarled oak tree. "It doesn't matter what I want."

I hovered a few feet away, drinking in the sadness that clung to Cirian's words. Maybe he felt the same pressures as Lynette, being in line to inherit great power yet beholden to the expectations of those who asked you to wield it. Did the weight resting on their shoulders feel like shackles? For once, I was grateful for my lowly status as an Adored male, if only for the freedom it provided me.

"We're nearly there," Cirian said after a moment.

"Where exactly is 'there?'"

"I told you. A sanctuary. A safe place where we can rest and make arrangements." He turned to me, his dark eyes soaking in the eerie glow of the orb in his hand. "I'll keep you safe, Toto. I swear it."

And in that moment, under his gaze, I fully believed him.

The sanctuary was off a dirt road, not far from the edge of the woods. The sounds of night returned as we stepped out from the cover of the dense foliage, starlight washing us in a pale glow as we made our way to the derelict A-frame building. Faded and dirty stained glass hung above the entrance, splintered in multiple places with spiderweb-like cracks that only added to their intricate designs. Two heavy, wooden doors adorned the front of the building, far sturdier than I anticipated them being as I pushed on one. It swung open with a creak, but before I could cross the threshold, Cirian grabbed onto the fabric bundled around my shoulders, keeping me from moving forward any further.

"Just a moment, Toto," he whispered, pulling gently to guide me out of the way. Once the doorway was clear, Cirian held out a hand, his palm pressing flat against an invisible barrier where the door had been. Taking in a deep breath, Cirian muttered a string of words under his breath, the air quickly taking on the distinct smell of ozone as a crackling ripped through the quiet, followed by the sound of splintering glass. Shimmering waves of magic rippled over the space around Cirian's hand, then peeled away like tattered strips of paper held to a flame. Once he was satisfied, Cirian nodded in my direction, taking a cautious step inside.

It was not lost on me the peculiar scenario I found myself in. It was true that I had known Cirian since childhood, having interacted with him dozens of times throughout the years at social functions, sparring sessions, and meetings held at Chateau Greene—at least, those were the moments I could recall—but that was well before I had shown up to the Cradle, flaunting my recently revivified self to the man who was tasked with leading the witch hunt for all things necromantic. And now I found myself alone with him, in a secluded place, miles away from anyone or anything. What were the odds Cirian allowed me to live through the night? As I lingered in the doorway, I weighed the options of risking it in the woods and making a run for it now.

Cirian glanced over his shoulder, already halfway down the aisle of the sanctuary.

"Are you coming, Toto?"

I had to decide quickly. Even Cirian would have a difficult time locating me if I was fast enough to disappear into the thicket. But what would I do once I was on my own? I had no magic—at least none I could use without debilitating side effects—and no other means of finding Bastien. *If* he had even made it out of the camp alive. A sinking dread bloomed in my stomach at the idea. Maybe Mother had been successful in her ploy, and the Rebellion had been stamped out in one fell swoop?

That would mean Lynette....

Cirian face appeared in the doorway, a quizzical expression twisting his brow. "I know it doesn't look like much, but I assure you that you'll be much safer in here than out there."

Perhaps I could just ask him outright? He'd always been painfully honest in the times I could recall. Why would that have changed now?

"Why are you doing this?" I asked, remaining planted in place. "Why are you keeping me safe?"

"Would you prefer I left you to the wolves?" Cirian asked, bemused.

"I want to know you're not going to slit my throat while I sleep."

Cirian laughed at that, his chuckle sharp and harsh. "Toto, dear, if I wanted you dead, I could have left you bleeding out in that field of wildflowers. Have I not done enough to earn at least a smidgen of trust?"

"I've had a very long and trying day," I said, running a hand through my matted curls. "So, you'll have to forgive me for my cautious behavior. You did threaten my life not twelve hours ago, in case you've forgotten."

Cirian leaned a broad shoulder against the frame of the door, expanding his chest with a deep breath. I tried valiantly to ignore the way the lithe muscle of his bicep bunched as he crossed his arms. "What else was I supposed to do, Toto? You waltzed into the Cradle with that heavy Veil, thinking that I wouldn't be able to *smell* the death that lingered on you. Really, you'd have better luck hiding from starving hounds after rolling around in yesterday's scraps."

I took an instinctive step back, inhaling deeply. If I smelled of death, then it must not have been an aroma with which I was familiar.

"I wasn't exactly given time to bathe," I said, face warming at the implication. "And I was dead for three days before Bastien got to me—I do not need to defend myself to you."

"Peace, Toto," Cirian managed through his hearty laughter. "The necromancer's magic doesn't leave you rank. But that's exactly what I could smell on you. *His* scent. His magic running through your veins. It made me—" he stopped, something flickering in his dark eyes that set me on edge. "He should have known better than to bring you there. If I hadn't reacted in the appropriate manner, I would have drawn even more suspicion. You can imagine that Sancha doesn't exactly support my involvement with the Rebellion, so I must keep up the charade on all fronts."

"And threatening our lives was you acting on your best behavior?"

His eyes narrowed. "When I am acting as the Acolyte of the Church, then yes, occasionally it is. You're not exactly one to stand on the moral high ground, Toto. Or have you conveniently forgotten the number of lives you've ruined in the name of your mother?"

I flinched at his words.

"I'm sorry," Cirian amended, his tone softening. "There's little room for me to judge. My hands are far from clean. We do what we must to survive."

At that moment, for the first time, I was glad for the memories taken from me, if only to avoid the phantoms of those Cirian referred to. I knew I couldn't hide from them forever, that if I survived the coming days, I would have to face the reality of who I was. The lives I had destroyed.

My stomach turned at the thought.

"Come inside," Cirian said gently, stepping aside to make room. "You're exhausted, and I swear on the Source that no harm will come to you under this roof."

I looked once again at the dark trail leading away from the man with fathomless eyes, and for more reasons than one, I finally conceded and stepped into the sanctuary.

# ELEVEN
## DEAD GIVEAWAY

"Power. Influence. Tradition. These are the hallmarks of Adored culture. Our people have been guiding the Magi toward a common goal for centuries. Can either of you tell me what goal it is that we strive for?"

The classroom was empty, except for Lynette and I, seated across from one another at a desk of rich mahogany. I glanced across to my sister, wondering why she didn't already have her hand raised. She seemed distracted, caught up in a swirling pattern she was drawing on her paper. So, I raised my hand instead, and the wrinkled woman standing in front of the chalkboard pointed her stick at me.

"Mother says that we're going to lead the Magi into the next Awakening."

The tutor smiled, the lines of her face sinking further inward. "That's absolutely right, Tobias. More than a thousand years ago, the Awakening brought us out of the shadows of mortality, sparking the gift of magic in our very souls. With these gifts, the Magi have been able to accomplish countless wonders. Grand cities rose from the ashes of mortal wars. Diseases that ravaged the population have been culled. Society flourishes under the guiding hands of generations of Adored women. This is the legacy that you will inherit, Lynette."

My sister didn't look up from her paper, still focused on the drawing, her hand moving in the same slow, intentional circles.

"And I'll help, too," I added to the tutor, straightening my posture.

"Of course you will, dear," our teacher replied, an amused smile curling the edges of her wrinkled mouth. "But it's Lynette who could bring about the next Awakening and, with it, another evolution of the Magi."

"Will the mortals be able to use magic, then?" Lynette asked, her hand never slowing its progress along the parchment.

"The mortals?"

Confusion hung from the tutor's face, much like her jowls.

"They don't have magic," Lynette continued, her face nearly obscured behind a wall of crimson curls as she worked. "So, when the next Awakening happens, we'll give it to them, right?"

"The mortals would not know what to do with magic, dear, so I don't think it's—"

"But we came from mortals," Lynette interrupted. "All of us. It's only fair, right? We should share the magic with them."

The tutor's expression pulled tight as she waved her hand in the air. "It's really not my place to determine that."

"It is fair," Lynette said, finally looking up from her spiraling design. "Or it will be. I know. I've seen it."

"Seen what, dear?" the tutor questioned, stepping over to Lynette's side. She picked up the parchment, holding it close so she could peer down through her half-moon glasses.

"The Awakening will come."

Lynette's voice deepened, her words slowing. She looked up from the desk, her eyes clouded white, and the tutor gasped, taking a step back as the parchment fluttered from her grip, landing between us on the desk.

"Lenny?"

I leaned forward, catching a glimpse of the fiery circles my sister had drawn. Lines of harsh red and bright orange converging into a spiraling inferno. The hair on the back of my neck stood up, my skin prickling as if the air itself was electrified.

"The Awakening will come," Lynette repeated, her head swiveling till her glassy eyes trained on me. "But only when it's called. Only when the Magi are one. Bind them together. Wake me, Son of the Second. I wait for you. I wait for you. I wait for you."

Lynette's voice trailed off into mumbled gibberish, and it was all I could do not to scream. The tutor seized Lynette by the shoulder, giving her a quick shake followed by a blow across the cheek with the back of her hand. Lynette slumped back in her chair, her pale face once again obstructed by a sheet of red curls.

I held my breath, afraid that if I moved, those haunting, milky eyes would find me again. That terrible voice echoed in my head, burning a hole through my subconscious till it leaked into my very soul, leaching all of the heat from my veins.

Our tutor stepped away from the desk, moving to the black box that hung on the wall beside her chalkboard. She removed the small wired receiver, spinning the dial on the front a few times before pressing the receiver to her ear.

"It's happened again. Please inform Madame Greene."

Lynette didn't move from her seat till the door to our classroom sprang open a few minutes later, Mother stalking into the space like a predator on the prowl. I hadn't taken my eyes off my sister, my own dread locking me in place.

"What did she say?" Mother questioned the tutor, keeping a distance between herself and Lynette.

"Same as before. She was drawing again. Tobias, show her."

I unfurled the roll of parchment I'd been concealing, showing Mother the strange fiery rings. The longer I stared down at them, the more I could swear I saw them moving across the page.

"Add this to the collection," Mother said quietly, snatching the scroll from the desk and thrusting it at the tutor. She then turned to where Lynette sat slumped in her chair. "Daughter, can you hear me?"

Lynette lifted her head slightly, an emerald jewel peering through the bramble of curls.

"Tell me what you saw," Mother ordered, her tone far from comforting. Comfort wasn't a tool in her repertoire.

My sister remained silent, staring up at Mother with wide eyes. The tutor bowed before leaving the room and closing the door behind her. I wanted to follow her, to get as far away from this version of Lynette as I could.

This wasn't the first time I'd seen her seized by whatever force made her speak in that terrible voice. Mother said it was a gift. I thought it closer to a curse. Something that hacked away at my sister bit by bit till there would be nothing left but a hollow shell.

"Lynette," Mother said, her voice echoing through the empty space around us. "I will not ask again."

"They're burning," Lynette muttered, her gaze drifting up to the ceiling. "They will burn. There's nothing you can do to stop it. You'll burn too, Mother. The most spectacular of them all."

Mother's posture stiffened. I had never seen fear on Mother's face before, but this was the closest thing to it, the way her eye twitched and the pull of her frown. She snapped her fingers and the door to the classroom opened, an Unseen servant moving silently into view. "Escort Lynette to her quarters and ensure she remains there till I summon her. Is that understood?"

The Unseen bowed his head. "Yes, Madame."

"Tobias," Mother addressed me, staring down with an icy intensity. "Walk with me."

I knew better than to refuse Mother's request, even if I wanted to more than anything, so I quickly followed after her as she turned and exited the classroom.

Chateau Greene was large enough that it would take us several minutes to make it back to the main house and Mother's office. I hoped that the journey would be a quiet one, but those hopes were quickly extinguished.

"I worry for your sister, Tobias. If things should continue as they are, I'm not sure she'll survive the days to come."

"But… she's the Successor."

"Pay attention," Mother ordered, snapping her fingers in front of my nose. "When she is taken by the Augur, a heavy toll is extracted from her body. If it continues to speak through her, then there may come a day when she doesn't recover."

"But she's the Successor," I said again. "There are none more powerful than her."

"Not yet, she isn't. She is young. You both are. Her power has not had sufficient time to mature. Which is why you must help her."

That stopped me in my tracks. "Me? What can I do?"

Mother turned to face me, annoyance masked behind the thinnest wall of sincerity. "You must always help Lynette," she said, clasping her hands in front of her. "And if it should come to it, you must sacrifice for her."

"Sacrifice?"

"There is no greater honor for an Adored male than to serve their family. So, I must ask you, Tobias. What would you be willing to give to protect your sister?"

I mulled over the question. I loved Lynette more than anything else in this world. But did it mean I would do whatever it took to keep her safe?

"Anything," I answered, though I wasn't fully convinced it was the truth.

"And everything?" Mother questioned.

I nodded.

Mother managed a small smile. "Good. You will make me proud, my son. Of that, I am certain."

"I'll do my best, Mother."

Our sanctuary's interior was just as dilapidated as the exterior. The entire structure riddled with decay, from holes punched through the sloped roof, allowing residual light to pour through in beams and spill onto the dubious wooden floors, to cracks running up and down the walls, plaster and other detritus raining down with the slightest of breezes.

I watched as Cirian walked down the moldy carpet that ran through the center of the room toward the raised altar on the far end. Above the dais, opposite where I stood, a large swirling pattern—the symbol of the Source—was painted onto the plaster wall; the deep blue color faded with the erosion of time.

"Come closer," Cirian called to me over his bare shoulder as he reached the altar. He sunk to his knees before the painted emblem.

"I much prefer the view from here, thanks." I shifted my weight from one foot to the other, the boards beneath them groaning with each adjustment. One wrong step, and I'd tumble into whatever cesspit awaited beneath the ruins of this place.

"You need a blessing," Cirian argued, lifting both hands face up into the air above his head.

"I've been faring just fine without a blessing for a number of years, thank you."

"Have you?" Cirian questioned, amusement permeating his voice. "I'm not sure I would consider someone who has been assassinated, resurrected, and almost killed a second time all in the same week as 'faring fine.'"

I let out a sigh. As annoying as I found it, he had a point. Even with my addled memories, I knew that the last twenty-four hours had been amongst the worst in my life. Not many experiences can compete with being murdered.

"What exactly does this blessing do?" I asked, trudging up the damp carpet path. My feet sank into the saturated material, drawing up memories of playing near the bog located on the outer edges of the Greene estate as a child. "I must admit, I don't have any experience with religion. Mother never allowed us to attend any services—not that I'd asked in the first place."

Cirian snorted a quiet laugh. "The blessing is merely that, Toto. A blessing. You have to place the intent yourself."

"Well, I suppose it can't hurt." I knelt beside the other man, pausing only to increase the distance between us by a few more inches. "What do I do?"

"Quiet your mind," Cirian replied, lowering his hands and resting them palm-down on the tops of his thighs, his smooth chest rising and falling with practiced breath. "The Source speaks to all of us through the very magic in your blood. Open yourself to it, and you'll be ready to receive the blessing."

I tried to mimic Cirian's posture but found it increasingly uncomfortable, so I ended up kicking my legs out from under me, spreading them till my feet butted against the base of the altar. After a moment, I risked a glance over at Cirian to find the edges of his mouth twitching.

The bastard was enjoying this. Whatever this was.

I ignored the heat nipping at the back of my neck, instead settling into my new seat as best I could. "Okay, my mind is quiet. What's next?"

"Your mouth is still making plenty of noise," Cirian replied, his eyes fluttering closed. His breathing was slow and steady. For a moment, I felt the gentle brush of Cirian's aura as it expanded from him. Gentle notes of spiced tea hit the back of my tongue before the iron-clad walls of my mental defenses rebuked the presence, repelling it.

A sharp stab at my temple caused me to suck in a breath. Again? Why did this keep happening to me?

I'll admit, I was rusty. Before my death, I would never have risked letting another person so close to my mind, even for a second. The walls always had to be up, always impermeable, lest I be rendered a liability to Mother.

"You'll never feel anything with that kind of reaction," Cirian interjected, a smirk still playing on his lips. "The Source can only speak if you're willing to listen. How can you expect to hear anything hiding behind all those layers?"

"I'm not hiding," I sniped, recoiling from the intensity of my own reaction. "I'm defending myself."

"They can often be the same thing if you're not careful."

I glowered at the man, but Cirian just kept breathing, in and out, at the same even pace. Was he really asking me to abandon the defenses around my mind? It could be a trap—a ruse to get me to lower my guard so Cirian could take anything he wanted.

I refused to be this man's prey.

"Nothing is going to hurt you here," Cirian said, his voice barely a whisper, yet it bounced around the space till it was coming at me from all sides. "You have my word, Tobias."

The truth is, I wanted to believe him. To place my trust in someone other than myself. How long had it been since I had felt that level of connection? I couldn't recall the last time. From what I could recall, Cirian and I had never been friends. Rivals seemed the more appropriate description when I looked back on the interactions that dotted my adolescence. But while Cirian had always been abrasive, he was never cruel.

So, perhaps the dangers were not as immediate as I first assumed.

The walls around my mind had buried themselves deep, rooting in my consciousness like ancient trees. Removing them was going to be a challenge. As I reached for them, I flinched as the familiar stabbing pain behind my eyes returned, a huff of frustration passing over my lips.

"What's happened?" Cirian's voice was beside me, a cautious hand on the small of my back.

"It's no use." I exhaled, dropping any attempt to alter the barriers in my mind and running a hand through my hair. "Something is wrong with my magic. Since Bastien removed that blasted gem from my chest, I can't manage even the smallest feats."

"Ah-ha," Cirian hummed in his throat. "So, that's why...."

"Why what?"

Cirian's gaze had grown distant, his attention leagues away. "If that's the case, then I should be able to replicate it. Even the odds...."

I snapped my fingers in front of Cirian's nose, startling him. "Now's not the time to get cryptic on me."

"Your necromancer," Cirian clarified, his attention returning to me. "You said he placed a stone in your body?"

"Yes," I confirmed with a nod. "And he's not *my* necromancer—he's not *my* anything. At least, not anymore." My hand rose instinctually to my mouth, a finger tracing my bottom lip where Bastien had kissed me just a few hours ago. A lingering heat spread out from my chest, leaving me flushed.

"He's smarter than he looks," Cirian muttered to himself, then he was on his feet. "Fortunate for you, I know how to solve this little conundrum."

"What, my magic?" I questioned, rising from the floor as well.

"Revivified corpses shouldn't even possess magic," Cirian continued, stepping up to the platform where the altar rested and pulling off the dusty cloth that draped over the surface. Beneath it, the altar was a faded white marble with small cracks spread throughout. He set to work, wiping down the tarnished altar as he spoke. "Magic leaves the body when you die, returning to the Source. The necromancer's spell would have brought you back to life, but it cannot provide you what has already been returned. So, he gave you another option."

"Another option?"

"A piece of his own magic, distilled down to physical form."

"Right, Bastien told me that he put some of his magic in the gem to keep me alive till he could perform an actual resurrection. What's all this fuss over?"

"The fuss? That's an ancient practice, Toto. From a time before the Awakening, when magic was far more rare. And this magic requires a certain… connection to achieve." Cirian trailed off, once again lost to his inner dialogue.

"What kind of connection?"

"I've read ancient grimoires from those times, hidden away in the Church's libraries," Cirian said, pausing sporadically to lock eyes with me as he worked. "Before magic lived in our veins. Those precious few who could access magic pulled it directly from the Source—a virtually endless supply. With it, they were able to reign over the mortals in an era known as the 'Time of the Magi King.' But there were limits to even the Magi-King's power, and those who tapped too frequently into the Source found their humanity slowly sapped, carved out by the all-consuming flow of magic. The kings, however, were infinitely clever. It was only a matter of time before one of them discovered that they could condense the Source's power into a physical shape, giving the potential for anyone to be able to use magic. At least, minor magics. They called these stones Anima. The Kings set to work, distributing this newfound power to a select few mortals and using them as powerful soldiers as they waged war over land and resources.

"As these battles raged, the mortals using the Magi-King's magic began to go mad in droves. The more they used the Anima stones, the more their bodies and minds were twisted into horrible Distortions."

I snorted a laugh, then choked it back as I realized that Cirian wasn't joking. Distortions were nothing more than fairy tales used to keep Magi children from playing around with magics outside of their capabilities. Surely, he wasn't implying they were real.

"This chaos persisted until one of the Magi-King's lovers, a woman who wished only to end the suffering of her people, begged for them to stop. The Magi-King was blinded by their power and refused the request. Seeing her chance, the lover seized one of the Anima stones, using its power to destroy the hoard of Anima the king had created.

"The magic unleashed on the world that day brought about the Awakening, and since then, magic has lived in the very blood of the Magi."

I stared at him, wondering if this little trip down the annals of Magi history was going anywhere. "A wonderful history lesson," I told him. "Really top-notch. So, you're saying that Bastien used the same process as these Magi-Kings to give me his magic? Why did I not go mad with his power, then?"

"I theorize that it's because there is some commonality between you and the lover of the Magi-King."

"Commonality? Oh, for Source's sake, speak clearly, man."

Cirian looked up briefly from his work, giving me a sly smile. "Piece it together, Toto. You can't expect me to do all the work, can you?"

I released a huff of frustration. What did this story have to do with my current situation? And why was Cirian so interested in how Bastien imbued me with magic? Why was he doing any of this, really? The two of us haven't had a conversation since we were teenagers—or at least not that I could recall.

A draft seeped through the gaps in the walls, sneaking a shiver up my spine.

"The grimoires refer to it as Soul-Binding." Cirian ceased his cleaning, tossing aside the cloth and running a hand along the polished altar. "The Magi-King's lover was so much a part of the king's soul that the magic allowed itself to be used by her, even though it didn't belong to her. It's incredible, really, seeing as the others who wielded the Magi-King's magic were twisted into Distortions."

"So, you're saying that Bastien is, what, Soul-Bound to me?" I extrapolated, drawing the statement out into a question.

This was nothing but more fairy tales.

"It's a working theory. You were able to use the magic from the gem he gave you, yes?"

I nodded in response, my hand drifting to the sore spot on my chest where the gem was embedded. "I haven't been able to draw on my magic since I was revived."

"Your magic was already absorbed back into the Source, so there's nothing for you to draw on. Every time you've tried to wiled your own magic, you've been drawing on your own life force. It's a wonder you're still standing, Toto. This resurrection ritual that the necro—*Bastien*—will perform is nothing more than a communing with the Source, where he will barter for your magic back."

"Barter? You mean he'll have to give something up in return?"

Cirian shrugged.

Bastien was willing to give something up to help me. I didn't know how to feel about it. My damn lips tingled again with the memory of his kiss back at the camp. Did he really still harbor feelings for me, or was this all out of some twisted sense of duty to Lynette and the Rebellion?

"Now then, Toto. On to my proposition."

My attention returned to Cirian, who stood behind the altar, bracing himself against it and leaning forward with an excited shine in his eyes.

"In lieu of the attack against the Rebellion, I think it unwise for you to be without the means to defend yourself."

"I can take care of myself," I argued.

"Says the man I found bleeding out in a field of wildflowers. Trust me, I know what you're capable of, Toto. I just want to ensure you're given every opportunity for survival, that's all."

I wanted to throttle him, but I knew he was right.

Cirian reached into the folds of his billowing harem pants, producing a small silver dagger. Holding his empty hand over the altar, he pressed the tip of the blade to the palm, drawing a trickle of red blood that rained down on the smooth, white surface.

"What are you doing?" I asked as the air grew heavy with the weight of magic.

"Testing a theory," Cirian replied, squeezing his blooded hand so that a few more drops fell onto the altar. "It stands to reason that if the necromancer was powerful enough to craft his magic into physical form, then it should be child's play for one such as me."

I rolled my eyes. So, that's what this was. A chance for Cirian to one-up Bastien. He never backed down from a challenge.

The blood sizzled and smoked where it hit the altar, and Cirian passed a hand over the spattered gore, chanting under his breath. I watched in fascination as the blackened blood drew together, pooling into the center of the altar as Cirian formed a sigil with his hands. The sanguine puddle bubbled as his chanting increased in fervor. With a flash of light, Cirian struck the viscous material with his fist, the ringing of metal against metal echoing through the empty sanctuary. Rearing back, Cirian struck again, a bloom of fresh blood running along the side of his fist at the point of impact, but he didn't seem to notice or care. Seven times, he struck the altar, sending ripples of magical energy through the air. With the final blow, a flash of light blinded me momentarily, and I shielded my eyes. The room quieted, the only sound now coming from Cirian's labored breaths and the pounding pulse in my ears.

Lowering my hand, I blinked away the burned images clouding my sight, the shadows from the corners of the room seeming to draw closer to obscure the man slumped over the marble altar.

"Cirian?"

I reached out a hand, halting as the figure on the altar shifted, a low groan emanating. A sigh escaped from my lips. At least Cirian hadn't killed himself with this foolish display.

"That was moronic," I said, keeping my distance. I tried to ignore the strained relief in my voice.

"Was it now?" Cirian croaked, brushing long strands of scarlet hair from his sweaty face. He held out his hand to me—the one soaked in blood—and brandished a small, blue gem that pulsed with light.

"Still foolish," I chastised him. "What good does that do either of us? If what you said earlier was true, then I would have to be soul-bound to you to even use that magic without becoming some sort of hideous beast."

"Hence the experiment," Cirian said through a wild grin. "I want to know if the grimoires speak the truth or if the details have gone hazy over the years."

"So, you want me as your lab rat?"

"Such harsh words," Cirian replies with a chuckle. "You're simply the only control group, Toto. You were able to use the necromancer's magic. You proved that already. Now I want to know whether or not it's because your souls are bound to one another, or perhaps you're just an enigma in and of yourself."

"Bastien," I reminded him, a flash of irritation coloring my tone. "And you can go fuck yourself. I won't be touching that thing."

Cirian laughed again, his voice hitting a squawking pitch. "Come now, Toto. Aren't you just a little bit curious? You know, it must be unbearable, that emptiness you're feeling right now. This magic could hold you over till your beloved necromancer can perform his unholy rite. Something tells me it wouldn't be the first unholy act he's afflicted upon your body." He held his free hand out to me, a small, blue flame conjured in his palm. "Just a little something to cast away the chill?"

Heat singed my cheeks as I turned from Cirian. "You're an arsehole. And even if I wanted to, you said it yourself. It could turn me into a Distortion. I didn't just survive the worst day of *both* my lives to end up some monstrous nightmare."

"Oh, I'd never let that happen to you, Toto. You have my word. Just a smidgen of basic magic is all I'm asking for. If there's any sign of trouble, I'll intervene." He stepped closer, a wicked grin curling the edges of his smooth lips. "I *did* save your life earlier this evening, in case you'd forgotten."

I fought back a second shiver, wondering if it was from the cold or something I was too afraid to speak out loud. "A favor I fear I will be repaying for years to come."

"Nonsense," Cirian huffed. "Just this one simple gesture of good faith, and we'll never speak of it again. You have my word."

It would be a lie to say I wasn't tempted. Ever since Bastien removed the gem from my chest, I'd felt a lethargy seeping into my limbs that honestly frightened me. It was like Death was crawling its way slowly through my body once more. But would this fragment of power that Cirian had conjured stave off the encroaching numbness? It was impossible for me to know unless I gave it a try. Cirian's magic still clung to the air around me. I could taste it on my tongue with each breath, acrid and smoldering, like smoke from a campfire. The thrill of it was intoxicating. And despite my hesitations, I couldn't argue the fact that I was drawn to it. My body craved the power, wanting nothing more than to reach out and accept the offer enthusiastically.

The pit in my stomach was the only thing holding me back.

"Your lips speak disapproval, but your eyes can't lie." Cirian was close now, bearing down on me with the gait of a predator. "You can't hide the question lurking underneath, Toto."

I squared my shoulders, raising to my full height, even if I was dwarfed by Cirian to the tune of several inches. "And what question might that be?"

"You want to know if the necromancer—Bastien—is still yours," Cirian purred, cupping his unbloodied hand under my chin and lifting it so I match his gaze. "Or has the end of your first life changed that fact?"

I yanked away from his touch, my face alight with heat. "Must you always touch me?"

Again, I felt the gentle pressure of Cirian's hand guiding my gaze, my chin pinched between his thumb and index finger. He was close enough now that I could feel his breath against my skin.

"You've never protested my touch before."

Once again, I felt the caress of Cirian's aura stroke the walls of my mind.

Memories burst through the surface from obscurity—*flashes of pale skin pressed into my own, the thrill of lips trailing my inner thigh, a mop of red and white-blond hair vanishing between my legs, and the wet heat of—*

I gasped, shuddering at Cirian's touch.

"There it is." Cirian's eyes narrowed, wisps of his fair lashes obscuring the dark brilliance of his pupils. "All of those days we spent sparring with one another. I was starting to worry you'd forgotten about me, Toto."

"How long—when did—" I sputtered, my pulse racing as more memories rose to the surface. Our trysts stretched through adolescence. Mornings spent sparring till my muscles ached, then Cirian following me up to my room where we would linger between silken sheets, practicing all the ways our bodies moved together that only two men could know.

"There's a good boy," Cirian whispered, the warmth of his words against my cheek. "Now, I'll ask you once again to reconsider my offer."

I shuddered once more, a molten heat building at the base of my spine. I couldn't think clearly, not when Cirian was so close, and our history was resurfacing in such vibrant detail. Without the will to resist, I finally sputtered, "F-Fine."

He released his grip on my face, taking a half step back and relishing in a knowing smirk. He offered the gem to me, the edges still wet with blood, darkening the color into more amethyst than sapphire.

Taking it, I ran my thumb over the smooth facets. It was warm to the touch, and beneath the surface, a thrum of power vibrated against my skin. I closed my fist around it, exhaling relief as a spike of warmth radiated through my limbs, easing the aching fatigue.

So far, so good.

Reaching for my aura, it reacted immediately, and I braced myself for the splitting pain in my head to return. But there was merely a pleasant humming in my ear as I wrapped myself in the magic and, with little effort, projected my aura outward, focusing it on the space at my palm. I held up my hand, a small flame bursting into existence and hovering over it.

"That's my boy," Cirian murmured, the fire dancing in the reflection of his eyes. "There you have it. The experiment is a success."

"What does it mean?" I asked, snuffing out the flame and allowing my aura to retract around me.

"There are a few possibilities to consider," Cirian replied, turning his back to me as he moved toward the altar. "One, the grimoires have been lying about the Magi-King's downfall as a way of controlling mortals and preventing them from revolting. Why would they ever think to rise against the rule of the Magi if the only weapon they could use against their oppressors twisted them into horrific monsters?" He paused once he reached the dais, taking a moment to round the altar before continuing. "The second possibility lies in the assumption that you are special in that you can somehow utilize the magic of other Magi without suffering any of the adverse side effects."

I couldn't help but snort a laugh. The theory that I was anything other than ordinary amongst the Adored was dubious at best. Mother had reminded me of my inadequacies at every opportunity. If there was anything more than mediocrity in my veins, Mother would have put it to use years ago.

Cirian braced himself against the altar, shaking his bloodied hand gently as blue light spread across the skin, sealing the wound. "And yet there's still another possibility…"

"Are you going to tell me what it is, or should I leave you alone with your thoughts?"

Cirian's eyes found me once more, his confident demeanor peeled away for the first time since he'd found me amongst the wildflowers. For the briefest moment, I thought I saw something I recognized glimmering behind those dark, calculating eyes.

Fear.

"The other possibility," Cirian continued, his words stretching between us. "Is that you're Soul-Bound to more than one person."

# TWELVE
## DEAD-END KID

"Azzy, is that you out there?"

I peeked through the cracked door of my bedroom and into the empty hallway. The sconce closest to me flickered with warm light, casting shadows along the floor that made the pattern on the carpet appear to dance. It was customary for the curtains to be drawn this time of day to block the harshest rays of the afternoon sun. Mother often complained that sunlight gave her headaches, so the curtains stayed drawn more time than not around the chateau.

Checking the hallway once more, I chalked up the noise I'd heard to my imagination, shutting the door behind me as I returned to my desk. But as I pulled my chair away from my work, a quick knock roused me once more. Scurrying back, I thrust open the door just in time to catch a glimpse of purple hair and the gentle squeak of the boy who dashed down the hall.

"I saw you!" I shouted, laughter bubbling up along with the words. Abandoning my coursework, I tore down the hallway, giving chase to the other boy. Around the corner of the hall, I skidded to a stop, finding no evidence of my target. Sucking in a deep breath to calm my thundering pulse, I panned my gaze from left to right, moving slowly down the stretch of hallway. I was almost at the next turn when something caught my eye—a glimmer of light from around the corner—and I reached out, grasping the boy by the shoulder as his image flickered into reality with a blur. "Got you!"

The purple-haired boy scowled. "Not fair! I had to scratch my nose! That's the only reason you saw me."

"Do you really want to get into what is and isn't fair, Azzy? We're playing hide and seek and only one of us can turn invisible." I gave him a playful shove. "Or at least mostly invisible."

The boy scowled back at me, baring a row of fangs. "Just wait till I get better at it! Papa says that I fidget too much, but soon I'll be able to disappear like that—" he snapped his fingers, the scowl morphing into a grin. "And you'll never find me!"

The thought made my heart flutter in a weird rhythm. "But you won't actually leave, right, Azzy? When you're older, I mean. You're not going to disappear on me, are you?"

I'd never considered it before. Azzy and I had been the best of friends since I collided with him in the hallway at the age of five. His father worked in the kitchens, so Azzy and I had spent many an afternoon hiding in the cabinets and scrounging for apple peels or the rare pastry. I couldn't imagine my life without him.

Azzy's smile faded a bit, the pointed ears on top of his head drooping as he looked away. "I don't know, Tobi. Papa told me that we'll stay as long as the madame is pleased with us."

"Then I'll make sure she never sends you away," I assured him, reaching out and taking Azzy's hand in mine. "That way, we can play together forever!"

"But I'm clumsy," the boy replied. "And I'm no good at the house chores. Papa told Mr. Chatterly about the madame being upset because I broke her favorite teacup. I didn't mean to—I was trying to help. Mr. Chatterly spelled it back together, but the madame said that his 'primitive magic' ruined the taste of the tea."

"Mother can be harsh sometimes," I said, giving his hand a squeeze. "But that's only because she wants us to be our best. I'm sure you won't break another cup."

The boy nodded solemnly, his ear remaining deflated atop his head. I couldn't bear to see my only friend so upset.

"I found you," I told him, releasing my grip on his hand. "So, now it's my turn to hide. Close your eyes! No peeking!"

That was enough to perk Azzy up, and he covered his violet eyes, beginning to count softly under his breath. I took off like a bolt, running down the hall and diving around corners, trying to put as much distance as I could between me and the other boy. All of my best hiding places had been exhausted by this point in our game, so I had to think quickly or be caught out in the open. Ducking under one of the maids as she dusted a framed painting in the hall, I slid through the next door—one of the many guest rooms—and dove under the ornately carved bedframe. The plush rug underneath cushioned the sound of my shuffling as I crawled deeper, slowing my breath as best I could.

Lurking in the shadows, I waited for Azzy to find me.

When the door of the bedroom opened a few minutes later, I sucked in a breath but quickly realized that it was not my friend in search of me but two other figures, shutting the door gently behind them.

"—out of your mind, Balthus? Where would you have us go? Back to the slums in the Magi City?"

"There are places outside of the city, Andres. Places where we Unseen can walk in the daylight and not be ridiculed. Where you could raise your younglings to aspire to be more than just servants—"

"Quiet!" hissed the other voice. "Don't let anyone hear you spouting off such nonsense. It'll get you locked up or worse. Then what would happen to little Azzy? Think of your son, Balthus."

"I am thinking of him," Balthus spat back. "What kind of life will he have if we stay here?"

"A good life," the other Unseen said. There was a twinge of sadness in his voice, as if he didn't fully believe his own words. "The best he could wish for. Please, Balthus, don't let your head get filled with these crazy ideas. It can only lead to trouble."

There was a pause and the wet sound of a kiss between the two. "I care for you, Andres. Really, I do. But I can't just stand by and watch our lives wither in the darkness. I'm tired of hiding away."

"You speak these grandiose plans," Andres replies with a sigh. "But don't you see? It's Azrael who will end up paying for your carelessness. Worry about him and leave all this foolishness behind. Now, come. The madame will be expecting her afternoon tea."

The door opened and shut, a quiet settling back over the room.

I'd never heard the servants speak that way before. In fact, I tried to remember the last time I'd heard Azzy's father say more than two words. Balthus was the head chef at our chateau, in charge of our meals and the goings on of the kitchen. Azzy had been trying to learn under him since he was old enough to hold a knife but had a proclivity for unintentionally setting things ablaze.

I lay still, mulling over the conversation in my head. Did Balthus really want to leave the chateau? Wasn't he happy here? I'd only ever seen him smile when I was nearby. He'd worked here longer than I'd been alive, according to Mother. Even when he was carrying Azzy, he took only a few weeks off after delivering, then was right back in the kitchen.

If he left, would he take Azzy with him? Suddenly, it wasn't just Mother that I needed to convince to let my friend stay, but Balthus as well. Digging myself out from under the bed, I moved for the door, but it swung open before I could reach for it.

A hand reached out, bopping me on the end of the nose.

Azzy beamed at me, his snaggletooth fang protruding over his bottom lip. "Found you! Wow, Tobi, you're really bad at this game."

"I am not!" I retorted, retreating further into the guest room and away from the purple-haired boy. "I was in a really good hiding space, but I had to get up because—" I stopped, not wanting to bring up Azzy's father in case he'd go searching for him. It was better to keep him here, at least until I could figure out what to do next. "Never mind. I'm it, so I guess I'll count again."

I'd keep him distracted until I figured out what I could do to fix the whole Balthus situation. There must be something.

"Before you do," Azzy said, following me across the ornate rug. He kept a distance from me, twiddling his thumbs together as he stared down at the floor. "I wanted to ask you something, Tobi."

The weird fluttery feeling in my stomach that usually preceded my conversations with Azzy intensified to the point where I thought it might lift me off the ground.

"Yes?"

"Did you mean it when you said that you wouldn't let the madame send me away?"

# THE SECOND AWAKENING

"Of course I did. You're very important to me, Azzy. You're my best friend."

The boy's cheeks flushed red, and he kept his eyes trained on the ground between us. "Okay. You can count now."

I nodded, letting out an exhale to try and calm my stuttering pulse. Azzy stepped closer to me, the toes of his shoes nearly touching mine. And before I could question it, the boy leaned it, pressing his lips gently to mine. My heart stammered, then pounded against my chest like a caged animal.

"Thank you," Azzy said as he pulled away, cheeks even more ruddy.

"For what?" I asked, breathless.

"For choosing me. You didn't have to."

I started back at the boy, confusion knitting my brows together. But before I could question him further, the door opened again, and I nearly fell over at the sight of Mother standing in the doorway.

"There you are, Tobias. You've kept me waiting for our lesson."

I stepped quickly in front of Azzy, silently wishing for him to turn invisible. "Mother, my apologies. I didn't realize how late the day had grown."

Mother's eyes narrowed as she looked through me to the boy who stood defiantly behind me. "Distractions can have that effect, Tobias. I would hope to avoid more of them in the future. Is that understood?"

"Yes, Mother. I'm ready to join you now." I stepped forward but paused as Mother held out her hand, her eyes still locked on the Unseen boy.

"Would you care to join us, Azrael? It would seem Tobias may need a hand with this afternoon's lesson."

"Yes, madame," Azzy replied, bowing to her. His eyes landed on me, and I could only shrug as we followed Mother from the room and down the hallways towards her office.

We dared not speak so close to Mother, but I allowed my hand to brush against Azzy's as we walked, my mind replaying the moment our lips touched over and over again. The thrill it sent down my spine kept me from dwelling on whatever was awaiting me at Mother's lesson.

The doors to her office swung open of their own accord as we approached, and there was not a hitch in her stride as she entered, quickly taking her place behind *the long wooden desk.*

*Azzy and I hovered awkwardly on the opposite side, awaiting further instructions.*

*"It's time for you to practice the most sacred of Adored magic, Tobias. Do you know of which I speak?"*

*Ice flooded my veins. I nodded, afraid that my teeth would chatter if I unclenched my jaw. Mother had taught me many of the minor magics by now, but I had little experience when it came to wielding the Command.*

*"Good. You've already selected the perfect partner for this exercise, as the Unseen hardly have a will of their own to begin with." Mother rounded the desk, propping herself on the corner as she folded her arms across her chest. "Now, what shall the order be? Something simple… ah, of course. I want you to command this boy to kneel."*

*"W-What?"*

*"Was I not clear, Tobias?"*

*The tone in Mother's voice was a warning. Azzy gave me a quizzical look, not understanding what it was Mother asked for me to do. I swallowed down the nausea rising in my gut, then turned back to Mother, giving her a quick nod.*

*I squared myself, reaching deep within to wrap the aura of my magic around me before projecting it outward. Azzy bristled at the touch of it, his eyes finding mine once more, now shining with a glimmer of hurt.*

*"Kneel," I merely whispered, the word burning hot in my throat.*

*Azzy sucked in a breath, his nostrils flaring, but did not move from his standing position. I flinched at the crack of Mother's whip.*

*"Again, Tobias. With feeling."*

"Azzy!"

The name tore from my throat, ringing out into the empty sanctuary and reverberating against the pallid walls. The details of the memory sank further as I clutched the back of the long bench that served as my bed, muddling with the events of the previous night.

# THE SECOND AWAKENING

My muscles ached, though I wasn't sure if the cause lay in my near re-death experience or from sleeping on the dilapidated wooden surface all night.

"Does something trouble you?"

I groaned, running a hand through my greasy hair before looking up to find Cirian standing over me. He'd somehow secured another tunic during the night, and I couldn't decide whether or not I was thankful for the fact that his body was covered once more.

"It's nothing," I said, standing quickly and taking a moment to refamiliarize myself with my surroundings. Dim light shined through the cracks of the walls and ceiling, casting patches of warm-hued light across the space. Cirian stood in one such spot, his hair mimicking blazing flames against the shadowy backdrop. It made it difficult to look away.

"I'll take you at your word," Cirian replied, fighting a smile. "How are you fairing this fine morning?"

"Like someone who slept on a plank," I muttered, rubbing at the small of my back.

This coaxed a laugh from Cirian, causing the emblazoned hair on display to bounce. "Are you feeling any lightheadedness? Lack of sensation in your appendages? Abnormal desires?"

The only desire I had was to relieve myself and take a scalding hot bath. And if I were being honest, for Cirian to discard his tunic once more.

I kept all of them to myself.

"I'm not becoming a Distortion," I replied, reining in the intrusive thoughts. I flexed my back till a series of popping noises relieved a bit of the pressure. "Is there a powder room in this hovel by chance?"

Cirian's smile didn't fade. "I'm afraid not. But nature provides a wonderful service just outside the doors. Our ride should be ready once you return."

"Ride?" I questioned, suddenly suspicious. "Where exactly are we going?"

"Back to Cradle for the time being," Cirian explained, stepping close enough I could smell the familiar scent of clove coming from him. "Adoranda's forces are likely still active in the area, so we need to be cautious about our next moves. Once we're safely under the Church's protection, I'll make contact with the Rebellion, and we'll get you back to your lovely necromancer."

"*Bastien,*" I corrected him with a scowl, my annoyance seeping through more easily due to my exhaustion. "I know you're intelligent enough to remember his name, so stop pretending otherwise."

"You assume I wish to commit anything about the man to memory. The fact of the matter is that I address him by the only quality in which I find interest. Besides his penchant for forbidden magic, he's otherwise dreadfully unexceptional."

"You speak as though you know him," I countered, eyes narrowing with suspicion. "Why is that?"

Cirian's obsidian eyes rolled back as he chuckled. "I assure you, Toto, yesterday afternoon was the first time I had the pleasure of speaking with the necromancer. I'm certain he's spent the majority of his life avoiding Hallowed like me for all the reasons you've already been made aware."

"Ah, that's right. So, your biases are the source of your contempt. Good to know that you are not as nuanced as I gave you credit for."

Cirian's knowing grin didn't falter at the ribbing. "Make all the assumptions you wish, Tobias. It's always been your forte."

"What's that supposed to mean?" I asked through gritted teeth.

The cheery demeanor spackled across Cirian's visage faltered. "You'll remember one day. If the Source sees fit." He reached into his pocket, producing a small receiver with a coiled antenna. It crackled to life in his hand, a voice speaking low in a language that I couldn't understand. He looked up at me after the message was relayed. "Transportation will be arriving shortly. I've already lowered the wards around the entrance, but be cautious of your surroundings while you relieve yourself, yes? I wouldn't want to have to come to your aid while you're holding your cock."

I huffed a sigh in his direction. What had he meant earlier about my making assumptions? Was there even more from our past relationship than the trysts I actively had to fight from resurfacing in my mind? I had enough distractions going on already.

Cirian moved toward the altar, then halted, turning to face me once more.

"Do you still have the Anima stone?"

I patted the protrusion in my pocket, the gem's warm surface pressing against the side of my thigh.

This seemed to satisfy him, and he gave a curt nod. "Good. Keep it close."

As he retreated to the dais at the front of the sanctuary, I could ignore the discomfort no longer and I turned to make my way outside in search of seclusion enough to release my basest of needs. Outside of the sanctuary, the morning was cool against my skin. Sunlight filtered down through the thick cover of trees overhead, washing the dirt road in equal parts shadow and brilliance. Without the wards surrounding me, the sounds of the woods swirled around—insects buzzing through the air, the skittering of leaves under rodent's feet, an incessant bird song that repeated itself like a record jumping the track—and as I walked around the back of the dilapidated building, my thoughts drifted nearly as aimlessly.

Lynette was alive. I hardly had the opportunity to relish in the fact before all hell had broken loose back at the camp. Not to mention the bombshell that was Bastien. Just the thought of him was enough to start the tempest of muddled memories again, springing up from the recesses of my mind— *A lazy afternoon, sipping coffee on my apartment balcony, books discarded on the table as Bastien's fingers tangled in the curls of my hair. An evening spent whispering sweet nothings back and forth in a dark booth, purple smoke hanging thick in the air. A bright morning spent walking through a crowded marketplace, rows of bright flowers in dazzling arrays across every direction*—at that moment, they felt like memories from another life. Like I was spying on someone else's romance.

Would I still feel that way after the ritual? Or would the affection I was supposed to feel for him return like the pieces of a puzzle falling into place?

I wish I could say.

Around the trunk of a thick oak tree, I stopped, unfastening my pants and allowing myself the momentary pleasure of an emptied bladder.

Retracing my steps to the sanctuary, I took my time enjoying the pockets of warmth brought on by the sun before pulling open the heavy wooden door. A few moments passed before I located Cirian, knelt by the altar at the end of the aisle. His soft voice carried through the still air, the words mulling together in a stream so fluid that it almost sounded like a song. Quietly, I made my way up the aisle, watching the man as he shifted his position, arms extending and the muscles along his back pulling taut as he shrugged off his tunic, letting it fall to the ground behind him. From his kneeling position, Cirian tucked a leg under him, balancing on one foot as he remained in a low squat, centering himself. The prayer, or whatever it was he was reciting, continued uninterrupted as he moved through a progression of postures, his skin quickly beginning to glisten with the fruits of his exertion.

I had never witnessed a communing ritual before. Mother had not allowed me nor Lynette to delve into the practices of the Hallowed during our studies, preferring that we focus on more 'appropriate' subjects. There was an abject beauty in the way Cirian's body moved, how he bent and twisted himself into shapes I would have thought impossible, all the while his concentration never faltering.

It was impressive, to say the least. And the longer I watched him, the more I wondered if my fascination was with the ritual itself or the beautiful man performing it.

Cirian's body seized suddenly, his limbs going rigid as the prayer ceased, casting the sanctuary into an eerie silence. I took a cautious step toward him but halted as Cirian's posture straightened, turning to face me. The whites of his eyes were swallowed by cerulean light. It poured from his orifices, nearly blinding me as his mouth opened, a guttural voice echoing through him:

*"Son of the Second, lost in the ether. You have been beckoned, Death is your teacher.*
*Awakening draws nigh, the fragmented power,*
*Longs to be whole, and late grows the hour.*

*"Bind them together, imbue them with might.*
*Test the connections betwixt shadow and light.*
*Keep close the prophet, cling to the seeker,*
*Stand firm with the rebel, wake not the sleeper.*

# THE SECOND AWAKENING

*"Son of the Second, your journey begins.*
*Wastelands and deserts, flee wide across the stems.*
*Look for the mirror, reflecting the truth.*
*Beware the distortion, trust only the sooth."*

Cirian fell quiet, the eerie light receding from his eyes, his chest heaving as he stood stark still. My own breath was cemented in my chest. When his gaze finally lifted to meet mine, confusion twisted his features.

"Sorry," he mumbled, shoulders sagging with fatigue. "I don't... I don't know what just happened."

Fear roiled in my gut, twisting my insides and rooting me in place. Memories of Lynette staring back at me with milky eyes set me on edge, but I shoved them down. My mind raced, repeating the words spoken by the ominous voice to try and commit them to memory as best I could.

"A pen," I said, and Cirian's expression only grew more confused. "Quickly! I need a pen and paper! Anything to write with."

Cirian moved then, circling the altar and retrieving a scroll of parchment then rummaging through a derelict chest of drawers until he uncovered a stick of charcoal. I played the words again and again while he searched, hoping that my addled mind wouldn't muck up the transcription.

Snatching the material from him, I unfurled the parchment onto the altar—the only semi-flat surface around—and began to write furiously.

"What in damnation are you doing?" Cirian asked, hovering over my shoulder.

"Quiet," I ordered, devoting every bit of my function to documenting the words. My mind had been a sieve since my rebirth, but surprisingly, I was able to complete the set of couplets, only faltering on a word here and there.

"What is this?" Cirian questioned as the charcoal fell from my hand and dusted the lingering residue off on the leg of my trousers.

"I think it's a prophecy," I replied, scanning over the smudged, hastily scrawled lines. "Direct from the Source, if I had to guess."

"The Source?" Cirian echoed, turning to face me. "What are you talking about?"

The absurdity forced me to bite back a laugh. "Are you telling me you don't remember reciting this, oh great Acolyte of the Source?"

Cirian's expression turned tortured. "You jest. This is an ill-timed joke, Tobias, so cease this at once."

"What's the trouble, Acolyte?" I pushed, the mocking tone welling up from someplace deep within my subconscious. "Proof of your faith in the Source is right here in front of you, and you're cowering like a mongrel pup."

Cirian moved with a determined haste, catching me at the wrists and pinning me in place. "I've had enough of your mockery," he growled. "Explain yourself plainly, or I swear on the Source that I will leave you here to rot in this place."

"They're your words, you devout imbecile! You looked right at me and spoke them just moments ago! Are you saying you don't recall reciting them?"

Fear flickered in Cirian's stygian eyes, his grip on me loosening. "No. I was simply praying. Going through my recitations, and then I was standing, looking at you."

Was his mind not his own while the Source spoke through him? The thought sent a chill down my spine. Is that where we Adored got the power to control others? Was it the power of the Source itself?

"The words were yours, Cirian. I swear it. I swear it on my sister's life."

Cirian held my gaze for just a moment longer before turning back to the altar, dropping his hold on me and rushing forward to seize the parchment. He held it up to the light, his lips moving silently as he read, his hands trembling. When he looked back at me, all I could see were the questions burning behind his eyes.

"Do you know what it means?" I asked.

He shook my head. "Not in the slightest. There hasn't been a prophecy delivered by the Source in nearly a century. Her Eminence thought the prophets extinct."

"Well, apparently, her holiness is lying through her teeth. Is that why she keeps you around, Cirian? I often wondered what made her choose a successor before the need for one had arisen. The Cardinal could serve for another hundred years or more before she needed to name a replacement, yet you've been at her side since adolescence."

"Do not speak ill of her," Cirian spat, his lips curling into a snarl. "If what you've said is true, then I trust Her Eminence is just as ignorant as I am on the matter. I must speak with her right away. Come, we can't delay any longer. We must return to the Cradle at once."

Cirian moved for the doors of the sanctuary, then paused, turning back to me with a look of mild amusement. "Oh, and I have some clothes waiting for you in the car. I may be the Acolyte of the Source, but not even I can't explain away an animated corpse wandering down the halls."

"I'm not a corpse," I argued.

Cirian's nose wrinkled. "You certainly smell like one."

"Fuck you."

"Ah, there's simply not enough time, I'm afraid. Let's be gone."

Walking through the entrance of the Cradle for the second time in the last twenty-four hours, my unease had not abated in the slightest. Even with the clothing provided by Cirian—a set of monastic robes that covered me entirely from crown to sole, complete with a porcelain mask to cover my face—I couldn't help but feel exposed just existing in this space. The vitriol that the Hallowed carried for those who had "cheated" Death was a weight I could feel in the air. It settled into my lungs like a fine powder, building until it became difficult to breathe.

"Good day, Master Cirian."

The greeting was expressed by every passing figure, Cirian responding with a polite nod and the occasional thanks. If he felt even a fraction of my discomfort, he certainly didn't show it. His calm façade of serenity held firmly in place, and Cirian knew better than to allow it to slip.

The ride from the sanctuary deep within the woods had taken nearly an hour, traversing roads that had long succumbed to nature. Cirian didn't speak much on the way, instead gazing out the window with a contemplative expression that I felt it rude to interrupt.

Once we reached Cirian's chambers, he moved swiftly to the wall behind his desk, removing a small receiver from the black box that hung there. After a moment, he spoke softly into it, then awaited a response.

My disguise felt suffocating, the heavy cloth of my robes scratchy and unyielding. Sweat pooled in the small of my back, and the stench of my own breath inside the mask was enough to leave me nauseated.

Perhaps Cirian wasn't *too* far off with his earlier comments about my aroma. The thought alone of Cirian drawing close enough to take in the scent was enough to make the nape of my neck swelter.

A swift knock on the door, and Cirian quickly hung up the device, snapping to draw my attention. He mimed the stance a monk should take, pointing to the corner of the room he wished for me to stand in. I quickly followed the silent instructions as he spoke, "Enter," and the Cardinal strode through the door.

"Ah, Your Eminence. I was just trying to reach you. Deepest apologies for my tardiness this morning. I'm afraid my nightly rituals left me feeling rather drained—"

"Silence," the Cardinal interrupted, her commanding voice perfectly matched to the intimidating presence of her physical stature. "Adoranda Greene has made her move against the Unseen Rebellion. Their camp was raided last night, and our reports say their numbers are diminished."

My breath faltered behind the mask. Diminished? What did that mean?

The Cardinal continued, seemingly oblivious to my presence. "The Madame has requested the Church's assistance with holding one of the prisoners apprehended during the raid."

"And why would she have a need for such a request?" Cirian questioned, his tone even. "Surely her militia has enough capacity to handle as many prisoners as she'd like."

"The prisoner in question has been confirmed as a Reviled practitioner," the Cardinal answered. "The Madame has him contained at her Chateau, but as the law dictates, all Reviled are to be judged by the Church. I will be leaving shortly to confirm the Reviled's identity myself and carry out their sentencing."

My pulse rushed in my ears. If Bastien had been captured, did that mean Lynette was taken as well? Had Mother already disposed of her quietly as she originally intended? The room was starting to spin around me.

"A Reviled amongst the Rebellion?" Cirian mused, the slightest edge in his voice. "How troubling. Do you know for what reason they enlisted the services of a necromancer?"

The Cardinal paused, her gaze drifting over to me for a brief moment. I stiffened my posture, pouring new diligence into holding the motionless pose.

"I have my theories," the Cardinal finally said. "But it matters not. This qualm between Adoranda and the Unseen is finally reaching its end. It won't be long before the bloodshed will cease and we can return to preparing the Magi for the second Awakening."

"I look forward to that day," Cirian replied, bowing his head slightly.

"Now, what was it that you needed to discuss with me?"

Cirian hesitated. "It's nothing of grave importance. We can discuss it at a more opportune juncture."

The Cardinal nodded, turning to exit when Cirian called out to her.

"Your Eminence, might you wish I accompany you to Chateau Greene? Adoranda has always had a certain fondness for me, and I should like to witness the first Reviled confirmation since my time as Acolyte."

The Cardinal pondered the request, her back turned to Cirian. But then she glanced over her shoulder and gave a curt nod. "We leave within the hour."

Cirian bowed his head once more. "You honor me, Your Eminence."

Once the door closed behind the Cardinal, I deflated with a sigh.

"Well, that's piss-poor luck," Cirian muttered, rubbing the stubble along his chin.

I ripped off the mask, no longer able to contain the gasping breaths that tore from my chest. "What will happen to Bastien?"

"If history has been any indicator, he won't be leaving Chateau Greene alive, which is a major problem...."

That seemed an understatement. "They're going to kill him?"

"And since he's the one who cast the initial revivification," Cirian continued muttering under his breath, moving to the large bookshelf on the far wall and running his finger along the spines as he searched.

"Cirian."

He pulled out a leather-bound tome, flipping through the pages quickly as he continued, "What if he can't perform the rite? Is there an alternative?"

"Cirian, please, don't leave me floundering."

He paused, looking up from the tome with a solemnity I'd rarely seen him display. "If he dies before he completes the resurrection rite, then there may not be another option."

"What does that mean?"

"It means you'll die. Again. And worse, without your own magic to guide your soul back to the Source, I'm almost certain you'll be lost to the ether."

*Son of the Second, lost in the ether.*

The line rang in my ears as if it were spoken again.

Was the prophecy about me? I quickly shook the idea from my head. There were more important things to concern myself with at the moment, like staying alive.

"We have to save him," I said, a twinge in my chest stifling my breath. To imagine Bastien being put to death was almost too terrible to consider, and I wasn't convinced it was only because of my own dire fate should it happen.

"Why do you think I convinced her Eminence to let us accompany her? It's not going to be easy, but we'll figure something out. At least for now, we've got our foot in the door. Now, there's no time to wait, and we need to make ready." He set the tome on his desk, crossing to the door in the corner of the chamber and opening it before stepping aside. "Your bath, as promised. I'll have to fetch you some new garments so you can accompany me as my steward."

I nodded, in no position to argue.

Cirian gave me a wide berth as I trudged over to the washroom. A luxurious marble setting awaited me, a tub recessed into the floor. Just seeing the promise of a bath made my bones ache with want, so I muttered my thanks and closed the door behind me.

With a turn of the knob, the fixture began to run, steam rising immediately from the stream of water. I reached down, plugged the drain, then worked on disrobing. The heavy disguise fell to the floor, pooling around me, and I shivered as I stepped out of its warmth, my feet bare against the frigid tile. I removed the blood-stained tunic Cirian had lent me next, then the rest of my tattered clothing, piling them all in the corner.

The numbing sound of the rushing water did little to calm the chaos of my mind. Mother had captured Bastien, but to what end? Was she aware of the connection between the two of us? Was I the reason that Bastien had been taken in the first place? Another sacrifice he'd be making on my behalf... they were starting to pile up like the laundry.

Carefully, I stepped down into the tub, blessed relief rolling over me as I sank lower into the nearly scalding waters. A few minutes later, I shut off the stream, exhaling a long sigh as I settled against the curved wall of the tub. The sapphire-like Anima stone that Cirian had created lay on the edge of the basin—I wanted to keep it close, just in case—and after a moment in the water to cleanse the lingering stains, I marveled at how the edges caught the light.

Magic thrummed from within the facets, and as I held it, a familiar tugging sensation pulled at me in the direction of the closed door. Was the stone drawing me towards the one who made it? I let it slide from my hand, settling once again on the tiled ledge.

After some much-needed decompression, I reached for the bar of soap at the edge of the bath, working it into a rich later with the help of the warm water. I started with my legs, scrubbing away the caked-on dirt of our nocturnal traipse about the woods and wincing as the suds touched the plethora of minor scratches and scrapes on my calves and ankles. As I worked over the other parts of my body, the surface of the water became obscured with bubbles. Once my arms were free of grime, my hands drifted down my torso, and I jolted as my fingers brushed against the base of my cock. It responded instantly, stiffening.

Even in the impossible situation I found myself in, the baser needs of my manhood would not be ignored. With the time to reflect and the rapidly growing urge to wrap my fingers around my cock, I couldn't help my thoughts from drifting back to Cirian and the newly resurfaced memories of the dozens of rendezvouses we'd had after our sparring sessions.

If the worst should happen, if I was going to die a second, even more gruesome death, this may be the last moment of self-indulgence I would be afforded. And so, I decided not to squander it.

The suds clinging to the surface of the water obfuscated my body underneath, making it all the easier to imagine my hand was someone else's as it wrapped around the base of my cock. A tingling sensation shot up my spine, causing my toes to curl as I closed my eyes, allowing my mind to drift once more to memories of silken sheets and supple skin, of hitched breath and soft groans, of two becoming one, transcending to something more.

Before too long, I could feel the heat building at the base of my spine as my legs began to quake with anticipation of what could be my final climax, and I pushed forward toward the edge of the precipice, waiting to topple over into—

The door of the washroom opened abruptly, Cirian stalking in and shutting the door behind him.

I was stunned into immobility, merely staring at him in shock as my hand was frozen around my cock beneath the surface of the cloudy water.

Cirian didn't say anything as he began to strip his clothes off, tossing them to the side and flexing his back in a stretch as he stood in front of the sink, observing himself in the mirror.

"What are you doing?" I finally choked out, my ruined orgasm evaporating like water on a scalding pan.

Cirian turned to look at me, and I quickly averted my eyes. "I'm getting ready to bathe," he said as if it were the most obvious thing. "Move over."

"I most certainly will not," I told him, pulling my knees to my chest in an effort to hide my exposed body. "Get out. You can bathe when I'm done."

He moved closer, but I still refused to look at him. "Oh, grow up, Toto.

We don't have time for this nonsense. Are you really that bashful? I assure you that I've already seen all there is to see."

"Fine, then I will leave," I said, trying to gain purchase on the slippery tile.

"You still reek of the grave," Cirian argued, sliding one foot into the water, then the other. "I'm sorry, but I can't let you get that close to the Cardinal without a thorough scrub down."

"I smell fine," I argued, hugging my knees closer as the lower half of his body sank into the tub opposite me. There was more than enough room for the both of us to bathe and avoid contact, but the realization did nothing to help the fluttering in my stomach. "You're torturing me. I know how you are. You're enjoying watching me squirm."

"I seem to recall you enjoying the squirming as well," Cirian fired back, pulling his long hair back and tying it with a restraint.

Now that he was partially submerged, I found I could look at him without wanting to immediately combust. "Enough. I don't want to discuss our past dalliances any longer."

"I can respect that," Cirian said, sounding rather rational. Then again, it wasn't rationality he typically lacked. It was compassion. "However, you do still smell, Tobias. I'm not fabricating that detail."

"I've already washed myself," I muttered, feeling more embarrassed than when I was only worried about exposing my body.

Cirian let out a sigh, straightening his posture and patting the surface of the water in front of him. "Come here, Toto."

"I'd rather die again, thanks."

"I'm serious. I need to make sure you're not going to blow your cover before I put you in close proximity to the Cardinal. Now, please."

I hesitated. Was this the first time he'd said 'please?' Once again, I forced myself to look him in the eye, expecting a cruel confidence or twisted enjoyment to be staring me back. But when I locked eyes with Cirian, all I found was an earnestness that caught me off balance.

"Okay," I agreed after a moment, in no hurry to leave the safety of my corner. "Close your eyes."

"How am I supposed to clean you if I can't see—"

"Just for a moment," I cut him off, fighting the urge to splash him. But that might disturb the layer of obscurity that was protecting my modesty, so I pushed the urge away.

Cirian sighed, nodding his head and closing his eyes. Moving as quickly as I could, I stood, crossing the few steps' distance between us and crouching back down into the water. Spinning my back to him, I settled under the suds, careful to keep as much distance between us as I could. His hand braced against my shoulder, and I shivered at his touch.

"Was that so hard?"

His voice was softer than before, given our proximity.

"Get on with it," I ordered, growing increasingly worried now that he was out of my line of sight. Who knew what was going on in his head.

Cirian's hand appears in my periphery, grasping a bar of soup and a washcloth from the side of the tub. There was only the sound of water sloshing to fill the space, then the scrubbing of cloth against my skin.

Cirian was gentle but thorough in his work. I couldn't help but feel a bit like a child, having him pass over me with the washcloth and the rich amber-scented soap. A few minutes in, I allowed myself to relax. The tension melting from my shoulders, I no longer flinched at Cirian's every touch.

I caught myself sneaking glances at the mirror, getting glimpses of Cirian's body as he worked. His pale skin had gone ruddy in the heat of the bath, his flushed cheeks nearly matching the color of the locks pulled back from his head.

His attention was fully concentrated on me, and as his hands drifted to my hips, then around to my navel, I jolted at the sensation. Memories flared in my mind once again, the ghostly sensation of Cirian's hands moving across my body, setting flesh alight with heat that threatened to burn me down to the core.

"Apologies," he said, his hands retracting. "I should have remembered how ticklish you can be."

I hated how much I missed his hand on my body, even just for that brief moment. But the crushing weight of what lay ahead of me—the reality of the slim odds of my survival—quickly quashed the hesitations that rose in my mind.

If I was honest with myself, I couldn't deny the fact any longer: I wanted Cirian's hands on my body.

"It's okay," I told him, reaching behind me and taking his hands in mine. I returned them to my hips, doing my best to hide the shudder that shot through me as his fingertips sunk into the flesh. My cock stiffened again, this time with a dull ache as if it mourned the release that never came.

Cirian sucked in a breath, his touch hesitant on my sides. He seemed… nervous. Which was a position I didn't think came naturally to Cirian. To be honest, it gave me a thrill. Thrill enough to push things a little further.

"You interrupted me before," I said, eyes trained on his expression in the mirror. "I was going to have the first and possibly last release of my second life."

Cirian's mouth opened, then shut again, his eyes boring a hole in the back of my head.

"But I guess there's no time for that," I continued, my hands trailing down my sides till they overlapped his around my waist.

He tugged then, pulling my body closer to him and pressing his chest to my back. Strong arms wrapped around my waist, holding me in place as a soft rumble emanated from his chest.

"You're wicked, Tobias Greene."

"You don't have to remind me."

One of his wandering hands drifted down my navel, running along the trail of fair hair till his fingers split around the base of my cock. My hips bucked instinctually, grinding out as much friction between us as I could, a sputtering gasp escaping my throat.

This wasn't just a memory any longer. I wanted it to be reality. Wanted a moment of reprieve from the pain of my second life.

He paused there, waiting for me to give the go-ahead. Reaching down, I pulled his hand away, only to reseat it along my shaft, closing his fingers around it. He took the hint, pumping his fist down the length of me, causing a ripple of quivering pleasure to stir my bones.

"Yes," I breathed, one of my arms reaching behind me to hook around the nape of Cirian's neck and pull him closer. "Keep going."

He did as he was told, stroking me with a comfortable rhythm that brought me back to the edge within a matter of moments.

My body was on fire with pleasure, heat radiating from my core, building hotter and hotter. With each stroke, my body ground against Cirian's, pressing his stiff cock into the small of my back.

It seemed I wasn't the only one enjoying themselves.

"Tobias." Cirian's heated breath in my ear nearly sent me over the edge. His voice was desperate. Like he was waiting for my permission. "I-I can't take much more."

I halted the movements of my hips, a soft whimper sounding against my ear. I stood, legs trembling beneath me as the slick water dripped from my stark body. Cirian looked up at me, an adoration in his expression that flared to life those memories in my head once more. Taking his face in my hands, I guided him onto his knees.

"Worship me, Acolyte."

A sly grin spread across his face as he nodded, knowing exactly what I asked of him. Leaning close, he took me into his mouth in one fluid motion, sinking to the hilt as the head of my cock hit the back of his throat. My hands fell to his shoulders, gripping tightly to keep myself upright as Cirian took me again and again, the heat from his mouth bringing me closer and closer to melting.

The memories I clung to molded together with the present until they were one in the same.

"I-I'm close," I told him, the building heat reaching its apex as the spasm of release gripped me. Cirian pulled off enough that the tip of my cock rested against his tongue, his hand continuing the constant motion that drove me past my breaking point. With a grumbled shout, I climaxed, the fruits of our labor pouring into Cirian's mouth and running down his chin. He kept his eyes on me the entire time, his opposite hand stroking his own member, and he finished just as my cock stopped twitching, entirely spent.

Sinking into the warm embrace of the water, I laid back opposite Cirian, watching him wipe the mess from his face.

"I think you won that point, Toto," he said finally, reaching for the washcloth.

The laughter that bubbled up from my chest made me feel lighter than I had all day.

# THIRTEEN
## FROM MY COLD, DEAD HANDS

"You never told me why."

Cirian lifted his head from the pillow, a piece of his crimson hair falling into his face. The two of us had spent the afternoon sparring with one another in the gardens, and now he was all mine, reclined in my bed, his body of pale marble draped in silken sheets as the golden light of dusk washed us in its radiance.

"Why what?" he replied, propping himself up on an elbow.

"Why you call me Toto," I clarified, rolling on my side to face him. The smell of sweat clung to us still, both from the activities outside and those that we practiced behind closed doors. It was easy, this time spent with Cirian. He pushed me, out on the fencing strip, till I was a panting mess. And I returned the favor here in the confines of my bed. He was far more agreeable with a cock in his mouth, or better yet, when I was sheathed fully inside him.

Cirian pursed his lips, rolling onto his back to stare up at the canopy that hung above my bed. He remained quiet long enough that I considered abandoning the topic altogether and drawing us a bath, but then he spoke, his voice soft.

"I had a sister before my time as the Acolyte. Emma was her name."

I waited for him to continue, my focus drawn back to the boy as he gazed past the canopy overhead, lost in thought.

"She was born...frail. The healers didn't know what to make of her condition, as it didn't respond to any of the poultices or magics they could think of. My mother knew that we had a limited amount of time with her. She would spend hours a day communing with the Source for answers. But despite her ailment, Emma was a rambunctious thing. She'd chase me around the cathedral, running up and down the aisles till her little lungs were about to give out.

"She didn't speak much, just jumbled words here and there. Names were especially difficult for her, so she would cling to sounds that were easier to make. Mother was 'mama,' and she would call me 'Cici.' She had her own names for everyone we were close to." He went quiet for a moment, his dark eyes searching the space overhead for something that wasn't there. "After Emma passed, Mother and I kept up the practice, calling those we cared for by those simple little names. It was our way of keeping her with us, even after she'd returned to the Source. I haven't given anyone in my life a new name since I went to live at the Cradle. But... when I met you, it was like I could hear Emma in my head, and that was the name she picked out for you."

"So," I said slowly once he'd fallen silent. "Does that mean you care about me, Cirian?"

He turned to look at me then, and I expected him to laugh off my comment or chastise me for my sincerity, but he reached for me instead, cupping the side of my face with his hand.

"Too much, Toto. It scares me, sometimes."

His thumb slowly traced my bottom lip.

"Why would that scare you?" I asked, transfixed by the immeasurable depth of his eyes.

"Because everyone leaves," he whispered, pulling his hand away but holding my gaze. "No matter how hard I try and hold on. They slip through my fingers."

I reached for him then, wrapping my arms around him as he rested his head against my chest. "I'm here, Cirian. You don't have to worry about me disappearing. I'm right here."

And I sealed the promise with a kiss, planted gently on his forehead.

I'd imagined what my return to Chateau Greene would be like since the start of my second life. Initially, I wondered if Mother would even bat an eyelash if I strolled in, pretending as though nothing had happened at all. Now, as I sat in the backseat of a car with Cirian, dressed in all the finery of the personal attendant to the Acolyte, I wondered how quickly Mother would have me removed if she recognized me at all.

"Are you alright?"

I looked up from the floorboard, finding Cirian watching me from the opposite side of the bench seat. We hadn't exchanged many words since leaving the Cradle and even fewer since extracting ourselves from the bath. If he wanted to discuss our actions, he certainly was hiding the desire well. Or perhaps he knew there were more pressing situations at hand.

"I'm fine," I said, my voice muffled by the porcelain mask that I'd been fitted for before leaving the Cradle. This one fit far more comfortably than the previous one and made me feel less claustrophobic. I'd insisted on the mask, afraid that I'd be recognized the moment I set foot in the Chateau, if not by Mother, then by one of the staff. "Or, I will be, at least."

Cirian didn't take the opportunity to mock me, which I found to be a surprising change of pace. Or maybe he's actually heard the uncertainty behind my words. Either way, he didn't press, only nodded.

As we neared the property, he gave me the run down on things to remember while acting as his servant. Ways to address him. Motions that he'd use if he needed something in the middle of a conversation. Times when it was and wasn't appropriate to speak. I did my best to commit them to memory, but the longer the list grew, the more I suspected I was fighting a losing battle. This was pure lunacy, waltzing into the very heart of enemy territory—my childhood home. It felt like a battleground long before this day arrived, but now it served that purpose in earnest. But instead of a battle of wills between children and mother, it was a fight for my future and possibly the future of the Rebellion.

Nausea swelled in my gut.

"I'll send you away as soon as possible without arousing suspicion," Cirian said as we pulled through the large, golden gates of the chateau. Members of Mother's private militia stood stationed at the gate, and we stopped long enough for the driver to show them identification. "It'll buy you some time to locate where they're holding the necro—*Bastien*. Don't try anything on your own unless you absolutely must. I don't know how long that stone is going to be able to sustain your magic, so use it as a last resort, do you understand?"

I nodded, gritting my teeth behind the mask and swallowing back bile. The Anima stone felt heavy against my leg, hidden in the pocket of my trousers.

"We're here," Cirian announced as the car rolled to a stop across from the stairs to the main entrance. More militia members walked the grounds outside of the chateau in patrols of four. Two more guards were stationed at the front door, armed and vigilant. "Adoranda sure seems paranoid that there will be a retaliation to her attack. That bodes well for us. It means she's still afraid and that the Rebellion hasn't lost its teeth quite yet. Come, open the door for me."

I did as he instructed, climbing out of the car and holding the door for him as he exited. An Unseen servant shimmered into existence at the base of the stairs, bowing to Cirian as he approached, his own mask of authority firmly in place.

A sliver of black material around the Unseen's neck drew my attention, and I shuffled a few steps closer to try and get a better look at it.

It appeared to be a thin strip of leather with a golden clasp in the front. A collar, perhaps? It felt immediately out of place, but I couldn't mention it now.

"Good day, Acolyte. You are expected by the madame. This way, please."

Cirian hurried up the steps after the Unseen, and I followed suit, doing my best not to draw attention. The guards eyed us as we approached but didn't speak as the Unseen pulled open the door and ushered us inside the foyer.

I stifled the gasp in my throat. Inside, the foyer had been transformed into what I could only describe as a war room. A long wooden table ran through the center, a large map unfurled and covered in annotations. Several higher-ranking militia members gathered around it, speaking in hushed tones, their attention focused on surveying the placement of small figurines atop the map. I tried my best to pick up on the conversation, but we moved too quickly to catch more than a few words. The Unseen led us down the familiar hall off the foyer, stopping in front of Mother's office. The doors were already open, a militia member posted on either side. The Unseen gestured for us to enter, and we found the Cardinal seated by the desk on the far wall.

"The madame will be with you shortly," the Unseen announces, closing the doors behind him after he exits.

Cirian moved for the desk, taking the seat beside the Cardinal. I did my best to hover in the background, not too far, but not too close, either. Being back in Mother's office sparked a new onslaught of memories, but I had to push them back into the slurry.

This was not the time for distractions.

"I've never seen such a force here," Cirian mused as he sunk into the plush chair. "Adoranda must be frightened of something."

"She is ready to seize a victory," the Cardinal replied, her hands folded neatly in her lap. "It is imperative, Cirian, that you only listen as we discuss the Reviled. Listen and observe, is that understood?"

Cirian nodded. "Yes, Your Eminence."

The doors opened then, Mother striding in, flanked by more militia soldiers. A decorated militia member flanked her, and it took me a second to recognize Renata through the fresh scars across her face. I was relieved to see that she was still alive, though it meant her hands were all the bloodier.

"Glad you could make it, Sancha," Mother greeted the Cardinal, then her eyes shifted over to Cirian. "And young Master Cirian. I wasn't expecting to see you today, but it is, as always, a pleasant surprise. Wonderful you should join Sancha on this most auspicious of days."

"The pleasure is mine, madame."

Mother took her seat at the desk, shuffling a stack of papers out of her way as she dug into a drawer for her pipe. After a moment, a sweet-scented purple smoke drifted from the end, and she returned her attention to the visitors.

"Well, let us get down to business, then. Renata, could you please share with the Cardinal how you came across our Reviled guest?"

# THE SECOND AWAKENING

Renata nodded. "Aye, ma'am. The Reviled was found amongst the rebels at their base camp. At first, we thought he might be a prisoner of theirs, but when I saw him tending to the wounded Unseen, I knew that they must have recruited him for his vile magics. Who knows what kind of deplorable experiments they were cooking up?"

I bit down on my tongue to keep from interjecting, anger steaming the flesh behind my mask.

"And what is the latest?" Mother asked, a plume of smoke exhaling from her mouth.

"He's yet to speak, Your Grace. But he can only resist for so long. We'll have the information you seek soon enough."

"What information are you intending to extract from them?" asked the Cardinal, her voice even.

"The leader of the Rebellion has managed to slip through our fingers once more," Mother answered, flashing a glance at Renata before continuing. "As well as a person of great interest to me. We believe that the Reviled knows to where they've fled, so once that information has been extracted, you may do with him what you wish."

A person of interest? It could only be Lynette. A wave of relief washed over me. Maybe things weren't looking as bleak. All we had to do now was get Bastien out of here.

"I will return to my efforts, Your Grace," said Renata, giving a bow before exiting. She didn't look in my direction as she went, and I wondered if she even mentioned finding me amongst the rebels last night.

"While we wait," said Mother, leaning back in her chair and focusing her attention on the Cardinal. "I was hoping that we could discuss a matter of business, Sancha."

"I don't see why not," the Cardinal replied, folding her hands across her lap. "Speak your mind, Adoranda."

"I was hoping that you would reconsider my standing offer once this horrible Rebellion issue has been resolved. Without the constant distractions, just think of what we would be able to accomplish. How quickly we would be able to bring about the second Awakening."

Cirian cocked his head to the side, glancing over at his mentor. Obviously, he was not privy to the details of whatever said offer entailed.

"I look forward to the day of the second Awakening just as much as you do, Adoranda," replied the Cardinal. "But the Church cannot take such a strong stance on this issue. At least not in the current climate. I'm sure you understand."

Mother huffed a laugh, spilling more of the purple smoke from her nostrils. "As cautious as ever, I see. No matter, Sancha. You'll see things my way sooner rather than later. And when that happens, I do hope that there is still a seat at the table for the Church."

The women stared each other down, neither breaking away until Cirian jumped in, breaking the tension. "Apologies, Your Grace, but I'm feeling a bit weary from the trip over. Would it be possible to send Reginald here down to fetch some us some tea?"

Mother looked over at me as Cirian referred to me as "Reginald," seeming to realize for the first time that I was in the room. I panicked for a moment, praying that she wouldn't see the need to reach out with her aura, but she simply nodded to Cirian.

"Sounds delightful."

Cirian snapped his fingers, summoning me to his side. I bowed deeply, doing my best to lower my voice as I replied, "Yes, Master Cirian?"

"Tea and perhaps something sweet from the kitchens. And don't dawdle, Reginald. I know how you like to fraternize."

"Yes, Master Cirian." I bowed once more and nearly lost my balance as I found Mother staring intently at me. Her lips parted as if she were about to ask me something, but then Cirian spoke again, allowing me enough time to escape.

"We've heard of your marvelous victory on the front of the Rebellion. Please, do tell us in your own words how the effort is going."

I slipped out of Mother's office as quickly as I could, waiting till I was clear of the soldiers by the door before I exhaled a shaky breath.

So far, so good.

Moving back into the main foyer, I couldn't ignore the signs of my mother's growing paranoia. The windows on the front of the chateau had been reinforced, the sparkling glimmer of magical wards distorting the view through them. Great Grandmother's statue watched from above as I crossed the space, once again moving past the giant map sprawled along the table. I spotted a mortal maid cleaning off a stack of dishes from the corner and figured I would follow her to the kitchen.

She noticed me as we moved in tandem down the hallway, and I offered a polite wave so as not to startle her. "Just looking for the kitchens. The Cardinal's Acolyte needs tea."

The woman's posture relaxed, and she gave a soft smile. "Of course. I can show you the way, love. Follow me."

There was far too much ground to cover in searching for Bastien, so I'd throw my lot in with the servants, as they were bound to know where Mother was keeping him, at least. Even prisoners had to be fed.

I hurried to match the woman's stride, ducking the random maid or soldier who marched down the hall. Memories assaulted my mind, shooting up from the depths of my subconscious like geysers. These halls held so much of my history I only wished there was more time to sort through it.

"There certainly is a lot going on around here," I said as we dodged a line of militia soldiers just outside of the kitchen.

"Tell me about it," the woman replied, using her hip to push open the door. The kitchen was sweltering as we headed in, a row of Unseen working along the center wooden-block-topped island, preparing dozens of plates. The stove top was overflowing with stockpots of simmering liquids, and across the way, the large double-oven belched steam each time the doors were opened to remove pans of bread and pastries. "You can speak with Eustace if you need a teapot," the woman tells me, pointing to one of the Unseen manning the stovetop.

"Thank you," I replied as she hurried off in the opposite direction. Feeling immediately in the way, just as I did when I was a child, I moved gingerly through the kitchen. It was more difficult than I remember now that I was too big to weave between the cook's legs as I went.

I noticed more of those strange collars, each of the Unseen sporting one. They were uniform in their appearance, just simple black leather with a golden clasp, but a certain unease settled in my stomach the longer I looked at them.

Finally, I reached the Unseen called Eustace, a younger man than I was expecting, with a shock of soft orange hair protruding up in a line between the pointed ears tufted in the same-colored fur. He eyed me as I approached, already looking annoyed.

"And who are you s'posed to be?"

"Apologies," I started, raising my voice over the din of the swirling action moving around us. "The Acolyte and Cardinal have requested tea—"

"I can't bloody understand you with that thing on, chap," the Unseen interrupted, lifting a heavy cast iron lid from a pot and stirring the contents with a long wooden spoon.

Glancing over my shoulder, I decided the chances of anyone recognizing me here were low, so I pulled the mask away, turning back to face the man. "They want tea," I said again, my voice carrying much further. "Just tell me where I can get a pot going."

Eustace groaned, muttering under his breath as he replaced the lid. "How do they expect me to feed an army if I keep having to heat up their stinkin' piss water—" he paused, his eyes going wide as he looked over at me again. "You. I know you."

I fumbled with the mask, shaking my head furiously. "You're mistaken."

"They said you were dead," Eustace continued, waving a wooden spoon in my face. "What the bloody hell is going on around here?"

"Keep your voice down," I begged, looking over my shoulder again, half-expecting a row of soldiers to be waiting for me. My hand clasped around the stone in my pocket, squeezing it as the comforting heat of magic spread up my arm. Last resort. It had to be a last resort. "Please, I'm here with the Rebellion."

His eyes only grew wider. "They're coming, aren't they? For the Reviled down in the cellar? Gods, this is going to get so messy. The madame's going to string us all up before the day's through."

Okay, the cellar. That confirmed the location. It was a good start.

"We're going to make sure that doesn't happen," I replied. "But if you blow my cover, then things are only going to get messier for everyone, so please, keep it quiet."

"You're different," Eustace said, seeming to calm a bit. "I can see it. You're different than before."

"I am," I confirmed because it seemed like the only appropriate response.

Eustace nodded after a moment, kneeling down to a shelf by the stovetop and producing a tea kettle. "Go fill it, and I'll get to work on the tea."

"Thank you," I said, packing as much sincerity as I can into the words. Hurrying over to the sink, it didn't take long for me to fill the iron kettle, returning to find a spot cleared on the stovetop. Eustace took it from me, setting it in place as the flames lapped up the side of the kettle.

"China's in the cabinet," he said, motioning to the large wooden structure around the corner. "Go ahead and gather what you need. We had shortbreads just come out the oven, so I'll have some plated up as well. That'll keep the madame happy."

"Right," I agreed, moving for the cabinet and assembling the necessary equipment for the tea service by gathering them onto a silver tray. By the time I'd found the matching sugar caddy and filled the boat with cream, Eustace was there, pouring the hot water into my teapot and setting the prepared tea bags onto the tray.

"Be sure to serve the madame first," he said softly, giving me a quick wink before turning and heading back over to the stovetop.

I could only hope Eustace would keep his word.

Brandishing the excuse for my reconnaissance, I headed out of the kitchen and back into the hallway, retracing my steps towards Mother's office. My mind raced through the details I was able to glean. They were keeping Bastien in the cellar, which meant there would be no easy way to gain access to him. We'd have to devise some sort of ruse to see him, which I hoped Cirian might already be plotting. Not only was his location a cause for concern, but the sheer number of militia members milling about proved an almost insurmountable obstacle. If it came down to a fight, there would be no chance of us prevailing. The odds were stacking against us at an alarming rate.

I rounded the last corner before reaching the foyer, stepping to the side to allow another line of soldiers to pass, their boisterous chatter reverberating in the cramped space. Once the coast was clear, I began to move again, but something latched onto my elbow, yanking me hard enough that I stumbled. The tray clattered in my hands, but then someone was steadying me, closing the door I'd been forced through and casting us into darkness.

My pulse hammered, and I contemplated dropping the tray if only to ready a defense against whoever had grabbed me, but then the light overhead illuminated with the pull of a string, and I was able to get a good look at the one responsible for my being in a broom closet.

"After all these years, you're still terrible at this game."

The voice—much deeper than I remembered—sparked memories like fireworks in my mind. The Unseen man grasped me by the shoulders, holding me at arm's length—a rather difficult task for two grown adults in a broom closet—and beamed a snaggle-toothed smile.

"Azzy?" I whispered, forgetting for a moment the cargo in my hands as I stepped toward him. He caught the tray, pulling it gently from my grip and setting it on a shelf beside us. I pulled off the mask, shoving it aside as well. "W-What are you doing here? Are you with the Rebellion?"

Azzy grinned wider. "I could ask you the same thing, Tobi. I take it by your fancy getup that the Hallowed Acolyte had something to do with it."

I nodded. "He saved me during the raid. We planned on staying at the Cradle till we heard from the others, but then he got word of Bastien's capture, and we had to improvise."

"Yeah, it wasn't our finest hour last night. I tried to make it to Bastien during the chaos, but the sneaky bastard had already wandered off looking for you, and I was knee-deep in Adored soldiers wanting to skin me alive. I wanted to come for you, too, of course. But I figured Lenny would have already saved your arse."

My heart skipped a beat. "Is she here too?"

He shook his head, bits of his violet hair escaping the soldier's cap he wore. He was decked out in an entire Adored militia member's uniform, only his piercing eyes giving any indication of his actual identity. He'd even managed to tuck his tail away somehow in the trousers. "She hadn't made it to the rendezvous point by the time I left," he said, pausing for a moment to close his eyes. Twitching movement under his hat told me that he must be listening out for something in the hallway.

"I'm sure she's rightly fine wherever she ended up," he continued, his eyes finding me once again. "We're here for Bastien as well as Crassus—one of our leaders who was taken. Stick to the Acolyte for now, and you'll know when we make our move."

I nodded, still in a state of disbelief. Azzy and I, playing hide-and-seek once again around Chateau Greene.

"Now, as much as I would love to stick around and reminisce about old times, I've got to get back to the other chaps before they start looking for me."

"Let me come with you," I said, squaring my shoulders. "I can help."

Azzy grabbed the tray from the shelf, offering it to me with a bit of reluctance. "Nah, Tobi. Even in that getup, you stick out like a sore thumb. You never did figure out how to blend in. It's probably my favorite thing about you."

I took the tray, stunned into silence as his hand drifted up to my face, stroking my cheek before he offered a quick wink. Then his body shimmered like a mirage before disappearing entirely, the door to the broom closet opening without a sound.

Taking a moment to compose myself and reattach my mask, I pulled the cord above my head to extinguish the light and made my way back to Mother's office.

# FOURTEEN
## KNOCK 'EM DEAD

"Madame Greene? To what do we owe the pleasure of your presence?"

I looked up from my coursework—a boorish set of fractions that I couldn't care less about—to see Mother standing at the door of our schoolroom. Lynette looked up as well, her face mirroring the same curiosity as mine.

What was Mother doing away from her office? She rarely ventured into the schoolroom while we had our lessons.

She entered the room in the same haughty circumstance that followed wherever she went. "Good day, lady Bask. My apologies for interrupting your lesson, but I will be taking over from here."

Our tutor paled, bowing her head. "Of course, Your Grace. Please forgive me if there has been any oversight on my part—"

"You may wait outside," Mother replied, not looking at the woman.

Bask bowed once more, abandoning her lesson and leaving through the still-open door. Mother hovered by our work table, eyeing the formulas scrawled on the chalkboard. She ran her hand along the edge of the table, her nails digging into the wood. "I have a lesson for you, my children. Put away these silly calculations and pay attention, now."

Lynette and I shared a look of worried confusion but did as we were told.

"You've been taught about the birth of the Magi, correct?" Mother asked, moving to the chalkboard and picking up the eraser with a look of disdain.

# THE SECOND AWAKENING

"Yes, Mother," we replied in unison.

"Tell me what you know," she ordered us, wiping the board clean from our previous lesson.

"The world was full of only mortals before the Awakening," Lynette answered. "They didn't take care of the land or each other very well, and there was a lot of fighting. Ms. Bask called them 'wars.'"

"That's right," Mother replied, now picking up the chalk and drawing a large triangle on the board. "And after the Magi were created during the Awakening, they quickly ended the suffering of the mortals, showing them that there was more to live for than killing one another. But this is not all of the story, dear children."

"It's not?" I asked, my curiosity piqued.

"Far from it. To the mortal eye, all Magi are equal, each of them gifted with magical talent through the Awakening. However, we know this isn't exactly true." Her hand drifted from the top of the triangle down to the bottom two points. "After all, there are plenty of Magi who lack the skill to cast more than the most basic of spells. And yet, there are those who have been given the responsibility to rule, to guide the Magi with their vision of what is possible."

Mother stepped back from the board, displaying her diagram. At the precipice of the pyramid was the Adored. Beneath them, forming the base two angles, Hallowed and Unseen.

"As you can see, the Adored are chosen to lead. We are predestined for greatness, children. Given the gift of influence, we can shape the future and steer it towards a brighter tomorrow. A second Awakening. Now, I'm curious. Can either of you tell me what role I fill?"

We both raised our hands.

"Lynette."

"You're the leader of the Council of Magi. They help make decisions about rules that Magi must follow."

"That's right," Mother replied, a smile devoid of warmth creeping onto her face. "A role that you will inherit one day, Lynette. It has been the duty of our family since the first Awakening. Our history goes back nearly a thousand years."

Lynette raised her hand again.

"Yes?"

"How did our family become the leaders of the Adored?"

Mother's brow furrowed. "It was a decision made long ago, Lynette."

"By who?" she pressed, leaning forward in her seat. "Was it the mortal leaders? Because we learned about them from Ms. Bask, and a lot of them were bad people."

"Does it matter?" asked Mother. "Adored have the power to unify the Magi. It is only just that we are the ones who lead them. The mortal leaders are no longer a concern of ours."

"But couldn't someone from the Hallowed or one of the Unseen be just as good at leading?" Lynette continued her questioning.

This actually garnered a laugh from Mother. "The Hallowed would never leave their precious sanctuaries long enough. They simply lack the backbone, dear. And the Unseen are not equipped with the higher mindset required. Their magic is primitive and affects their composure. How can they expect to remain level-headed in the face of adversity?"

"So, they have to be servants?" I asked, Lynette giving me a nod of approval. My mind was on Azzy and his father. Would he still want to be my friend if he didn't work for my family?

"They have found their role in our society," replied Mother, her tone curt. "Just as we have."

"And who tells them it's their role to serve?" I asked, getting caught up on the flawed logic. Maybe it was Lynette's presence, or perhaps the burning need to keep Azzy close by, but I would have never questioned Mother like this before. "Because you've always told us that our role is to lead, but what if there was something else we wanted to do?"

"Because that is what is expected of you," Mother snaps. "Society guides the roles of each of its members—"

"But you guide society," Lynette interrupted. "You hold the power. If you wanted to, you could change things. Could make it so that the Unseen could do more—"

"That is enough," Mother cut Lynette off, the air growing heavy around us as power emanated from her. "You will sit down and cease these questions at once!"

# THE SECOND AWAKENING

The magic of her Command washed over me like a smothering wave of heat, spurring my body into motion as I straightened in my seat, my jaw clenched so hard that I was sure I would crack a tooth if I held much longer.

Lynette struggled against the Command, her ability to resist far greater than my own, but she, too, eventually succumbed to our mother's wishes. Once silence fell over the room, Mother returned to the chalkboard.

"I don't know where you are getting these impossible ideas from, but it is clear you're your education must be amended. And I am just the person to take on the task." She straightened her blazer, tugging on the ends and dusting off a bit of chalk. "Where was I? Ah, yes. My role as the leader of the Council means that I must make difficult decisions, as will you one day, Lynette. I have one of those decisions that needs to be made today. Would you like to hear what it is?"

I couldn't open my mouth, so I nodded instead, but Lynette remained perfectly still, eyes staring daggers at our mother.

"Out there," said Mother, pointing to the window. "Is a group of rebels who want to see nothing but the destruction of our way of life. These monsters would do harm to our family in the name of what they seek, and if they are not stopped, they will destroy everything we have worked for.

"And as if that wasn't disturbing enough, I have been told that there is someone here in the chateau who wishes to align themselves with this cause. As the madame of this house, I have a duty to protect those who dwell here. So, what should be done about this most personal betrayal?"

The pressure holding my jaw shut slackened, but Lynette was the first to speak.

"Does it matter what we say? If you don't agree, you'll silence us again. Just like you do all the others."

Mother exhaled an exasperated breath. "Lynette, one day you will stand in my place, and you will understand the weight of our charge. I only wish to prepare you for that moment."

"Then listen to me, Mother. Please, at least consider the course of action."

"What would you have me do, daughter?"

"Spare their life," Lynette replied, standing from her seat. Mother loomed over her like a mountain, but she didn't falter. "Show mercy. Try and speak with them, to understand what it is that drives them away. Then you can make your decision."

Mother pondered Lynette's words for a moment her arms crossed as she shuffled her weight from one foot to the other. Was she actually considering it?

"What of you, Tobias?"

I flinched at the mention of my name, looking up to find both of them staring. "M-Me?"

"Yes, you. What would you have me do with this dangerous individual? Tell me, would you feel safe walking the halls of your home if you knew someone could be lurking behind every corner, just waiting to slip a knife into your back?"

I shook my head. "I don't want to be afraid."

"Ah," Mother cooed, leaving Lynette's side to come and crouch beside me so she was at eye level. "You've stumbled on something, Tobias. Therein lies the solution."

"What solution?" I asked.

"Fear. It is a powerful tool. Used correctly, it can inspire even the most devout rebels to abandon their ideals."

"But, Mother," Lynette started, but she faltered as Mother rose once again to her full height.

"I will take your counsel into consideration, children. Lynette, you have my word that the individual's life will be spared. At least, I will not order it to be taken from them. And Tobias, I will make sure that the ideals which radicalized them are dismantled from the ground up, even if I must tear them from their mind bit by bit."

Lynette turned to me, a look of horror on her face.

Mother clapped her hands, her lips curling into a cruel smile. "A wonderful lesson, children."

Azzy was supposed to meet me outside my bedroom an hour ago. I checked the watch in my pocket for the tenth time before deciding I would go looking for him. Perhaps his chores had taken longer than expected, and he was still in the kitchen helping his father.

# THE SECOND AWAKENING

The kitchen was bustling like always when I arrived, but the air was heavy, like a great sorrowful cloud hung overhead. There was no music to be heard between the Unseen as they went about their tasks. No humming or whistling or murmured cordiality back and forth, only the stark silence and gentle clattering of dishes.

"Excuse me," I asked one of the mortal maids close by. "Have you seen Azzy?"

The maid's eyes widened, and she looked like she was about to cry. "He... he's not here, young master. He left this morning."

"Left?" I repeated, not understanding. "Where did he go?"

"I don't know. Nobody does. I'm sorry."

The woman bowed, hurrying away from me. Shock rooted me in place as I processed the news. Where was Balthus? Surely, he would know what happened to his son. Willing my feet forward, I ran through the kitchen in search of him, but he was absent as well.

"Did you need something, young master?"

One of the older Unseen with greying hair and a long, crooked nose had spotted me frantically pacing by the pantry.

"Where is Balthus?" I asked, breathless.

The Unseen winced, his eyes crinkling with deeper wrinkles. "He's out in the gardens, I would imagine. But you should know, young master—"

"Thank you!" I didn't wait for the rest of the answer, already bolting through the servants' entrance and around the back of the chateau. The gardens sprawled ahead of me, rows of hedges and rosebushes, but I wouldn't be deterred. I ran down each row, panting as I searched for Azzy's father. Questions buzzed in my mind like a swarm of insects. How could he have left without telling me? Where would he have gone that his father didn't accompany him? Why was there a terrible pit in my stomach?

Near the edge of the garden, I found him knelt in the dirt, spreading what appeared to be a layer of fertilizer around the base of a rose bush. He looked up as I approached, his violet eyes—so much like Azzy's—widened, and he scrambled to his feet.

"Tobias!" he nearly shouted, reaching for me with his sullied hands and then thinking better of it. "Please, tell me. Tell me he's safe, that's all I ask. I beg of you, just tell me he's safe."

"I don't understand," I replied, taking a step back from him. "Are you talking about Azzy? Where is he?"

Balthus sank to his knees, tears spilling down the lavender stubble on his cheeks. "Please, just tell me my boy is okay. That's all I ask."

"Your boy is fine, Balthus," a voice called from behind me. The Unseen stiffened at those words, his gaze moving past me.

I turned to see Mother standing by a rosebush, admiring the blooms. She gave me a slight nod before coming over, careful to keep a distance from the stench of the manure and the man who wept at our feet.

"Tobias, I'm glad you're here. You can see the fruits of your labor."

"My what?"

"Balthus here was the one whispering conspiracy around the hallways, trying to get others to join him in abandoning their duties for a doomed rebellion. Now, Balthus, I had every mind to order your execution without a second thought. However, my daughter saw fit to err on the side of mercy. You have her to thank for your head still being attached. But Tobias here," she paused, resting a hand on my shoulder. "He reminded me that there was something more effective I could rely on than magic to get what I wanted. See, Tobias, all I had to do was inflict enough fear in dear Balthus that he'd never think to question the status quo ever again."

Cold dread pulsed through my veins. "What did you do, Mother?"

"Please, Madame Greene," Balthus pleaded, snot dripping from his nose. "I never meant you or your family any harm. I just wanted a better life for my son. That's all I wanted."

"And he'll have it," Mother replied, her grip on my shoulder tightening. "You can rest every night knowing that dear Zazzy—or whatever his name is—is well taken care of and will remain that way so long as you remain loyal to this house. Am I understood?"

"Y-Yes," Balthus managed through his sobs, bowing lower to the ground. "Yes, I understand."

I wanted to vomit.

"Good. See, Tobias? You and your sister were right. I didn't need to stoop so low *as to have someone killed. He's so much more useful to me alive. Balthus, don't forget my peonies. They won't bloom fully come Spring if they aren't swimming in shit by the end of the day, yes?"*

*I slowly walked back to the house, my breath coming in short, shallow gasps.*

*It was the first life I'd ruined.*

*It wouldn't be the last.*

"I was beginning to think you'd died, Reginald."

Cirian addressed me as I entered Mother's office, carrying the silver tray.

"Apologies, Master Cirian. The kitchen was overrun with hungry soldiers, and it took some time to get everything in order." I set down the tray, making it a point to set Mother's place first, then the Cardinal's, and finally Cirian's.

Mother scoffed, her nostrils flaring. "Those lollygaggers have been slacking ever since we made the Chateau into a base of operations. I mean, really, their entire purpose is to cook, so you'd think they'd be excited to do it for more people?"

I poured Mother's cup, then set the plate of shortbreads down in front of her. She eyed them with gluttonous intent. Not matter how powerful she was, her head could always be turned by a sweet.

"Good help is so difficult to find these days, isn't it, Adoranda?" Cirian asked, motioning toward me. "Sure, Reggie here may have dedicated his life in service to the Source, but does that mean he can slack off when I'm not looking? I say, no way."

The Cardinal let out a quiet huff, a dissent to the conversation if I'd ever heard one.

"Tell me about it," Mother responded, picking up one of the cookies and dunking it into her steaming tea. "I always knew I felt a kinship to you, Cirian. You're a man who knows what he wants and isn't afraid to ask for it—nay, demand it. It's a rare trait in Adored men, unfortunately. Most lack the gumption to even speak to me, let alone commiserate over the staff."

"That is their loss, then," Cirian replied, raising his teacup in a gesture of goodwill to Mother. "Because every conversation with you is a delight."

I could practically hear the Cardinal's eyes rolling around her head.

A soft knock on the door and one of the maids poked her head through the opening.

"Yes, what is it?" Mother barked after swallowing her mouthful of cookie.

The maid hurried over to the desk, bending down to whisper in Mother's ear. I kept a comfortable distance from them, so I wasn't able to make out any of the message.

"If you'll excuse me," Mother said, sliding her cup forward as she stood and dusting the crumbs from her jacket. "There's a matter that requires my attention. A lady's work is never done, aye, Sancha?"

"I suppose not," the Cardinal responded coolly.

"Don't take too long, now," Cirian added, standing as Mother exited the room. Once the door shut behind her, he sank back into his chair.

The Cardinal shifted in her seat, straightening out her robes. "Must you be such a shameless flirt, Cirian? I am finding it difficult to keep my breakfast down."

"This is why I told you I needed to be here," he replied with a sly grin. "If I'd left you to your own devices, you two would be sitting here in an awkward silence."

The Cardinal made a noise I can only assume was a laugh. "This is no improvement, I assure you."

Cirian bowed his head toward his master, though his smile was still prominently displayed. "My apologies, Your Eminence. I will do better to dim my charm and wit so it does not offend you."

"Any dimmer and you'd be acting like her tawdry son, may his soul find peace."

Cirian's smile faded, and he did his best not to look at me.

"You trained me to use every tool in my arsenal in service of the Source, so I must remind you that this shameless flirting is all your fault."

The Cardinal let out another clipped laugh, reaching for her teacup.

# THE SECOND AWAKENING

I couldn't help but empathize with Cirian. I'd spent the majority of my first life using my charms and magic to woo and flatter and ultimately manipulate others into doing what I wished. Well, what Mother wished, but that didn't absolve me. How many lives had I ruined in the process? How many hearts had I fractured with promises I never intended to keep?

How many of those promises did I give to Cirian during those long afternoons spent in my chambers?

And perhaps that explained the moment Cirian and I shared earlier today. It was the ghostly remnants of a decade-old affection, heightened by the urgency of the moment, nothing more. Another empty promise divvied out.

I couldn't consider it more. Not now.

The door sprang open again, Mother reentering the room with a familiar blonde woman in tow. I sucked in a breath, hoping my mask muffled the noise enough to go unnoticed as Lorelei Orion leaned against the corner of Mother's desk, her eyes locked on Cirian.

"Apologies," said Mother before sinking back into her seat, her expression sour. "This is Lorelei, a Truthsayer from the house of Orion. She's been leading the interrogation against the Reviled practitioner, but he's proving stubborn. I need him to remain in our custody for a while longer, Sancha."

"His judgment cannot be delayed," the Cardinal replied, her tone stern. "You know the law, Adoranda. You must release him to us immediately."

Mother rose to her full height, looking down on the Cardinal. "You misunderstand me. I am not asking for your permission. That man will not be leaving this place until I get what I want from him."

"Why not order him to speak?" Cirian interjected. "Surely, no one would be able to resist you, Your Grace."

"My magic can make him speak, yes," Mother replied, her edge softening a bit as she addressed Cirian. "But it does not ensure that his words are truthful. He could merely babble for days, and we'd be no closer to finding the answers I seek. Truth is hard earned, I'm afraid."

The Cardinal didn't seem impressed as she also stood, her robes falling around her body in a hoop. "Take me to the Reviled. Now."

"You don't give the orders here," Mother scoffed. "You can have him when I'm done with him and not a moment sooner. If you'd like to wait around, be my guest. I'll have a room prepared."

"Madame Greene," Cirian inserted himself once again. "There must be a middle ground we can find here. There's no need for hostility."

Lorelei snorted a laugh, pulling out her little leather notebook and flipping it open. "That's rich, coming from you. What's the matter, Acolyte? Are you mad that we're holding one of your little friends?"

Cirian didn't falter, staring down Lorelei before replying, "I'm sure Her Eminence and the madame would love to hear the story of how you walked into the Cradle yesterday with said Reviled and the madame's recently resurrected son?"

The Cardinal and Mother broke their stare down, turning to Cirian.

"What?" they echoed one another.

The doors flew open, the conversation evaporating as a number of militia soldiers poured into the room, including Renata.

"Barricade it," Renata ordered, the soldiers setting to work quickly to move bookshelves in front of the door.

"What is the meaning of this?" Mother questioned. Shouting came from outside of the room, and then a deep rumbling shook the floor beneath us.

"Apologies, Your Grace, but a small Rebellion force has infiltrated the chateau," Renata spoke quickly. "Our forces are working now to contain them."

"Preposterous!" Mother shouted, her fist slamming into the desk and leaving an indent of splintered wood. "How could they have gotten in? The wards in place should have stopped them in their tracks."

Renata grimaced. "We believe they had help from within the chateau, Your Grace. We don't have confirmation yet, but—"

"Those animals," Mother seethed, her teeth gritted and her eyes burning with a fiery rage. The air thickened around her, sparks of gold igniting sporadically. "It was the mongrels I keep. I know it. I open my home to them, and this is how they repay the kindness? So be it. Captain, I want you to issue the order. All of the Unseen are to be rounded up and brought down

# THE SECOND AWAKENING

to the cellar. Lorelei will extract the truth from them, and then they will *all* face the consequences of their actions."

Lorelei frowned. "That's not really part of my contract—"

"Silence," Mother ordered. "You'll receive ample compensation."

"You can't be serious, Adoranda." The Cardinal's voice sounded shaken, as if Mother's barbaric actions had finally thrown her off balance. "You mean to punish those who had nothing to do with the Rebellion?"

"Their silence is their crime," Mother continued, moving from her place by the desk to where Renata stood, supervising the barricade's construction. "Give the order. If there is any resistance, they are to use whatever force is necessary. Activate the collars, and any that attempt to leave the premises will be exterminated. Am I understood?"

Renata blanched but nodded. "Yes, Your Grace."

This couldn't be happening. Mother was going to cull the entire Unseen staff? That was dozens of lives. People I'd grown up with, loyal and kind people who didn't deserve this treatment. I had to stop this. I had to get to them before the soldiers did. Would Azzy be able to help? Would we be able to spirit the Unseen staff away before Mother's wrath would be unleashed?

That would all depend on whether or not I could get out of there.

The Cardinal and Cirian muttered to each other, casting glances at Mother as she barked more orders to the captain. Lorelei was writing in her notebook, an almost bored expression on her face, and I was stuck pretending to be a servant when all I really wanted was to bust down the doors and run screaming down the halls. Thankfully, the opportunity would come shortly.

Another rumble rocked the floor beneath us, the shouting intensifying from outside the doors. Renata pressed a finger to her ear, her gaze going distant as she received a message. "They're headed for the cellar. Our attempts to stop them have failed thus far."

"Idiots," Mother seethed, pushing aside one of the soldiers, her golden aura expanding from her body as she raised a hand into the air in front of her. With a deafening screech and a shower of sparks, the barricade was shoved aside, the door flung open, and a plume of smoke poured into the room. "We make for the cellar, Captain. Sancha, Cirian, you're coming with us. If you want to take your precious prisoner, you'll have to help us keep him here."

"Madame," Renata said, stepping toward the imposing woman, then shrinking back. "It's not safe for you. Please allow us to—"

"I am sick of your failings," Mother retorted, pushing up the sleeves of her emerald-shaded jacket. "There is not a Magi alive who can best me, so I would cast your fears elsewhere. Now, *move*."

Searing heat washed over me, stirring my body into motion. Looking around the room, everyone but the Cardinal—and, more surprisingly, Lorelei—did the same, our bodies locking into step behind Mother as she charged through the open doors and into the smoke-filled hallway. Shouting quickly overtook us, the soldiers moving to flank Mother and Renata while Cirian, the Cardinal, and I brought up the rear.

"This is madness, Adoranda," the Cardinal spat, raising her voice above the din of chaos. Being so close to her, the strength of her aura, wrapped tightly around her body, sent electric trills across my skin.

Mother let out a sharp laugh as we rounded the corner. "If you're frightened, Sancha, you can see yourself out."

The smoke cleared a bit when we reached the foyer, the high ceiling allowing a better vantage. The large table where the map had been sprawled earlier was overturned, papers scattered across the marble flooring, and there were several gouges taken out of the stairs leading up to the second floor as if some large-mawed creature had taken bites from it. Renata shouted orders to the lingering soldiers, giving instructions to sweep the first and upper floors for Unseen staff and bring them down the cellar. Cirian glanced at me, his expression grim, and I knew immediately we were of one accord. If we let Mother do this, we would be just as guilty for the slaughter.

We had to do something.

As if he had read my mind, Cirian nodded slightly, holding up a single finger as if to tell me to wait for his signal. My hand clasped the stone in my pocket, the surge of warmth it provided steeling my nerves.

The time had come. We would see what this Anima stone could do.

# THE SECOND AWAKENING

The group of us moved from the foyer then, heading towards the kitchen which would lead to the cellar entrance. As we reached a branch in the hallway, Cirian suddenly cried out, staggering to the side as he struggled against an invisible force.

"Get it off!" he shouted, hands grasping at the air in front of him.

This was the interruption I'd been waiting for. As the group erupted into chaos—soldiers running over to Cirian, only to be bowled over by him turning wildly and slamming into them, the Cardinal producing a blade the length of her arm from within her robe that she brandished with ease, Mother watching on with an amusement that only came from violence—I took the opportunity to slip down the opposite direction, knowing that it would take a while for anyone but Cirian to notice my absence.

Now that I was free of the others, I tore down the familiar halls, throwing open door after door in search of any staff.

Mother was unmoored. Her years of animosity toward the Unseen seeming to have concentrated into a miasma that now filled the hallways. I couldn't let those who had done no wrong bear the brunt of her wrath. As I neared the conservatory towards the back of the chateau, a soldier shouted, his voice carrying down the corridor.

"On the ground! Now!"

Peering around the corner, I spotted the two soldiers, their weapons—one, a long, narrow blade, the other a short club—drawn against the huddled group of Unseen. They outnumbered the soldiers two-to-one, but it was apparent they were scared out of their wits, cowering against the wall of paned glass, their bodies flickering in and out of the ethereal as their magic spiked with fear.

One of the Unseen—Eustace, the chef from the kitchen—stepped in front of the others. "Why are you doing this?" he questioned. "We've done nothin'!"

"Madame's orders," replied the soldier with the club, stepping forward and jamming the base of the handle into Eustace's gut. The air left his lungs in a wheeze as he doubled over, and that was all I needed to see.

Clasping the stone so tightly I thought my skin would break, I charged the soldiers, propelled by the jolt of warm magical energy that infused my muscles. The soldiers were trained for combat, but I had the element of surprise. I ran full force into the soldier with the blade, knocking us both to the ground and sending their weapon clattering away. The soldier recovered quickly, landing a glancing blow across my face, knocking the mask off. It was obvious I wasn't going to overpower the soldier physically, so I gripped onto their uniform, pulling them close to me as I enveloped him in my aura, crushing the meager defenses he tried to raise around his mind.

"*Get up and go home,*" I issued the Command, a searing heat rolling off my words like molten honey. Another flash of pain in my hand, but I ignored it.

The soldier's body went slack, his struggle abating all at once. With a grunt, he clambered to his feet, shuffling off down the hall without another word. I rolled onto my side just in time for the other soldier to kick me in the ribs, pain ricocheting through my body as my breath sputtered. They reared back again, but I quickly projected my aura around them, their walls crumbling like a sandcastle under pressure.

Fear filled my mind, echoing off the soldier, but I pushed it away, staggering onto my feet before giving the Command, "*Smell the roses.*"

The soldier's panic faded as my orders set in, burning in my throat like a hot coal. They walked calmly over to the other side of the conservatory, where rows of rosebushes waited for them, bending down to take in a deep inhalation.

My hand ached, and for a moment, I thought I had lost hold of the stone. But when I examined my palm, my stomach turned. The gem had embedded itself into my hand, the smooth facets protruding from it, refracting light.

There would be time to worry about that later.

Rubbing my bruised ribs, I turned back to the Unseen, who watched me with mixed expressions. "You need to leave," I told them, reaching down to retrieve the soldier's blade from where it was discarded on the ground. It was heavier than I was used to wielding, but I would make do. "Adoranda suspects all Unseen of betrayal and has ordered you be rounded up."

"That's insane," Eustace replied, the other Unseen murmuring to each other. "We've got nothing to do with the rebels!"

"It doesn't matter any longer. If you stay here, they will take you. And you need to believe me when I say that she won't hesitate to kill each and every one of you."

Eustace ran a hand through the shock of hair between his ears. "We don't have anywhere to go...."

"That's not entirely true. The rebels are here. They can help get you to safety."

"We're not soldiers," Eustace replied. "We can't fight for them."

"We won't ask you to," came a deeper voice from behind me. I turned to see another Unseen shimmer into existence. He wore the same militia outfit as the Adored soldiers but was missing the hat, revealing hair of deep navy cut short and a pair of pointed ears, much like Azzy's, the left one with a chunk missing out of it.

The other Unseen bristled, huddling further into the corner, but the blue-haired man held his hands out to them. "My name is Kaine, and I'm with the Rebellion. Rest assured, we only require what you are willing to give. Nothing more. Whether you see eye-to-eye with us or not, let me get you to safety first. The rest can follow."

Eustace looked back at the other Unseen, then turned to Kaine. "Alrigh', we'll go with you. But we make no promises."

Kaine moved in a blur, suddenly standing beside Eustace and offering him a small, silver blade. "Cut off the collars. They'll try and kill you the moment you step outside the door."

The cook blanched at this but nodded, quickly severing the band of leather around his own neck before moving to help the next.

Kaine gave a nod, then directed his attention to me. "You must be Tobias. I was told you'd be around. Are you looking for others?"

"Yes. I'll do my best to convince them to leave."

He handed me another of the small silver blades from a holster at his side. "Get the collars off, then get them outside, and we'll take it from there."

Turning back toward the others, he leveled his stare at each of them. "With me. Move quickly, and don't get too comfortable. The militia have spyglasses that see through our magic, so don't assume you're safe till we've made it far from here. Are you ready?"

They looked frightened out of their minds but nodded along, gathering around Kaine in an uneasy clump. Together, their magic caused the air to shimmer like a mirage as each of them disappeared from sight, the sound of their soft steps drifting down the hall.

Leaving the remaining soldier with their head buried in a bush full of thorns, I headed back down the hallway and toward the opposite end of the chateau. I hid the blade I carried as militia soldiers ran past, shouting back and forth. None I met seemed to have taken any of the Unseen captive, so that was a small relief.

Upstairs, in one of the guest bedrooms, I pushed open the door to find another small group of huddled Unseen. One of them lunged at me, wielding a poker from the fireplace, and I quickly deflected it with the blade I'd taken, then put some distance between us before holding up my hands.

"Master Tobias?" the Unseen asked, the poker falling to the ground in a clatter. A yelp sounded from the wardrobe, and the other adult opened the door to comfort two younglings concealed inside. "What are you doing here?"

"We need to get you outside," I told them, checking over my shoulder down the hall before shutting the door behind me. "Mother has taken leave of her senses. It isn't safe for you here anymore."

"They've already taken so many of us," the Unseen closest to me said. "We can't—We can't leave them behind."

"The Rebellion is here. They're going to do their best to ensure everyone is freed. But right now, we need to get you out. Are there any other Unseen on this floor?"

"No, they've already fled or been taken."

"Understood. The collars you wear need to be removed." I handed them the small silvered blade.

They took it with shaking hands, quickly cutting the band from their neck as I checked the hallway. Smoke still clung to the ceilings, but otherwise, the bulk of the conflict seemed to have migrated to the main level.

Once their collars had been removed, the two adult Unseen scooped the younglings into their arms.

"How will we get through the soldiers?" one of them asked.

"Leave that to me."

Our egress from the chateau was quiet, for the most part. The bombastic sounds of the clash between Adored and Unseen had drifted to the far corners, and by the time we made it down to the main level and through the desecrated foyer, the tension in my gut was primed to burst. Pushing open the heavy wooden door, the daylight from outside was blinding. I paused, listening for any signs of the conflict before waving for the others to follow me.

I heard it before I could see it, the whistling sound that sapped every bit of warmth from my blood. The bolt of light streaked into sight just as I turned to those following me, shouting, "Down!"

We all hit the ground, a streak of fizzling magical energy zipping just over our heads and colliding with the stairs, carving out a hole the size of my fist. The younglings began to cry as the adults whispered strained comforts.

I cursed under my breath, rolling to try and get a better view of where the bolt came from. Since when did Mother's militia have access to long-range magical weaponry? Those were instruments of war.

We were out in the open now and the closest cover was the gardens at least thirty yards away. There was no way I could cover that distance with the others before they'd fire on us again. I could try and cast a ward to catch the projectile, but I was never very good at physical shields and this didn't seem like the best time to be testing out the limits of my borrowed magic.

So, I took the only option left.

"You need to run as soon as I tell you," I said, digging my fingers into the pavement and tensing my muscles in preparation. "I'm going to dash straight ahead and draw their fire. You need to make it over to the hedges. From there, keep moving through the garden till you hit the edge of the property. Hopefully, the Rebellion will find you before you get too far."

"Master Tobias," the Unseen said, his eyes wide with fear. "Thank you."

I couldn't help but see Balthus in the man's eyes. This wouldn't make up for what I did to Azzy and his father, but maybe it would help tip the scales back towards balance.

"Don't thank me till your family is safe," I replied, taking a deep, steadying breath. It was now or never, so I nodded to the Unseen, then sprang forward, my feet catching on the pavement as I dashed in a straight line down the open driveway and toward the main gate.

I didn't get far before the whistling noise returned. Another bolt of pulsating magic trained on me, impossibly fast. Reaching for my aura, I poured my strength into it, focusing it forward and adding layer upon layer till the air in front of me shimmered. The impact was sudden, and the shattering noise deafening as the newly formed ward splintered then gave, the bolt of light hitting dead center, then deflecting to clip my shoulder with searing pain. I didn't stop moving, even as blood poured down my arm, wet and warm. I pushed through, still heading in the same direction as the bolt's origin, my feet thundering against the pavement. The Unseen should have made it to the garden by now, so there was no reason for me to continue onward, and yet I kept moving, reaching into my magic stores once again to rebuild the ward that had narrowly saved my second life. My head was spinning by the third layer, and a familiar pain split through my skull. Cirian's loaned power was waning, and I was running straight toward a return trip to my grave.

Another whistling sound, and I braced for the impact.

A streak of grey and purple in my periphery, and the bolt skittered across the driveway, exploding in a flash of light. I skidded to a halt, holding up the stolen blade toward the newcomer on the pavement, dressed in soldier's garb. They had their back turned to me, facing away from the chateau and towards the entrance gate.

I lacked the strength to Command them, so I would have to hope I could best them with my blade.

"You're bleeding, Tobi."

The deep voice sent chills along my exposed skin. Another whistle, another bolt of light bursting into existence from the tower a few hundred feet away. Before I could react, the newcomer moved in a blur, their hands glowing with purple light as they batted the bolt away, and it drove into the ground like the last one. Their hat slipped off their head in the motion, revealing lavender hair and a pair of pointed ears.

"Azzy." My voice was weaker than I anticipated, and my head swam as the strain of holding onto my ward took its toll.

He was beside me in a second, wrapping an arm under mine and bearing the brunt of my weight as he moved us off the driveway and towards the gardens. "Remind me that we need to have a serious conversation about your incessant need to stand out."

I wanted to laugh, but the best I could do was chuckle, the ward around me crumbling as I reached the bottom of my reserves, and the pounding headache set in.

"Did the others make it?" I asked as we cleared the hedges, ducking down long enough that Azzy could get a look at my shoulder. He tore a shred of fabric from the edge of my disguise as if it were paper, tying it quickly around the wound. I hissed a breath as he tightened it down.

"Kaine has them," he replied, inspecting his work. "I came out to cover their escape before I join the force inside. They're working on breaking into the cellar."

"Guess I should thank you," I said, trying to laugh again, but what came out sounded broken and harsh.

"Not necessary," he replied, peeking over the hedges and then ducking down quickly as another bolt soared over us, setting a row of rosebushes on fire across the path. "I was already in the neighborhood."

"What kind of weapon is that?" I asked, needing to distract myself from the growing list of pains threatening to relieve me of consciousness.

"No bloody idea. I've not seen anything like it before. Leave it to Adoranda to save the most dangerous toys for herself." He went quiet for a moment, but then his face was in front of mine, concern bending his features.

Shit, I must have passed out for a second. Gods, he was pretty. Especially when his violet eyes were wide, and his lavender hair was pushed back off his forehead so he couldn't hide behind it.

"You still with me, Tobi?"

"Mostly," I confirmed, giving my head the slightest nod. "Sorry, I flew a little close to the sun earlier, and I'm paying for it."

"No troubles. If we can hide out long enough for Kaine to get back, I'll send you with him to—"

"No!" I shouted, sickly adrenaline flooding my veins with icy panic. "I'm okay. I need to help get Bastien out of there. They're going to kill him."

"I know," Azzy replied, a hand on my uninjured shoulder to keep me in place. "But you're in no shape to move right now, Tobi."

"I'm fine," I lied, shrugging him off. "And it doesn't matter. If Bastien dies, then I'm dead all over again."

Another whistling, and we both flinched as the explosion went off, filling the air around us with dust.

"Shit, they're getting closer." Azzy hooked a finger under my chin, raising my gaze to meet his. "Stay put. I'll be right back."

"Wait, Azzy, please don't leave me here—"

His body shimmered in a haze, then vanished.

I was alone in the garden.

Without the whistling sound, I could hear the bubbling fountain a few dozen yards away. I wasn't far from where Cirian and I used to spar one another. On the other side of the garden, a bird sang a hopeful song, oblivious to the destruction around it. I focused on its song, hoping that it would keep me from slipping away again.

Before long, I heard footsteps, followed by what sounded like the wheels of a wagon on the paved driveway. Azzy was right. They were getting closer. And I was an easy target, bleeding on the azaleas.

"This way," a soft voice came from my right.

I turned to see a pair of eyes looking at me from the bushes, followed by a clawed hand, outstretched and beckoning me with a come-hither motion. The other footsteps grew even louder, the rattling wagon noise unmistakable now.

"Quickly," the voice said again, the hand disappearing into the brush.

What did I have to lose? If I stayed here, they were going to find me eventually. Gritting my teeth and doing my best not to lean on my injured arm, I crawled over to the bushes in question, pushing aside branches till I found the owner of those peering eyes.

"Balthus…" I breathed, coming face to face with the grey-haired Unseen. He wore a dirty pair of coveralls, his beard long and unkempt, and his eyes sunken into his head. But it was him. Of that, I was certain.

"Quickly," he repeated, turning around and moving in a crouch through the cover of the brush.

With great effort, I followed, wincing with each branch that dug into the wound on my shoulder. My mind raced. Did Balthus know that his son was here, in the garden that he'd been sequestered to for all these years? Did he realize that he was closer to liberation than he'd ever been before? Did he recognize me, the man responsible for sending his son away?

Moving out from under the brush, Balthus deftly maneuvered over to a glass-paned greenhouse, ducking behind one of the walls, his outline becoming obscured by the frosted glass. I did my best to mimic his movements, but I was far less graceful in my weakened state, and I knocked into one of the large clay pots in rows outside of the greenhouse. The resounding noise of the pot colliding with glass echoed through the garden like the lone songbird, calling all who could hear to its location.

"Over there!" someone shouted.

I rounded the greenhouse, coming alongside Balthus and lowering myself down. Through the paned glass, I could see two shadows approaching from the main path, moving quickly. The stolen blade hung off my belt, and it would take some maneuvering to draw it in my position.

Balthus silently reached over to one of the pots, producing a small trowel from the dirt and clutching it to his chest. He gave me a look that told me he understood fighting was the only way either of us were getting out of here. I only wished I could have spoken, could have told him that his son was out there. That if we could somehow make it through the next few minutes, he could see him again.

"Come out of there," the commanding voice ordered us.

Neither of us moved.

"Angle thirty-two degrees east," the voice continued, speaking so softly I had to strain to hear them. "Fire in three, two, one—"

A sharp whistling, and the greenhouse walls imploded. Glass rained down on us, thousands of tiny daggers slicing into our skin and burrowing where they could. Without the cover of the greenhouse, we could see the two soldiers standing just a few yards away and further down the path, some sort of contraption on wheels, smoke billowing from the end of a long barrel.

Mustering the last bit of strength, I pushed myself from the ground, drawing the blade from my belt. The handle was slick, and I realized it was my blood oozing from the dozens of cuts sprawling across my hands. Balthus took his place beside me, giving me a solemn nod as we accepted the fate ahead of us.

How fitting it was that I would die beside the man whose life I had destroyed. A sort of cosmic karma, trying to balance the infinite scales of reality. It brought a moment of eerie calm to me at that moment. To know that my life was nearly over. Maybe if I was quick enough, I could make sure Balthus had the best chance to escape.

It was the least I could do for him now.

The soldiers eyed us, their wariness fading by the second, replaced by a foolhardy confidence. One of them raised a device to their mouth, speaking into it.

"Prepare another round, same coordinates. Fire in three, two, one—"

Balthus and I braced ourselves, and I wrapped whatever dregs of magic I could pull into my aura around him, hoping it would be enough to keep the damage from being lethal.

But the shot never came.

The soldiers turned to look back at the weapon, and then one of them swore, a fresh rivulet of blood pouring down his cheek from a slash across his face. He reached for his weapon, but the shimmering image of Azzy flickered into reality as he struck, his clawed hand wrapped in violet light as he dug into the soldier's chest, ripping out a chunk of flesh. The man collapsed to the ground, moving no more. The other soldier moved to strike, but Azzy was faster, knocking them off their feet. As he knelt down to deliver a slash across the soldier's throat, Balthus let out a whimpering breath.

"Azrael?"

The Unseen man looked up from his kill, flicking his wrist to rid his claws of the bits of flesh that clung to them. His eyes widened as they fell on his father, for what I knew was the first time in decades.

"Papa?"

Balthus moved to greet his son, but then a whistling filled the air, and all I could do was watch as the older man shoved Azzy off his feet, the bolt of light striking him squarely in the chest. He hung in the air for a moment, his hand still outstretched, reaching for his son. Then he crumpled to the ground.

I couldn't think. Couldn't process what happened. My body moved of its own volition, running for the weapon, fingers gripping the bloodied handle of my blade as I drove it into the back of the soldier who clung to it as weakly as he clung to life. He uttered his last breath, and then the garden was quiet.

So, so quiet.

# FIFTEEN
## DEAD ON ARRIVAL

The gardens surrounding Chateau Greene had always served as an escape for me. Whether I was a teenager, fencing with Cirian, a child playing hide-and-seek with Azzy, or strolling along with Lynette on one of our many walkabouts, talking about all the ways she wanted to change the world we lived in.

It was a place where I could be at peace, even when the rest of my life was chaos.

It was also the place where I destroyed a man's soul and ripped his child away. Now, it was the place where I watched that same man die, nestled in the arms of his beloved son.

"Papa," Azzy muttered, cradling Balthus' head in his lap. "I'm sorry it took me so long to make it back. I always wanted to come back for you. Always."

Balthus' eyes fluttered, a wet breath sucking in. The bolt had carved a perfect hole straight through his chest. Any hope of getting him to a healer would be a fool's errand.

"I… I never… wanted you to come back."

"Don't say that." Azzy's face crumpled as he hugged his father's head.

"Better off… out there… so proud, Azrael. So…."

Balthus didn't speak again.

Azzy wept, his body shaking as a wail built in his chest, bellowing out a noise that was more beast than man. After a moment, he lay his father to rest, folding his hands over the wound on his chest and closing his eyes.

I felt numb, rooted in place a few feet away from my childhood friend as he mourned. Mourned the life he'd never get back. Because of me. Because of my mother. Because of the imbalance in the world.

For the first time since I'd been brought back to life, I wondered at that moment if I had suffered enough. The more I learned about my cruel first life, the more I knew that there was no punishment befitting my actions. I was the source of so much suffering, and yet I had been given not just one life—filled to the brim with privilege—but a second. A courtesy extended to so few. And what was I doing with this second chance? Sure, I had helped some of the Unseen escape, but that was so little compared to the opposite side of the scales. Drops of water contrasting a vast ocean of transgressions—with more coming from every memory that unearthed itself in my mind.

Tobias Greene was a blight.

"Tobi."

Azzy—no, *Azrael*. He was no longer the boy who caused my stomach to flutter—stood now, looking down at his father, the late-morning light warming his skin to a deep russet. He'd grown in our time apart. Where I'd always been the taller one as boys, he now bested me by a few inches. The color of his hair had changed as well, lightening with age to a gentle lavender. And even through my melancholia, I couldn't ignore his beauty.

"Yes?" I replied, my voice cracking around the lump in my throat.

"We need to go."

"Right."

There would be time for us to talk, I told myself. Once our task was finished, and Bastien and the other Unseen were safe. If I survived the coming hours, then there would be time.

Maybe I could figure out a way to make up for a fraction of the misery I'd caused him.

Leaving Balthus at rest in the garden, Azrael and I made our way back up to the Chateau, circumventing the main entrance for the servant door that led directly to the kitchen. Inside, a small group of Unseen stood by the cellar doors. They were each in the militia's uniforms, but they'd been torn and bloodied in various places. One of them looked up as Azrael approached, and I recognized them as Kaine, the blue-haired one who had helped the other Unseen to safety.

"We've cleared the rest of the chateau, Azrael. Adoranda has warded the door herself, so we're having some trouble getting through."

Kaine spoke to Azrael as if he were waiting for further orders. Was Azrael leading this operation?

"I can break it," Azrael responded, his voice still thick. He looked up at the rest of the Unseen, taking the opportunity to match each of their stares. "Thank you, my brothers. My heart is heavy with the loss we share. Friends. Lovers. Fathers." He paused, taking a moment to regain his composure. "I carry those burdens with you. But we're another step closer to the end and another step closer to a brighter future. I'll ask you once more, are you with me?"

The Unseen each placed a closed fist over their heart. It wasn't just a sign of respect but of devotion, I realized. These men would follow Azrael to their own deaths without hesitation.

What kind of magic gave Azrael such influence over them?

"We're with you, Azrael," said Kaine, the others nodding in approval. "Let's make the heartless wretch wish she never drew breath."

Azrael stepped up to the cellar doors. The wooden frame recessed into the floor shimmered with a golden translucence as his fingers ran along it. He closed his eyes, taking a deep breath in. Suddenly, his hand began to glow with a violet light, and he raised it high over his head, then brought it down with a speed nearly invisible to my eyes, landing with a thunderous collision. The floor underneath my feet rumbled as cracks appeared in the golden ward laid over the doors. Azrael raised his hand again, a trickle of blood pouring down and dripping onto the crown of his head. He struck again, another blow that widened the cracks in the ward and sounded like the shattering of a pane of glass. On the third strike, the golden magic gave way, breaking into a thousand tiny fragments that drifted into the air like confetti before dissipating. Reaching down to the round handle, Azrael pulled the door open, stepping aside and grinning at Kaine.

"Easy as that," he said, shaking his bloodied hand.

"Come on, lads," Kaine said, the edges of his body becoming translucent with shimmering magic. "Stay close, and don't let Azrael get himself killed." The others quickly followed suit, vanishing one by one.

"The confidence is very reassuring," Azrael called down the stairs of the cellar. He looked up at me then, his smile fading. "What is it?"

"Just what is your role in the Rebellion?" I asked, trying to fit the pieces together in my mind.

Azrael huffed a laugh. "Why does it matter?"

"They trust you implicitly."

"And I trust them. We grew up together. Kaine and the rest of them found me when I was young. Looked after me. We came up under Rudderkin himself. He took us in when we had nowhere else to go."

Because of me. He had no place to go because of me. I had handed him over to a life of warfare and pain. And he had no idea.

"Are you ready?" he asked, motioning toward the stairs.

I nodded, joining him at the top of the staircase. Without another word, we descended into the darkness.

The air was stale and moist underneath the chateau. Azrael produced a glass orb from his coat, and it illuminated in his hand, shedding light around us in a halo. At the base of the stairs, the dirt floor was littered with footprints—signs of the flurry of activity the cellar had seen. Barrels of wine lined the far wall, the opposite stacked with shelves piled with sacks of vegetables and cured meats. There were no signs of the supposed prisoners, not even the sound of stifled breaths trying to conceal themselves. My skin itched with the thought of being underground, and I could taste the earth in my mouth, but then Azrael motioned for me to follow him, and we moved deeper into the space. Between two barrels of wine, there was a single door, double the width of a normal opening and reinforced with steel rivets. Even I had no idea what lay behind the door, my adolescent explorations having always halted in this room, as the steel door was consistently locked.

Azrael ran a hand over the lock, then handed me the light. I took it, relishing in its warmth as I realized my limbs were icy cold.

"Maybe we should try knocking?" Azrael suggested, flashing me a quick grin.

I rolled my eyes. "I'm not sure announcing ourselves is the best strategy."

Azrael knelt to examine the keyhole. "You'd be surprised. One thing is for certain: your mother is much better at Hide-and-Seek than you are."

"Do you think this orb would break if I smacked you upside the head?"

Azrael laughed at this, the deep sound rumbling in his chest. "Temper, temper. Glad to see some things never change." He placed his hand over the lock, muttering a string of words as his skin glowed with violet light. With a soft click, the lock gave way. He pushed the door, and before it was even halfway open, a voice called out.

"Glad you could finally join us! My patience was wearing thin."

Azrael entered slowly, and I followed, taking in the unfamiliar space with a growing horror. Half of the space was filled by a giant cage, iron bars forming a cube, with a dozen or so Unseen huddled in the center of it. The other half served as a grotesque torture chamber, with shackles hanging from the walls, a cluster of tables each fashioned with restraints, and a selection of "instruments" hanging in neat rows along the perimeter. Mother stood in the center of this space, a jeweled dagger pressed to the throat of Bastien as he struggled against the restraints that confined him to the chair. Behind them, Cirian, the Cardinal, Renata, and Lorelei watched on, all but Lorelei displaying varying levels of disgust.

"Adoranda," Azrael addressed my mother, positioning himself between her and the cage that held his brethren. "Of all the times I imagined my return to Chateau Greene, I never expected such fanfare. You have my deepest thanks. However, I'm going to have to ask for you to release these men to me."

Mother scoffed, the tip of her dagger drawing a trickle of blood on Bastien's throat. "Am I supposed to remember you? You will have to excuse me, mongrel, but I do not know you from Adam. Though, I assume that you speak for your kind. Such a shame, really, that your treachery would force my hand. I had grown rather fond of at least a few of you. Now, I will have to start over from scratch."

"Then let us speak civilly," Azrael continued, commanding the room nearly as well as Mother did. "Neither of us wishes to see any more precious blood spilled today."

Mother chuckled at this, her fiery gaze locked on Azrael. "That is where you are wrong, mongrel. Your blood is nothing but a part of the slaughter. There have been countless animals before you, and there will be countless after you have been bled dry."

"Then what of him?" Azrael said, pointing to Bastien. "Will you deny the Church their right to judge him for his supposed crimes against the Source?"

The Cardinal and Cirian stiffened at that, both of them tense as they stood shoulder-to-shoulder.

"That does not concern you, mongrel."

Azrael's eyes scanned the room in search of something. "How about your other prisoner? Crassus? What has become of him?"

"Ah, yes, the unbreakable mongrel. My Truthsayer had quite the ordeal getting through to him. I am afraid the process left him rather drained." She points a finger at the far corner of the room where a body lay slumped against the wall. "I must commend you. His loyalty is unmatched."

Azrael took a step toward the body, and Adoranda pressed the knife further into Bastien's neck, causing a groan to escape his lips.

"Stop!" I yelled, moving into the room properly. A splitting pain shot through my skull as I realized I had tried to issue a Command to halt her. Without the aid of my mask, Mother's eyes were on me in an instant, the controlled calm on her face slipping.

"Tobias."

On her tongue, my name was a curse.

Azrael stepped in front of me, but I pushed him aside, facing my mother head-on. "Release him at once, Mother. This is over."

"Over?" she repeated, her voice resonating against the walls till she came from every direction. "Has your death robbed you of your senses, boy? There is none who can stand against me. Not even an army of these *mongrels—*"

she snaps with fingers, a shower of golden sparks falling to the ground as a pulse of magic rolls over me like a wave. To my left, near where the Unseen lay unconscious, two of Azrael's companions became visible as the magic collided with them, knocking them against the wall. A third by the cage door appeared blasted backward as well. Renata lunged to hold a blade to his chest, moving him away from the cage. "It was a noble effort to resist, but ultimately pointless."

She moved the knife from Bastien's throat to the side of his face, running the tip of the blade along his cheek, carving a thin line of crimson. "I will give you one last chance. Where is my daughter?"

Bastien's eyes were on me as he gritted his teeth but gave no answer.

"*Speak.*"

The force of Mother's magic sucked the air from my lungs. Azrael clawed at his throat beside me, Cirian slapped a hand over his mouth, and even Renata began to babble incoherently. Only the Cardinal and Lorelei seemed unaffected by the strength of Mother's Command.

"She was with me… during the attack," seethed Bastien, his eyes bulging as he spoke. "Couldn't… see where she went. I don't know… where she is now."

Mother looked over at Lorelei, who gave her a curt nod.

Bastien was telling the truth.

"Then you're of no further use to me," said Mother plainly, any passion in her voice drying up as she straightened herself. With a flourish, she maneuvered the knife till the blade faced downward, then plunged it into Bastien's chest.

A sickening cracking sound filled the room as he let out a wet gasp.

"No!" I cried, lunging for Bastien.

"Now!" Azrael shouted. Kaine burst into existence beside him.

Chaos erupted around me as I reached Bastien, kneeling down and grabbing his shoulders to steady him. His body was limp, though his eyes still found me, something sparking behind them, even as blood began to spill over his bottom lip.

"Stay with me," I told him, working on the knots that held him in place.

"Bastien, stay with me."

From the corner of my eye, the two Unseen reached the body of the prisoner, hefting him onto his feet. On the other side of me, Azrael was trading blows with Mother, showers of golden sparks firing in every direction as his claws made contact with the wards around her body. She cackled like a madwoman when she landed a blow, knocking Azrael back a few feet in the process.

"You can't best me, mongrel!"

Cirian was at my side by the time I unfastened the ropes, catching Bastien before he was able to fall to the floor. The wound in his chest seeped blood, and it smeared across my clothing as I pushed him back into the chair.

"Help him," I begged Cirian, my voice hoarse.

Cirian nodded, placing a hand around the hilt of the knife and muttering a string of words as his skin began to glow. Swearing, he pulled back to reveal his palms covered in blood and the wound just as deep. "Damnation. It's a Sanguine blade. It's leaching my magic away. We need to remove it."

One of the Unseen crashed into the table beside us, tumbling to the floor. From the far side of the room, I could see Azrael and Mother locked in step while Renata and Kaine were having a standoff of their own. Lorelei had somehow disappeared in the chaos.

"Hold on," said Cirian, taking my hands and placing them around the hilt once more. "Keep pressure on it. I need to convince Sancha to intervene here."

"But he's Reviled," I argued. What was he thinking? The Cardinal would never agree to help him.

Cirian stood, his gaze drifting from Bastien to me. "Put your trust in me."

I nodded, and Cirian was gone.

Bastien let out a groan, his weight shifting forward, and I leaned my shoulder against him to keep him in place. He tried to speak, but more blood poured from his mouth, dripping down onto my arms and slicking my skin through my clothes.

"Shh," I coaxed him, my eyes burning as I looked at his bloodied face. "It's going to be okay. You're going to be okay."

His hands wrapped around mine, his grip weak but there. His lips moved again, but there was no sound, only the pleading in his eyes that twisted a blade of its own into my chest.

"Azrael!" one of the Unseen shouted as Azrael fell back from a second blow. But he picked himself up with ease, engaging Mother once more. Taking a moment to watch him, his attacks seemed…reserved. As if he were merely wanting to occupy her rather than inflict damage.

Kaine had made it to the cage now, one of the other Unseen holding off Renata's assault as he worked on the lock.

"Tobias," a strong voice came from behind me, and I looked over my shoulder at the Cardinal.

My hands shook as I removed them from the wound, my skin dyed red. The Cardinal knelt, getting eye-level with Bastien as she placed a hand on his forehead. His labored breathing quieted, his wide eyes watching the woman as her hands moved down to the blade protruding from his chest.

"I'm going to remove it," she said calmly. "Deep breath now."

With another gut-wrenchingly wet noise, the blade dislodged from Bastien, and the Cardinal let it clatter to the ground. Using both hands, she covered the wound, her skin glowing so bright with cerulean light that I had to look away.

After a dozen or so agonizing seconds, she removed her hands, her skin clean of any blood.

"The Source has blessed you," she said softly, leaning down and planting a gentle kiss on Bastien's forehead. He stared at her, bewildered. "Do not squander it."

"Thank you," I breathed, the twisted knot of anxiety in my gut loosening ever-so-slightly.

"Get a move on, Tobi!"

Azrael's exclamation snapped me back to reality, and I hooked an arm under Bastien's armpit, hoisting him to his feet. Renata was backed into a corner, the two Unseen carrying the prisoner had almost made it to the door, and the Kaine had just managed to get the lock on the cage open while Mother and Azrael continued their scuffle in the center of the room. As

# THE SECOND AWAKENING

Mother caught sight of Bastien, she knocked Azrael aside with a wave of her hand, the air around her shimmering with magical energy.

"*Halt!*"

The Command rolled over the room, all movement ceasing as our bodies locked in place. Even the Cardinal, who seemed unaffected till now, was immobilized.

Mother took advantage of the situation, retrieving the sanguine blade from where the Cardinal had discarded it and walking towards those closest to the door—the two Unseen rebels carrying the now-stirring Unseen captive. Crassus, Azrael had called him.

"This is all an effort of futility," Mother said, dragging the tip of her weapon along the arm of one of the rebels. "Even after all you've endured, your fate is inevitable. Let it be known that I will burn every last one of you from existence until there is nothing left but ashes and sorrow. And when your world has been reduced to atoms, and memory of your kind has faded into the annals of history, know this—I will endure. I will be there to make sure the Magi forget every detail of your so-called rebellion." She stood in front of Crassus, his eyes—one swollen shut from the injuries to his face—flickering open, then widening as she sunk the blade of her dagger into his stomach. "Remember this: No one will mourn the mongrels."

A whimper of pain escaped the captive's mouth as Mother sank the blade to the hilt, twisting it with a sparkle of glee in her crystalline eyes. I never wanted to pluck my own out so badly, if only to cease sharing a trait with her.

My limbs refused to budge. Had I reached the end of my brief second life? I had to admit, dying at the hand of my mother had been on the table ever since I learned it was her who orchestrated the attempt on Lynette's life. But to be there, standing mere feet from her and completely paralyzed by the control she had mastered over nearly two centuries—my body quaked with fear.

"What?"

Mother's voice shook me from my terror, her expression twisted in confusion, her grip still on the hilt of the dagger, but Crassus' hands wrapped around hers, holding her in place, claws sinking into her flesh.

"You're wrong," he spoke, voice hoarse but unflinching. "They will remember us. They will remember when the lowest among them refused to yield." Crassus' body began to flicker, like he was trying to turn invisible, but the magic wouldn't hold. "When the Unseen made a place for themselves. They will know because you cannot erase us."

*"Release me!"* Mother's voice reverberated, the power of her words once again forcing the air from my lungs.

But Crassus held fast, the frequency of the flickering image of his body increasing, till he strobed like a malfunctioning light. The incandescence of his skin grew brighter till he was difficult to look at.

Then he spoke his final words.

"We will not be forced into the dark."

Burning white hot, Crassus broke free of the hold of his fellow Unseen, wrapping his arms around Mother as the light of his body reached blinding status. Mother shrieked, her clothing catching fire. All at once, the oppressive pressure of her magic dissipated, and we all stumbled forward, our bodies catching up to the willed momentum.

"Hurry!" Azrael shouted, moving to the cage and ripping open the door.

I clung to Bastien, pushing him forward as Mother continued to scream. I couldn't look at Crassus directly, but the heat coming from him was enough to singe my skin at this distance, so I could only imagine the intensity of it up close.

We made it through the door to the wine cellar, a stream of bodies eclipsing the brilliant light pouring through the doorway. The wooden frame of the door began to smoke as Azrael made it through, the smell of singed hair burning my nostrils as we hit the staircase. Mother let out another shriek, her voice nearly drowned out by the crackling of fire that was swiftly consuming the room. Bastien and I made it up into the kitchen, dark smoke billowing now, heavy and choking, as I continued to pull him toward the exit. Kaine led the rescued prisoners out first, making sure all were accounted for before ducking through the door leading outside. As Cirian and the Cardinal made it up into the kitchen, the floor beneath us rocked as an explosion sounded below. A jet of fire shot through the open door, blasting Azrael up the last few steps and landing him atop the long wooden table. He roared with laughter, patting out the small fires that smoldered on his jacket. A terrible groaning noise sounded, and plaster rained down from the ceiling above.

Cirian pulled Azrael off the table, helping put out the rest of the flames on his clothes. Another groan from above, and more plaster fell, long cracks appearing along the ceiling.

"Let's get out of here!" I shouted, pulling Bastien along with me. We weren't far from the door and its promise of fresh air.

After the third step, the ground beneath us lurched as another explosion sounded, the door to the cellar belching fire once more. I stumbled over my feet, disrupted by the sudden movement, and took Bastien down with me, the two of us landing in a heap. The ceiling above us gave way then, splintered wood and plaster thunderously raining down. I rolled, covering Bastien with my body as best I could, and braced for the impact. But it never came. Bastien pushed me off of him, both of us staggering to our feet as the debris and furniture that fell through floated in the air just above our heads, suspended by a strange blue light. A few steps back, the Cardinal held out her hand, her brow twisted in concentration as she slowly moved her arm, the detritus moving along with her, then falling harmlessly to either side.

She didn't look fatigued in the slightest by the effort.

"Thank you, Your Eminence."

The Cardinal gave me a slight nod. "Let us move quickly."

Outside of the Chateau, the air was clear and inviting, the warm sun still hanging high in the sky. Kaine and the other Unseen were already at the gate, it appeared, and once Azrael had cleared the door, that was everyone. Well, almost everyone.

"What about Crassus?" I asked, turning to Azrael.

"There won't be anything left of him," he replied. "We should keep moving. There's no telling if another explosion will blast the roof off this place."

"What of us?" asked the Cardinal, motioning to herself and Cirian. "Should we consider ourselves to be hostages of the Rebellion?"

Azrael shook his head. "Not at all. You're free to go whenever you like, and I thank you for your help. However, I can't let you take Bastien. I've made a promise to someone very important to me to see him returned safely. If that's going to cause a problem, I'm sure there is something we can work out."

Cirian looked to the Cardinal as if he were trying to get a read.

After a moment, the Cardinal nodded. "No judgment will be passed today. Come, Cirian. We should report to the Council of Magi what has transpired here."

"Yes, Your Eminence." Cirian's dark eyes lingered on me before he hurried away, catching up to the Cardinal's long strides.

"You're safe," Azrael said to Bastien, clapping a hand on his shoulder. "I need to handle one more thing, but you two should head outside of the gate. Kaine will be there to get you to the rendezvous point."

Somehow, I knew that he was going back for Balthus. Guilt swelled within me, but I couldn't express it at the moment. Bastien seemed to pick up on my desire to stay with Azrael. "I'll be okay to make it outside the gate, Tobias. You should help Azrael."

I nodded, releasing my death grip on him. He limped a bit but managed to hit a stride as he headed for the gate at the end of the drive.

"Guess it's just you and me, then." Azrael smiled sadly, moving past me and heading into the garden. By the time I'd caught up with him amongst the hedges, the fire had spread to almost half the Chateau, the sound of glass breaking and cracking wood echoing through the gardens.

Balthus lay where we left him, his hands folded over the wound in his chest. Here, surrounded by the blooms, he looked almost peaceful, though his death had been far from it.

Azrael knelt next to him, his fingers brushing through the dulled, grey hair at his father's temples. "Come sit with me a moment," he said, motioning to the other side of Balthus.

I mirrored his position, rubbing my palms across my thighs.

"I always hated this place," Azrael said eventually, his eyes trained on Balthus. "Papa and I used to talk into the night about all the places we wanted to see when we left Chateau Greene. He'd worked in that kitchen nearly his entire life, you know. Decades of hard work, with almost nothing to show for it. Except for me, I guess. He told me that I was the happiest accident. That his lover wasn't ready for younglings, so when I came along, it sped up their split. He wasn't resentful or anything, just honest. He wanted nothing more than for me to escape this place. Yet, when the day finally came, and they stripped me from his arms, all I could think about was what I would give to have stayed."

Tears burned in my eyes, spilling over and onto the grass beneath me.

"Papa," Azrael continued, his own violet eyes shining as he took his father's hand. "Look, I made it back. I've seen so much, so many things I wanted to share with you. I always hoped that you'd find your way out of here, that you would break free from the madame and all of the pain of this place. But it doesn't matter anymore. I made it back. And now I'm going to take you with me."

Azrael leaned down, kissing his father's forehead.

"It's my fault," I said before I could think better of it. "When they took you away, it's my fault it happened."

Azrael's eyes were on me as he straightened.

"I didn't know that it was happening," I explained, hoping beyond hope that he'd understand. "You were my best friend, and I didn't want you to leave. You know that. But Mother... she'd found out about Balthus' plans. He wanted to leave the Chateau, and she took you as leverage to hold over him. She kept him trapped here, telling him that if he remained loyal, you'd be safe. I'm sorry, Azzy. I'm so, so sorry."

Azrael watched me for a moment longer, then stood.

"Help me lift him."

Did he hear anything I said?

With a bit of struggle, we managed to get Balthus balanced on Azrael's shoulder.

Without another word, Azrael headed for the edge of the garden. Once we passed through the gate, we kept moving till we hit the tree line. Turning back one last time, I watched my childhood home burn in the distance and wondered if Mother would burn along with it.

# SIXTEEN
## PLAY DEAD

"She's awful, Lenny. Truly dreadful. I don't know how you stand her."

Lynette cut a sideways glance at me, pausing at the crosswalk as we waited for the light to change. How many more times would we be able to wander around the Magi City like this now that she was set to assume Mother's position in the morning? The Ascension ceremony had lasted far longer than I had hoped and proved to be quite boring as far as parties go. Lots of handshaking and arse-kissing and whatever it is that Mother does to prove her superiority over the other houses.

At least the Floating Gardens had served as a picturesque backdrop. I should remember to add it to the list of places I take my "dates" should my role continue under Lynette's instruction.

"You complain too much, Tobi. Don't worry, I won't make you spend any alone time with Amelia."

"Or her dolls," I added, shivering at the memory of a night filled with porcelain faces and lifeless eyes.

"Or her dolls," Lynette agreed, moving into the crosswalk after the light changed. The streets were nearly empty this time of night, and it only struck at that moment, the oddity of Amelia hosting an event so late in the evening. But my head still buzzed with the alcohol from the party, and the promise of more libations awaiting at the VanDoughtens was enough to keep me moving forward.

"So, what is your first plan of action, oh mighty Ascendant? Tell me how you're going to start fucking with Mother's reputation."

"There are lots of things that I want to change," Lynette replied, her heels echoing along the pavement like the ticking of a clock. Steady and consistent. "But I'll have to be careful not to come in blazing. Mother says that influence is a practice in subtlety. I have to make the others think that they're coming up with solutions of their own volition."

I snorted a laugh. "Says the woman who can bend anyone to her will. Priceless."

"What would you do, Tobi? If our roles were reversed?"

"Well, that would never happen as I've got this thing between my legs—"

Lynette stopped, and I had to retreat several steps back to her. "I'm serious. What would you do if it were you stepping into Mother's role tomorrow?"

"I'd do whatever she told me to do," I answered honestly. "Because there's no way that she's giving up that control, even if she has to give up the title."

Lynette stayed quiet, her head tilting back to gaze up at the stars peeking through the space between the buildings.

"Did I say something to upset you?"

She shook her head, adjusting to look at me again. "No, you have the right of it. She will not rescind control of the council, even if I sit at the head. Try all I might, I simply lack the resources to defy her. She has the wealth of knowledge that far exceeds my own and the trust and loyalty of those in power. I am the youngest on the council by nearly a century—even if I could defy Mother, they'd never heed my word over hers."

I took her hand in mine, holding it to my chest. The night air had chilled her skin. "Then they are fools, the whole lot."

Lynette smiled, but there was a melancholia that clung to her still. Was it just the lingering shadow of our mother, hanging over the two of us as it had done since we were old enough to be aware of it?

"We spoke once," Lynette said, her hand firmly planted against my sternum. "When we were young, and the world was much more vast than it turned out to be, of the life we would lead if we no longer belonged to Mother. Do you remember it?"

"I do."

"An equal share, that's what I wanted. A chance to right the scales of balance across our world. I've dreamed about it ever since I was little."

I nodded along, a sobering clarity starting to sink in. "I told you it sounded like a fairy tale."

"You also said that you would help me make it come true, should the opportunity come."

"Did I?" I said with a chuckle.

"Would you still say it today, Tobias? If I asked you to risk it all for a chance at the dream I shared with you all those years ago, would you consider it?"

"Of course," I agreed, though my voice jumped an octave. "But what are we actually talking about here? We were children then."

Lynette pulled her hand back, shaking her head. "Right, of course. We can talk about it later. I just… I wanted to make sure that my brother was still on my side."

"I'm always on your side, Lenny."

We crossed the street, leaving the hypotheticals behind as we approached the VanDoughten residence. It wasn't their full estate—that was in the countryside among rolling green hills—but rather the place where they stayed while conducting business within the city. A rowhouse, three stories tall, clad with bleached brick and adorned with golden gilded windows. It certainly gave the impression of pomp.

Lynette navigated the stairs leading up to the front door, pausing before she reached for the knob. She turned back to me.

"Promise me something before we go in, Tobi."

"Why do I suddenly feel like a doe trapped in the maw of a steel trap?"

"Relax," Lynette teased with a laugh. "I may not have been completely honest with you about the reason we're here tonight."

"If you are about to tell me this is a birthday party for one of the dolls, I will walk home, Lenny. I'm not joking—"

"It's a bit more serious than that," she said, catching me by the wrist before I could turn away. "Just… keep an open mind, okay?"

I nodded, the intensity of Lynette's gaze extinguishing any further pith. She looked nervous. More nervous than she had been in front of a hundred of the most important members of our society earlier that night.

# THE SECOND AWAKENING

*What was I walking into?*

With a gentle knock from Lynette, the door opened. A mousy, blonde-headed girl answered, wispy curls hanging around her face where they'd pulled free from her bun. She wore a simple knit sweater and a skirt that fell past her knees, both riddled with wrinkles.

"Oh, Lynn. I'm so glad to see you." Her pale eyes fell on me, and her smile faltered. "And Tobias."

I gave her a polite nod. "Lovely to see you as well, Amelia. May we come in? The evening has grown a bit cold for my taste."

"Come in," Amelia replied, stepping aside. "They're all in the parlor, Lynn. Everyone's here."

*Everyone? Just what did that mean?*

Amelia led us to the parlor and into a sea of familiar faces.

*My face burned hot. Dear gods.*

Heirs of the Adored houses waited for us, gathered in clumps around the parlor and murmuring with one another. All eyes drifted to Lynette and me when we entered and I immediately wished that I shared the Unseen's magic because I truly wanted to disappear.

"Take a seat, Tobias," Lynette tells me, motioning to an empty spot on the sofa by the window.

I moved through the crowd as quickly as I could, wondering just how many of these heirs I had seduced on the orders of my mother. Sinking into my seat, I directed my attention to Lynette as she addressed the room.

"I'm glad to see so many of you," she said, moving to stand on the rug in the center of the room. Her voice was strong, those nerves I'd caught wind of before all but vanished. "I come to you tonight to speak of a chance at change. Real change."

"What choice did we have?" A brunette close to me asked. "You're the Ascended."

"Exactly, you've identified the issue right there. Too few times we are given an option. The agency to choose for ourselves. I may be the Ascended in title, but rest assured, my mother will cling to her control no matter what the cost. You've all felt the influence of Adoranda Greene, whether it be firsthand or inflicted upon your loved ones. You know what she is capable of. Even as we speak, she plots for the demise of the Unseen Rebellion. Total annihilation. And it will only be the beginning. Once she's squashed the rebels, she'll be ready to expand her influence beyond the Magi Cities and into the lands of mortals."

A wave of murmurs ripples through the room.

"What are you proposing we do to stop her?" asked another heir, a girl with short black hair and eyes like smoldering coals.

Lynette straightened her stance, giving her plea to all. "It will take all of us united against her and the council she's held captive for decades. You represent the future for the Adored, and it will be through our efforts that we will force the hand of change.

"I'm committed to do whatever it takes."

"Then how are you any different from Adoranda?" A young man asked from the opposite side of the room.

Lynette looked around the room, matching the gaze of all who looked upon her. "Because once my mother is removed and her power turned over to me, I will resign it."

The rendezvous point was a clearing in the woods about a mile or so away from the chateau. The smoke from the fire still clung to my nose as we moved into the open space, and I exhaled a sigh of relief at the sight of Bastien. He was propped up against the trunk of a tree, his shirt peeled back around the spot on his chest where Mother had stabbed him.

"Azrael," Kaine greeted us, moving to take the body from Azrael's shoulder.

"It's my father," Azrael explained, handing over Balthus's body to the other Unseen. "I'd like for him to come with us, if you think we can spare the room?"

"Of course," Kaine replied, motioning for two more Unseen to come and join him. He handed the body over, muttering instructions to them.

My eyes were fixed on Bastien. He prodded the thin line where the wound had been with a finger, examining the works of the Cardinal.

"Go to him," a voice came from behind me, and I turned to find Azrael alone now, the others heading back to the groups of Unseen refugees. "He'll want to know you're safe."

I nodded, pausing for a moment before wrapping Azrael up in a hug.

He returned the embrace, strong arms pressing me to him and bringing a sense of comfort I had not yet felt in my second life.

"Thank you," he muttered in my ear.

"For what?" I asked, pulling back to marvel at the way his eyes changed to lavender in the sunlight.

"For choosing me."

He repeated the words from all those years ago, summoning a heat at the nape of my neck that spread like wildfire. He smiled, leaning forward to press his lips to my forehead in a quick motion before releasing his hold on me.

"Our transportation will be here shortly," he said. "I need to go speak with the others."

I nodded, my mouth suddenly too dry to speak. As Azrael left, I wondered just when the boy I'd grown up with became such a beautiful man.

Bastien was still at the base of the tree when I approached, his fingers nimbly fastening the buttons on his shirt. He looked up, his eyes lightening as he spotted me.

"Is there room for one more?" I asked, motioning to the space beside him on the grass.

He nodded, scooting over a bit to allow me to nestle myself against the smooth trunk.

"I'm so relieved you're safe, Bastien."

"I'm so sorry," he says, a sniffling sound causing me to turn and look at him. Tears welled in his eyes as he stared ahead, his hands trembling until he curled them into fists atop his knees. "I tried to get to you at the camp. I shouldn't have left you by yourself. I should have kept you safe, but I couldn't get through—"

His words cut off with a broken sob, and I couldn't help but wrap an arm around him, pulling him into my side.

"You don't have to apologize," I told him, secretly relishing in the way his body fit against mine. "If anything, I should be the one. It was my mother's militia who captured and tortured you, Bastien. They almost got me, too."

Bastien rested his head on my shoulder, his breathing beginning to regulate. "They were awful to the Unseen that was with me. My treatment was child's play compared to what they did to him."

Crassus' swollen face flashed in my mind, and I shivered.

"You're safe now," I said, my hand reaching up to brush the moisture from his cheek. He caught me by the wrist, pulling the hand away from him to investigate the blue gem embedded in my palm.

"What is that?"

Damn. I'd forgotten all about the Anima stone till now.

"Oh, uh, Cirian gave it to me. He wanted to make sure I could defend myself. You know, since I don't have any magic of my own right now."

Bastien's body stiffened, his head lifting off my shoulder to get a better look at the gem. "Cirian *made* this?"

"He's the one that saved me back at the camp. I tried to escape on my own, but I got caught up in the scuffle and ended up bleeding out in a field. He found me there. Healed me and brought me back to the Cradle till we could devise a plan to come after you."

"Why *did* you come after me?" he asked, his grasp on me falling away. "Wait, let me guess, Cirian explained that I would be the only one who could perform the resurrection rite?"

"That was a part of it, sure. I would be lying if I said it wasn't. But there's more."

Bastien turned to me, the warm honey of his eyes pooling in the shade of the leaves above.

"What more?" he asked, his voice almost pleading.

A gentle tug in the pit of my stomach stalled the words on my tongue. That string that I felt when I first awoke into this second life, the attachment I had to Bastien, went taut. Could he feel it, too? This invisible connection that drew me to him like a lifeline?

"There's still something here," I said, finding it harder and harder to catch my breath this close to him. "I know things ended between us, and I still can't remember how or why. But something remains. You can't deny it. It's why you kissed me before, isn't it?"

Bastien nodded, his throat bobbing.

"Did you want to know? How things ended, I mean. I could tell you."

"I'm scared to find out," I admitted. "The more I discover about the life I led before you brought me back, the more I wish I could forget it all. I wasn't a good person, Bast. And if things ended the way I assume they did, then I don't need you to tell me. I know I fucked it up along the way."

Bastien didn't deny the claim. But when he did speak, he said, "You're not a bad person, Tobias. I think sometimes you just need a little reminder."

He reached for me, cupping the side of my face in his warm hand as he leaned in, pressing the lightest of kisses to my lips.

When he pulled away, he took with him all of the fear I'd been hoarding, allowing me to exhale for the first time in what felt like forever.

Bastien nodded off on my shoulder at some point, the tree overhead shielding us from the late morning sun. Azrael came back eventually, explaining the game plan.

"I'll take the refugees with me, and Kaine will escort you and Bastien to the train station. You two can't turn invisible, so there's a different route you'll need to take to the new ops site."

"We're splitting up?" I questioned, suddenly anxious at the thought of being separated from Azrael.

"Just for a little while," he said, a small smile playing across his lips. "Bastien needs to rest. You do, too. It looks like you're about to fall over."

He was right. I was exhausted. My shoulder—not the one Bastien was snoring softly against—was still caked in dried blood, and it ached with each beat of my pulse. Bastien's wound may have been healed over, but he was still worse for wear. Dark circles swelled under his eyes, and his wrists were covered in ligature burns from the restraints.

"Will Lynette be there?" I asked, a bit of shame burning in my cheeks that I hadn't asked about her sooner.

"That's the plan," Azrael replied. "We've had sporadic communication with her since the raid, but she's safe for now."

For now. The words hung over me like a thunderhead.

"We need to get moving," Azrael continued. "Word will have spread about what happened at the Chateau. There will be Adored forces crawling all over this place soon enough."

I nodded, giving Bastien a gentle shake. He bolted upright, then swore under his breath, pressing the heel of his hand against his temple.

"Your transportation is already waiting," Azrael told us. "You two stay safe, and I'll see you both at the site."

"Wha's going on?" Bastien asked sleepily, blinking in rapid succession.

"Come on," I told him, rising to my feet and offering a hand to help him up. "Our chariot awaits."

Azrael gave a small wave before heading over to where the other Unseen waited. As they grouped together, listening to Azrael speak in a hushed voice, the group shimmered like a mirage, then disappeared completely from my sight.

"Where are we going?" Bastien asked, taking my hand and hoisting himself up.

"Azrael says that we're going to a new site for the Rebellion."

"You two seem chummy," Bastien said, his brow furrowed. "I take it you know each other?"

I nodded. "Since we were kids. He and his father worked at Chateau Greene."

"Oh, I guess that makes sense. I'm still not used to hearing folks call him by his first name. Everyone at the Rebellion base was just calling him Rudderkin."

I stopped, turning to look at Bastien. "What did you say?"

Bastien gave me a confused look. "Rudderkin. That's who we were just talking to. You know, the leader of the Rebellion."

Azrael? The leader of the Rebellion? That couldn't be possible. It started when we were merely children. His surname was Fritz, not Rudderkin. Bastien must be mistaken.

Kaine met us by the line of trees at the edge of the clearing, no longer wearing the militia garb he had before. He now wore a plain pale brown sweater and a pair of jeans, the edges frayed at the bottom. "It's a short walk to the road," he said, his gruff voice less harsh outside of life-or-death peril. "Then we're off to the train station."

I nodded, Bastien and I following him as he led us through the wooded area.

"Kaine, may I ask you something?"

"You just did," he said, tossing a sly grin over his shoulder at me. "Speak your mind, Greene."

I flinched at the use of my surname but continued, "Azzy—I mean, Azrael. Is it true that the others call him Rudderkin?"

"Aye," Kaine replied, seemingly not surprised by my line of questioning. "They do. Those close to him still know him as Azrael, though. We trained together as younglings, we did."

"And he's the leader of the Rebellion?" I prodded, still having trouble wrapping my mind around the idea.

"Aye, he is."

"Since when?"

"Since the first Rudderkin up and died."

Oh. Maybe Rudderkin was more of a title, then?

"How long ago was that?"

Kaine eyed me, his stride slowing. "A while ago. You'll have to get the rest of the story from him. It's not something that gets talked about."

His answer didn't do much to alleviate the anxiety buzzing in my stomach, but I nodded, falling back in line with Bastien. About a half hour later, we broke through the trees and found ourselves on a dirt road. An automobile sat in the embankment, hidden by the brush lining the woods. It looked dated, with faded paint and long scratches across the sides. Kaine produced a set of keys from underneath the chassis, using them to unlock the trunk and handing us both a set of clean clothes to change into. Bastien helped me dress the wound on my shoulder, promising to heal it once he was able to get some rest. After changing, Kaine climbed into the driver's seat. Bastien and I took the back seat, and soon enough, we were on our way.

The afternoon sun had stretched long by the time we arrived at the train station just outside of the Magi City. The station itself was quiet, with only a few figures lingering on the platform as we waited for the train to arrive. Kaine had already handed us our tickets while we drove, and I took the time to read over the stub.

One-way ticket to Brierwood. Travel time: three hours. Private cabin.

Bastien's ticket read the same, and by the time the train had pulled into the station, my eyes were heavy, and my shoulder ached, and I yearned for sleep.

Kaine ended up in a separate cabin than we did, but he was just next door, so he warned us that he could hear everything that went on in our cabin.

I didn't get the joke at first, but Bastien wouldn't look me in the eye, which clued me in.

The train departed with a whistle, and we were on our way to Brierwood.

"This is cozy," Bastien said, leaning back in his seat and propping his feet up. "It's like that place we stayed when we went to the opera house in the city. You swore that you'd never let me book accommodations again and that the room looked like a fancy closet."

The specific scenario didn't rise through the din in my mind, but I nodded along, not wanting him to know how much I'd forgotten of our past. Even now, I could barely conjure up a memory at random without a flood of others tagging along, resulting in a deluge of flashing faces and conversations with zero context.

It was exhausting, to be frank. Most of the time, I just pressed them all down, withdrawing into the cramped corner of my mind where I was able to process the current happenings around me.

Bastien's eyes fluttered closed a few minutes into the ride, his breathing evening out and his mouth slightly open. I lay across the seat opposite him, the distance between the two of us minute, but it felt like a chasm that only grew wider the longer I stared at him.

He obviously still cared about me. Why else would he have risked his life to come and find me during the raid? Why else would he have given so much just to bring me back to life?

So, what was this terrible dread that kept swelling in my gut? It was as if that lifeline I'd felt, the connection between Bastien and I, had become twisted and tangled, clinging to all the anxieties and doubts I couldn't abate, until it sank into my stomach, a knotted, thrashing beast.

I wanted to sleep. To calm my mind and dull the edge of pain from my shoulder. But the longer I lay there, the faster my thoughts bombarded me till I was gasping for air, and my pulse thundered in my chest.

Bastien stirred, but I didn't want to face his questions, so I hurried out of the cabin and down the long corridor to the vestibule at the end of the carriage. The door slid open silently, the whipping wind filling my senses all at once and quieting the noise inside my head.

I braced myself against the railing, focusing on taking deep breaths through my nose. The landscape moved by at a dizzying pace, streaks of greens and greys blurring together to create an endless feed of muted colors that lulled me into placidity.

With my mind quieted, I was able to reflect on the last few hours.

One question rose above the others: what fate befell Mother?

Surely, whatever feat of magic Crassus had performed, he'd saved our lives. But, was it enough to stop her for good?

Unlikely.

Azrael had returned to the Chateau. Not only that, but he came as the leader of the Rebellion his father longed to join all those years ago. Balthus was still there, waiting for him. And now he was dead. Just another life shoved through the grinder of my family's influence.

Bastien was safe, which meant that he would be able to perform the resurrection ritual, and I wouldn't have to rely on other's magic. I stared down at the cerulean stone embedded in my palm, running my thumb over the smooth surface.

Would Cirian try and continue his support of the Rebellion from the shadows? Had his previous involvement been revealed to the Cardinal? And why did she let Bastien go so easily? The Reviled and Hallowed were supposedly the gravest threat to one another, and yet she healed his wounds and sent him on his way. Was it a political move so as to not upset the Rebellion? Or was there something more going on behind the curtain of the Church?

Something to do with a prophecy spoken by their very own Acolyte?

The pieces on the board were in motion, though not in patterns I could recognize at that time. For now, it seemed like chaos, simply a dozen different individual gambits, each vying for their place in the world. But there was too much coincidence for it to be naught but serendipity.

Perhaps once my addled mind had been made whole, I would be able to glean more answers. Or perhaps there were none. Only the beautiful chaos of the world on full display before me. If that were the case, I would want to bury my head in the sand, if only to keep from being driven mad by the machinations surrounding me.

At least then, I would be able to rest.

# SEVENTEEN
## DEAD IN THEIR TRACKS

"We'll have your most expensive bottle of red," I told the maître d', his eyes swelling to the size of saucers.

"That won't be necessary," my date quickly added, dropping the menu onto the table in front of him. "I'll have an iced tea, please."

The maître d' looked back at me, his eyes begging for some direction.

"Perhaps just a glass to start off with, then," I told him, handing back the wine list and shooing him away. This "Bastien" was going to be playing hardball. I could tell from the moment he sat down.

Bastien tugged on the cuffs of his sleeves, unrolling them. "You know, when you asked me to join you for dinner after work, fine dining wasn't exactly what I had in mind."

"I have a standing reservation here," I explained. Hoping to put him more at ease, I unfastened a button on my shirt, but the effort prompted an eye roll from the man. "If it's a question of monetary concerns, rest assured that I'll be more than happy to cover—"

"Are you saying I can't afford to eat at a place like this?" Bastien interrupted, raising an eyebrow. "I'm a barista, so this level of elegance is outside of my means?"

"No, I wasn't thinking that at all. I was just offering to cover the—"

"I don't need you to. I'll take care of my own bill, thanks."

"Right. My apologies. Forget I mentioned it."

The night was off to a rough start. Had I been wooing some Adored socialite, they would have swooned at the bottle service and the sterling silver cutlery on the table. But this Bastien character merely scanned the menu, his frown deepening the longer it went on.

"Do they serve anything here that isn't garnished with edible gold? I'm not really a fan of heavy metals in my meal."

"I'm sure they could accommodate such a request," I answered. Bastien gave me a quizzical glance, and I realized I had missed the joke entirely. "Ah, but what fun is life without a little risk?"

Bastien gave a polite chuckle, his attention returning to his menu.

Where the hell was my wine?

"What do you do for work, Tobias?" asked my date, glancing up from his menu.

"I work for the Magi Council, actually. My Mother is Ad—"

"The Council?" interrupted Bastien, leaning forward in his seat. "You mean, you actually work for those power-hungry bastards who make all the rules?"

I abandoned Mother's introduction entirely.

"Yes, you could say that."

"And what do you do for them, exactly?"

"I am an ambassador of the Adored," I explained. "So, mostly, I do this. I entertain those designated by the Council and help them feel comfortable in the city. It can be overwhelming for those that live outside of the hustle and bustle."

"Ah, so you party for a living, then?"

"That's a bit of an oversimplification—"

"I've never met an Adored before. At least none who identified themselves as such. But now that I think about it, you certainly fit the mold of what I expected."

"What's that supposed to mean?"

Bastien motioned to the surrounding restaurant.

"Oh, come now," I said, my words tinged with exasperation. "What would you have preferred? Some dirty little watering hole with loud music and drinks that peel paint off the floor?"

"Sounds like a better time, to be honest."

"Then why did you agree to come tonight?" I asked, anger flaring before I could contain it.

Bastien set down the menu once more, his eyes narrowing at me. "Maybe I thought I saw something else. Something that made me believe you were a different person."

The maître d' returned, setting down our glasses, but Bastien was already standing up. He pulled a billfold from his pocket, handing a bill over to the man. "Thanks for the tea," he said, pushing his chair in.

"Wait, Bastien," I started, but he was already turned, heading for the exit. The maître d' gave me a confused look, but I just told him to put the items on my tab and bolted after the barista.

Outside, the wind whipped up, blowing the tails of my coat around me. Snow blustered into the air, blinding me momentarily, till I was able to spot the dark figure stalking away down the sidewalk.

"Bastien!" I called after him, careful to avoid the icy patches on the pavement beneath me. The figure didn't stop moving, so I called out again, "Bastien! Please, just a moment of your—" My foot slipped out from under me, and I crashed to the ground, landing on my tailbone as the wind was knocked from my lungs.

This halted the figure, and they turned around, slowly approaching the spot where I landed. He leaned over me, fighting a smile as he offered me a hand. "That looked painful."

"It was." I took his hand, and he hefted me to my feet with ease. "Thank you."

He dusted the snow from my shoulders. "Don't mention it."

"I am sorry about before," I continued, ignoring the pulsing aches from my fall. "I realize that I'm used to entertaining a very specific crowd, and I foolishly assumed you would fall into that category. That was my mistake."

Bastien took a step back from me, folding his arms across his chest. "Do you know why I finally approached you at the café?"

"I assume it wasn't because of my devilish good looks?" I joked, my face still hot with embarrassment.

"You came in every day for two weeks, Tobias. You weren't exactly being subtle. And for the most part, I treated you like any other regular customer. Learn your order. Make small talk. Figure out how to get you to leave a bigger tip. The usual.

I watched you flirt your way through at least four different men during that time, each of them handsome and well-dressed and drooling over you like you were the most succulent meal."

He moved closer, fixing my tie, then pulling the fabric of my vest with a quick tug. "After our chat, when you asked me to dinner, all I could think about was how different I was from those men. How you obviously had a type, and I was the farthest thing from it. So, I turned you down and I thought that would be the last of it. But you showed up again the next day. And the day after that."

"I'm impeccably consistent."

"Mhm," Bastien hummed with a nod. "But do you know what changed my mind about you?"

"I'm hoping you don't say my ability to walk on sidewalks without falling."

"It certainly wasn't your sense of humor," Bastien answered, another smile playing across his lips. He stepped closer again, his words bursting into the air with puffs of steam. "Three days ago, you were sitting in the café. You looked irritated as you kept checking your watch, so I assumed that your man-of-the-hour must have been running behind. As you sat, staring a hole through the front door, one of our regulars came in and took the seat next to you. Gladys is her name. She comes in every Tuesday and enjoys a pot of oolong tea and a good book. She used to come in with her husband, Timothy, until he passed away last spring."

I wracked my brain for the interaction, trying to place a face with the description.

"When I delivered her teapot to the table, you'd already scooted closer to her, discussing the book she'd brought in that day. When I checked in on her an hour later, you were still there, engrossed in conversation. You seemed… different. The haughty façade stripped back to reveal a tenderness I hadn't seen before. That's the person I wanted to go out with tonight. The man who would spend his afternoon entertaining a lonely widow. So, if you think there's a chance that man is still available, I'd love to go find a—how did you put it? Dirty watering hole?"

I stared back at the man, feeling vulnerable for the first time in what felt like forever. Had he been watching me as intently as I'd been watching him?

"I did say that, didn't I?"

"You certainly did."

Taking a deep breath, I brushed off the remaining snow from my garments, then extended a hand out to Bastien. "Would you permit me a do-over? Hello, I'm Tobias, and I'd love to get a drink with you."

Bastien considered my offer for a moment, then took my hand in his. "Nice to meet you. And I know just the place."

As the train began to slow, I returned to the cabin to find Bastien snoring into the cushion, his arm bent at a strange angle above his head. The squealing of the brakes caused him to stir, and when his eyes landed on me, a smile crawled across his lips, so precious that I wanted to lean in and take it from him.

But instead, I knocked on the door of the cabin next to us. Kaine pulled it open, running a hand through the shock of hair between his ears.

"What's all the knocking about?"

"We're arriving at the station," I told him. "I just thought you should know."

"I got ears, haven't I?" Kaine asked, but then his scowl morphed into a playful grin. "Alright, give me just a tick, and I'll come gather the two of you. We've got a little ways to go into town, but we're not far now."

"Far from what?" I asked, still curious as to the destination.

"You'll see, Greene."

The door shut in my face, and I returned to Bastien, who had managed to rouse himself enough to sit upright.

"That was a quick ride," he said, voice thick with sleep. A trail of dried drool lined his mouth, and I had to stop myself from wiping it away.

I moved to the window, looking out at the small town that grew closer with each passing second. The buildings were squatty and old, with slanted roofs of rusting metal and trees far too tall to be outside of the forest.

"What kind of place do you think Brierwood is?"

I had never been this far outside of the Magi Cities before, so it felt a bit like landing on an alien planet.

"It's a mortal town," Bastien answered, pulling his shoes on one at a time.

"We used to get some of the dairy into the café from around here. I'm surprised I can't spot any cows from the tracks."

A mortal town? I guess it made sense that the Rebellion would be better off hiding amongst mortals. If they were going for a place that the Adored would be less inclined to look, they'd found the right one.

The train settled into the station, a whistle signaling when it was clear to disembark. Once we were on the platform, Kaine guided us out through the station and into the quaint little town. The train station was off the main thoroughfare, a collection of buildings lining the narrow road on either side with a shabby-looking city hall sitting at the end of it. Old vehicles spewing plumes of smoke puttered down the street, mortals traversed the sidewalks with bags and strollers and dogs on leashes. It was sort of picturesque in that quaint way that only a greeting card could capture.

"I've got to go ahead and make sure everyone made it," Kaine announced as we departed the train station. "You two should be safe around here but don't wander too far. I'll come get you in an hour or so."

"We can't just come with you?" I asked, not too thrilled at the idea of wandering around a new environment when I couldn't defend myself from what else may be lurking out there.

"Patience," Bastien muttered beside me.

"I won't be long," Kaine reiterated. "Don't cause a ruckus, and you'll be just fine." With a final nod, he headed off into the town, disappearing around a corner and leaving Bastien and me standing in front of the train station.

I nearly jumped out of my skin as the train whistled behind us, signaling its departure.

"You need to relax," Bastien said with a laugh. "Come on, let's take a walk."

"Not like we have much of a choice," I muttered, following Bastien's lead.

We emerged onto the main street just as the lights overhead came on, a buzzing electrical noise permeating the air. The sun had nearly set at this point, the late afternoon warmth still lingering on the pavement below.

"Wow." Bastien marveled at our surroundings, peering through a storefront at the mannequins displayed in garments that seemed years out of fashion.

"It's nearly the same as the town I grew up in."

"You didn't grow up in the city?"

He shook his head, looking back at me with eyes of seeping honey. "No, I stayed with my grandmother in a little town like this. It was easier to hide there. Not a lot of Hallowed hanging around a quiet place filled with mortals."

And it hit me then that there was so much of Bastien that I didn't know. Even if my memories returned in earnest, they would only be of the man he allowed me to see. The mortal barista with a penchant for sleeping late and a disdain for loud noises.

But what was he *really* like? Who was the powerful Reviled practitioner who snagged me from Death's grasp? Which was the real Bastien?

"Hey, look, a coffee shop." Bastien pointed to the storefront across the street. "I could certainly use a cup. You mind?"

I shook my head, following him across the narrow street and into the small shop. Bells rang over our heads as we entered the cramped space rich with the smell of coffee and baked goods. The front of the shop had a comfortable-looking sofa nestled against the wall by the window and a side table stacked with books. The coffee bar ran along the rest of the wall on the left, while the opposite wall was lined with tables, half of them occupied with patrons—a woman absorbed in a book with a colorful cover, an older couple sitting in silence as they sipped from steaming mugs, a young man dragging charcoal across a sketchbook he held in his lap.

"You want the usual?" Bastien asked me, sparking a stream of memories of him in an apron, sliding glasses of iced espresso to me across a wooden counter.

"Yes, thank you."

I found my way over to the table furthest from the door, nestled in the back corner of the shop. I could sit with my back to the wall, allowing myself full vantage of anyone entering the shop. Maybe that would help with the pulsating anxiety in my chest.

Bastien joined me a few minutes later, setting our drinks down along with a plate of croissants. I would have hugged him if my shoulder hadn't hurt so badly.

"I miss this," he said, holding his drink up to his nose and taking a long inhale.

"What, coffee?"

He laughed, then pulled a sip. "No, I meant the life I had working at the café. My mortal life was far less complicated. Don't get me wrong—" he looks over to the young man closest to us, then lowers his voice, "being a Magi has its perks. But things were infinitely simpler when my job was making really great coffee for the masses."

"Why did you stop, then?" I asked, seizing the opportunity to gain further insight into Bastien's past.

He leaned back in his chair, chest deflating with a sigh. "My grandmother passed. It was a few months back. It wasn't sudden or anything. She'd been getting weaker as the years went on. But it was still… a shock. I told you before, Death is a comfortable companion to me. It's been a part of my family, our culture, for centuries.

"Granny Yvonne was the one who taught me about our history, just like she did for my mother. My great-grandmother was one of the Elders that fled during the schism of the Revered, and she brought all she could from the sanctuaries where they used to practice their craft."

"Before the Hallowed took over," I concluded.

"Exactly. You see, my mother wasn't good at the whole 'stay under the radar' thing. Even though she'd been born after the schism, hiding her power never came naturally to her. She'd grown a reputation in our town for being a healer. Someone the mortals could come to when their medicines failed. Granny said that she even brought a child back from the dead, but it was long before I came along.

"But that kind of action draws unwanted attention. They came for her one night before I could even walk. I always assumed it was the Church, but to be fair, I can't confirm it. Granny hid me and herself, but she couldn't get to Mom in time. Then, it was just the two of us. I don't have many memories of my mother, but Granny helped her live on in my dreams."

"I'm sorry," I said, wishing I could wipe the sadness from his expression. What must it have been like, to have such a connection with a parent, only to have them ripped away from you? At least Father died when I was an infant....

Bastien scratched the end of his nose, then shook his head. "Anyway. Granny was the one who gave me my markings." He rolled up the sleeves of his sweater, baring arms free of blemish. But then there was a crackle in the air between us, and the glamours faded from his arms, revealing the black ink that swirled across his skin. The designs started at his wrist, spiraling up his arms, forming an intricate circular pattern that disappeared under the sleeves of his shirt. He closed his eyes, muttering something under his breath, and the markings vanished once more. "The markings are how we Reviled channel our magic. They connect us to Source, or at least that's what my grandmother used to say. I'm not so sure I believe every bit of the teachings.

"Granny kept me safe during that time. Enrolled me in a mortal school so I could better learn how to blend in. Then, at night, she'd teach me about our culture. About the Elders that came before us and the wonders they were able to perform. Most of the practice was in theory, as she was extra cautious of drawing attention, but as I got older and her health began to fail, I was able to put some of my learnings to good use."

He paused, a finger tracing the rim of his cup as he stared down into it. I watched him, completely transfixed.

"She passed a week after we broke up," he continued, his voice suddenly husky and thick. "I'd been distracted that week, and I wasn't checking up on her as much as I should have. She missed our weekly call, and I got worried, so I went back to that town, and that's where I found her."

He cleared his throat, then tucked his hands tight against his body, arms folded over his chest. "I tried to bring her back, of course. But I should have known better. She wasn't interested in coming back."

"What do you mean?" I asked, the idea sticking in my mind like a thistle. "Are you saying she had a choice?"

"Of course she did," Bastien replied. "Everyone does. I can't just force someone back into this world. They have to be willing."

Was I willing when he did the same for me? Obviously, I must have been. But I remembered feeling so at peace, alone in the darkness.

"You're wondering about your own, aren't you?"

I looked up to find Bastien smirking at me.

"Am I that easy to read?"

"Not always."

There was another question that stuck out as I mulled over the new information. "Was I the first? The first person you brought back, I mean."

Bastien nodded, once again preoccupied with tracing the rim of his cup. "Did you want to hear about it?"

"Please."

"The process isn't as complicated as some might think it is. I mean, there's a lot of prep work, like crafting the Verdant gem and being able to completely center yourself. But the actual reviving part is simple. All I have to do is find you, out there in the ether, and bring you back. Once your soul occupies your body again, I just give you a quick kick-start and that's that."

Ether. There was that word again. The line of the prophecy rang in my ears.

*Son of the second, lost in the ether.*

*You have been beckoned, Death is your teacher.*

"When you say 'find me,'" I repeated. "What exactly does that look like?"

"I project my consciousness into the ether—the place where we pull magic from to create glamours and Veils. It's the space between the living and the dead. Remember how I told you I thought it might have been too late by the time I got to your body? That's because souls don't typically linger in the ether that long. They're drawn to other places, places of rest or retribution. But yours was easy to find. It was like you were waiting for me, and all it took was me pointing in the right direction for you to come back."

Was it really that simple? Kudos to my incorporeal soul.

"Cirian told me a bit about the process of death for us Magi," I said, piecing together the details. "He said that our magic returns to the Source, and that's why mine is gone. That it already returned."

Bastien nodded. "He's right, mostly. As Magi, magic runs in our veins. When your heart stops beating, that magic retracts, gathering in the body to be released with your final breath. That magic gets absorbed back into the ether, but it doesn't surprise me that the Acolyte believes it finds its way back to the Source. He's a man of faith, after all."

"You don't believe in the Source?"

Bastien chuckles. "Do I believe there's a source of magic? Sure. But it's not some deity to be worshipped. It's like the ancients worshipping the Sun. They saw how it brought life to their world, and they bowed down to it. Nowadays, we know it's simply a resource, and we can choose whether or not we wish to utilize it. The Church has spent centuries building up the case for devotion to the Source, but it's merely a façade behind which they hoard power. For who better to communicate the wishes of a god than those who sit closest to its feet?"

"And what of prophecy," I asked before I could think better of it. "Where do you think that comes from, if not the Source?"

"Prophecy?" Bastien repeated, his eyes narrowing. "I'm afraid Granny never spoke of prophecies. Why do you ask?"

"It's nothing," I said, heat flooding my face as I shook my head. "Just something I heard in passing while at the Cradle. Please, forget I mentioned it."

He eyed me for a moment longer before continuing, "Your memory problems, Death's Touch, is theorized to be caused by prolonged exposure to the ether. I think that's why yours is particularly severe. Your soul was there for nearly three days. I've never heard of one hanging around that long without being corrupted."

"That sounds ominous."

"Sort of," Bastien replied. "If a person's soul clings to the ether for long enough, they can manifest back into the physical world in a number of ways. They'll possess someone's body or the body of the recently deceased. Or they may appear as an apparition, visible to those here in the physical realm."

"Ghosts," I concluded.

"You could call them that, yes."

"So, would I have started haunting people if you didn't bring me back?"

Bastien shrugged, taking another sip of his drink. "You tell me."

The thought of lingering in that place, numb to all that was going on around me, suddenly filled me with a dread that twisted my stomach into knots.

"That brings us to the true resurrection ritual," said Bastien, drawing my attention back from the spiraling scenarios bouncing around my head. "Which should let me restore your magic. Once I locate it in the ether, I'll extract it and then funnel it back to you. If everything goes well, you should regain all the power you once held."

"And if it doesn't go well?"

Bastien squirmed in his seat. "I don't know. This probably isn't what you want to hear, but all of this is theoretical for me, Tobias. I'm only going off the books I've read. I've never seen it performed in person."

It certainly wasn't what I wanted to hear. "I trust you," I said, both for his sake and for mine. This was Bastien. I had no reason not to put my faith in him. "You'll do great."

That seemed to relax him a bit, and he took another sip from his cup.

It was nice being with Bastien in this way. Easy. I could see why I was drawn to him all that time ago in the café. Even when he was hiding a piece of himself from me, there was this airiness to him. A light-weighted joy that seemed to permeate everything he did. Even now, as I watched him enjoy a cup of coffee, those moments shined through.

He had kept secrets from me when we were together. But the need for secrets was gone, so I asked, "Could you tell me more about your childhood? I want to hear about your grandmother if that's okay."

His brow shot up as if he were surprised by my inquiry.

"I'm sure we have more important things to talk about."

"Please," I insisted, reaching across and laying a hand over his. "Even if things between us are… strange right now. I'd like to know what she was like."

He blinked at me, his smooth forehead creased with confusion before it slowly melted into something more relaxed. "Our town was a lot like this one," he started, his eyes trailing down to where my hand covered his.

# THE SECOND AWAKENING

"Pleasantry, that's the name. Granny ran a laundry service out of the back of our duplex. She made enough to keep the lights on but not much else. Our neighbors next door—an elderly couple, the Prescotts, married for over fifty years when we first moved in—took it on themselves to look after us. They'd bring over food on the nights that Granny was too busy to make anything. We'd listen to recordings of old radio shows, and Mrs. Prescott would tell me what it was like when she was a young woman, and Mr. Prescott worked at the factory on the edge of town that had shuttered decades ago. In return for their kindness, Granny offered to help Mr. Prescott. He was sick for a long time, you see. A disease that robbed him of the use of his limbs and left him trembling in his chair most days.

"At first, Mrs. Prescott rejected Granny's offerings, saying that they'd spent the majority of their later years visiting every doctor in the surrounding area, spending every bit of money they'd saved their entire lives to try and find the answer to what ailed her husband. They were tired of the promise of hope and had long accepted the reality of their situation. But they didn't know that the frazzled old woman next door was once one of the most renowned healers across the Magi Cities.

"Then, one night, I couldn't have been more than six or seven, there was this loud knock on the door that woke me. I peeked from my bedroom and saw Granny letting Mrs. Prescott inside. She was upset, speaking quickly about her husband and the urgent need to take him to a medical facility. She asked Granny if she could drive them, but Granny simply told her that she would do more than that. Mrs. Prescott didn't argue when Granny told her to bring her husband over to our side of the duplex. As she waited for the Prescotts, she closed the curtains over the windows and then caught me spying from the hall.

"'Come here,' she told me, reaching for my hand and taking me into the living room where she'd unfolded a table in the center that she typically used for ironing. 'It's time for you to see for yourself the power you hold.'

"I didn't know what she meant at the time. Sure, I'd seen Granny use the odd bit of magic here and there. Healing my scrapes and bruises. Closing the windows at night with a flick of her wrist, when she was sure no one was watching. But what she was preparing for, this would be the first time I'd seen what it meant to be Reviled.

"Mrs. Prescott returned after a few minutes, wheeling her husband through the door and stopping cold when she saw the table. She asked Granny what she was doing, and Granny told her that she was going to help, just like she'd promised. Mr. Prescott's eyes were closed, and his skin was paler than I'd ever seen before. His breathing rasped, wet like the gasps of a drowning man. Even then, I could smell Death on him, heavy and smothering. It could have come at any time. Unable to argue, Mrs. Prescott wheeled her husband up to the table. Granny, though she looked frail, lifted him out of his chair with ease, resting him on top. She called me to her side, her wrinkled fingers unfastening the buttons on Mr. Prescott's shirt.

"She set to work, her hands glowing with power as she worked over Mr. Prescott's body. His wife stood on the opposite side of the table, her eyes wide, but she didn't speak a word. After a few minutes, Granny moved to stand over Mr. Prescott, her hands on either side of his head. She murmured words that made my skin itch, and the light from her hands filled the entire room."

Bastien paused, retracting his hand from me and pulling it into his lap. "When Mr. Prescott woke up, the trembling had stopped. Mrs. Prescott cried and cried, and they both thanked Granny. She told them that they had to keep it quiet, that there would be no safe place for me and her if word got out about what we were. The Prescotts agreed to keep our secret, returning to their home after the happy tears had dried. Granny sat me down and told me about where we came from and the work that she used to do. She told me that it was a heavy responsibility and that even though it was dangerous for her to expose herself, the work was important.

"A few weeks went by, and the Prescotts didn't visit us again. One afternoon, Granny was outside, hanging a line of sheets to dry while I played in the yard. Mr. Prescott came out of their side of the house and started yelling at Granny. His wife followed him out, trying to calm him down, but he kept yelling anyway. Granny told me to go inside, but I didn't want to leave her.

Not when Mr. Prescott sounded so angry.

"They stood in the yard for what felt like hours, speaking in hushed tones. Granny didn't yell back or even raise her voice. She looked… sad. But not surprised. When the conversation finally fizzled out, Granny came over to me, scooped me into her arms, and carried me inside. I asked her why the Prescotts were angry, and she told me they were scared. Scared that they would be punished for what she did for Mr. Prescott. He said that she had cursed him, and nothing good came from the magic that had saved his life."

Bastien's gaze drifted, meandering over the other café goers before moving to the window. "The Prescotts left shortly after that. I'm not sure where they went, and we never asked. Years later, when I was old enough to understand what had happened, I asked Granny why she wasn't angry about their reaction. Why it didn't upset her that she was berated for saving that man's life? She merely smiled and said that it was his life, and he got to do with it whatever he wished.

"'That is the beauty of life, my Bast,' she told me. 'All the possibilities. He was angry, yes. But I knew that anger would pass, and he and his love would go on to have many more happy days together. This is why I could never be upset with what I did. I gave him life so that he may choose what to do with it.'"

He came back to me then, honey-like eyes finding me as they retreated from visions of the past. "That's the kind of person she was."

"You carry her with you," I said, hoping he understood the context.

"In more ways than one," he muttered.

"Thank you for sharing with me. I understand why you had to hide this part of yourself from me before. I would like to think that I would have understood, if you told me."

Was that the truth of it? It was easy to say these things now when I couldn't remember the details, the intricacies of whatever relationship we had during my first life. If I never had died, would I still feel the same way about him?

The space between my certainty and doubt stretched wide, a chasm between us.

"I would have told you," Bastien said, and once again, his voice was quiet, like he didn't want me to hear. "Eventually, I would have told you, Tobias."

"It doesn't matter. You've told me now. More than that. You've done what your grandmother did all those years. You gave me my life back with no thought of yourself."

"It's not true," Bastien replied, wrapping long, spindly fingers around his glass again. "I'm nothing like Granny. The first time I use my magic outside of her training, it's to bring back the man I never got over. Some altruist I am."

His words buzzed in my ear like a swarm of insects. What was he saying? Obviously, there was still something between the two of us, this unspoken attraction that drew me to him like a moth to its demise in clandestine flame.

The bells rang above the door, and Kaine entered my periphery before I could ask anything else. He spotted us in the back corner, striding as casually as he would down the sidewalk over to us.

"Just got the all-clear," he said over the two of us. "We need to move."

Bastien was out of his seat in a blink, downing the last of his beverage and setting the empty glass on the counter. I started down at my untouched espresso, then made the decision to chug what I could.

It was nowhere near as good as Bastien's.

Outside of the café, Kaine led us away from the main street, weaving through passages between brick buildings and never traveling in a single direction for too long. It would make remembering the route to our destination nearly impossible, even in the daylight. A precaution I'm sure had served the Rebellion well in the past.

When we reached the outskirts of the town, the buildings growing scarcer the further we traveled, Kaine finally stopped in front of a dilapidated warehouse, a faded sign above the battered door reading "Paradise Pastries" in faded script under a flickering light.

I hesitantly eyed the entrance. "Is this it?"

"Now, now," Kaine said with a chuckle. "It's not a chateau, but what better place to set up shop than Paradise, am I right?"

Bastien seemed to share my concerns as he peered through a broken window pane. "There's no one inside. Are we early or something?"

"Not at all," Kaine replied, pushing the door open with a bit of force. It shuddered, then gave, all at once. "Inside, you two."

"You're not coming with us?" I asked, alarms blaring in my head.

Kaine laughed again. "You've got a healthy dose of suspicion, Greene. I'll give you that. I'll be right behind you, rebel's honor." He held up a hand, palm out as if pledging himself.

I looked back at Bastien once more, his own concern evident in his expression.

"Come on, chaps. Paradise awaits," Kaine added, staring us down with an intensity that set my teeth on edge.

With nowhere left to go but forward, I ducked through the entrance and into the dimly lit space.

# EIGHTEEN
## DON'T SPEAK ILL OF THE DEAD

"Do you think they'll support my decision?"

The door to the VanDoughten house closed behind us, the pool of light from the street lamp casting a warm glow on Lynette from the sidewalk.

"I don't know," I answered honestly, still trying to wrap my head around the night's events. Lynette was planning what essentially boiled down to a coup against our own mother, and a half hour was not the appropriate amount of time to digest the reality. "There were some who seemed enthusiastic, but most of them just looked scared."

Lynette deflated with a sigh as she hit the sidewalk. "And you?"

"I... don't know," I repeated.

Lynette nodded, muttering something under her breath that I didn't catch. She looked up at me then, reaching out for me to take her hand. "It's so nice out tonight. Would you mind walking me home?"

I looked up at the cloudless sky. She was right. The weather was perfect, with only the slightest chill in the air. Lynette's apartment wasn't far from the VanDoughtens', so I agreed, taking her hand in mine.

We moved in silence down the streets of the upper Magi City. Here, there was little foot traffic this time of night, so the only encounters we had were those of the pigeon or squirrel variety.

"Oh, look." Lynette pointed to the iron gates across the street, the sign above reading 'cemetery.' "I forget that it's so close, sometimes."

"I haven't visited Father in a long while," I admitted, shoving my hands deeper into the pockets of my jacket as the wind kicked up. "Did you want to stop by?"

Lynette thought for a moment, then nodded, hooking her arm through mine as we crossed the street. Our father, a rather unremarkable man when compared to Mother, died shortly after we were born of an illness that claimed him far younger than the norm. Mother wasn't the sentimental type, but once Lynette and I were old enough to learn about him, we'd made it a tradition to lay flowers on his grave at the change of the seasons.

A tradition that had become less important as the years marched on.

We followed the familiar path through rows of headstones, stopping on the second to last on the left. Father's plot had always been well maintained, but there, in the middle of an autumn evening, we had to brush away the layer of leaves that hid his epitaph.

> **HERE LIES TOBIAS GREENE.**
> **TAKEN TOO SOON FROM THE SCENE.**
> **FATHER. HUSBAND. ADORED.**
> **MAY HIS SPIRIT FIND REST IN THE SOURCE.**

"Hello, Father," Lynette said, squatting down to run her hand along his name.

I had always felt awkward about sharing a name with my father, and I'd often wondered what his surname was before he took Mother's. I hadn't really known the man, and what little information I could find out about him didn't leave me with strong feelings one way or another. He simply was. As he died shortly after our birth, the term 'Junior' never seemed appropriate, so it was easy to forget most days that someone had shared my name at all.

He was forgotten, just as I would be one day.

"Are you really going to give it up?" I asked after a moment of silence bloomed between me and my sister.

"Give what up?" she asked, straightening.

"Your position. Our family's power. All those things you said back there. Are you really going to throw them away?"

Lynette stiffened, folding her arms over her navel. "I'm not throwing anything away, Tobi. I'm simply relinquishing it. Our family doesn't deserve the power that Mother has amassed. It needs to be given to those better suited."

"And who determines that?" I continued, my stream of consciousness flowing freely now. "A popular vote? Then, you'll be handing the reins over to someone who can manipulate emotions better than the next Adored. That doesn't exactly seem wise. So, what else can you look at? Maybe the Council will be able to hold a search for the right candidate. But they're all in Mother's pocket already, so it's dubious whether or not we can trust the lot of them."

"Then we'll reform the Council. It's unfairly balanced as it is. It's supposed to be the Council of Magi, yet the Adored and Hallowed are the only ones appointed. We can bring in the Unseen."

"Right," I scoffed, folding my arms across my chest, "because that will ever happen. You hand over power to one of them, and you've got a war on your hands before they can hold a single gathering. The people would revolt, Lenny!"

She balked at me. "Where is this animosity coming from, Tobi? I thought you were sick of working for Mother's agenda. What, did you get scared because you might have to give up your swanky bachelor pad on the upper side?"

"Oh, fuck you, Lenny. You know this isn't about that."

"Isn't it?" she pushed, stepping toward me. "The only reason you're asking me this is because you're afraid that I'll fly off the handle and rid our family of its wealth. Well, here's a novel concept—maybe we should!"

Anger flared in my gut, spurring me on. "And that would make you feel less guilty, huh? Maybe if you give away enough money and resources, people will forget you're Adoranda's daughter? Never. You're stuck with the name Greene just like I am."

"Then let's make it synonymous with hope!" Lynette retorted. "Let's show the world that we're not the monsters that everyone has made us out to be."

"Exactly! And if you give away your most effective tool—power—how do you think you'll accomplish any of it? The minute you vacate that seat, they'll just replace you with someone worse, someone who will do whatever they want, and we'll be right back where we started."

Lynette stepped back, and I advanced another step toward her.

"Not to mention, Mother will still be there, waiting in the wings. If your plan to remove her fails, then there's nothing stopping her from just taking over the Council again through whatever figurehead gets established."

"But that won't happen—"

"How can you be sure? How can you know for certain that what you're proposing will work? What kind of assurance can you—"

"Because I've seen it!" Her voice filled the empty cemetery, reverberating off the rows of polished stone. "I've seen it all happen, Tobias. Flames will consume the world, and it happens because of her. She'll be the death of everything good and beautiful if I don't stop her. If I don't...."

Lynette's gaze trailed down to our father's grave.

I halted my advance, her revelation throwing me off balance. "You've seen it?" I questioned. "Like the visions you used to have? How long have they been back?"

"They never left, Tobias." Lynette's shoulders sank, her voice cracking. "I merely stopped talking about them once I was old enough to understand that's what Mother wanted."

"But they can't be real, Lenny. Don't you see that? You can't throw your life away because of a couple of bad dreams—"

"Do not mock me, Tobias. I know the difference. These are no dreams."

"Then let me help you!" I pleaded with her. "Clue me in on what's going on, and maybe I can help think it through. But giving up the power you'll need to enact change isn't the right move. You'll only clip your wings—"

A sound from the bushes a few feet away silenced me. Movement out of the corner of my eye and someone—

If this was Paradise, I struggled to imagine what the opposite must look like.

The warehouse was vacant, except for a few cardboard boxes stacked against the wall that seemed to be melting into one another. Dark stains on the brown exteriors oozed some sort of mysterious liquid onto the floor, and I didn't want to get closer to investigate exactly what it might be. Lights flickered overhead, throwing shadows that danced across the floors. Kaine followed us inside, just as he promised he would, closing the door behind him. Without the dying sunlight streaking through the doorway, the room was even more dim, and I squinted into the dark, searching for any reason as to why he brought us here.

"This way," said Kaine, moving away from the entrance and further into the barren space.

"What are the chances we're about to be murdered by this guy?" Bastien whispered as we begrudgingly followed at a distance.

"Definitely not zero," I replied, clutching my fist over the stone embedded in my palm, even though it was most certainly drained of magic. Would Bastien be able to fight Kaine off if he turned coat? He'd probably never used his magic to defend himself before. I would have to show him the basics sometime. That was if we survived our trip to Paradise.

Kaine came to a stop near the center of the warehouse, four structural pillars surrounding us but nothing in between. He knelt, brushing aside some scraps of newspaper to reveal a small silver handle embedded into the concrete floor. As he pulled on the handle, the floor creaked and groaned but gave way, a panel of stone coming up in the shape of a hatched door.

"You must be joking," I said, peering down into the darkness of the opening. The rungs of a ladder disappeared in the pitch a few feet down.

"You didn't think we'd be hiding out in the open, did you?" Kaine asked, raising an aqua-colored brow.

He had a point. But it didn't alleviate the twist of anxiety in my gut. If he meant us harm, there would be no better place to commit it than in a hole under an abandoned warehouse. But I had to remind myself that Azrael trusted this man. Enough that he called him a brother. That had to count for something.

Summoning my courage, I crossed over to the hatch, lowering myself down onto the first rung.

"Careful now, Greene. It would be a nasty fall. Even if you are already half dead." He gave me a wink and I contemplated giving him a finger, but decided I needed all ten if I was going to survive my descent.

Once the light vanished from above, it felt like I was alone in the dark, even though I could hear Bastien and Kaine above me. The descent was slow going, as I had to grope around for each wrung before I could put my whole weight on it, and my shoulder still ached something terrible. When my foot finally collided with solid ground, it was such a shock that I stubbed my toe hard enough to provoke a yelp.

"Found the bottom, did you?" Kaine teased from above.

"What do I do now?" I asked, still clinging to the ladder. I could have been standing on the edge of the void and not know any better. "I can't see a thing down here."

"Back up a few steps and make room," Kaine ordered with a grunt.

I did as he instructed, keeping one hand on the side of the ladder as I took two steps backward. My muscles stretched to keep me attached to the metal tube, but I wasn't willing to let it go yet.

Once I heard Kaine hit the ground, he muttered something under his breath, and a deep violet light burned into existence in front of his face. The magical flame flickered, throwing wild-looking shadows against his face in a way that set me on edge.

Kaine stepped back from the ladder, eyeing my hand still clinging to the side, and chuckled. "Almost there," he called up to Bastien, and we watched as he descended the final stretch of the ladder.

We'd climbed down into a tunnel, as far as I could tell from the strange purple light that stretched on further than I could see. The walls were a cool concrete, stained with time and untold layers of grime.

"What now?" I asked as Bastien's feet hit the ground beside me.

"There's only one way to go," Kaine replied, pointing down the tunnel. "Now, let's get a move on, or we'll be late for dinner."

I looked back at Bastien, who rolled his eyes. "Well, we can't be late for dinner, can we, Bastien?"

The tunnel continued in one direction for what felt like half a mile before making an abrupt turn to the left, followed by a fork. Kaine showed no hesitation taking the path to the left and was just as confident at the next fork. Before I knew it, we'd taken half a dozen turns, and the tunnel still stretched ahead of us, seemingly endless.

"What are these?" I asked as we rounded another curve of concrete. "They're not sewer channels."

"They're left over from the mortal wars," Kaine answered, still leading the way by flickering violet light. "A network runs under Brierwood above and goes for miles. Not really sure what they used them for, and a couple of branches have collapsed from age, but don't worry your pretty little heads. You're safe as long as you stick with me."

Somehow, his words didn't make me feel that way.

"How did the Rebellion find this place?"

Kaine didn't answer, as we'd come across another branch. He stared at the diverging paths, hesitating for a moment.

"Everything okay?" I asked him.

"Yeah, it's just difficult to see this one. You've got to really know what you're looking for."

"What *are* you looking for?"

Kaine walked forward, nearly colliding with the wall of the tunnel, but his head never made contact with the sloped surface as his form moved *through* the wall of stone and disappeared. The glow of his violet light illuminated the space around us still, shining through the cracks in the concrete.

"It's a Veil," Bastien breathed, moving up to the glowing section of stone and placing a hand against it. He reached his other hand back, beckoning me to join him. "A really good one. I swear, I can feel the texture of the concrete. Even Granny's weren't this convincing."

"How do we get through?" I asked.

"By knowing it's not real." He moved his hand over a few inches, his arm disappearing through the wall up to his elbow. Then he closed his eyes and walked through the wall, vanishing from my view.

# THE SECOND AWAKENING

I braced a hand against the tunnel. It felt solid to me. The grit against my palm dug into my skin enough to be uncomfortable. This was so much more than a normal glamour. They were only illusions. Illusions couldn't feel this real.

I closed my eyes and stepped forward, bracing for an impact that never came. When I opened them, my lungs deflated with a sputtering exhale.

We stood on the side of a cliff path that wound down and away from us. The ceiling of brown stone expanded high above our heads, forming a dome shape hundreds of feet above. Under the domed roof, an expanse of short buildings spread over the cavern floor, forming a grid pattern with pathways in between. Lush patches of earth sprang up among the structures, with neat rows of crops lining the outer rim, encircling the structures. Above, along the sloped roof, massive glowing crystals illuminated the space, shining down as if the sun itself were presiding over the underground town.

At the center of the buried oasis, a large fountain shot geysers of water into the air, refracting that artificial light into an arch of rainbow hues.

It was breathtaking.

"Paradise," Bastien muttered.

Kaine had already begun down the winding path to our left, and we quickly hurried to catch up with him.

"What is this place?" I asked as we went. From above, the space hadn't appeared more than a mile or so wide, but the further we descended from the apex, the bigger the buildings became and the steeper the walls around us grew.

"A settlement," answered Kaine. "Refugees fled here in search of a better life. They've been kind enough to allow us to stay with them for the time being."

Once we reached the bottom of the path, I stopped and looked up at the blinding lights on the domed roof. It felt as though we stood beneath a hollow mountain.

"Come on," Kaine urged us forward. "I wasn't kidding about dinner. I'm starving."

Bastien seemed just as awed, his eyes wide as we took in the rows of corn and wheat that lined the flat path that led into the town. Now that we were on the ground floor, I could tell that the buildings were not dwarfed as I originally thought. In fact, some of them were two or three stories tall.

As we moved through the rows of crops, a flicker of movement caught my eye and a child carrying a woven basket crossed our path up ahead. Their skin was pale, and their grey hair was pulled back into a braid that hung down their back. Their dark eyes widened as they saw us, but it wasn't fear I saw in them. It was excitement. They dropped their basket to the ground, waving with both arms over their head.

Bastien made a choking sound beside me.

I looked back at the child, wondering what could have caused such a reaction that he would—then I saw them. Markings of intricate black ink woven up the child's arms to their exposed shoulders. They looked familiar.

They looked like Bastien's markings.

"Reviled," Bastien exhaled the word, and it hung like a miasma over his head.

Another figure appeared from the rows of plants, this one much older than the child with a stooped posture and a basket strapped to their back. Their skin was less pale than the young one, their face wrinkled and worn, but a pleasant smile parted their lips. They, too, bore the markings of a Reviled, the ink faded with age.

"Good day," Kaine called to the duo, waving from our approach.

The child ran up to us, bowing once they reached a few paces away. "Hello again, Mr. Kaine!"

"Hello again, Thessa." Kaine motioned at the two of us, "These are my friends, Tobias and Bastien."

The child gave us a wave, eyes lingering on Bastien longer than expected. "Are you staying with us, too?"

"Yes," I replied, Bastien still stunned into silence beside me. "At least, for a little while."

The older figure—a woman with long grey braids tied back from her creased face—had caught up with the child now, setting down their basket of harvested greens. "Welcome to Paradise. Kaine, Wilhelm was asking about you. She's in the community hall now, so you should probably catch her before she starts making the rounds."

Kaine nodded. "Let me get these two settled in, and I'll head right over."

"You look frightened, child." The woman was looking at Bastien now, her warm, umber eyes trained on him. "You needn't be. You can rest here."

Bastien opened his mouth but didn't speak.

"You won't be needing those, either." The woman extended her hand, the air around it shimmering briefly with an acidic green light.

Bastien gasped as the glamour faded from his arms, revealing the intricate lines of black ink. He ran his hands over them, tracing the designs. His breath hitched in his throat.

The woman moved over to him, wrapping wrinkled hands around his. "Paradise welcomes you, child. Do not hide from her embrace."

Bastien nodded, swallowing.

"Come, Thessa," the woman said, releasing her grip on Bastien. "We'll need more rampion for our guests tonight."

"Okay, Gran." The child gave us another slight bow. "It was nice to meet you!"

"Likewise," I replied, my attention focused on Bastien as he stood stark still, looking down at his hands.

The child and woman moved back up the path, the child chattering excitedly. "Why was he hiding his marks, Gran? He looked really sad."

"You know, there are markings that are always invisible," the woman replied, balancing the basket on her hip as she went. "And they can make even the happiest people sad sometimes. I think our new friend carries some of those as well…"

Their voices trailed off, words swallowed up by the greenery as they returned to their work.

"Are you alright?" I asked Bastien, placing a gentle hand on his shoulder.

He flinched at my touch, blinking a few times before nodding. "Yeah, sorry. I'm… let's keep going."

"Stay strong now," Kaine told Bastien. "There's a lot more to see."

Bastien nodded once more, squaring his shoulders. As we began to move up the path once more, approaching the collection of buildings, he reached for my hand.

It was a simple gesture, his fingers wrapping around mine. It was something that we'd done countless times during my first life. But this was different from those times. He needed strength in this moment, someone to lean on as the world he knew was being rewritten around him. It meant everything to me, that I could be the one to provide that support for him when he'd already given me so much.

It would do little to even the scales. But that didn't keep me from tightening my grip.

Paradise was more than either of us expected. Buildings made of colorful stone rose from the earthen floor of the massive cavern with rounded doors and windows of colored glass. We walked past residences and shops, fountains bubbling with crystalline waters, grassy knolls with flora of all kinds, blooming as if it were the peak of spring. And people. So many people that all bore the markings along their arms and upper body. They greeted us in the street with smiles and friendly faces, one after another. The laughter of children carried above it all, rising as they played with toys of beautifully carved wood.

Everywhere we looked, there was joy. There was peace. There was something the world had thought long gone for people like Bastien.

Hope.

"We're this way," Kaine instructed us, and I realized that we were near the center of the cavern now. A row of buildings, three stories tall, sat on one side of the street, with pallets of goods stacked outside of the entrance—evidence of the hundreds of displaced Unseen. "Azrael should be here soon with the majority of those from the camp. They had to take a longer route to avoid attracting attention. It should go without saying this place is to remain a secret at all costs."

"Only for the time being," a voice called, coming from the entrance of the building opposite the row of housing. A woman with dark skin emerged from the doorway, approaching us with a confident stride. She was tall, even taller than Bastien, with thin braids of black hair pulled back and held by a band of golden fabric. Her clothes were just as colorful as the rest of paradise—a loose tunic that cut off just before her navel with billowy sleeves and cropped pants. "We won't be kept in the dark forever."

"Wilhelm," Kaine addressed the woman. "Azrael should be here soon. These two are a special delivery ahead of our main contingent."

"Tobias Greene," the woman said, approaching me without hesitation. She extended her hand to me, and I dropped Bastien's to take it, wincing at the strength of her grip. "Never in a million years did I ever think I would be welcoming a Greene into Paradise. Even a reanimated one. The universe has a unique sense of irony."

"I'm grateful," I replied, my diplomatic instincts taking over. "You'll forgive my incredulity. This is a lot to take in."

"That it is," she agreed, her attentions shifting to Bastien. "And you, seeker? I can see the chaos that's consumed your thoughts. Share them with me."

Bastien's nostrils flared, his breathing reaching near-panting levels of exertion. "How... have you been here all this time?"

"You're upset," Wilhelm concluded, her expression soft as if she were speaking with a child. "This is a natural response. Come with me, seeker. I will provide you with any answers you seek."

Bastien looked at me, and I gave him a nod of encouragement. He had been disconnected from his people since his grandmother died. I knew this was something he had to do.

"We won't be far," Kaine added, pointing to the row of housing. "You can come find us once you've talked things through. Wilhelm, I'll send word once Azrael shows up."

"Thank you, friend." She motions for Bastien to join her, steering him towards the building she came from. "Ask your questions."

The two of them disappeared into the building. Kaine gripped my shoulder gently, and I realized that my hands were clenched into fists at my side. "He'll be fine," Kaine said, "You can go with them if you want. I'm sure Wilhelm will make an exception for lovers."

"No, it's not—we're not lovers," I sputtered, face warming at the allegations. "Not anymore, I mean."

"Ah, and you're upset about that fact?" Kaine questioned.

"I'm not upset," I argued, the high pitch of my voice in perfect juxtaposition. It wasn't like that. I didn't think I had some weird claim over Bastien. He was free to do what he wished. But this stupid tether I felt for him—the tugging at my chest whenever he left—was getting uncomfortable.

Kaine nodded slowly. "Right. Well, that's none of my business. And if it were, I would have told you that boy is coming apart at the seams right now. And even if the history between you two is complicated, he's got no one to lean on."

The invisible tether hooked into my chest pulled taut at that as if reacting to Kaine's words. It's not that I didn't *want* to comfort Bastien. I couldn't imagine the rush of emotion he must be feeling right now. Paradise has shown him a world he never knew could exist. It must ache, knowing that this place was here while he suffered alone.

But I wasn't exactly the best at comforting others. And there's nothing I could offer him but a physical presence. A hand to hold. Would that be enough? He needed more. He needed someone who could care for him completely and who understood the pain he felt.

He deserved someone better than a selfish, arsehole-of-an-ex-boyfriend with holes in his brain. Someone who didn't fear each memory that resurfaced and wasn't forced to reconcile their own self-image a dozen times a day.

Bastien deserved better than me. But that fact did nothing to slacken the tug of the invisible line that drew me to him.

"Kaine!"

A familiar voice shook me from my daze as Azrael appeared at the end of the row of housing.

Kaine bolted from my side, running toward Azrael at full speed. The two collided with an embrace, laughing as Kaine lifted Azrael into the air and spun him around as if he weighed nothing. The two swatted at each other, speaking in a hushed tone as I approached slowly, not wanting to intrude on the moment of surprising affection.

Behind Azrael, figures began to flicker into existence as the crowd of Unseen allowed their magic to peel away. I recognized a few faces from the chateau, including the family with the younglings, who still clung to one of their fathers, and Eustace from the kitchens. But there were far more than just those that escaped Chateau Greene.

"Sorry we're late," I heard Azrael say. "We ran into some trouble on the road, so we had to take the long way around. They're all exhausted."

"What about you?" Kaine asked a twist of worry in his expression.

"Never been better," Azrael replied with a grin, patting Kaine on the chest. "Can you see to them?"

Kaine nodded. "The support crew from camp has been making ready the housing. We'll get them cleaned up and fed, and then we can discuss where to go from there."

"Thank you." Azrael pulled Kaine in close, resting his forehead against the shorter man's. They closed their eyes, taking a moment to synchronize their breathing. It was an intimacy that forced me to look away lest I feel a voyeur.

When they pulled away, Kaine quickly addressed the crowd of Unseen. "Follow me, everyone. There's warm beds and a good meal waiting for you all."

There's a murmur of relief through the group as they trudge after the blue-haired man, streaming into the entrance of the housing.

Azrael was looking at me, I realized, so I told him, "I'm glad you're okay."

"I feel the same," he replied with a chuckle. "What happened to Bastien?"

"He's with Wilhelm," I explained, motioning back to the community hall. "They have a lot to talk about, I'm sure."

Azrael nodded, scratching at the nape of his neck. "Aye. He'll have a few choice words for me later, I'm sure. He's been with the Rebellion for weeks, and I never told him about this place. Then again, I'd been sworn to secrecy, so only me and a handful of others knew it existed."

And it dawned on me again that this wasn't just Azrael, my friend, that I was speaking with. This was the leader of the Rebellion. It was amazing how much the same he seemed, even with that enormous burden on his shoulders.

"Come on," Azrael said, motioning for me to follow him. "I'm starving, and I know a place down the way."

I followed, hurrying to match his confident stride.

"Have you heard from my sister?" I asked as we went, weaving our way through the street.

"Lynette should be showing up soon. She insisted on traveling with a small company, as she had an errand to run before she joined us. Being the person she is, of course, she didn't tell me what that errand was, so I couldn't tell you how much longer she'll be. But not to worry, she's got a communicator that connects her directly to us, so I'm sure we'll get an update soon."

"How long has she been working with you?" I continued my questioning, looking to piece together some of the fragments of my understanding.

Azrael's ear twitched, and he didn't look at me when he answered, "Since I almost killed her a few years back now."

I stopped in my tracks, and he slowed his pace, finally turning to look at me. "I wanted to wait till we had some food before I dove into everything, but I guess we can talk on the way? I'll have to start at the beginning, or it won't make any sense."

"Keep talking," I said, restarting my stride.

"When your mother banished me from the chateau, she had one of the mortal butlers drive me into the city. He was a nice man. Bertrand, I think, was his name. He gave me what little money he had on him and dropped me off in the safest place he could find. Before he left, he offered a warning, saying that the madame had ordered her guard to seize me should I try and return home and that my Papa would suffer the consequences if I tried.

"I had never been to the city before, but Papa always told me that we'd go one day. For the briefest moment, I was sort of excited, surrounded by the hustle and bustle of the Magi City. But reality quickly began to set in as I realized I had nothing but the shirt on my back, which inadvertently also had a target. Adored gave me baleful stares as I walked down the sidewalk, just trying to get my bearings. And the mortals just ignored me. Funny, I didn't even have to use magic to be invisible to them. I nearly got run over a few times before I realized how traffic worked, but all in all, by the time night was approaching, I had found myself alone in a dark alleyway, bawling my eyes out and wishing I was home.

"It took a few days for me to work through what little I had. By the end of my first week on the street, my hunger had reached a ravenous state, and I felt more beast than man with each passing hour. It was there that Kaine and the others took me in. A group of fellow urchins, they had found themselves in similar situations and had banded together to survive in the Magi City. They taught me what I needed to know to survive, the best places to steal food, where to bed down come winter so you won't freeze to death, and on and on.

"By the time we'd grown into adolescents, we'd mastered the art of urban survival. It was then that Rudderkin showed up. This grizzled old man with grey fur and fangs that never quite receded. He caught one of us trying to pickpocket on the corner and convinced them to bring him back to our hideout. He sold us on a tale of comforts that none of us had known in years if we channeled our talents. He told us he was looking for soldiers. Those who could turn the tide of the Unseen struggle. Rudderkin spoke with such passion nearly half of our group agreed on the spot. The rest of us were reluctant, but rather than split up the family that we'd worked so hard to hold together, we ended up accepting his offer.

"The training was intense. In those days of the Rebellion, Rudderkin had earned a reputation for his swift and brutal tactics. He educated us in those ways. I excelled in the training, quickly outpacing the others. Kaine and I rose to the top of the recruits in a manner of a few months, besting others twice our age. Rudderkin pushed us to be ruthless, but we never quite agreed to the level of violence that he demanded from us. He said that the path to peace for our kind would be paved in blood, but Kaine and I had other ideas, and our fellow recruits began to look to the two of us for guidance.

"When the time came for us to graduate to soldiers, Rudderkin came to me privately, asking if he could discuss a topic of discretion. He told me that there was no place for someone with my beliefs on the front lines but that me and the other Urchins, as we'd grown to be known, would be better suited for another task. So, he formed us into his own personal strike force. For ten years, me and the Urchins carried out his orders. Kidnappings, assassinations, covert reconnaissance, you name it. He gave his expectations in the form of orders, but I quickly began to push back in my decisions as leader. Rudderkin was growing more bloodthirsty the longer the conflict went on. Strategic maneuvers became acts of revenge, and both sides saw their casualties skyrocket.

"That's where Lynette entered the picture. The Urchins were given the order to eliminate a target. We were told it was a member of Adoranda Greene's staff and that it would sow disruption into the Adored's military actions, allowing a long enough break in the fighting for the Rebellion to catch their breath. But once we arrived on site, the orders were clarified. We were there to kill Lynette, the heir-apparent to Adoranda's seat on the Council. I refused the orders, telling Rudderkin that this would only fan the flames of Adoranda's ire, that it would lead us head-first into more bloodshed. He argued that the Greene family was the catalyst for the entire affront against the Unseen population, and as long as they drew breath, the Unseen would never know peace. We had to end their line of succession to ensure the freedom of our people.

"It was a hard argument to ignore. How much blood did I have on my hands, all because of your mother's crusade? I'd been fighting for over ten years, Tobias. And this was a way out. A way to end the suffering. The price would be a single life, and for once, I decided that the price was worth the outcome.

"I told the Urchins that I would go in alone. They each had their tasks on ensuring my extraction once the job was done, but I was the fastest, and I'd grown up alongside you and your sister. I had been touched by your magic before and would know if she were about to dominate my will.

"We waited for them to leave the chateau—some diplomatic trip to an outlying Magi City where they had to squeeze the local Adored to align with your mother's latest political leanings. When the time finally arrived, I snuck into Lynette's quarters late in the evening, ready to accomplish the mission. I wasn't expecting her to be awake at that hour, and in my haste, I was spotted.

It took her only a moment of touch with her magic to recognize me. I braced myself to resist her control, but instead, she merely greeted me by name, pulling me into an embrace as she told me how happy she was that I was still alive. I was speechless, waiting for the ruse to end and for her to defend herself. But that moment never came. Seeing the way I appeared to her, Lynette merely nodded, telling me that she understood what I was there to do. She told me that she knew that someone would come for her eventually and that she wished for a peaceful way to end the conflict, and if her death was the best option to avoid further violence, she'd give herself up willingly.

"I was floored by her reaction. Lynette and I never had the kinship that you and I shared, but she was always kind to me back at the chateau. It was bizarre seeing how much of that kindness survived a life alongside Adoranda. I would have thought it all wrung out by then. She turned her back to me, saying that she didn't blame me for my task and that she hoped she would be the last life I would have to take in the name of peace. Once again, I defied my orders and told her that I wasn't going to kill her, but maybe her being alive was the best path forward. After all, she was the next in line to power. If she was an ally to the cause, then there was no reason for her to die. We merely had to speed up her ascension to end the conflict.

"We talked into the night, discussing ways that she could begin to work from within on pushing the conflict toward a peaceful resolution. She explained that her mother would never heed her counsel, but perhaps there were others she could recruit to help apply pressure at the right moments. Negotiations would be our path forward, and all we needed was a plan to get them to the table.

"When I returned to Rudderkin empty-handed, he was less than pleased. In front of the other Urchins, he condemned me as a traitor. I explained to him, as I had to my brothers, that Lynette would be the lynchpin to a peaceful resolution, but that only angered him further, as he had devolved past the mindset of any outcome that wasn't total annihilation."

He paused there, and I realized we had stopped in front of a vendor's stall, the smell of smoke and charred food hitting my nose, making my stomach growl.

Azrael held his story long enough to order us some food, handing me two skewers with chunks of potato and vegetables roasted with a dark glaze. The smell was heavenly, and we found a spot to settle in around the corner so he could continue.

"Rudderkin was beyond reason at that point. He ordered that I go back and bring him Lynette's head, but I refused. It was then that he attacked me. Rudderkin was rusty in his advanced years, so it wasn't difficult to overpower him. The Urchins restrained him after that as we began to argue over what happened next. Kaine was especially upset with me for how things had turned out, and the conversation quickly became heated. Before it came to blows, Rudderkin snapped and broke free of his restraints, lunging at me with the intent to kill. Kaine pushed me out of the way, taking the blow and crumpling to the floor.

"So, I did what Rudderkin trained me to do. I neutralized the threat. It was only once my claws tore a hole through his chest that I realized what I had done. Rudderkin was dying, right there in my arms. The man I had looked up to as a father, and I'd ended his life. He seemed calm in those last few moments. No longer clouded by hate like the months leading up to that point. He told me that he'd always known I was the only one who could pick up his mantle for our people and that if I thought peace could be reached, I'd better be damn sure."

Azrael paused, taking another slow bite.

"Kaine barely survived the wound, and the other Urchins were the only ones who knew what happened to our leader. After we talked things through, they agreed that I should continue on and become the new 'Rudderkin' to lead the Rebellion. So, I took up the mantle as agreed. Once our contact with Lynette was established, it didn't take long for the others to get on board with the new mission—peaceful resolution."

"But Mother would never allow it," I surmised, polishing off my second skewer.

He shook his head, exhaling. "It became apparent quickly after I took over. Adoranda wanted nothing more than the erasure of my people. We wouldn't stand a chance as long as she held the reins. Maybe Rudderkin was right. Some problems can only be solved with blood."

We sat in silence for a moment, mulling over his conclusion. A crackling noise broke my concentration, and Azrael pulled out a small device, turning a knob on top till a voice spoke.

"Azrael, acknowledge."

"Acknowledged," Azrael responded, holding a button on the side of the device. "Speak freely."

"Our scouts have reported seeing Lynette Green enter the Magi City unaccompanied. She was due to arrive in Paradise nearly half an hour ago, and all attempts to reach her have failed. Her party just showed up without the fuzziest idea how they got here."

Azrael swore under his breath. "Acknowledged. Contact the Urchins and tell them to meet outside of the community hall in ten."

"Acknowledged."

The device went silent, and Azrael's eyes were on me. "Why would she go into the city?"

I'd been asking myself the same question. It didn't make sense. She knew that she was being hunted by our mother. What would make her want to go back there?

It hit me like the broadside of a blade.

"The Council," I concluded. "They're set to replace Lynette tonight if she doesn't show up. She's trying to take Mother's seat while she's not there to force the hands of the Council members."

"But why would she go alone? If Adoranda is still alive, she's bound to show up."

"If Lynette thought that she had a chance at ending things between the Adored and the Rebellion, she would have seized the opportunity. She may have a fighting chance if Mother doesn't show, but with her there, Lynette is done for."

The device sounded once more. "Azrael, additional reports are coming in. There is movement at Chateau Greene. I repeat, there is movement being reported at Chateau Greene. It appears the madame is still in play."

Fuck. If Mother was still alive, that meant Lynette was walking into a slaughter. She'd never make it to the Council in time, which means that Mother's plans to consolidate her power had never been closer to fruition.

"Acknowledged. Prepare transportation at once." He turned to me once more, eyes burning. "I'm going after her."

"Please, let me come with you. I can't let my sister face our mother alone."

Azrael hesitates. "Bastien should be ready to prepare the resurrection ritual by now. You should stay and take care of that."

"If Lynette is killed, then there's no point in me coming back."

He watched me, a deep confliction under sparkling violet eyes.

"Fine. But you need to let Bastien know what's going on. Meet me at the entrance to Paradise in half an hour."

"I'll be there."

# NINETEEN
## RAISE THE DEAD

Inside Paradise's community hall, I found Bastien seated in front of a large mural, staring up at the artwork. The familiar, spiraling designs of his tattoos were displayed throughout the artwork, and I wondered what it must be like to feel such a deep connection with something you'd never seen before.

"How goes it, seeker?" I asked, repeating what Wilhelm called him. I ignored the common word from Cirian's prophecy, squirreling that thought away for another time. I simply lacked the luxury of prophetic deciphering at the moment.

His gaze found me, his stoic contemplation melting away. "It's... incredible, Tobias. There's so much here that I thought was lost forever. Scattered to the wind. Before now, I had never even met another Reviled outside of my family."

"I'm happy for you," I said, wanting to reach for him but thinking better of it. I couldn't be distracted from the task at hand. "Listen, something has happened, and I have to leave."

"What?" Bastien scrambled to his feet, his brow drooping in confusion. "What are you talking about? Wilhelm is gathering the materials we need for the resurrection ritual as we speak. We shouldn't delay it any further."

I explained the message Azrael received and the plan to pursue Lynette. His eyes grew wide at the news of Mother.

"But without your magic, your mother will kill you, Tobias."

"It's Lynette, Bastien. I have to go. I have to help her. It's the entire reason I was there that night, to keep her from dying. If I can't stop it from happening again, then what was the point of all this?"

"The point?" Bastien repeated, his eyes narrowing. "The point is that you deserve to live, Tobias. There are people who care about you. Lynette included. So, stop talking as if your life has no value."

"You don't have to sell me on the value of my life, Bastien. I remember enough to know that I harmed far more people than I ever helped. And yes, I'm terrified of facing my mother again, but I won't stand by and let her kill my sister."

"Please," Bastien said, his voice suddenly pleading. "Please, Tobias. Don't do this. Just stay with me. Let me fix this—" he takes my hand in his. "Let me fix you."

"You can't fix me," I tell him, pulling my hand away gently. "I did this to myself, Bastien. I was fractured long before you ever brought me back. It's only because of your kindness that I've got this second chance. And I want to spend it making sure that Lynette lives."

He goes to argue, but I grasped him by the fabric of his sweater, pulling him closer. I kissed him, and his words melted away at the touch of my lips, the tension of his body dissolving as his arms wrapped around me, urging me even closer.

The tether, that invisible connection between us, pulled taut once more, vibrating at a frequency I swore I could hear, as his lips parted and we shared a breath between us that settled into the warm recesses of my chest.

"You can't go now," he whispered, clinging to me.

"I have to. But that doesn't mean that I'm not coming back. Prep your ritual, and I promise that I'm all yours as soon as I return with Lynette."

"Promise me," he replied. "Promise that you're coming back."

"I promise."

He nodded, pressing one last soft kiss against my lips before he released me. I didn't enjoy lying to him.

"Here," he said, digging through his pockets. "I'd feel better if you held onto this."

He handed over the green gem that had once been embedded in my chest. It sparkled in the light, the inner facets lined with shadows. He held it out to me, and I took it, but he covered my hand with both of his, muttering under his breath. The gem grew warm to the touch, Bastien's hands surrounded by a green light.

"What are you—"

That invisible thread pulled at my chest once more, and I was stunned to silence as a voice filled my mind. It was a familiar voice. Bastien's voice.

*"Keep him safe. Bring him back to me. Keep him safe. Bring him back to me."*

His intentions poured into the gem till it burned against my hand, and as he pulled away, I looked down to see it buried into the flesh of my palm, opposite the blue one that Cirian had given me.

"You didn't have to do that," I told him, cupping the side of his sweat-dampened face.

"Now you have to come back," he said, his breath coming in small gasps.

"Bastien, I—"

"Bastien, we've prepared the ritual space." Wilhelm approached with the staccato of her shoes against the polished floor. "Are you ready to begin the preparations?"

"I'm ready," Bastien said, giving me a slight nod. "We'll be waiting for you, Tobias. Don't take too long, now."

Confusion flashed across Wilhelm's face, but I hurried away before she could know what had transpired between us.

Heading back outside of the hall, I retraced our earlier path, finding it simple to navigate the narrow streets. The entrance had been toward the fields, so I kept that in mind with each turn, trying not to let the rising panic in my chest spur my pace.

Yes, I was heading back into the viper's pit, but abandoning Lynette was not an option. And I wasn't going alone. Azrael would keep me safe. A subtle warmth bloomed in my chest at the thought, but I didn't have the opportunity to dwell on that fact as I spotted Azrael standing by the path out into the fields. He was speaking with another Unseen, this one with fiery red hair and a long scar that ran across his cheek. He nodded as Azrael spoke, then darted off back into the settlement without a word.

The authority that Azrael commanded caught me off guard sometimes. It was hard to imagine this man was the little boy I used to play with all those years ago at Chateau Greene.

The boy I had shared my first kiss with.

Now was *really* not the time to dwell on that.

"I'm a bit surprised to see you alone," he said, craning his neck as if he expected someone to be hiding behind me.

"Bastien is preparing for the resurrection ritual. But he isn't letting me take off empty-handed." I showed him the stone embedded in the palm of my right hand, and something flashed behind his violet eyes.

"Ah, so that's *his* magic I smell on you. I should have known."

He smelled Bastien's magic on me? I didn't know what to do with that information.

"And to whom does that one belong?" He asked, pointing to my left hand. His warm fingers cupped my hand, drawing it upward so he could inspect it.

"Cirian, the Source's Acolyte. He made this after rescuing me from the raid on the camp. I depleted the magic at the chateau, though, so I guess it's merely ornamental at the moment."

Azrael watched me, the smile on his face fading as he did. "So many lay claim to you, Tobi." His hand dropped from mine, his thumb rising to my face to gently stroke my bottom lip. "But don't forget, I was the first."

A trill shot down my spine, and I shuddered away from his touch, heat blooming across my cheeks. I cursed my body's reaction, pulling away before it could betray me further.

"Kaine is waiting up ahead," Azrael said, pointing down the path toward where the sheer wall of the mountain rose. "Go and meet him. I'll catch up when I can."

"Catch up? You're not coming with us?"

"I'll be right behind you, Tobi. I promise. There's just one more thing I have to take care of here before I can leave."

Guilt swelled in my gut. Azrael was dropping everything to help Lynette—to help me—but he was still the leader of the Rebellion. His people came first.

"Okay," I agreed.

"Right behind you," Azrael said again, pulling me into an embrace. His strong arms enveloped me, pressing me into his firm chest. My head fit perfectly under his chin, and he rested it on my crown for just a moment, breathing in deeply. A low rumble sounded in his chest, but then he released me and strode away, back towards the settlement without another word.

The nape of my neck prickled as I gathered myself, willing my feet down the path. The rows of crops blocked my view to either side, but I was able to make out the silhouette of Kaine before long, waiting for me by the spot where the wall met the ground.

"Something tells me you're terrible at staying in one place," he said as I approached, a playful grin spread across his lips.

"You're not wrong," I muttered, rubbing at that prickling spot on the back of my neck. "Guess I ruined your dinner plans, huh?"

He snorted a laugh. "Come on, Greene. We've got a ways to go."

Kaine led me on the path along the wall, and it quickly dawned on me that we weren't traveling the way that we'd come in.

"Where are you taking me?" I asked, wincing at the suspicion I wasn't able to keep from my voice.

Thankfully, Kaine didn't seem offended. "There's a faster way out of Paradise," he explained, his pace not slowing. "It's only one-way, however. But it's great for a quick escape."

I didn't like the sound of that.

A staircase, carved from the stone of the mountain itself, rose up alongside us, and Kaine transitioned us onto it, beginning the ascent. Our position became quickly dizzying as I peered over the edge, watching the rows of crops become smaller and smaller.

My skin was flushed by the time we'd reached what I assumed was the halfway point. The stairs ended abruptly, emptying us out onto a small platform that jutted out from the wall. A lift—a primitive pulley system of ropes attached to a makeshift wooden platform—dangled over the side, two sets of levers flanking it.

"Hop on," Kaine told me, pointing to the device.

My knees quaked under me.

"You must be joking."

"Time's a wasting, Greene. Get on the platform, or you can stay behind. It's that simple."

I wanted to scream, but instead, I stepped out onto the swinging platform, my stomach dropping as it swayed beneath me. Kaine pulled one of the levers, quickly hopping onto the platform as it began to rise, running along the sloped ceiling and transporting us even higher.

Paradise lay sprawled below us, the colorful buildings forming a grid that wove its way across the stone floor. Bastien was down there, preparing the ritual that he'd promised would restore my magic. I wish that he could be with me now, but I clenched my fist around the stone, and the warmth of his magic soothed my raw nerves.

"Have you ever seen anything more wonderous?" Kaine asked, holding onto one of the ropes attached to the lift before leaning over the edge to peer down.

I shook my head, the fear for his safety far outweighing any sense of wonder I felt at the moment. We were quickly approaching where the stone roof leveled out, the slope of the ceiling curving drastically the higher we went till we were practically moving straight up.

"We're going to the top?" I questioned, looking above us into the dark recess of the uppermost portion of the ceiling.

"Almost," Kaine replied, his hand resting on the lever attached to the pulley system in the middle of our lift. "Don't worry, we're nearly there now."

Kaine pulled the lever a moment later, the lift coming to a shuddering stop. He reached out to a place along the stone wall, running a hand over a knob of stone that sunk into the wall with a clicking sound. As if on a hinge, a section of the wall opened up, lifting outwards.

Wind roared through the opening, buffeting us with a burst of cold air. I shielded my eyes, and Kaine fastened one of the ropes to the side of the wall, holding the lift in place.

"End of the line, Greene. Let's get a move on." He gives me a smile before stepping through the opening and into the night air. The stars shone brightly overhead, offering just enough light to make out my surroundings.

I followed him cautiously, finding another platform of rickety wooden planks outside. Two other Unseen were out on the platform, one holding a pair of binoculars to their face and the other taking readings from some handheld device that kept beeping incessantly. I recognized them both as members of Azrael's group from before—the Urchins—though I hadn't learned their names yet. I took a moment to orient myself, finding us on the side of the mountain overlooking the mortal town below. Dark buildings lit from within, spilling warm light throughout the valley below.

"Just how are we supposed to get down from here?" I asked, then immediately regretted it when I saw the contraption Kaine was fiddling with.

A line of thick braided metal hung above our heads fastened onto the rocky face of the mountain. A harness of sorts was attached to the line, and I started to piece together our trajectory.

"No," I said to Kaine, tracing the line of metal wire until it disappeared into the night. "No way."

"It's the fastest way down," Kaine said, pulling on one of the harness belts from a box on the corner of the platform. "Time is of the essence, right?"

"This is insanity!" I cried, my voice getting swallowed by another gust of wind that nearly knocked me off balance. "How long has it been since these were last used? How do we know it won't snap, and we all fall to our doom?"

"Well, if it makes you feel better," Kaine said, latching his belt onto the hook that hung down from the wire and giving it a tug. "I'll be going first. If I die a horrible, painful death, then I give you explicit permission to chicken out. But when I make it, then you'll be next."

"Take me back down, Kaine," I said, moving toward him. But he was already going for the edge of the platform, positioning himself for the takeoff, his cerulean eyes glinting with amusement in the dim light.

"Sorry, Greene. If you want to yell at me, you'll have to catch me." He tipped himself forward, allowing his body to fall over the edge of the platform. The line on the harness went taut, the sound of the wheel moving on the metal wire zipping loudly. He rocketed away from us, howling with laughter and disappearing quickly into the darkness over Brierwood.

"I've got eyes on him," the other Unseen with the binoculars said. "He's going to hit the first brake in three… two… one… There he goes. He's almost at the bottom now."

Was it really that quick? It had only been a few seconds.

"Success," the Unseen with the binoculars said. The other Unseen—with flaming red hair that matched the one I'd seen talking with Azrael back in the settlement—typed something into the device he held, then nodded as if he were logging data. Then he turned to me, his eyes the same fiery red, and said, "You're up next."

I wanted to jump back through the cavern door, but that wouldn't solve any of my problems in the long term.

"There's a harness over there," the redhead pointed out. "Let me know if you need help getting it on."

The other Unseen snorted a laugh, and the redhead slapped his shoulder with an open hand.

"Don't blame me, you git. You're the one who said it."

The two continued squabbling like children while I convinced myself that leaping off a mountain was a good idea.

I grabbed a harness from the box, taking a moment to figure out exactly what parts went where. Once it was on, the redhead came to double-check my work, tugging on a few spots to ensure that the fit was tight enough.

"Kaine will be at the bottom to catch you," the redhead told me. "Try not to kick him in the process."

"What if he really deserved it?" I asked, humor distracting me momentarily from the paralyzing panic running through my veins.

Staring up at the wire that ran above my head, I reminded myself that this was for Lynette. If our roles were reversed, I knew she would brave far worse for me. And with that, I swallowed my fears, stepped up onto the edge of the platform, and cast off.

Wind deafened me as I struggled to hold my head up against the buffeting force. My skin was peppered with stinging impacts of what I could only assume were insects, and I clamped my mouth shut even tighter, determined not to swallow the entrails of the creatures I was eviscerating with my descent. My hands ached as I clung to the rope connecting my harness to the cable. After a few moments of disorientation, I seemed to level out, and I risked cracking an eye open to check on my progress. Below, the quiet town of Brierwood was still quite small, but I was close enough to make out the headlights from vehicles, and the chiming of the clocktower by city hall. I wondered if they could see me, too, rocketing through the sky high above. If I carried a light, would they think I was a shooting star? How many wishes would go wasted on the likes of me?

I was almost to the point of enjoyment with my ride when I hit the first of the brakes, the arrested momentum hurling my feet forward and up till I was upside down, the soles of my shoes turned toward the sky. Rocking back, I continued the descent in bursts, hitting brake after brake till my feet were almost skimming the tops of trees below me. Darkness overtook me as I cleared the tree tops, zipping down toward the pitch-black forest floor and finally coming to a stop dangling above a wooden platform attached to the trunk of a tree.

Kaine was there, holding a lantern as he waited for me, an amused grin displaying his fangs.

"Wasn't that fun?"

I stared daggers at him. "Get me down. Now."

He laughed as he unfastened the harness, giving me little warning as it suddenly gave, dumping me out on my ass.

"Ooo, sorry about that. Good thing you've got some cushion to break your fall."

Was he commenting on my ass now? I needed to get away from this maniac in a hurry. When would Azrael be back?

The other two Urchins zipped in a few minutes later, wearing a tandem harness. The redhead—Irwin, Kaine called him—and the one with dark hair shaved close to his head.

"Grab the bikes, Reed," Kaine told the dark-haired one as he tossed a rope ladder down from the platform. "And leave Azrael's alone. You know how he gets if anyone touches his things."

Reed's eyes flickered to me for a moment, then he let out a hearty laugh, disappearing down the ladder.

What was that about?

"Irwin, we're headed for the City. Go ahead and make a call to the scouts in the area to see if they've got any updates."

"Aye, Kaine." Irwin vaulted over the railing of the platform, ignoring the ladder altogether.

Kaine sighed, shaking his head. "Those two are going to be the death of me," he muttered, reaching a hand down to help me up.

"Did you say bikes?" I asked him, my voice colored with confusion. "Wouldn't it be faster just to catch the train?"

Kaine merely laughed again, dropping down onto the rope ladder and descending with a speed and grace I would never hope to achieve, even if I had two working shoulders. Clumsily, I followed suit, my foot getting caught only twice as he watched me from the ground, his expression bordering on leering.

"This way," he said, beckoning me to follow him.

We were outside of the town, trees towering overhead, taller than most of the buildings I'd seen there. Kaine led me out onto a worn path through the leaves and underbrush, his footing confident, even in the darkness. We moved in silence for a few minutes, but my curiosity got the better of me, so I made the most of the time we had.

"You've known Azzy—Azrael—for a while, yeah?"

"More than a while," he replied.

"Were you the one who found him? When he was on the street, I mean."

Kaine glanced over his shoulder at me. "Yeah, I was."

"How was he? When you found him, I mean."

He stops then, turning to face me. The playful smile he usually wore had faded, and when he spoke, his words were all fangs, sharp as a warning. "He was a child, Greene. How do you think he was?"

I swallowed down the next question, giving a slight nod.

Kaine resumed his way down the path, his steps heavy as the atmosphere around us had grown. Thunder rumbled in the distance and I couldn't help but imagine Azrael, cold and alone on the streets because of a foolish decision I made.

I would make it up to him should my second life continue past what lay ahead.

Before the rain could set in, we happened upon Irwin, who stood leaning against a tree, a bar of chocolate between his lips. Beside him, three motorbikes stood in a row, each more ghastly in appearance than the last. They looked as though they'd been made from a scrap heap, with rust spreading across the majority of the surfaces.

"There you are, Kaine. We were about to send a search party," Irwin teased, his bottom lip covered in melted chocolate.

"Greene here isn't used to all this hiking back and forth," Kaine explained, walking over to the larger of the three bikes. "I'll have to thank Azrael for saddling me with babysitting duties."

Reed shimmered into existence beside Irwin, the glimmering magic fading from his tanned skin as he said, "The path to the road is clear. We shouldn't have any trouble."

Peering through the branches above, I eyed the swelling grey clouds. "And we're sure the train isn't an option?"

"Aw," Irwin hopped on the smaller of the two remaining bikes, kicking the engine to life. "He's afraid to get a little wet."

I shoot him a look. "I'm not afraid of rain. I'm wary of skidding off the road on one of those death contraptions."

"Good thing you're not driving, then," said Kaine, patting the space on the long seat behind him.

"Gods, save me."

Climbing onto the bike, I did my best to maintain a polite distance between Kaine and me, but as the engine rumbled to life and the bike kicked off, my arms wrapped around his waist to keep me from flying off the back.

Irwin howled with laughter as he took off past us, the trees streaking by in shadowy smudges. Behind, I could hear the engine of Reed, who seemed to be the most reserved of the trio, but even he was smiling when I chanced a glance back at him.

Once we left the woods behind, hitting the paved road that led away from the quiet mortal town, Kaine took point, revving the engine as our speed climbed and climbed. The wind whipping past my ears was the only thing I could hear, and as we reached the open road, the sting of raindrops against my skin felt like electricity biting into me.

Lightning streaked across the sky, lighting the way for us in spurts. The rumbling thunder indiscernible from the rumbling engine beneath me as I clung to Kaine, burying my face into his back to escape the painful impact of the rain.

The ride would be long and grueling if this rain persisted, however, when we reached our destination, Death may very well be waiting to greet me.

If these were to be the moments leading up to my finale, I couldn't have asked for a more dramatic backdrop.

Loosening my grip on Kaine's waist, I lifted my head from his back, squinting into the streams of stinging rain. Each collision reminded me I was alive. I was still here, no matter what happened, no matter what memories still lurked beyond the chaos of my mind. I was alive.

Spreading my arms wide, they caught the wind as it rushed by. And in the next rumble of thunder, I let loose a howl of my own from the very depths of my soul, crying along with the heavens.

I was alive. At least for the time being.

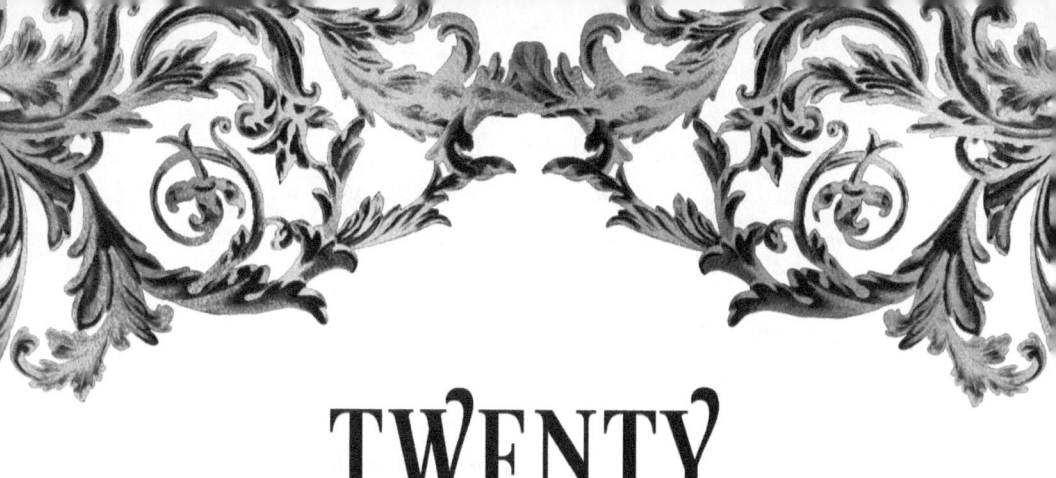

# TWENTY
## OVER MY DEAD BODY

We made it into the Magi City in a little over an hour. Kaine was right. The train would have taken at least double the time. Irwin and Reed split off from us once we hit the outskirts, each with their own assignments I wasn't privy to. Kaine seemed to operate as the de facto leader when Azrael wasn't around, and the other took their lead from him.

"We'll lay low for now," Kaine told me as we stopped to let me stretch my legs and regain feeling in my ass. "The Council isn't scheduled to meet till later this evening, so that gives us a few hours to get eyes on the key players. Adoranda will show, no doubt about that, but Lynette still hasn't been sighted again."

I wrung the hem of my sweater out, the rainwater spattering the ground like an animal relieving itself. Thankfully, the rain moved on just as we entered the city, but the oppressive clouds stayed behind, blotting out the stars. With the wind funneling through the buildings, I couldn't escape the chill.

"My apartment isn't too far from here," I told Kaine. "There's no need for us to skulk on the street like a couple of vagrants. Plus, we can get dry. And I think I owe you dinner, if I'm not mistaken?"

"That's not part of the plan," Kaine argued, brushing the rain-slicked hair from his eyes.

"Plan or not, I need dry clothes. There's no chance they'll let me anywhere near the Council looking like a drowned rat."

Kaine seemed to chew on the idea for a moment longer before conceding.

"I go in first, and if there's anything suspicious, we hightail it outta there. Understood?"

"Whatever you say," I agreed.

I gave him the directions, and we were off again, thundering down the familiar city streets. Once we arrived at the high-rise that contained my apartment, Kaine stashed his bike in the alleyway, muttering a string of words under his breath to make it vanish before my eyes.

"That's handy," I said, eyeing his work.

"Being 'Unseen' certainly has its perks."

The air around him shimmered and he disappeared next, tapping me on the shoulder to alert me that it was time to move.

Inside, the doorman thankfully let me by without a fuss. He even provided me with my spare key so I wouldn't have to resort to breaking in my own door. The lift carried Kaine and I up to the twenty-seventh floor, and a short walk down the hall later, we were inside my apartment.

I had only been gone for a few days, so the space still felt lived in. Materializing, Kaine went straight for the fridge, rummaging around and making the odd comment about how I didn't have any real food.

"Order something," I told him, pointing to the stack of menus by the rotary phone on the wall. "Tell them to bill it to my account."

This seemed to please Kaine as he excitedly flipped through the pages.

Down the hall to my bedroom, I closed the door behind me, exhaling a sigh of relief at the sight of my own bed. The cleaning staff had been in since I last left, so the sheets were tucked tightly, and the pillows arranged just so. Peeling the wet, mismatched clothes from my body, I tossed them into the bathroom. No amount of laundering would ever get the smell of wet-Kaine off of them, so I'd probably end up burning them after this was all over.

I took a moment to refresh myself, washing my face and passing a comb through my damp hair. My reflection was hardly recognizable at this point, the dark bruise-like circles under my eyes, something I would normally conceal, on full display, my shoulder bandaged together, and my lips splintered from the wind. It was hardly the time to care about such things, however.

Pulling on a clean pair of jeans and a sweater that actually fit, I swapped the dirty sneakers for my favorite pair of boots and headed back out into the hallway.

"What kind of food did you decide on?" I called ahead of me, stopping short of the living room to grab a jacket from the hallway closet.

Silence.

"Kaine?"

The hum of the lights above my head was the only thing I could hear. Dread swelled in my gut, and I moved slowly toward the end of the hall.

I spotted Kaine first, sitting straight up on the end of the sofa, a scowl on his face as he stared in the opposite direction of me, his claws digging into his knees where he clutched them. Moving further in, I found the reason.

"Nice place you got here," Lorelei said, standing at the opposite end of the sofa from Kaine, a long-barreled metal contraption in her hand, pointed at him.

Was that a gun? I had only read about them in novels set in times before the first Awakening. Magic had made most mortal weapons obsolete, so if it were real, it must have been a relic.

"Hands where I can see them," Lorelei ordered.

I raised them slowly above my head, palms facing outward.

"My, my. You've been a busy little boy, Tobias. No sudden movements, now. I wouldn't want your friend here to ruin this beautiful sofa. I must say, your taste in furniture is far better than your taste in company."

Her escape from Chateau Greene seemed to have left Lorelei unscathed, her appearance just as immaculate as the first time we'd met. Not a curl out of place.

"What do you want?" I questioned, throwing a quick glance at Kaine, then back to her. "My mother can't possibly be paying you *that* much money. Why are you still—"

"Quiet," Lorelei snapped, her blood-red lips curling into a snarl. "My reasons are my own, and what I want is for you to come with me without any more lip, you brat."

"Come where?" I questioned, hoping if I talked long enough, I'd draw her attention fully to me, leaving Kaine a window of opportunity. But right now, the barrel of the gun was still trained on him.

"To a little family reunion," Lorelei answered, her focus uninterrupted. "It's sure to be an evening to remember."

This wasn't working. I had to do something, or I'd be playing right into her hand.

Reaching for the magic in Bastien's gem, I pressed my aura outward, hoping to catch her off guard. If I could just get a command through for her to drop the gun, that would be all the time Kaine would need—

"Just like your mother," Lorelei said with a sigh.

A deafening *bang* sounds and Kaine exhales a wet breath. My eyes were drawn to him as the scarlet stain bloomed across his chest, and he slumped back against the sofa cushion.

"No!" I shouted, my legs propelling me forward, but Lorelei was there, standing between us with her sights on me now.

"Want to try that little move again?" she asked.

I gritted my teeth, my vision narrowing in on Kaine. He was still breathing. I could hear the ragged sounds from where I stood. If I could get him to a Hallowed soon enough, maybe I could save him. But how was I going to convince her to allow that?

Taking the risk, I moved slowly toward the sofa. Lorelei's gun made a noise, like the next bullet loading into the chamber, but I didn't let it stop me. I assumed she needed me alive for whatever awaited me. But that didn't mean she couldn't hobble me, so I did my best to seem non-threatening, still holding my hands above my head.

Kaine's eyes were half-lidded when I got to him, his breaths coming in quick, shallow spurts. There was so much blood already. It oozed from the entry wound and pooled behind him in the cushions.

"You're a terrible host," he joked, his eyes half-focusing on me.

"I know," I went along, my voice hollow. "I didn't even ask if you wanted something to drink."

"Do you think I'll get to haunt your apartment now? Gotta say, I'm not looking forward to watching you wank on the daily."

A broken laugh escaped alongside my tears. "Then don't look."

He tried to laugh, but then he was coughing, and his mouth was filled with blood. My mind raced, my hands going to the wound out of panic, applying pressure that was too little, too late.

I cursed under my breath. I was powerless. If only Bastien were here, or Cirian. They could fix him up in seconds with their magic.

But Bastien's magic *was* here. Or at least, in the Anima stone he gave me. Did that mean…?

I didn't know the incantations. I didn't speak the language typically required to draw on the magic that could mend flesh. I was Adored. Our magic was tied to emotion. Intention. Bastien had entrusted me with his magic, but did that mean it was truly mine? And if it were, did that mean I was limited to only feats the Adored could manage?

The questions buzzed through my brain till they were silenced all at once by the reality of the situation.

I had to try.

I'd never be able to face Azrael again if I was the reason his right-hand man died. I'd taken enough from him already.

So, I did what felt natural. I extended my aura to Kaine, wrapping him up in it. His pain flared in my chest, but it was dull. Fading. He was fading. I'd have to be quick. I focused in on that spot, the wound that seeped blood under my palm. The gem burned hot against my flesh, but I couldn't tell if it was working, not when the wound was covered up. Still, I didn't relent. I poured every bit of intention I could into the spot I focused on, willing it to close. Willing the skin to knit itself together. For the arteries to regenerate. For Kaine to keep drawing breath. I wished, and I hoped, and I prayed to the gods who had always been silent that this would work.

"It's time to go, Tobias."

Lorelei's voice was close like she was standing right behind me. I didn't care. I would stay with Kaine until the magic worked. Or until he left this place. Either way, I wasn't moving.

"Mourn on your own time. We're running late."

"Fuck you," a sputtering voice sounded. "We're having a moment."

I gasped, my hand retracting in surprise. Kaine's skin was smooth once more, a clean spot amidst the blood smeared across his chest.

I had done it. But... how?

Lorelei clicked her tongue, then moved to point the gun at Kaine once more. I quickly moved between them, pushing my chest into the barrel. "I'll go with you," I said quickly. "I'll go if you just leave him be."

She pondered that for a moment, a manicured finger on the trigger that could end me. "Alright, I guess you've learned your lesson."

Lorelei lowered the gun, lifting her other hand to her mouth. She stuck two fingers between her lips, letting out a sharp whistle. The door to my apartment opened, and a hulking man hurried to her side.

"We're taking this one to go, Grigori. Wrap him up."

"Yes, ma'am," the hulking man answered, his voice thick.

A weak grip on my hand made me turn, Kaine holding me by the wrist. "No..."

"I'll be fine," I lied.

The man pulled a shroud over my head, the room going dark. My arm was yanked out of Kaine's grip and forced behind my back, tied to the other. With little effort, he hefted me over his shoulder and whisked me away to whatever venue would see my second life end.

# TWENTY-ONE
## DEAD MAN WALKING

"Grigori, has anyone ever told you that you have very soft hands?"

The car remained silent, as it had since I was shoved into what I can only assume was the back seat. Light peeked through the fabric of the shroud over my head, so I was able to at least make out a couple of shadows ahead of me in the car—my captors.

My hands were bound tight behind my back, my shoulder throbbing something fierce. There was little chance of me being able to wiggle my way out of the restraints at this angle, and Lorelei seemed impervious to any of my magic, so it would have been a waste to try again.

So, instead of plotting a daring escape, I spent my downtime pondering the implications of what just happened with Kaine. I had healed him. Or at least, I was pretty sure that's what happened. I'd never heard of an Adored being able to wield healing magic before, so I could only assume it was because of the Anima stone that Bastien had provided me. But did that mean I would be able to wield *any* Reviled magic?

The possibilities were enough to occupy my mind till the vehicle came to a stop. Grigori grabbed me from the back seat, once again hefting me over his shoulder as if I weighed nothing. Lorelei spoke softly in a language that I didn't understand, taking pauses long enough that I parsed together she was on a call. We were outside for only a brief moment before conditioned air and bright light told me we'd entered a building. Elevator music drifted over me as we stepped inside, the door opening and closing with a soft *ding*. I could swear I heard Grigori humming along tunelessly with the song, but then we were moving again.

When we finally stopped moving, Grigori placed me in a cushy chair, unfastening my hands long enough to refasten them to the armrests. Once I was secured, he yanked the bag off my head and I had to blink a few times before my location sunk in. I was sitting in the corner of the enormous board room in which the Council of Magi met. It was located on the sixtieth floor of the building and offered stunning views of the Magi City. I'd been here more than a few times as Mother's delegate, so I was slightly annoyed with myself that I hadn't recognized the path here.

Lorelei hung up her call, sitting herself on the edge of the long table that ran through the center of the room.

"Not long now," she said, stowing the device into her pocket. She wasn't brandishing her gun any longer, but I'd have been foolish to assume it wasn't on her person.

"Why exactly did you bring me here?" I asked, craning my head to see if anyone else was present in the room. Grigori lurked in the corner behind me, and Lorelei watched me with a bored expression.

"Isn't it obvious?" Lorelei asked, reaching into her blazer and retrieving her little leather notebook. "You're here to sit there and look pretty while the grown-ups talk about important things."

I rolled my eyes. Obviously, I wasn't going to get any useful info out of her. "Great, well, why don't you wake me when my mother finally decides to show up, and we can just cut out all this middle-man banter."

Lorelei laughed—a sharp and disconcerting noise.

"You're as dense as ever, aren't you? Haven't you put it together yet?"

"You'll have to elaborate, dear. If you don't remember, my brain got scrambled when I died that one time."

"Patience, Tobias. You don't have long to wait. Then we'll see just what that second life is worth to you."

I didn't like the sound of that. I was in the midst of crafting another quippy response when the door opened on the far end of the room, and my heart nearly jumped out of my chest.

"Lenny!" I shouted, pulling against my restraints in an attempt to jump for joy. It ended up more of a flail for joy, but I'd take it.

Lynette walked into the room unaccompanied, her sights set on me as she moved. Her coppery hair was pulled back off her face, her body covered in a long brown trench coat tied at the waist.

I was saved! Lynette would make quick work of these two and we would be able to come up with a plan for when Mother decided to show up.

As Lynette got closer, her trajectory changed slightly, and she stopped at the end of the table, standing beside Lorelei, who looked up from her notebook with a smile.

"Right on time," Lorelei said, setting the notebook down as Lynette wrapped her arms around the blonde woman and then leaned in for a kiss.

My blood ran cold. I blinked a few times, willing the sight away, but they were still embracing each time I opened my eyes.

What the hell was happening?

"Did you have any trouble out of him?" Lynette asked, pulling away from Lorelei.

"Eh, I had to shoot one of his pets to get him to show me. But other than that, it was smooth sailing."

And just like that, the frozen river of my veins turned to boiling lava. I pulled against my restraints with renewed strength. "Come closer and say that again, you bitch!"

"Now, now," Lynette chastised the two of us. "Let's keep this civil."

"What the hell, Lenny?" I demanded. "What's the meaning of this?"

She walked over to my chair, running a cool finger across my cheek. "It's going to be okay, Tobi. I promise."

I pulled away from her touch, glowering at her. "What have you done? Why are you working with her? She's mother's stooge."

Lorelei laughed again, another sharp jab to my eardrums.

My sister doesn't answer, her attention too wrapped up in something. She grabbed one of my hands, turning it over—with some difficulty, thanks to Grigori's knot-tying skills—to reveal Bastien's green stone. "This was the one?" she asked, turning back to Lorelei.

The blonde woman nodded in response. "He put it right over the wound. It closed up without an incantation."

"Really?" Lynette questioned, her eyes wide. "Tobi, I didn't know you had it in you."

"Untie me right now, Lenny. We can talk this out. Whatever is going on, it's not too late—"

"Too late for what, hm? I'm simply doing what I told you I was going to do, Tobias. Unlike some people in this world, I keep my promises." She lifted my other hand, inspecting Cirian's stone, then turned back to Lorelei. "Has he shown any other signs?"

"None so far," Lorelei replied, jotting something down in her little book. "He didn't put up much of a fight, to be honest. Are you sure you're related to him?"

"Don't talk about me like I'm not here," I spat, straining once again. "I'm your brother. How could you treat me like this?"

Lynette looked down at me, her expression colder than I've ever seen. "My brother? Oh no, Tobias. You lost that privilege the moment you decided to try and murder me."

"What are you talking about?" I demanded.

Magic, heavy as a boulder, bared down on me. Lynette leaned in close, her eyes burning with golden magic as she whispered, *"Remember."*

"Do not mock me, Tobias. I know the difference. These are no dreams."

"Then let me help you!" I pleaded with her. "Clue me in on what's going on, and maybe I can help think it through. But giving up the power you'll need to enact change isn't the right move. You'll only clip your wings—"

# THE SECOND AWAKENING

*A sound from the bushes a few feet away silenced me. Movement out of the corner of my eye and something darting out of the brush, dark as a shadow and fast as lightning. They closed the distance in a fraction of a second, the flash of steel glimmering in the lamplight as the figure thrust a short blade at Lynette.*

*She catches them at the wrist, her other hand moving in a blur, but she's too slow to catch the assailant's other hand as they slap something across her mouth. Lynette grunts in pain as the device locks over her lips, keeping her from speaking—or commanding the assailant with magic.*

*"S-Stop!" I shouted, attempting to wrap the figure in my aura, but their defenses were too strong for me to overwhelm, and they stabbed back into my mind, causing me to flinch. Instead, I charged them, shoving my shoulder into their side to try and throw them off balance, but it was like colliding with a brick wall, and even with mine and Lynette's combined strength, the assailant shoved me with their hip, knocking me to the ground.*

*"Don't interfere," they barked, voice harsh behind the black mask that obscured their face. They pushed the blade closer, the tip biting into Lynette's abdomen. She whimpered but held fast, keeping the attack from advancing any further.*

*I attempted to wrap the foe in my aura once more, wincing as they retaliated, a splitting headache ripping through me. From the ground, I kicked at their feet, but they were too quick, pushing Lynette forward a few steps out of my reach.*

*"What do you want?" I asked, desperate. Obviously, I wasn't going to be able to overpower them, but if I could distract them long enough for Lynette to get that thing off her mouth, then no one would be able to stand against her.*

*"Do not interfere," the assailant ordered. "I act on behalf of Her Grace, Adoranda Greene."*

*"Liar!" I cried, kicking at the woman, but she drove her heel into my side, knocking the air from my lungs.*

*"Has your sister told you what role you play in her visions, Tobias?" the assailant asked, their gaze drifting to me with cold indifference.*

*I froze there on the ground. "What?"*

*Lynette struggled harder to free the blade, a trickle of blood staining the front of her dress. The assailant swept a leg under her, knocking her down to a knee.*

Bearing down on her from above, the blade sunk deeper into her abdomen, and she howled against the muzzling device.

"What are you talking about?" I asked the figure.

"Her visions from the Augur. Madame Greene has been logging them for years. They all involve you, Tobias. You are the key to unlock the calamity that will burn the world the ash."

I turned to my sister, her eyes burning with fiery hate toward the assailant as they struggled for control over the blade. "Is this true?"

The veins in her neck were bulging under the strain, but after a moment, she nodded.

"You are to be the sacrifice that lights the flames, Tobias," the assailant continued, still bearing down on Lynette.

"Sacrifice?" I echoed, looking to Lynette, her wide eyes pleading. "You were going to sacrifice me? For what? So Mother wouldn't get her way? Gods, Lenny!"

She shook her head, losing her focus enough that the blade sunk in another inch. Another stifled groan, but I didn't care. I needed answers.

"How… how could you, Lenny? I'm your brother!"

Her eyes shined, and with a final grunt from the assailant, they broke her hold and plunged the blade fully into her gut. But she held my gaze, eyes begging me to understand something that was beyond my comprehension.

I turned to the assailant. "Are you going to kill her?"

They nodded, yanking the blade out in one swift motion. The edge was glowing with ruby light—a Sanguine blade. The wound would sap Lynette's magic away if it wasn't healed properly. Lynette groaned, writhing on the ground. Her fingers were slick with blood, and they couldn't find purchase on the edges of the muzzle over his lips.

"Are you going to interfere?" the figure asked me, poising the blade to strike the killing blow.

I looked down at my sister, my Lenny, wanting to tell the assailant to stop. But all I could see was her, leading me to this secluded area, alone, next to a freshly dug grave.

She was going to kill me here and leave me in the ground next to our father.

What other reason would she have?

Tears welling in my eyes, I turned back to the assailant.

"No."

With a muffled shriek, Lynette pounds the ground with her fist, the dirt shimmering with golden dust as it rocked beneath our feet. The assailant dove for her, looking to sink the blade into her chest, but she was ready this time. Catching the blade between her hands, golden sparks showered the ground beneath her. She wrested it from the assailant's grip, rolling far enough away to regain her footing. Using the edge of the knife, she cut the muzzle from her mouth, leaving a long gash down her chin. The device fell to the ground, and in a split second, her aura crushed the air from my lungs as she ordered, "Stop."

Both mine and the assailant's bodies went rigid, completely at Lynette's mercy. She held out the blade, still slick with her blood, and for a moment, I thought she was about to slit the woman's throat right there. Instead, she held it out handle first. "Take this back to my mother and tell her she's too late. It can't be stopped. I can't be stopped. And soon enough, she'll burn alongside all the others."

The assailant took the blade with a trembling hand, utterly powerless to ignore the Command of my sister.

"Go."

Knocking the woman back with the power of her word, Lynette straightened as the assailant fled from the scene. When she turned to face me, her expression was tempered steel. She'd been preparing for this moment, I imagined. The moment when she would fulfill this delusion that plagued her day and night.

And here it was.

She moved toward me, wincing as she clapped a hand over her wound to stymie the flow of blood. It hardly slowed her down. I was surprisingly calm as I met her gaze, acceptance hitting all at once.

"I won't help you. If you're committed to destroying the world, you'll have to do it without me."

Lynette held up a finger. "Not the world, Tobi. The Magi. We're the blight that's created this chaos. This violence. The Second Awakening will come with the lapping of flames and will bring balance once more. I've seen it."

*I tried to break from her hold. To make a run for it. She was deranged. Unmoored. Overtaken completely.*

*She wasn't my sister any longer.*

*But my limbs remained motionless, no matter how much I urged them. With a wave of her hand, however, I moved along with her, headed for the empty hole in the ground just across from the grave of our father.*

*"What good can I do you if I'm already dead?" I asked. "Some sacrifice a dead guy makes."*

*"Don't worry, Tobi. Death is only the beginning for you."*

*With a violent twist, I felt my spine snap, and my legs give out as I tumbled forward into the dirt. Along a shower of golden sparks, the loose earth began to bury me, another grave for another Tobias Greene.*

My eyes snapped open with a start, my breath coming in gasps.

Lynette watched me, her eyes mirrors of my own staring back.

"You were going to let me die," she said plainly.

"You fucking killed me!" I argued, the rage bubbling up all at once. "You actually fucking killed me!"

"Oh, calm down," Lynette said, rolling her eyes. "I was always planning on bringing you back. Or at least, having someone bring you back. Your boyfriend took longer than expected to show up, though. I was getting worried he wouldn't make it before you started to smell."

"You already knew about Bastien?"

"Of course I did," she scoffed. "I'm not oblivious, like most men. You really should have noticed your boyfriend exuding death magic, Tobi. Those glamours on his arms didn't hide jack shit from me."

"So, what, you brought me back to life just so you could kill me again?"

"Not exactly," Lynette said, turning back to Lorelei and giving her a nod. "You'll see soon enough, but I'm afraid there are some friends joining us for an important meeting, so you'll have to sit tight and be patient."

"If you think I'm going to sit here while—" my words were muffled by the gag Grigori shoved in my mouth, pulling the binding around my head.

Lynette turned to the brute. "If he doesn't quiet down, rip out his tongue. He won't be needing it for much longer."

Grigori chuckled. Stupid Grigori. I was starting to think that we could have been friends.

The doors opened on the opposite end of the room once more, a stream of bodies moving into the meeting space. Lynette and Lorelei moved to the center of the table, standing by the high-backed chair that was elevated slightly above the rest.

Gasps rippled through the crowd as they entered, more of them seeing Lynette for the first time. A silver-haired man with half-moon glasses stepped forward, bearing the crest of the Hallowed on his vest. "What is the meaning of this?"

"You've been lied to," Lynette addressed the Council members as they trickled in. "I'm sure my mother has told you a great number of things, including news of my disappearance. Yet, here I stand. Ready to take my place as the Ascended amongst the Council."

Near the back of the crowd, I spotted a familiar robe of aqua blue. The Cardinal, Saint Sancha, stood in the entrance, leaning over to whisper to none other than Cirian. I groaned into the fabric, but Grigori put a hand on my shoulder, and I quieted down. He couldn't see me, at least not clearly, from where he was. But that didn't mean that he wouldn't eventually. I just had to wait for the crowd to thin.

Murmurs of confusion rippled through the Council members, but the grey-haired man approached the table opposite Lynette, picking up a small wooden gavel and pounding it against the table. "Silence! We will get to the bottom of this nonsense, I assure you all."

"This is the truth of it," Lynette addressed the crowd. "My mother attempted to end my life prior to my Ascension. She feared what I would do should I be allowed to speak unfettered. Now, I tell you all, here I am. Ready to enact the changes necessary to lead us into a new dawn of prosperity. I will bring the second Awakening here and now."

The second Awakening? What was she talking about?

I struggled against the gag, trying to make any sound that might carry over to Cirian. But there were too many bodies between us, and like the others, Lynette held his full attention.

The grey-haired man continued, "That is a staggering accusation, Lynette—"

"Councilman Briggs," Lynette addressed the grey-haired man. "You've known me for nearly thirty years. You've known my mother for far longer. I would ask that you take a moment to consider which of us you believe carries the want of a brighter future for all Magi." She moved her attention to the gathering crowd, planting a foot on the chair reserved for the Ascended and standing upon it. "Please, friends. Take your places. Let us discuss this bright future together."

Another round of murmurs from the crowd, but they began to file around the table, each taking their place amongst the others. As the Cardinal sank into her chair directly across from Lynette, I was finally able to catch Cirian's eye. He glanced over me at first, then his dark eyes narrowed in, his lips pulling into a thin line. With the slightest of nods, he gave me the sign I'd been waiting for. He knew that I was there.

Once the council had taken their seats—twelve Adored and twelve Hallowed, fanning out from the center—Lynette lowered herself down into the chair, still flanked by Lorelei on one side.

"Friends," she spoke in a high, clear voice, raising her hands outstretched. "Since the first Awakening, we Magi have been blessed with the responsibility of guiding our world. A thousand years of perspiration has led us to this point, and we've never been closer to achieving a second Awakening. Another leap forward in the evolutionary line of the Magi people—"

"A thousand pardons," Councilman Briggs interrupted. "We're all aware of the benevolent history of our people. We do not require a history lesson."

Lynette chuckled under her breath, Lorelei moving from her side and walking towards the doors. "Yes, I'm well aware of the *history* that we've been taught, Councilman. We've all been given the same falsehood, sweetened beyond recognition to paint us in a favorable light. But there is a point to my lesson tonight. A reason why I wanted you all to hear me."

"And what is that?" Briggs asked, folding his arms across his chest.

Lynette smiled sweetly, leveling her gaze at the man. "So you'll understand why you'll burn alongside the rest of them."

Chaos erupted from the Council members. Shouting quickly overtook the room as Lorelei stood in front of the exit, her gun drawn and pointed toward anyone who got too close.

I spotted Cirian in the bedlam, moving closer and closer to where I was being held as the crowd continued to rage. Grigori must have been caught up in the mess because he didn't even notice when Cirian slipped behind us, moving silently up to the brute's ear and whispering a few words, his eyes flashing with electric blue light.

Grigori's head drooped, his chin falling to his chest as he began to snore softly beside me. Cirian was there in a flash, removing the gag, then pulling at my restraints and cursing under his breath. "Fucking Greenes."

"It's good to see you, too," I muttered, relief sinking into my shoulders.

He'd almost got my hands free when Lynette's voice rose above the din, the room suddenly filled with the crushing weight of her Command.

"*Silence!*"

The Council members fell quiet, eyes bulging from their sockets as they looked back and forth to each other in a panic. Lynette was standing on her chair again, her chest heaving as she wiped a bit of spittle from her chin.

My mouth clamped shut, my limbs so heavy I couldn't lift them any longer.

"That's better," she said softly.

"Was that necessary, Lynette?"

My eyes moved to Saint Sancha, still seated across from Lynette, her expression calm as could be. She showed no sign of strain, like the others at the table languishing under the effects of Lynette's power.

Moving with surprising speed, Lorelei was beside the Cardinal in a flash, her gun trained on the side of her head. "I would think twice about trying anything funny, Your Eminence."

"I do not wish violence against either of you," Sancha said calmly, her hands planted on the table, palms down. "I merely want to offer counsel to someone whom I think desperately needs it."

"Liar," breathed Lorelei, a clicking noise emanating from her weapon.

Lynette snorted a laugh. "You're no better than the rest of them, Sancha."

"And what makes you think I claim to be otherwise?" the Cardinal responded. "You see the injustice in the world, and it makes you angry. I understand. I share in that anger with you. But this is not the way to bring about change—"

"*Shut. Up.*"

The pressure intensified, the windows behind Lynette quivered with a resonant tone, and several of the council members fell unconscious as blood dripped from their noses.

Sancha flinches, even her cool demeanor faltering for the briefest moment.

"You sit there," Lynette spat, "and try and convince me, convince yourself that you're not complicit. I know the skeletons you keep in your closet, Saint. I could kill every last person in this room, and my hands wouldn't have but a fraction of the blood that soaks yours. So, do not patronize me with fairy tales of tolerance for corruption. Necessary evils are never truly necessary. They exist only to alleviate the responsibility of any who profit off the backs of those beneath them.

"Look around you, Sancha. A room filled with the most powerful, the wealthiest of our kind. My mother has rendered them docile. Made them fat and happy, reaping the rewards of a system that benefits those who already hold power. You can see it plain as day if you'd only open your eyes to it."

"I… do… see it…." the Cardinal managed through clenched teeth, a stream of red blood flowing from her nose. "Please, let me help you—"

A sickening crack sounded through the room as Lorelei slammed the butt of her gun into the side of the Cardinal's head. She crumpled forward onto the table, speaking no more.

"Fucking Magi, and your need to feel superior," she muttered, nodding toward Lynette.

## THE SECOND AWAKENING

"Ladies and gentlemen of the Council," Lynette addressed those still conscious. "I would like to introduce someone very special. We are joined tonight by my brother, Tobias." She waved a hand, producing a shower of golden sparks. The pressure restricting my movements lifted, and the restraints around my hands fell away. "Come join me, brother. There's something that we must see done."

Was this it? Was I about to be ritualistically sacrificed in front of the entire Council in some horrific display of power? My limbs quaked as I stood, slowly making my way over to where Lynette waited.

"I've been given a vision," Lynette said, taking my hand in hers and pulling me the rest of the way. "A glorious premonition of a second Awakening. Together, Tobias, you and I will make that vision a reality. Together, we will bring forth a new era of magic that will last for another thousand years."

"Lenny, please. Mother is gone. You don't have to do this. You don't have to stoop to her level. You're better than her."

Another cruel laugh spilled from her mouth. "Mother has been running away from this moment since the first visions came, promising the flames that would put an end to her reign. I am doing this because I *am* better than her, Tobias. Open your eyes."

The door to the council chamber burst open with a bang, and Lorelei's head snapped toward the sound, but there was no one there.

Lorelei hurried over to close the doors once more before training her gun back on the unconscious Cardinal.

Lynette reached for my other hand, taking it in hers and pulling us to the wall of windows overlooking the city. "This is your moment, Tobi. Ever since we were children, you've spoken about wanting to show your usefulness. The reason you belong in this family. Now's the time. Don't be afraid. We were born for this."

Her grip on my hands tightened, and the crushing weight of her aura pinned me in place. She locked eyes with me, the edges of her form glowing with golden light. My hands burned where the Cirian's and Bastien's stones were embedded, and the pain only intensified as Lynette's aura squeezed around me.

"What are you doing?" I demanded.

She didn't respond, the scalding heat in my hands changing again. That empty place inside of my chest that had been dormant since the start of my second life began to fill, not with my magic, but with something that felt wrong.

Was she funneling her magic through the stones?

"Stop!" I shouted, but she didn't break eye contact, the vice grip on my hands nearly cracking the bones.

In matter of seconds, that space in my chest had never felt so full, brimming with this vile, burning magic that made me want to wretch. I tried to draw it out, to force it from my body with my aura, but it only swelled more, pushing against my skin like a caged animal dying to get out.

I was going to burst. The magic would tear me apart if she continued. Was that what she wanted? Was this the sacrifice she was looking for?

A groan tore from my throat as the pain spiked to new heights, my knees shaking as she clung to me, funneling a seemingly endless supply of magic into my body.

I felt it then, the tearing of my soul, bursting at the seam from the force of my sister's magic. What would be left of me once it shredded its way through?

My second life was almost over. What would come next? If Bastien was right, then there may be nothing waiting for me on the other side.

Bastien. My promise to him was about to be broken, like so many that had come before. I wasn't coming back from this. There would be no miracles, no magic that could piece together whatever would be left—

Lynette's hands were ripped away from mine as she was hurled into the high-back chair, shattering the frame into a heap of splintered wood. I collapsed to my knees, the swelling sensation holding steady in my chest, but the heat fading from my hands where the stones glowed red-hot. Shimmering into existence over me, Azrael wrapped me up, lifting me into his arms.

A deafening *bang* went off, something shattering the window behind us as Lorelei took aim for a second shot across the table. Just as she pulled the trigger, a long gash appeared on her arm, causing her to recoil and her shot to go wide. Irwin pulled a bloodied claw back, his lithe frame becoming visible as he ducked Lorelei's flailing haymaker, laughing as he rolled under the table. Reed appeared next, behind the seething blonde, wrapping her up in a bear hug and lifting her off the ground.

We were moving then, Azrael carrying me across the room where Cirian waited, shaking out his limbs as he regained control of them. Others stirred as well, a handful of the Council members lifting their heads from their stupor. The Cardinal raced from her seat, hurrying over to her Acolyte in a swirl of billowing fabric.

"Get close to me," she ordered. "I will shield you from her magic as best I can."

"What did she do to him?" Cirian questioned at Azrael's side. He pressed a hand to my chest, and the swelling pain flared, causing me to cry out.

"I don't know," Azrael said, the rest of his words getting swallowed by the pounding of my pulse in my ears. Whatever Lynette had put inside of me, it wasn't happy being contained. It expanded like it was breathing, squeezing the air from my lungs and pushing on my ribs till they cracked.

"Bastien! Over here, quick!"

My eyes fluttered open, searching for his face amongst the scrambling crowd around me. A man with greying temples, a patchy beard, and familiar honey-colored eyes broke from the crowd, kneeling next to me. The Veil peeled away from Bastien as he leaned closer, and I couldn't take my eyes off him.

"*Bring me Tobias!*"

"Shit, they're coming for him!" shouts Irwin.

Azrael set me gently on the ground, then handed something over to Bastien from his pocket. "In case you need it," he said, then bolted, snarling.

Bastien lifted my hand, touching the green stone, then recoiled as if it burned him. "That can't be good."

"What's happening?" I asked, the words coming out like a croak.

"I think Lynette's overloaded your system with magic," Bastien said, checking my other hand with the same results. "Now it's trying to come out all at once."

"I can't focus it," I told him. "Can't force it out."

"Look out!" Cirian shouted, and I raised my gaze quickly enough to see him release a bolt of blue lightning into the crowd, bearing down on the group. Three council members fell in a heap, but more waited behind them.

Another swell in my chest and my limbs shook violently, my body seizing as the burning magic expanded, crushing me from the inside.

"Gods, it hurts!" I gritted through my teeth.

"Hold on," Bastien said, pulling at the buttons of my shirt. He pressed something sharp to my chest, muttering a string of words under his breath.

It took nearly all of my strength to lift my head enough to catch a glimpse of the violet-colored stone in my chest as his hand pulled away.

*"He's mine. And I am his. He chose me. I choose him."*

"Azrael?" I choked out.

"He came and asked me to help him make it," Bastien explained, wiping the blood from his hands. "Said that he wanted to make sure you'd make it back for your resurrection. He also told me that I was a fool for not coming with you, and I agreed."

The pressure in my chest lessened some, allowing me to draw in a full breath.

"I think it's helping," I said, unclenching my jaw.

"Try and spread the magic out evenly," Bastien instructed me. "It's all focused in one place right now."

Reaching into that bursting reserve of magic, I pulled it forward, spreading the energy between my hands and chest. Immediately, the relief was enough that tears rolled down my face. My ribs ached, my head pounded, but I was whole. Lynette's magic hadn't broken me.

"That's it, Tobias," Bastien coaxed me, his hand on my cheek. "Keep at it. You're almost through."

And here he was, this beautiful man, bringing me back from the brink of oblivion for a second time, his gentle voice guiding me through the haze. The pressure continued to abate, that horrid magic moving from the place deep in my chest. As it carved its way through my body, I could feel it change, adapting to the energies of each of the stones as they absorbed the excess.

My senses came back to me, the noise of the conflict raging around us sinking in as they did. Lifting my head, I watched Azrael tear into a councilwoman's arm as she dove towards me, rending a layer of flesh before tossing her back into the crowd of bodies that clambered toward me.

"Down!" Cirian cried from the other side of the front, a streak of blue lightning crackling to life from his hand, immobilizing the next wave of puppeted bodies.

Sancha stood in the center of the group, her deep umber skin glowing with a halo of cerulean light as she chanted under her breath. She must be keeping Lynette's magic at bay. I wondered how long she'd be able to hold out.

"Brother!" Lynette's voice filled the room, surrounding us from all sides. "This is your destiny!"

This wasn't going to end until Lynette was neutralized somehow.

"Help me up," I told Bastien, struggling to lift myself from the floor. He hauled me to my feet, bracing me until I gained my footing.

"We need to get you out of here," started Bastien, steering me toward the doors, but I held fast, planting my feet.

"No, we can't just let her get away."

"But no one can stand against her," he argued. "The Saint won't be able to protect us forever."

My mind raced, running through our options. Lynette wanted me so we could leverage that. Draw her away from the council members, decrease the casualties. It was a start.

Reaching for the power now held in the stones attached to me, I wrapped myself in my aura, marveling at the rush of strength I felt from the magic. Bastien was right about me being supercharged. This was more power than I'd ever been able to conjure before. Maybe that would make the difference.

"We can draw her out. Let me get over—"

The doors to the council room blasted apart, shreds of metal and wood spraying across the room. A lone figure stood in the opening, a flickering golden light wreathing their form in an ethereal light.

"Daughter!"

All eyes were drawn to Adoranda Greene—or what was left of her. Her clothing was tattered and blackened, with patches being indecipherable between melted cloth and her skin. Her hair hung in singed clumps from her head. But her face was the most horrific of all. Blackened, charred flesh hung to the left side of her face, peeling away from bone and sinew in a stomach-turning fashion, the opposite side scarred with angry red welts and blisters. It appeared as though she'd chewed her lips away, her teeth barred in an inhuman snarl that sent tingling fear spiking up my spine.

She was Death, walking.

Raising a skeletal hand in the air, the golden light flared, a blast of magical energy clearing a path between her and Lynette. Council members flew through the air, landing haphazardly in crumpled heaps.

Lynette's magic brushed against my aura once more, but the pressure was like a finger running across my arm instead of the crushing weight of a boulder. To my right, Sancha groaned under the exertion—keeping us safe from the power that roiled off of my sister.

The remaining Council members under my sister's control abandoned their pursuit of me, turning instead to charge at Mother with twisted, broken limbs and vacant expressions. Mother cast them aside like a child playing with their toys, advancing on Lynette with a limping gait.

With the assault on our group paused the others rallied around me. Azrael and his Urchins spattered in blood that didn't belong to them. Bastien beside me, his hand on the small of my back as he watched on with horror. Cirian came beside the Cardinal, whispering incantations under his breath as he healed a wound that ran along his forearm.

Another wave of magic roiled over us as Mother crushed a councilman's skull between her clawed hands, and Sancha's knees buckled.

"Your Eminence!" Cirian exclaimed, catching her before she could crumple.

Shit. Without her protection, we were as good as dead. Thinking quickly, I pressed my aura out, enveloping the others. Before now, I found covering more than one person with my aura to be exhausting. But this felt easy, like I was wrapping my arms around each of them.

Now, I'd just have to hope it would hold.

# THE SECOND AWAKENING

A thunderous collision rattled my bones as Mother reached Lynette, the two of them clashing together in a blinding display of power. The wall of windows shattered from the force, glass debris raining down around us like sheets of snow in a blizzard.

Those council members still standing halted their movements, a dozen statues standing stark still as the pressure of magic spiked in the room. The waves of power rolled over us, butting against my aura like the ocean crashing against a cliffside, but my ward held fast, the pull on my power far less than I expected.

"Are you doing this?" Azrael asked, eyeing the violet stone over my heart.

I nodded, still focused on the struggle between Lynette and Mother.

Mother struck a blow against Lynette, sending her reeling, and she crashed against the framing of the massive window, her arm dangling over the edge and over the city sprawling below.

"You will not take this from me," Mother seethed, limping toward her daughter with determined malice. "My power will stay with me till my dying breath, and I will destroy anything that stands in my way. Even you, daughter."

Mother raised a hand into the air, an orb of pure golden light pulsating in her palm. Then, a shot rang out, a spray of fresh blood bursting from Mother's shoulder. Lorelei was standing atop the wreckage of the council table, the barrel of her gun smoking as she leveled a steely glare at Mother.

"Get away from her!" she ordered, the weapon clicking, then firing again.

The second shot hit Mother in the back, and she wheeled around, bellowing with bestial rage at the mortal. Seeing her opportunity, Lynette moved, wrapping her arms around Mother's torso. With a kick off the window frame, she heaved the two of them over the ledge, and they disappeared into the night air without so much as a whimper.

The room fell deathly quiet, then, all at once, the standing council members crumpled to the floor, a chorus of groaning beginning amongst those still breathing.

Slowly, I pulled away from Bastien's hold, making my way over to the window and peering over the edge. It was dark on the street below, too dark for me to be able to confirm exactly what happened, but in my heart, I knew.

Mother had met her end.

Withdrawing the ward from my friends, I projected the aura downward, feeling for either of my family. There was something—Mother's aura, I recognized, flickering like the flame of a candle. I wrapped my aura around the feeble presence, cradling it.

Did she know I was there?

In the end, it didn't matter. A moment later, the flame flickered out, and Adoranda Greene was no more.

# TWENTY-TWO
## DEAD WRONG

"Your Mother's body was recovered and laid next to your Father in the Upper Magi City."

I sat across a small table from the young woman, her tawny hair wrapped in a tight bun at the crown of her head. She was one of those who met that night at the VanDoughten house before Lynette had ended my first life.

Cynthia Creedy.

I wondered if her brother had told her about me ahead of our meeting.

"We didn't find any sign of Lynette in the wreckage, so the Council is considering her still at large. Until she's apprehended, we are suggesting that you stay in hiding, Tobias. For your own safety."

I snorted a weak laugh, nodding along. "Sorry, but it's rather cute that you think anyone will keep her from what she wants."

Cynthia frowned, scratching at the back of her neck. "There's more. The Council has made the decision to seize all of the assets of the Greene family as a recompense for last week's tragedy. Amelia and I were able to convince them not to pursue retaliatory action against you so long as you sign these documents forfeiting your rights to the Greene family trusts and properties." She pulled a stack of paperwork from her satchel, setting it on the table between us.

I stared down at the summation of my family legacy, boiled down to a pile of paper and ink, shocked at the emptiness I felt towards it. The Tobias who had lived a life of wealth and privilege would have mourned the loss. But I gladly signed the documents, a weight lifting from my shoulders as I crossed the final line.

"Thank you for coming all this way," I told Cynthia, sliding the documents over to her. "I know that it wasn't easy for a Council member to come all the way to Brierwood."

"Think nothing of it," she replied, waving away my thanks. "You should know that negotiations have already started with the Rebellion leaders. Hopefully, it won't be long till we can put all of this unpleasantness behind us."

"Let's hope you're right."

"There was one more thing, Tobias. If we could speak off the record for a moment." Cynthia glanced over her shoulder, then leaned over the table, lowering her voice. "We tracked down Lorelei Orion after the incident, our scouts reporting that she was staying somewhere in the Lower Magi City, near the Mortal Row. But before she was spotted leaving the city a few days ago, there was an incident. An Adored couple was attacked by some kind of monstrosity that Lorelei was transporting. The male was killed, and the surviving party reported that the creature tore something from the victim's chest, consuming it on the spot. Something that looked a lot like those gems you sport."

My hand drifted to the stone embedded in my chest.

"Be cautious, Tobias. I fear there are greater evils in this world, waiting to fill the vacuum your mother left behind."

I nodded once again. "Thank you for the information, Cynthia."

The woman straightened in her seat. "Of course. We'll be in touch if there's any development on the front of your sister. Until then, I hope you keep well."

"Tobias?"

I looked up from the table, spotting Bastien standing a few paces away.

"Sorry to interrupt," he continued. "I can come back if you need me to."

"That won't be necessary," Cynthia replied, gathering her satchel and the paperwork under her arm. "Till next time, Tobias."

"Next time," I agreed, rising from my seat. Cynthia gave a small wave before exiting the café, immediately stepping into the large, black vehicle that drew the eye of every passerby outside.

"Do I want to know what that was about?" Bastien asked, raising a brow.

"Just tying up some loose ends," I assured him, then wrapped him up in a hug. "I'm sorry, I didn't realize how late it had gotten."

"Don't be. Cirian just arrived a few minutes ago on the train, so he's waiting outside."

"I guess we're doing this, then," I said, a swell of anxiety pressing against my stomach. We'd delayed the resurrection ritual long enough as it were, setbacks occurring each time we'd attempted it over the last week. The Anima stones were proving to complicate things more than Bastien originally anticipated.

"Wilhelm got everything set up at your apartment," Bastien said, rubbing the small of my back. "So, we can head over whenever you're ready."

My 'apartment' in Brierwood was not much more than a bed, and some clothing scavenged from the second-hand store in town. Since we returned to the mortal town, I didn't feel right taking up space in Paradise while they were still housing the Rebellion, so Bastien helped me find a place to stay on the surface.

Bastien and I exited the café, stepping out onto the sidewalk lining Brierwood's main street. A tall figure leaned against the brick wall a few paces down from the entrance, their fiery hair pulled back in a ponytail. It took me a moment to recognize Cirian, his pedestrian outfit of dark jeans and hooded jacket a far cry from his religious paraphernalia. He took a long drag off the cigarette in his hand, then dropped it to the ground, stamping it out with the heel of his boot.

"There you are, Toto."

"Here I am," I replied, still taking in the stark difference of this Cirian.

"Azrael is waiting at the apartment already," Bastien tells us, leading the way up the sidewalk.

"Why are you staring at me?" Cirian asked as we rounded the corner.

"I've never seen you without your vestments," I explained.

"That's not entirely true," Cirian replied, flashing a wicked smile.

"You know what I mean."

"I know what you mean. I figured, what with the secret society of Reviled living nearby, it would be rude of me to parade around in Hallowed paraphernalia. Plus, when else would I get the opportunity, you know?"

"How considerate," Bastien chimed in, his words drenched with sarcasm.

"I can always get back on the train," Cirian joked, pointing toward the station.

Bastien leveled a stare at him. "Don't tease me unless you intend on following through."

"Knock it off," I chide them both.

"Whatever you say, Toto."

The walk to my apartment only takes a few minutes, the three of us scaling the exterior flight of wooden stairs to reach the door. It sat over a shuttered shop front, so it was quiet enough that Bastien was comfortable with us performing the rituals there without drawing unwanted attention from the mortals in town.

I opened the door, letting the other two enter first, then took a deep breath before heading in. The smell of incense in the small space made my head swim as Azrael bounded over to me, wrapping me in a bone-crushing hug.

"There you are, Tobi. I was starting to get worried."

"Sorry, I had a member of the Council come to tell me that I'm broke now."

"Really?" Bastien asked, his voice filled with surprise.

"Are you okay?" Cirian added.

"Surprisingly, I'm relieved. It's just another part of the Greene legacy that I get to bury. I'll probably have to get a job soon to pay for this dump, but that's a future Tobias problem."

"We'll figure it out," Bastien said, giving me a reassuring smile. "First things are first. We've got work to do. Now, if you two will follow me, I need to talk you through the extraction ritual."

Cirian and Azrael followed Bastien into my bedroom, where they had prepared the space for the ritual. Feeling slightly nauseated from the stifling air, I stepped into the small bathroom off the kitchen, shutting the door behind me. Splashing cold water across my face helped, and as I dried off,

# THE SECOND AWAKENING

I couldn't help but observe the violet gemstone poking out the deep cut of my shirt. I placed a hand over it, closing my eyes as I felt the invisible connection twinge, vibrating extra strong due to the close proximity to Azrael. The connection had only grown stronger the longer the stone stayed in my skin. The same went for the cerulean counterpart in my left and the verdant stone in my right palm. I ran my thumb over one, the invisible connection transferring to Cirian, his soft voice drifting into my head.

*"There you are, Toto."*

Bastien connection was the strongest of the three at the moment, as I barely had to brush against the green gem for the connection to snap into place.

He was worried about me. It radiated down the line like a pulsing heartbeat.

*"This has to work. I'll fix him. I promised."*

These connections were becoming a part of me. But what would happen if the extraction was a success? Would I lose the tethers to each of them? Was that really what I wanted?

My conclusion was a resounding no. But what if it were the only way I was going to be able to retrieve those memories that had continued to evade me? Now that I was more than a week into my second life, the kaleidoscope of memories had slowed, and gaps in my memory had become more apparent. Without fixing the fracture, I didn't know if I'd ever be able to recover them.

Selfishly, I wanted them to stay gone. But I couldn't keep running from my past. I had to face it head-on if I was going to have a future.

A soft knock on the door brought me back to reality.

"Come in."

Bastien pokes his head through the cracked door. "We're ready for you."

I nodded, taking one last look in the mirror before leaving the bathroom.

In the other room, my bed had been pushed to the side, a long table with restraints in the center of the room. The previous attempts at extraction had proven difficult, as my body reacted violently of its own accord, so the restraints were probably for the best. Cirian stood on the side of the table, while Azrael stood at the far end, where my head would go. They both smiled at me as I entered, and a pulse of warmth steadied my trembling hands.

"Tobias," Wilhelm greeted me. "Are you ready?"

"As I'll ever be," I replied, peeling my shirt off and tossing it onto the bed. Hefting myself onto the table, Wilhelm and Bastien worked to secure my limbs at the wrists and ankles. Cirian watched with delighted fascination while Azrael only looked into my eyes, his fingers padding through my hair.

"Okay, like we discussed," Bastien addressed the others. "We attempt to remove them at the same time. You have your instructions."

Azrael and Cirian nodded, each placing a hand over their stone. Bastien took his place last, wrapping his hand around mine so that his palm pressed into the smooth facet.

Wilhelm began to chant, the lights above us flickering as an acidic green haze drifted into the air around us. All at once, the three points of contact lit up with searing heat, my mind pulled in three different directions as the invisible threads connecting me to each of the men drew taut—

*"The Source has never made something more beautiful."*

*Cirian cupped the side of my face, his dark eyes mooring me to him. His pale skin glistened in the moonlight that poured through the window across from the bed we sprawled across. My flesh burned with desire at every connection of his body to mine, his free hand wandering the channels of my thighs, then directing his cock to press against my entrance, slipping inside with ease as I roiled against the cool sheets, a whimper on my tongue as I begged him for more.*

*"I love you, Toto," he breathed into my ear, the eager pace of my stroke driving me over the edge. "I love you, I love you, I love you—"*

Shocked back into the present moment, I cried out as the gem embedded in my palm burned white hot, Cirian's tugging sending a shooting pain straight up to my chest.

"Keep going!" Bastien shouted, clasping tighter to my hand as the thread between us pulled tight—

*"How was work today?"*

*I looked up from my plate, watching Bastien from across the dinner table. The small apartment was pleasantly warm, with candles glowing in the periphery and soft music drifting from the other room.*

"I couldn't wait to get home," I replied, knocking my foot against his under the table.

He let out a deep, contented sigh, sipping from his wine glass. It stained his top lip blood-red, and I couldn't help myself any longer.

Setting down my utensils, I rose from my seat, rounding the table and lowering myself into Bastien's lap. He made a surprised noise as I wrapped my arms around his neck and devoured him in a kiss. Warm hands held my hips as he breathed into me, the two of us abandoning our dinners for the comfort we found in each other—

Another cry poured from my mouth as pain ricocheted up my arm. I was fracturing again, this time my entire body coming apart at the seams. These threads I held were the stitching holding me together, and the others' efforts were trying to unravel them.

My body seized, muscles aching as I strained against the bindings that held me in place.

"Bastien!" Azrael's voice came in a growl.

"Keep going! They're almost free!"

Azrael's hand was in my hair again, trying to comfort me as the pain radiated through every pore—

"He has your nose," Azrael said, holding the bundled youngling in his arms, his head propped against a wall of pillows. His russet skin was still flushed, a sheen of sweat covering his brow as he cooed over the newborn.

"You did so well," I told him, leaning into his shoulder but careful not to jostle the sleeping babe. "Is it always that terrifying?"

"From what I've heard," Azrael chuckled. "Papa told me horror stories of his labor with me. I'm glad this one didn't put up as much of a fight."

The youngling stirred in his arms, one of the furry, pointed ears protruding from the crown of his head, twitching as he yawned, then settled back in.

"You still haven't decided on the name," I reminded Azrael, resting my head against his.

"Would you be angry if we called him Balthus?" he asked, watching me with violet eyes full of worry.

"I could never be angry with you," I assured him, planting a soft kiss across his lips. We looked down at our creation. "Welcome to the world, little Balthus—

"No!" I cried, tears streaming down my face.

"Just a moment longer, Tobias!" Bastien shouted, his voice strained.

All three tethers pulled at me, threatening to rip me apart. I couldn't let them do this. I didn't want to rid myself of the connection I held for them. Reaching down into that place in my chest, I drew out my aura and wrapped the connections up inside of it, reinforcing the threads till they braided together into a single cord, connecting the four of us—

*"Are you coming to bed?"*

*Bastien looked across the sofa at me, the question still worn on his brow.*

*I set my book aside, pulling out the watch from my pocket and checking the time. "Shit, I didn't realize the night had grown so late. Yes, I will be up in a minute."*

*He nodded, leaning over to plant a kiss on my head. "Don't take too long."*

*My heart sputtered at that, and I quickly marked my place as Bastien ascended the staircase. Heading down the hallway, I peeked into the office where Cirian sat at his desk, one hand tangled in the locks of his fiery hair, the other tapping the end of a fountain pen against the parchment beneath.*

*"Writer's block?" I asked, leaning in the doorway.*

*"The worst," he replied with a sigh, returning the pen to the ink well across from him. "Are you turning in for the night?"*

*I nodded. "You know, if you're looking for a little help breaking through that block…"*

*Cirian was out of his chair in a flash, wrapping me up in his arms and trailing kisses down my neck. "I was hoping you'd offer."*

*"Head upstairs. I'll be right behind you."*

*He held me for a moment with his stygian gaze. "Don't get lost, love."*

*Cirian disappeared down the hallway, headed for the staircase as I rounded the corner, nearly running into Azrael as he came out of Balthus' room.*

*"Another nightmare?" I asked, wanting to smooth the furrow from the man's brow.*

*"Hm? No, no, not tonight. He just wanted me to check his closest one last time," Azrael explained. "I'll be glad when we get through this monster phase."*

"I think we all will. Bastien almost got stuck under his bed last night. I had to drag him out by his ankles."

Azrael smiled as I grabbed him by the waist, pulling him against me.

"We're headed to bed. Would you care to join us?"

He grinned back at me. "Let me guess, writer's block?"

"You know Cirian needs all the help he can get."

"Yeah, yeah, I've heard that before. Tell you what, if you can catch me, I'm in." His smile turned mischievous as his body shimmers, then disappeared.

Holding back laughter, I chase my invisible partner up the stairs, managing to grab hold of his tail just as we clear the bedroom door, and he becomes visible again in time for me to crash into him with a kiss.

Waiting in the bed, Cirian and Bastien are already locked in a kiss, and as I push Azrael over the edge of the mattress, I join them, tangling myself between a mess of limbs and lips, and lose myself—

"Stop!"

The restraints holding my limbs snapped as a rush of heat pulsed through me. Azrael, Bastien, and Cirian were thrown backward with a flash of brilliant light, and Wilhelm's chanting ceased.

My chest heaved as I tried to catch my breath, the visions sinking back into my subconscious as Bastien appeared in my periphery.

"Are you alright?" he asked, eyes wide with concern.

I glanced down at my hands, the gems still firmly sunken into my flesh, and breathed a sigh of relief.

"What the hell was that?" Azrael asked, regaining his footing. "I thought for a second we had it."

"I don't think those things are coming out," Cirian added, poking at the stone on my chest. I flinched, suddenly feeling ticklish.

Wilhelm stepped up to the table, inspecting the Anima stones one by one. Her lips pulled into a hard line. "I'm sorry, Bastien. But we can't perform the resurrection ritual while these are present. Besides, there may not even be enough of Tobias' magic left in the ether to return to him. I think it's time we start thinking about alternatives."

Bastien nodded, disappointment evident on his face. "Thank you for trying."

"Of course, seeker," Wilhelm replies, her tone apologetic. "I must be gone, but do come see me tomorrow, and we'll go through the archives again to see if anything sticks out, okay?"

He nodded, and Wilhelm embraced him, kissing him on both cheeks before exiting the room.

Azrael helped me sit up, my head spinning. "How are you feeling?"

"Fine, I think. Just a little fatigued."

"So, I come all this way and have to leave empty-handed?" Cirian complained, folding his arms across his chest. "That's right fucking rude."

I swung my leg over the edge of the table, then kicked him in the shin. "Give me a few minutes, and we can have a bout. Just like old times. Hope your sword skills haven't diminished in your old age."

His eyes lit up at that. "Are you taking a piss?"

"Never."

"Right then, I'll need to get the strip set up. Can we use the alleyway outside?"

"Go for it," Bastien answered.

Cirian bolted from the room, humming a happy tune. Azrael watched him leave, then turned back to me. "I told the Urchins I'd touch base when we were through. Kaine's been asking about you, so I figured I should at least let him know you're alive."

"Tell him that if he's got a crush on me, he needs to tell me to my face like a real man."

Azrael barked a laugh, pulling the device from his pocket. "I'll be sure to do that."

"The Urchins are invited to dinner," Bastien joined in. "If I can squeeze enough chairs into the other room. And don't worry, I'm cooking."

"Hey, what's that supposed to mean?" I asked, frowning at the two of them.

Azrael laughed again, knocking his shoulder into mine. "We'll be there. Kaine can come see for himself that you're right as rain."

Still laughing, Azrael headed out, leaving me and Bastien to put my bedroom back together. I pulled my shirt back on as he cut what remained of the restraints from the table, then folded it up.

"I'm sorry, Tobias." He paused by the window, his expression pained as he gazed through at the drifting clouds.

"What for?" I asked, moving to his side.

"I promised you that I would help you get your memories back, but I failed."

"Hey." I caught him at the hip, pulling him to face me. "You've done more than enough for me, Bast. More than I ever deserved. You're the reason I'm alive right now. And if I'm being honest, I'm more than happy to leave my first life buried."

He nodded, pulling me into an embrace.

"I'm just glad you're here," he whispered.

And I couldn't agree with him more.

There, in the derelict apartment, penniless and battered, I had never been happier. Death was just the beginning for me. A chance at the life I never knew I was missing. And if anyone out there thought they could tear it away from me, they were wrong.

Dead wrong.

# EPILOGUE
## DEAD AND BURIED

Walking through the iron gates of Adoracia Cemetery, I pulled the ends of my tattered coat tighter around me. It was a far cry from the usual luxurious garments I had worn in a previous life, but it kept me warm and Bastien had commented on how it brought out the color of my eyes, so I'd worn it every opportunity I could.

Now that autumn was drawing to a close, the trees had nearly all finished their annual shed, littering the ground with a trove of multi-colored ornaments that shifted around my feet as a breeze kicked up. It was quiet today, much like all the other days I'd visited my father's grave. The same rows of polished marble epitaphs, the same visitors with their heads cast down in silent lamentations, and the same melancholia that gripped me by the gut, twisting my insides till they were nothing but brambles and thorns.

"It's peaceful here," Azrael said, breaking the silence as he traveled at my side toward the last row where Father was waiting. "I didn't know such places existed inside the Magi City."

"They're rare," Bastien replied from my other side. "And typically reserved for those who can afford the exorbitant price."

"He's over there," I said after a moment, leading them down the short path off the main trail to where Tobias Greene awaited. A new addition since my last visit stuck out in glaring disproportion—a large obelisk of white marble, seated in the ground beside Father's grave. I didn't have to look to know whose name was carved on the front of it, nor did I care to know what words the Council had used to immortalize my mother. Her grave was a continuation of her life—ostentation for the sake of reputation. I wanted no part of it.

Kneeling down, I brushed the stray leaves from Father's humble gravestone, then set the modest bouquet I'd brought against it. I didn't care for the act of prayer, or even know where to begin if I did, but here in these moments in the cemetery with my Father, I'd find myself wanting to speak to him. Wherever it was that he found himself.

"I don't think Lenny is going to make it this time," I spoke softly, hoping that my words would get carried away in the breeze like the late falling leaves. "But I'm still here. For better or worse."

From behind, I heard Bastien mutter something that sounded like a prayer, and I nearly jumped when Azrael landed on the soft grass beside me, sprawling his legs out in front of him as he leaned back, soaking in the late afternoon sun.

"You're sitting on the grave," Bastien pointed out, his recitation ceasing.

"And? Have you ever tried it? It helps you feel closer to the departed. I sit on my father's grave all the time back in Brierwood. Though, the grass is not nearly as soft." He ran his fingers through the plush vegetation. "We need to find out what kind of seed they use."

I choked on a laugh as Bastien rolled his eyes. Leave it to Azrael to bring levity, even on the somber occasions. The invisible tether between us pulled taut as he grinned at me, the golden light beaming down transfiguring his hair into a dozen different shades of lavender. I could feel it now, almost all the time, but especially when one of them was close by. Emotions would trickle down the line, giving me brief glimpses into their heads.

Over the last few weeks, since the death of my mother and the massacre at the Magi Council, life had taken on an almost mundane quality back in Brierwood. Bastien shared my apartment with me on the surface, as he wasn't ready to join Paradise full-time. He always led with caution, so it only made sense that he'd want to spend the time to acclimate to the community before making any long-term decisions. Most days he spent in their libraries, pouring through the history he thought lost.

Azrael joined us for dinner most nights, as long as his schedule permitted, and despite the cramped quarters, I was always glad to see him bring along an Urchin or two. The Rebellion hasn't seen a drop of blood spilled since Mother's death, and Azrael seemed determined to keep it that way.

Cirian visited whenever he could get away from the Cradle, spending long weekends sparring with me in the alley outside the apartment and learning how to ride Azrael's motorbike. The way the Urchins talked about Azrael's inability to share made me question his willingness to teach Cirian, but they get along surprisingly well. At least, as long as I was there to supervise.

Cirian's connection flared in my chest, and I quickly turned, scanning the rows of marble for the familiar head of flaming hair. I spotted him, strolling slowly up the main path, his vestments sticking out of place in the most adorable way. He never missed an opportunity to see me when I was in the Magi City.

But my smile soon faltered as I realized he wasn't alone.

"Source's blessings," Saint Sancha greeted us, standing at the edge of the grass, her arms tucked into the sleeves of her vestments.

"What are you doing here?" I asked plainly, the days of worrying over decorum long behind me. I stood, brushing the dirt from my faded jeans. "If you've come for Bastien, then you'll have to put me back into the ground before you take him."

Bastien chuckled at that, knocking his shoulder into mine. "So dramatic."

Azrael was on his feet now too, standing behind the two of us, a low growl emanating from his chest.

"It's not like that," Cirian interjected, stepping closer. "Please, Tobias, just hear her out. I've spoken with Her Eminence about the prophecy given to me by the Source."

Bastien's eyes were trained on me, his brow raised in surprise. I hadn't shared the prophecy with another soul since Cirian spoke it into being.

"I've had enough of prophecies, thanks," I replied. "I want no part of this one or any other."

"Your hesitation is understandable, Tobias," the Cardinal commiserated. "But I would still ask you to hear me, if only to know what it is that waits for you out in the world."

I looked to Cirian, his dark eyes pleading. The tether between us twinged with a resonance of longing. He needed me to understand.

"Fine. Speak your piece."

"Something moves amongst the Source. A shadow that looms over all Magi. We can see the ripples of its existence even now, spreading. I believe this to be the 'distortion' mentioned in Cirian's prophecy."

"And what does that have to do with Tobias?" Azrael asked, the growl not fully distilled from his words.

"Not just Tobias," the Cardinal corrected, glancing between the three of us. "But you all have your part to play in what's coming as well." She reached out a rested hand on Cirian's shoulder. "The prophet." Her eyes drifted to Bastien next, "The seeker." Then she looked to Azrael, "The rebel." And lastly, her gaze fell on me, "The Son of the Second."

The words of the prophecy burned in my mind. I had my suspicions before, but I'd turned a blind eye to the correlations. I wanted to enjoy the peace I'd managed to squeeze from my second chance at life. Prophecies didn't fit into that picture.

"It's not enough," I said, leveling my stare at the Cardinal. "You can keep your prophecy. I don't want any part of it."

The Cardinal nodded solemnly, her arms once again retracting into her robes. "I know the hardship you've faced, Tobias. But there is one more thing I wish for you to consider. This… distortion precursing havoc across the Source—I believe it is your sister."

Another growl from Azrael and my stomach twisted.

"What are you talking about?" Bastien stepped in, launching into a slew of questions. Azrael joined him as they moved to close the gap between them and the Cardinal, and I turned to face the obelisk rising from my mother's grave.

# Dead Wrong

I knew that Lynette was still alive. I knew it the moment I reached out my aura that night when she fell from the window. Still, I'd hoped that she'd disappear. Retreat into obscurity, if only so I wouldn't have to face her again after everything she'd done. *We'd* done. The curse of the Greene family.

But she was still alive. And if what Sancha said was right, and Lynette had become some sort of monster, leeching off of the Source of magic, then maybe I wouldn't be able to escape this prophecy after all.

The marble pillar towered over me, just like Mother used to. My hand clenched at my side, a swell of magic drew from the stone in my chest, and I slammed my fist into the monument, the marble cracking at the impact.

Behind me, the conversation fell silent as half of the marble obelisk fell to the ground, breaking further into pieces.

"I'll find her again," I said, not bothering to look at the others. "But I'll do it alone."

I wouldn't risk their lives. I'd been running on borrowed time as it was.

A strong hand clapped down on my shoulder, spinning me in place. The three of them stood there, staring me down with mixed expressions.

"Like hell you will," Azrael snarled, retracting his hand.

"You're hopeless on your own, Toto," Cirian scoffed. "You'll be bleeding to death in a field of flowers before you even find Lynette."

Bastien's eyes found me last, brimming with defiance.

"Where do we start?"

# ACKNOWLEDGMENTS

Hello! Thank you so much for reading my debut adult novel! DEAD WRONG marks my first foray into the Adult Romance world, and I can't wait to share more of Tobias's story with you all. But first, I wanted to take a moment to thank those who have helped me along the way.

First off, I'd like to thank my husband, Cecil. Thank you for choosing to love me, on good days and bad, and for all of the encouragement you give. I'm not always the perfect husband, but I am a better person because of you, and I know you feel the same.

I'd also like to thank my narrator, Joel Leslie, for bringing my characters to life in the audio version of DEAD WRONG. If you haven't heard Joel's incredible voice work, you are really missing out. You can find out more about his services and other titles at JoelLeslieNarration.com. You won't be disappointed!

Next, I'd like to thank my cover designer and format wizard, Molly Phipps from We Got You Covered Book Design! Molly, as always, I'm in awe of your work and your advice and guidance is par none. You always make my books shine!

And of course, I'd love to thank my Beta readers for their time and awesome feedback for DEAD WRONG. As an author new to the space of Adult M/M fiction, I was nervous about whether or not this book was going to be any good. But you were all so gracious and I appreciate each and every one of you!

Lastly, I'd like to thank you, dear reader. Whether you're new to my work, or you've followed over from my YA novels, I want to thank you from the bottom of my heart. It's readers like you who keep me going on days when life gets too loud and writing my little fictional worlds seems impossible. Thank you, thank you, thank you!

Till next time,
**- ALEXANDER**

# ABOUT THE AUTHOR

A Metro Atlanta area native, **ALEXANDER** has had a passion for writing from a young age. As he grew into his Queer identity, so did his works, and he is dedicated to bringing Queer stories to life in new and imaginative ways.

Alexander has penned over half a dozen titles, from Young Adult works exploring topics of Faith and Queer identities, to an Adult Urban Fantasy series, packed with magic and just the right amount of spice.

When not crafting quality Queer fiction, Alexander works for a local service company. He still lives outside of Atlanta with his husband and their children (dogs).

*Find him online at:*
**WWW.ALEXANDERCEBERHART.COM**

www.ingramcontent.com/pod-product-compliance
Lightning Source LLC
LaVergne TN
LVHW091710070526
838199LV00050B/2333